ROGUE SUN

ROGUE SUN, VOL. 1. First Printing. August 2022. Published by Image Comics, Inc. Office of publication: PO BOX 14457, Portland, OR 97293. Copyright © 2022 Ryan Parrott & Abel. All rights reserved. Contains material originally published in single magazine form as ROGUE SUN #1-6. "Rogue Sun," its logos, and the likenesses of all characters herein are trademarks of Ryan Parrott & Abel, unless otherwise noted. "Image" and the Image Comics logos are registered trademarks of Image Comics, Inc. No part of this publication may be reproduced or transmitted, in any form or by any means (except for short excerpts for journalistic or review purposes), without the express written permission of Ryan Parrott & Abel, or Image Comics, Inc. All names, characters, events, and locales in this publication are entirely fictional. Any resemblance to actual persons (living or dead), events, or places, without satirical intent, is coincidental. Printed in the USA. For international rights, contact: foreignlicensing@imagecomics.com. ISBN: 978-1-5343-2237-0.

Volume One
Cataclysm

Writer
Ryan Parrott

Artists
Abel
with Simone Ragazzoni *(Issue Five)*
and Francesco Mortarino *(Interludes)*

Colorists
Chris O'Halloran *(Issues One to Four & Interludes)*
and Natalia Marques *(Issues Five & Six)*

Letterer
Becca Carey

Production Artists
Tricia Ramos
Deanna Phelps

Logo Designer
Fonografiks

Editor & Designer
Michael Busuttil

Rogue Sun created by
Ryan Parrott & Abel

Chapter One
When The Knight Falls, A Son Will Rise

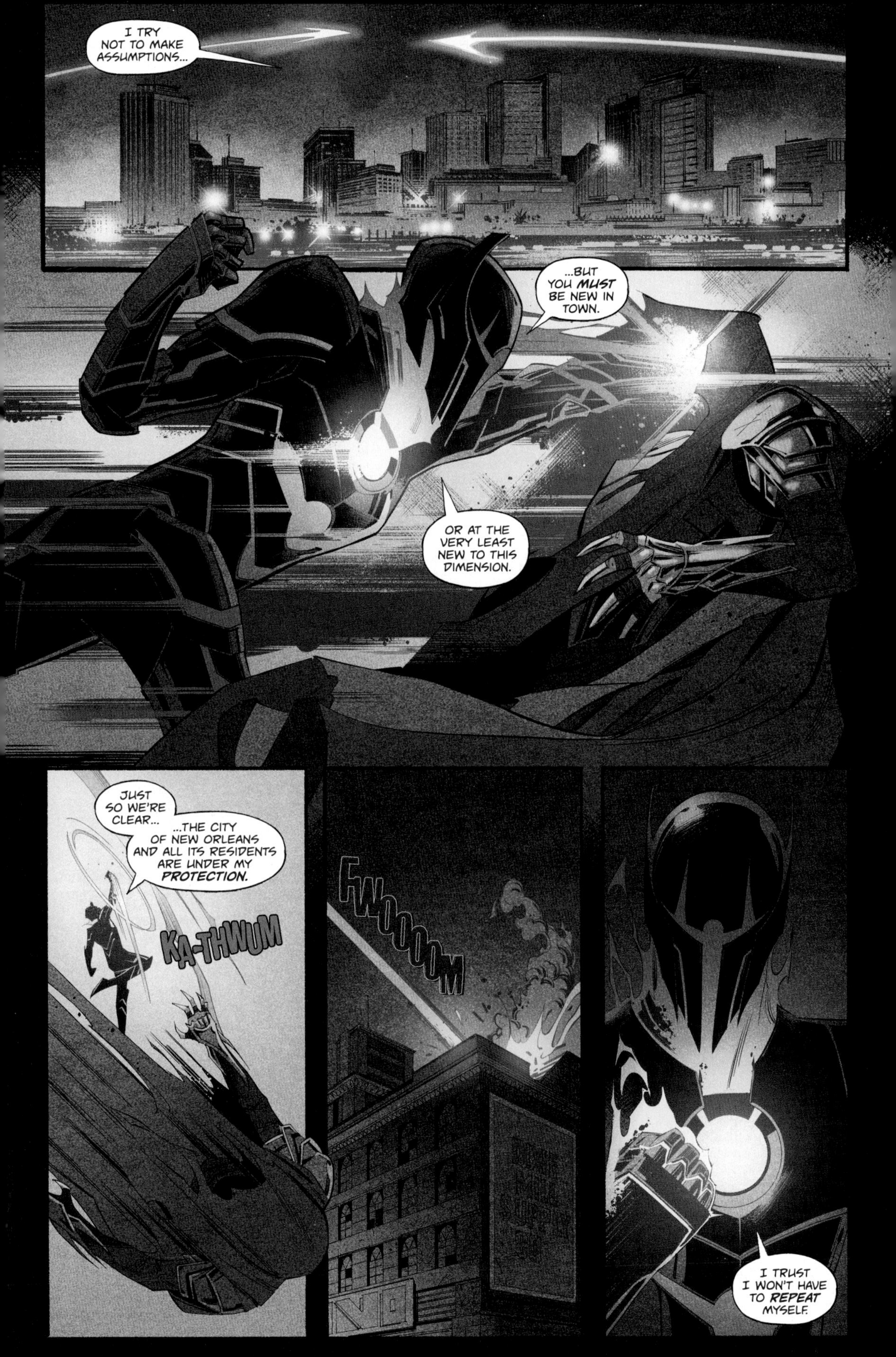
I TRY NOT TO MAKE ASSUMPTIONS...
...BUT YOU MUST BE NEW IN TOWN.
OR AT THE VERY LEAST NEW TO THIS DIMENSION.
JUST SO WE'RE CLEAR...
...THE CITY OF NEW ORLEANS AND ALL ITS RESIDENTS ARE UNDER MY PROTECTION.
KA-THWUM
FWOOOOOM
I TRUST I WON'T HAVE TO REPEAT MYSELF.

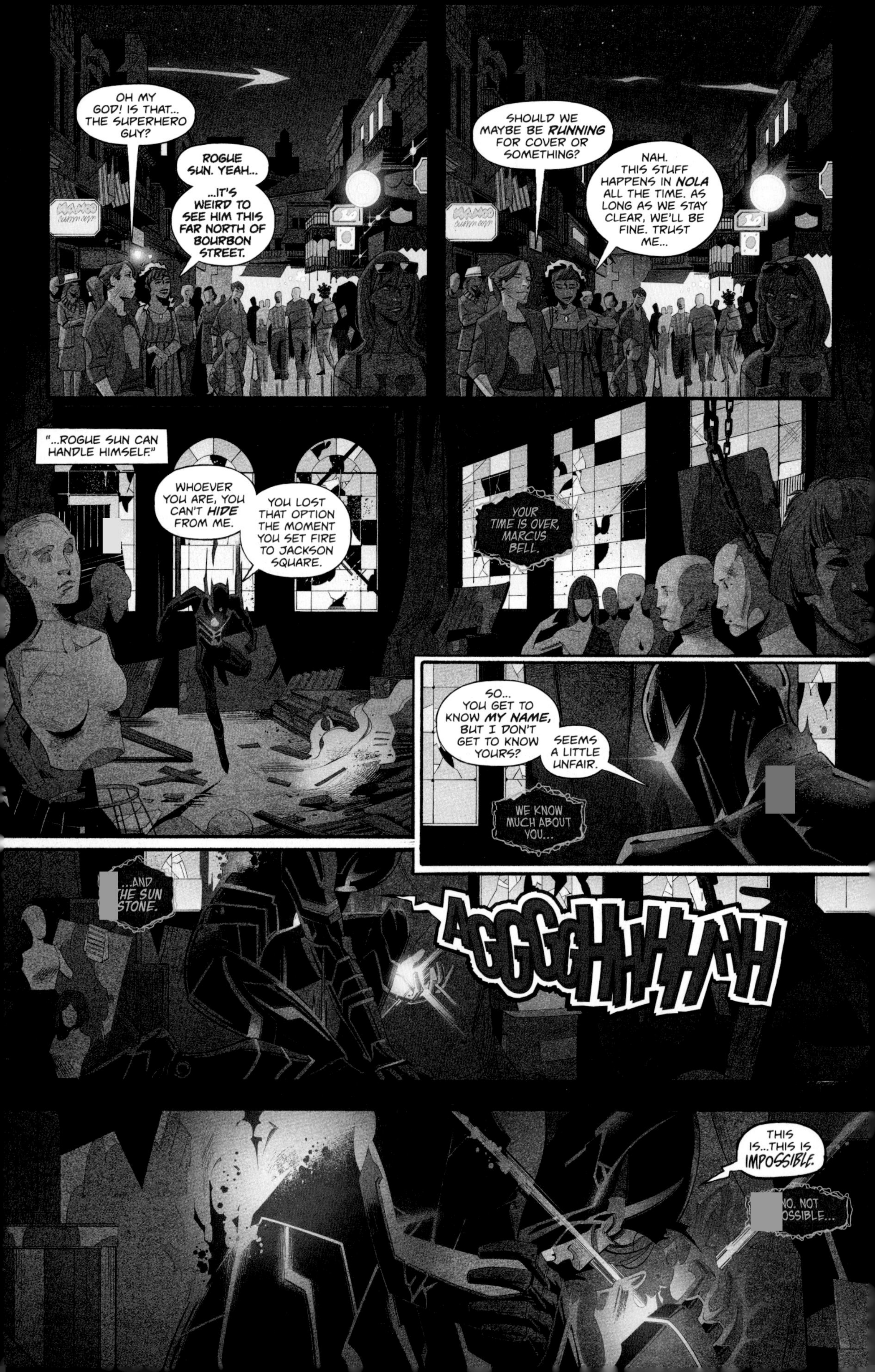
OH MY GOD! IS THAT... THE SUPERHERO GUY?
ROGUE SUN. YEAH...
...IT'S WEIRD TO SEE HIM THIS FAR NORTH OF BOURBON STREET.
SHOULD WE MAYBE BE RUNNING FOR COVER OR SOMETHING?
NAH. THIS STUFF HAPPENS IN NOLA ALL THE TIME. AS LONG AS WE STAY CLEAR, WE'LL BE FINE. TRUST ME...
"...ROGUE SUN CAN HANDLE HIMSELF."
WHOEVER YOU ARE, YOU CAN'T HIDE FROM ME.
YOU LOST THAT OPTION THE MOMENT YOU SET FIRE TO JACKSON SQUARE.
YOUR TIME IS OVER, MARCUS BELL.
SO... YOU GET TO KNOW MY NAME, BUT I DON'T GET TO KNOW YOURS?
SEEMS A LITTLE UNFAIR.
WE KNOW MUCH ABOUT YOU...
...AND THE SUN STONE.
AGGGHHHHAH
THIS IS...THIS IS IMPOSSIBLE.
NO. NOT
OSSIBLE...

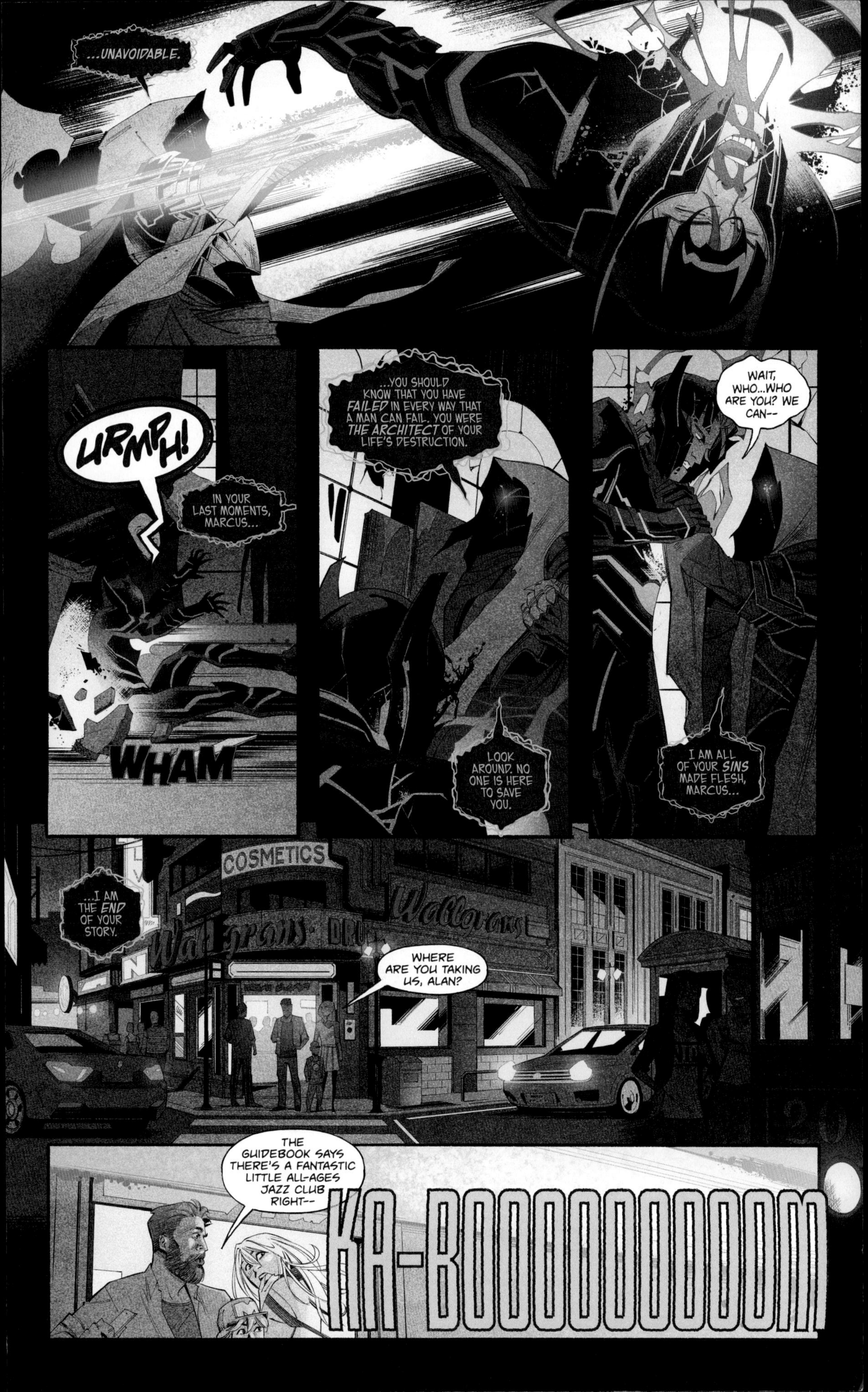
...UNAVOIDABLE.
URMPH!
IN YOUR LAST MOMENTS, MARCUS...
WHAM
...YOU SHOULD KNOW THAT YOU HAVE FAILED IN EVERY WAY THAT A MAN CAN FAIL. YOU WERE THE ARCHITECT OF YOUR LIFE'S DESTRUCTION.
LOOK AROUND. NO ONE IS HERE TO SAVE YOU.
WAIT, WHO...WHO ARE YOU? WE CAN--
I AM ALL OF YOUR SINS MADE FLESH, MARCUS...
COSMETICS
...I AM THE END OF YOUR STORY.
WHERE ARE YOU TAKING US, ALAN?
THE GUIDEBOOK SAYS THERE'S A FANTASTIC LITTLE ALL-AGES JAZZ CLUB RIGHT--
KA-BOOOOOOOOOM

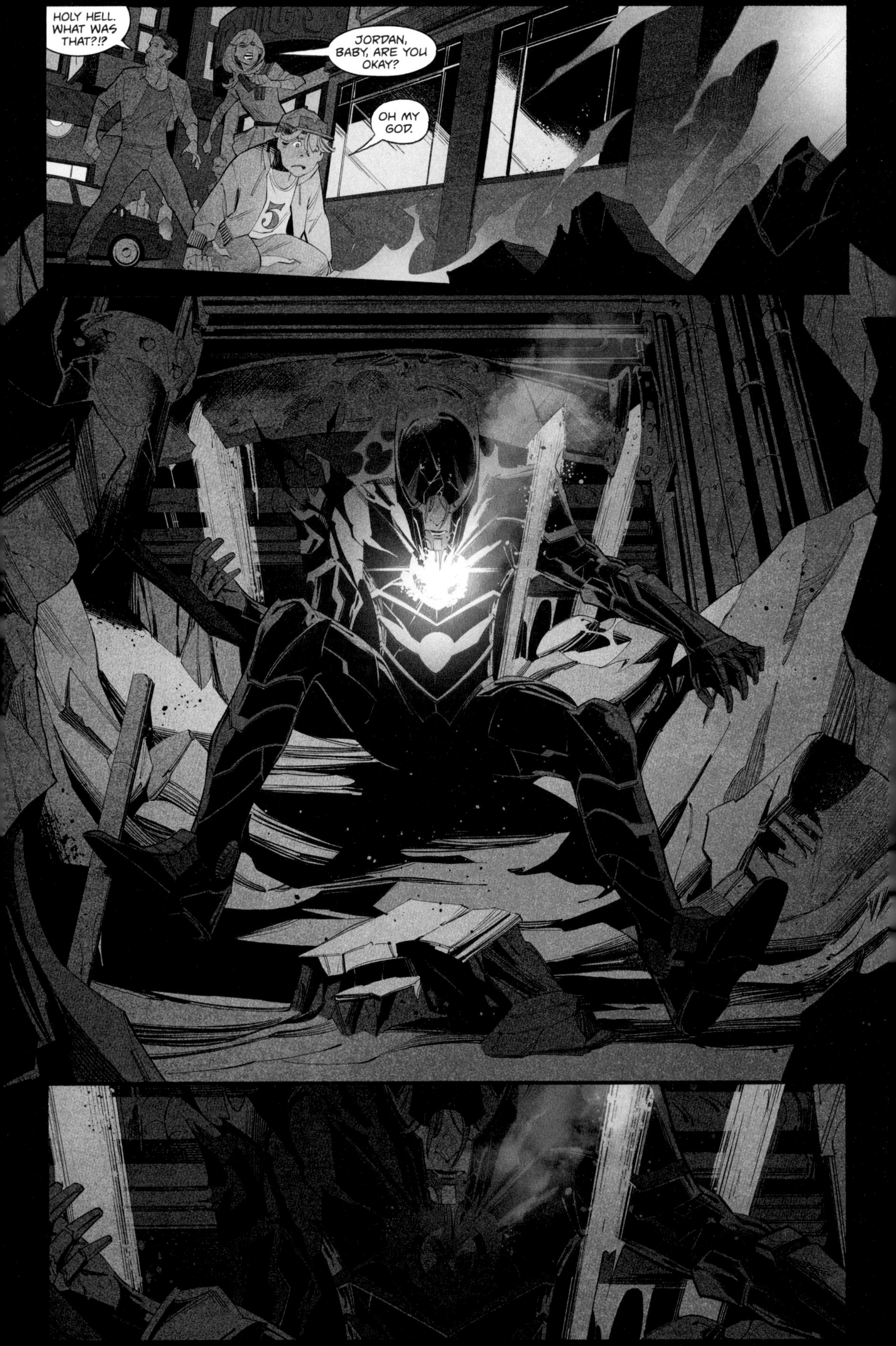
HOLY HELL. WHAT WAS THAT?!?
JORDAN, BABY, ARE YOU OKAY?
OH MY GOD.

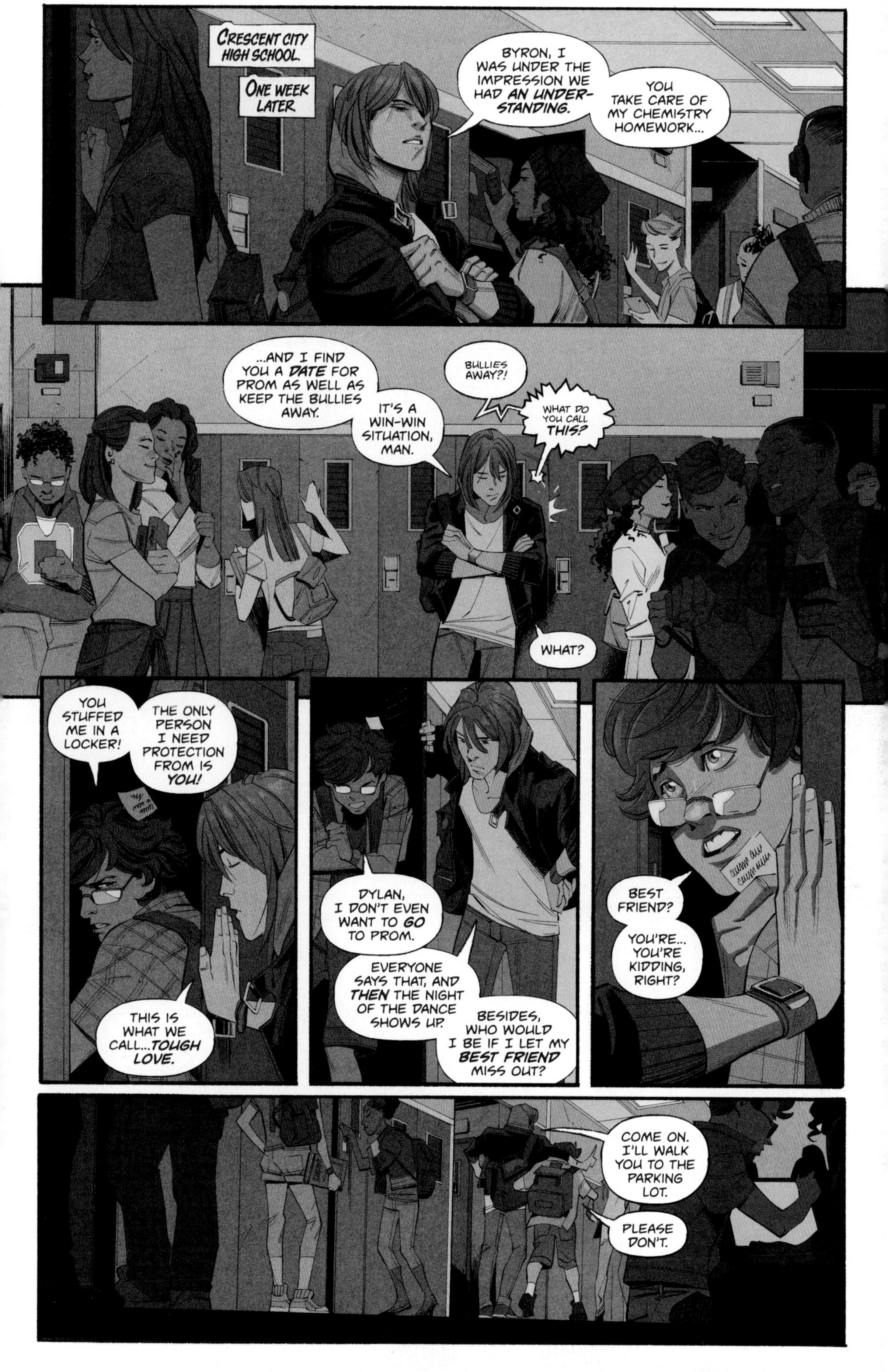

CRESCENT CITY HIGH SCHOOL.
ONE WEEK LATER
BYRON, I WAS UNDER THE IMPRESSION WE HAD AN UNDER-STANDING.
YOU TAKE CARE OF MY CHEMISTRY HOMEWORK...
...AND I FIND YOU A DATE FOR PROM AS WELL AS KEEP THE BULLIES AWAY.
IT'S A WIN-WIN SITUATION, MAN.
BULLIES AWAY?!
WHAT DO YOU CALL THIS?
WHAT?
YOU STUFFED ME IN A LOCKER!
THE ONLY PERSON I NEED PROTECTION FROM IS YOU!
THIS IS WHAT WE CALL...TOUGH LOVE.
DYLAN, I DON'T EVEN WANT TO GO TO PROM.
EVERYONE SAYS THAT, AND THEN THE NIGHT OF THE DANCE SHOWS UP.
BESIDES, WHO WOULD I BE IF I LET MY BEST FRIEND MISS OUT?
BEST FRIEND?
YOU'RE... YOU'RE KIDDING, RIGHT?
COME ON. I'LL WALK YOU TO THE PARKING LOT.
PLEASE DON'T.

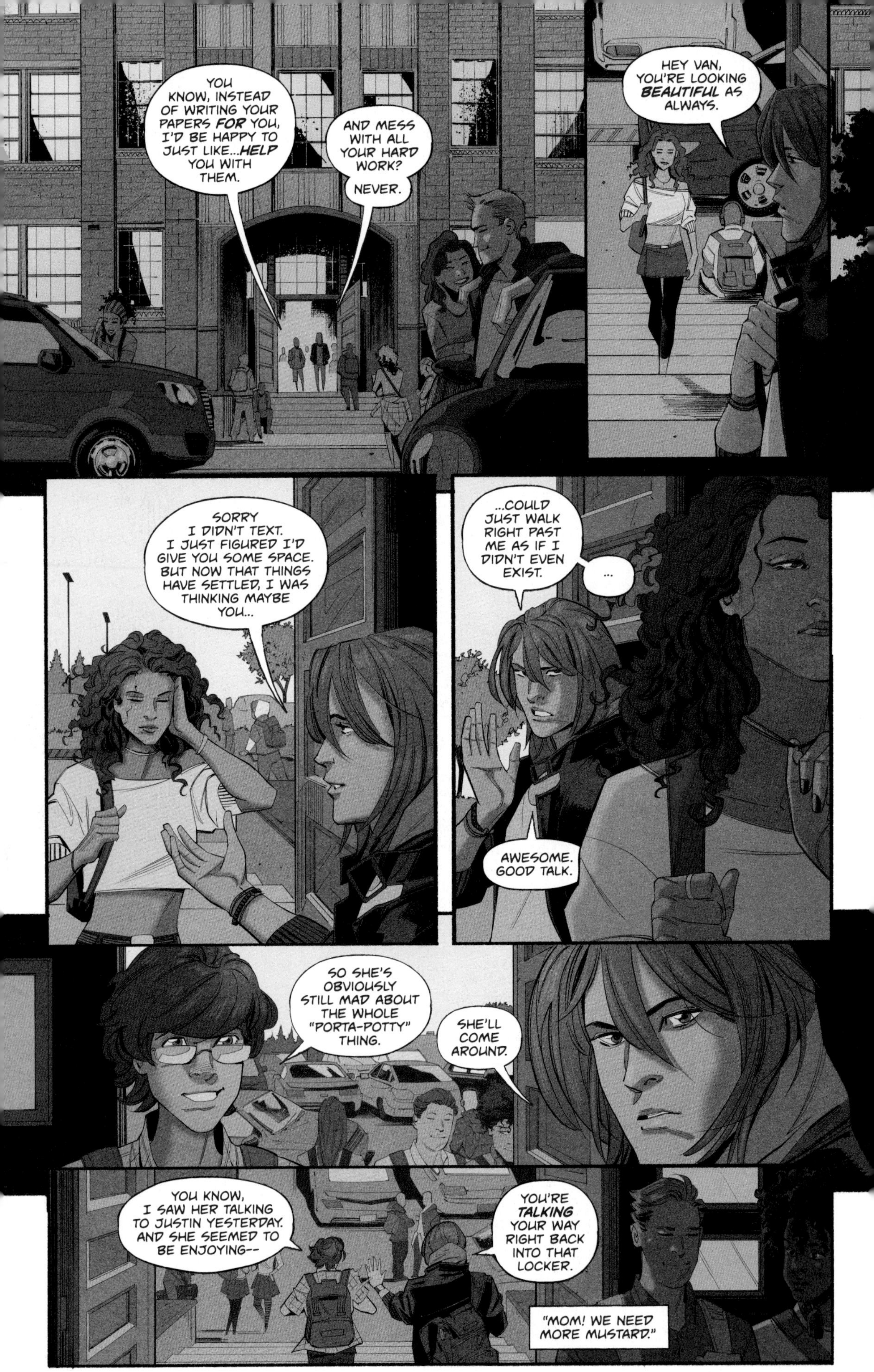
YOU KNOW, INSTEAD OF WRITING YOUR PAPERS FOR YOU, I'D BE HAPPY TO JUST LIKE...HELP YOU WITH THEM.
AND MESS WITH ALL YOUR HARD WORK?
NEVER.
HEY VAN, YOU'RE LOOKING BEAUTIFUL AS ALWAYS.
SORRY I DIDN'T TEXT. I JUST FIGURED I'D GIVE YOU SOME SPACE. BUT NOW THAT THINGS HAVE SETTLED, I WAS THINKING MAYBE YOU...
...COULD JUST WALK RIGHT PAST ME AS IF I DIDN'T EVEN EXIST.
...
AWESOME. GOOD TALK.
SO SHE'S OBVIOUSLY STILL MAD ABOUT THE WHOLE "PORTA-POTTY" THING.
SHE'LL COME AROUND.
YOU KNOW, I SAW HER TALKING TO JUSTIN YESTERDAY. AND SHE SEEMED TO BE ENJOYING--
YOU'RE TALKING YOUR WAY RIGHT BACK INTO THAT LOCKER.
"MOM! WE NEED MORE MUSTARD."

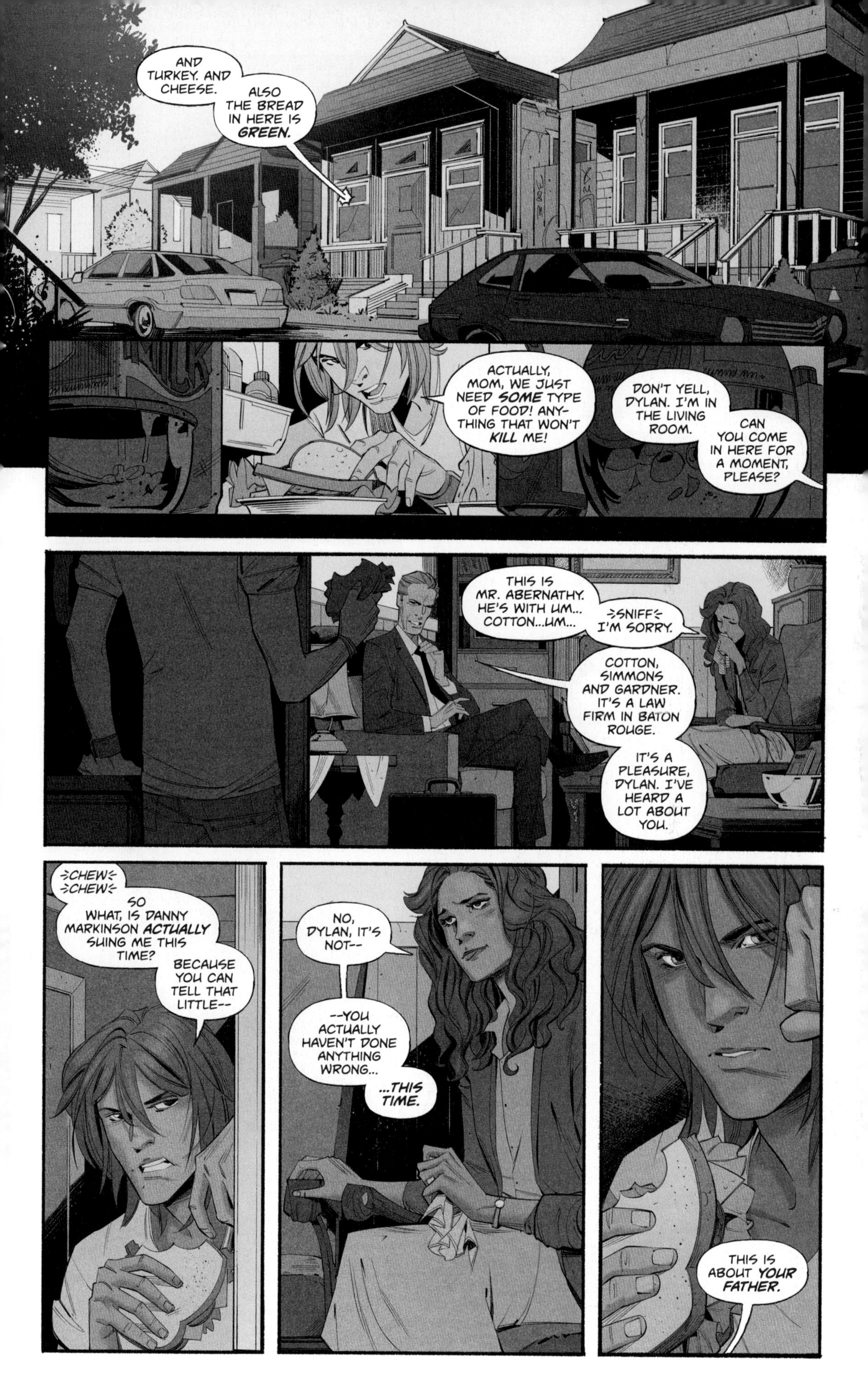
AND TURKEY. AND CHEESE.
ALSO THE BREAD IN HERE IS GREEN.
ACTUALLY, MOM, WE JUST NEED SOME TYPE OF FOOD! ANYTHING THAT WON'T KILL ME!
DON'T YELL, DYLAN. I'M IN THE LIVING ROOM.
CAN YOU COME IN HERE FOR A MOMENT, PLEASE?
THIS IS MR. ABERNATHY. HE'S WITH UM... COTTON...UM...
SNIFF I'M SORRY.
COTTON, SIMMONS AND GARDNER. IT'S A LAW FIRM IN BATON ROUGE.
IT'S A PLEASURE, DYLAN. I'VE HEARD A LOT ABOUT YOU.
CHEW CHEW
SO WHAT, IS DANNY MARKINSON ACTUALLY SUING ME THIS TIME?
BECAUSE YOU CAN TELL THAT LITTLE--
NO, DYLAN, IT'S NOT--
--YOU ACTUALLY HAVEN'T DONE ANYTHING WRONG...
...THIS TIME.
THIS IS ABOUT YOUR FATHER.

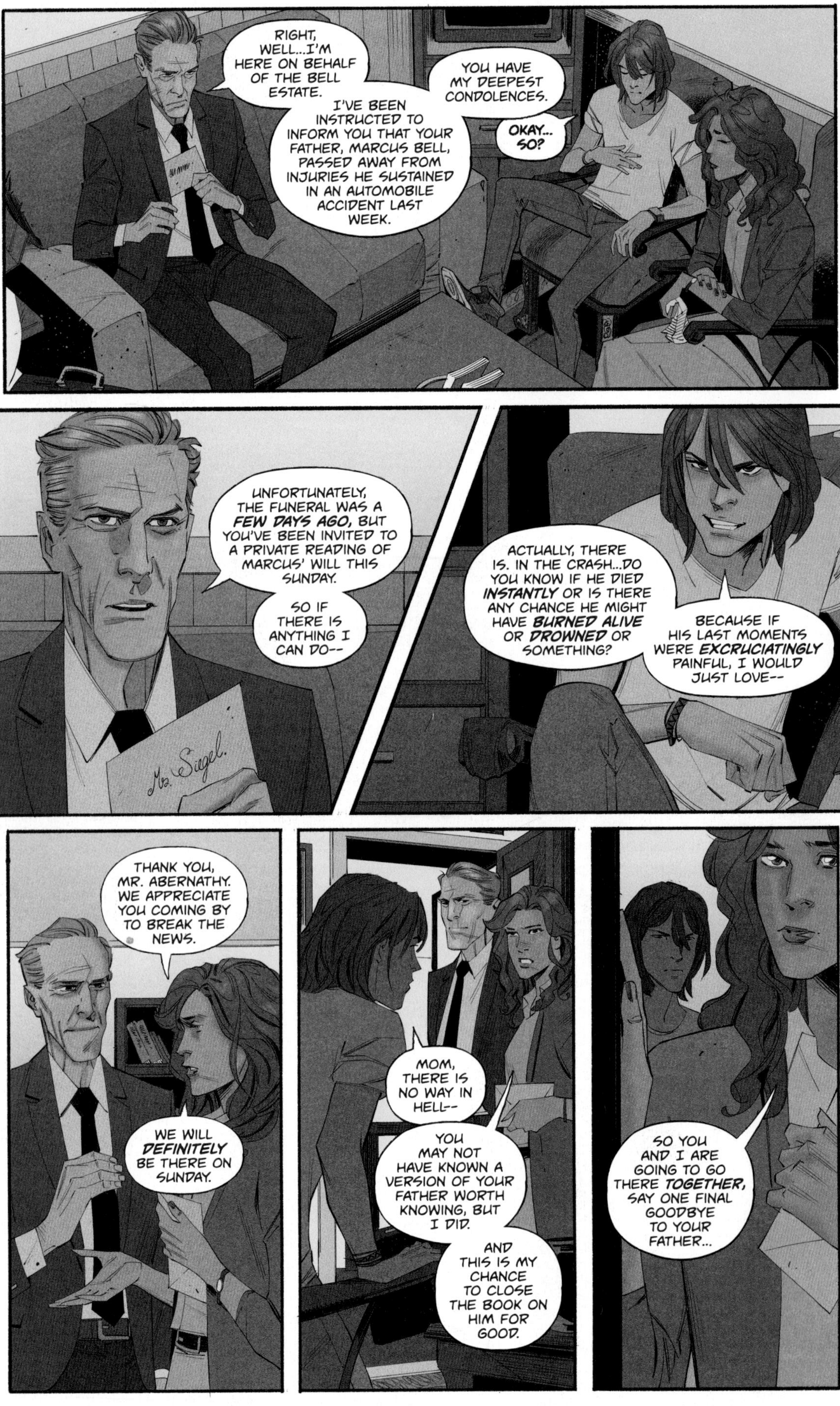
RIGHT, WELL...I'M HERE ON BEHALF OF THE BELL ESTATE.
I'VE BEEN INSTRUCTED TO INFORM YOU THAT YOUR FATHER, MARCUS BELL, PASSED AWAY FROM INJURIES HE SUSTAINED IN AN AUTOMOBILE ACCIDENT LAST WEEK.
YOU HAVE MY DEEPEST CONDOLENCES.
OKAY... SO?
UNFORTUNATELY, THE FUNERAL WAS A FEW DAYS AGO, BUT YOU'VE BEEN INVITED TO A PRIVATE READING OF MARCUS' WILL THIS SUNDAY.
SO IF THERE IS ANYTHING I CAN DO--
Ms. Siegel.
ACTUALLY, THERE IS. IN THE CRASH...DO YOU KNOW IF HE DIED INSTANTLY OR IS THERE ANY CHANCE HE MIGHT HAVE BURNED ALIVE OR DROWNED OR SOMETHING?
BECAUSE IF HIS LAST MOMENTS WERE EXCRUCIATINGLY PAINFUL, I WOULD JUST LOVE--
THANK YOU, MR. ABERNATHY. WE APPRECIATE YOU COMING BY TO BREAK THE NEWS.
WE WILL DEFINITELY BE THERE ON SUNDAY.
MOM, THERE IS NO WAY IN HELL--
YOU MAY NOT HAVE KNOWN A VERSION OF YOUR FATHER WORTH KNOWING, BUT I DID.
AND THIS IS MY CHANCE TO CLOSE THE BOOK ON HIM FOR GOOD.
SO YOU AND I ARE GOING TO GO THERE TOGETHER, SAY ONE FINAL GOODBYE TO YOUR FATHER...

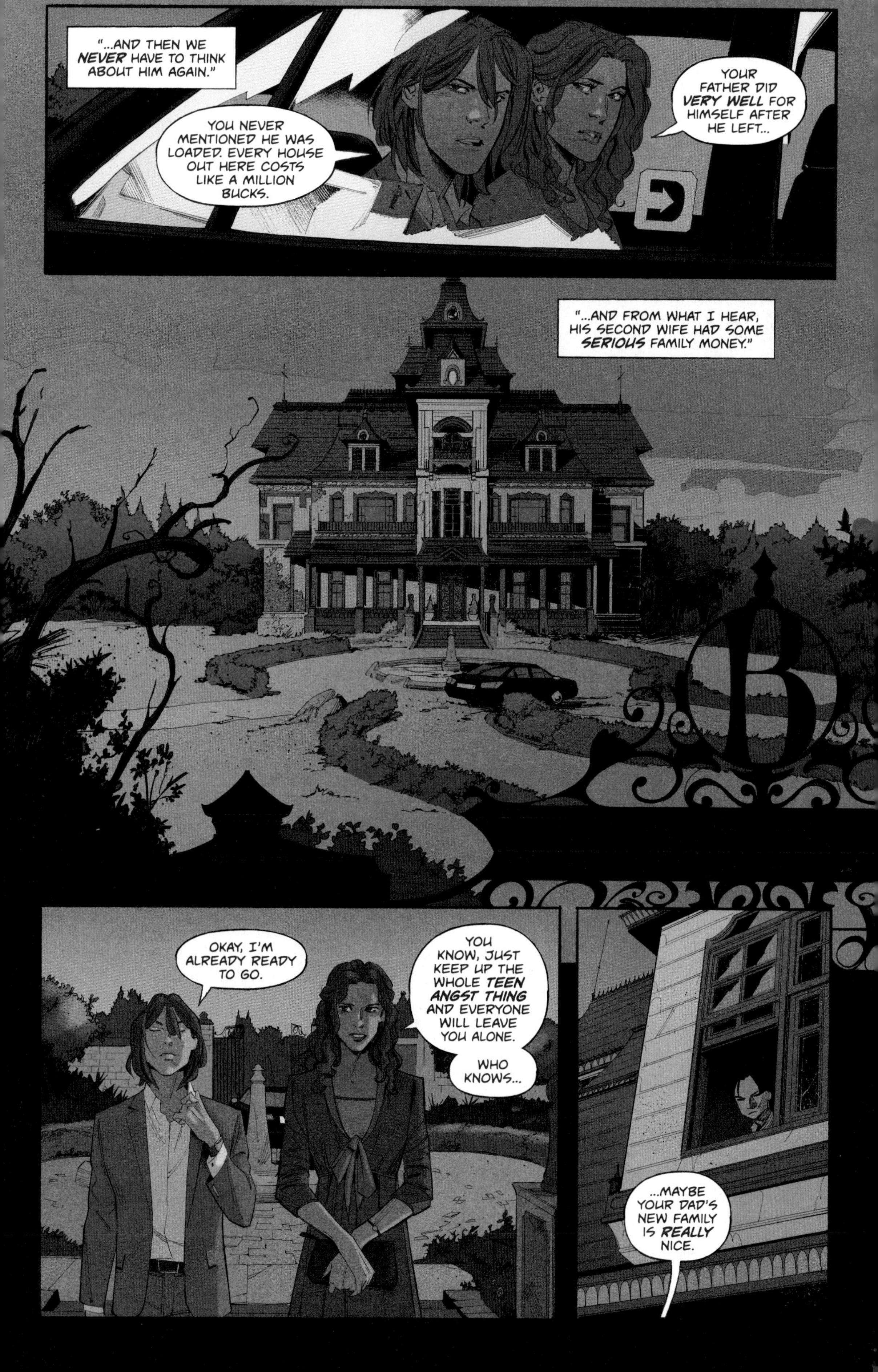
"...AND THEN WE NEVER HAVE TO THINK ABOUT HIM AGAIN."
YOU NEVER MENTIONED HE WAS LOADED. EVERY HOUSE OUT HERE COSTS LIKE A MILLION BUCKS.
YOUR FATHER DID VERY WELL FOR HIMSELF AFTER HE LEFT...
"...AND FROM WHAT I HEAR, HIS SECOND WIFE HAD SOME SERIOUS FAMILY MONEY."
B
OKAY, I'M ALREADY READY TO GO.
YOU KNOW, JUST KEEP UP THE WHOLE TEEN ANGST THING AND EVERYONE WILL LEAVE YOU ALONE.
WHO KNOWS...
...MAYBE YOUR DAD'S NEW FAMILY IS REALLY NICE.

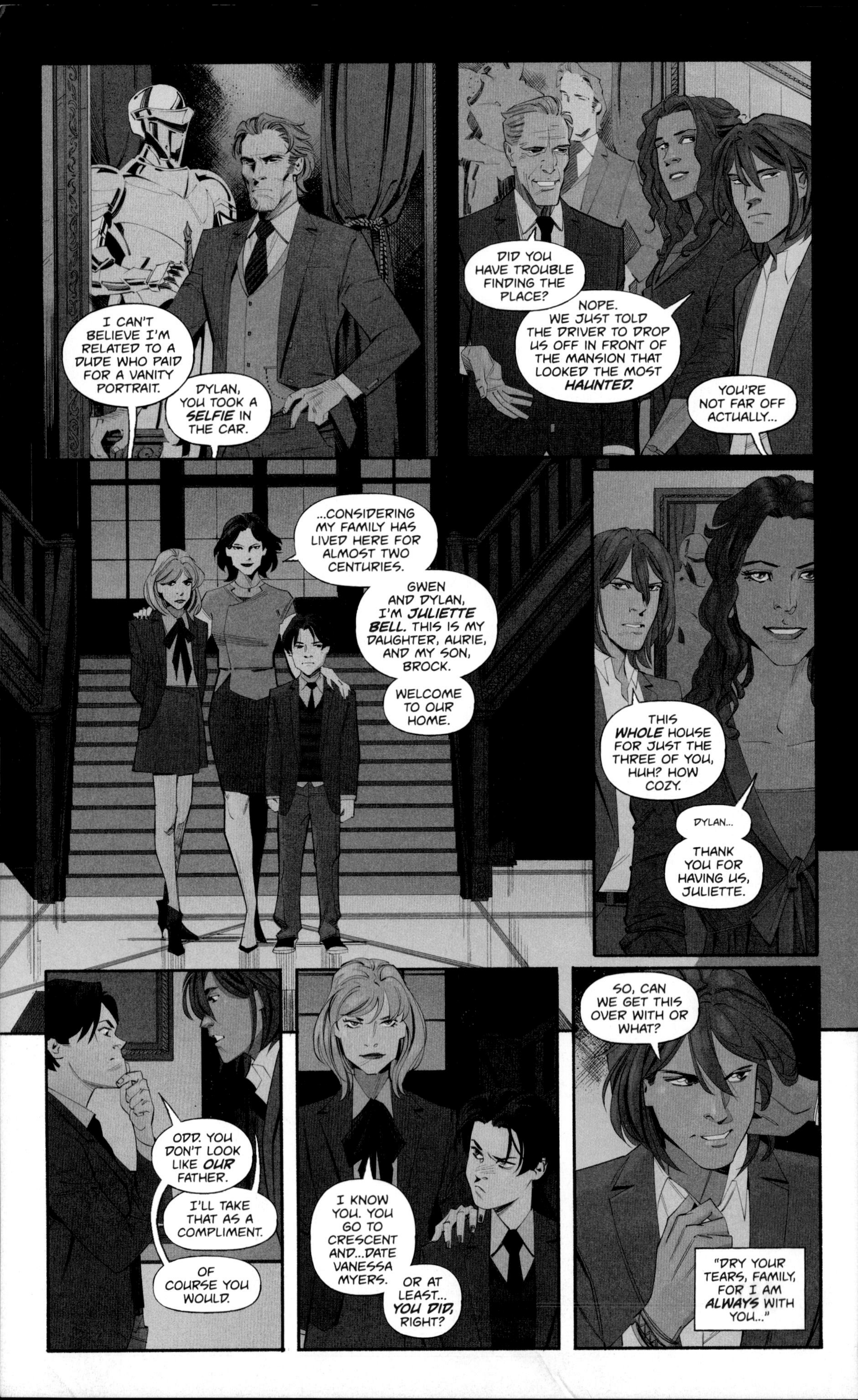
I CAN'T BELIEVE I'M RELATED TO A DUDE WHO PAID FOR A VANITY PORTRAIT.
DYLAN, YOU TOOK A SELFIE IN THE CAR.
DID YOU HAVE TROUBLE FINDING THE PLACE?
NOPE. WE JUST TOLD THE DRIVER TO DROP US OFF IN FRONT OF THE MANSION THAT LOOKED THE MOST HAUNTED.
YOU'RE NOT FAR OFF ACTUALLY...
...CONSIDERING MY FAMILY HAS LIVED HERE FOR ALMOST TWO CENTURIES.
GWEN AND DYLAN, I'M JULIETTE BELL. THIS IS MY DAUGHTER, AURIE, AND MY SON, BROCK.
WELCOME TO OUR HOME.
THIS WHOLE HOUSE FOR JUST THE THREE OF YOU, HUH? HOW COZY.
DYLAN...
THANK YOU FOR HAVING US, JULIETTE.
ODD. YOU DON'T LOOK LIKE OUR FATHER.
I'LL TAKE THAT AS A COMPLIMENT.
OF COURSE YOU WOULD.
I KNOW YOU. YOU GO TO CRESCENT AND...DATE VANESSA MYERS.
OR AT LEAST... YOU DID, RIGHT?
SO, CAN WE GET THIS OVER WITH OR WHAT?
"DRY YOUR TEARS, FAMILY, FOR I AM ALWAYS WITH YOU..."

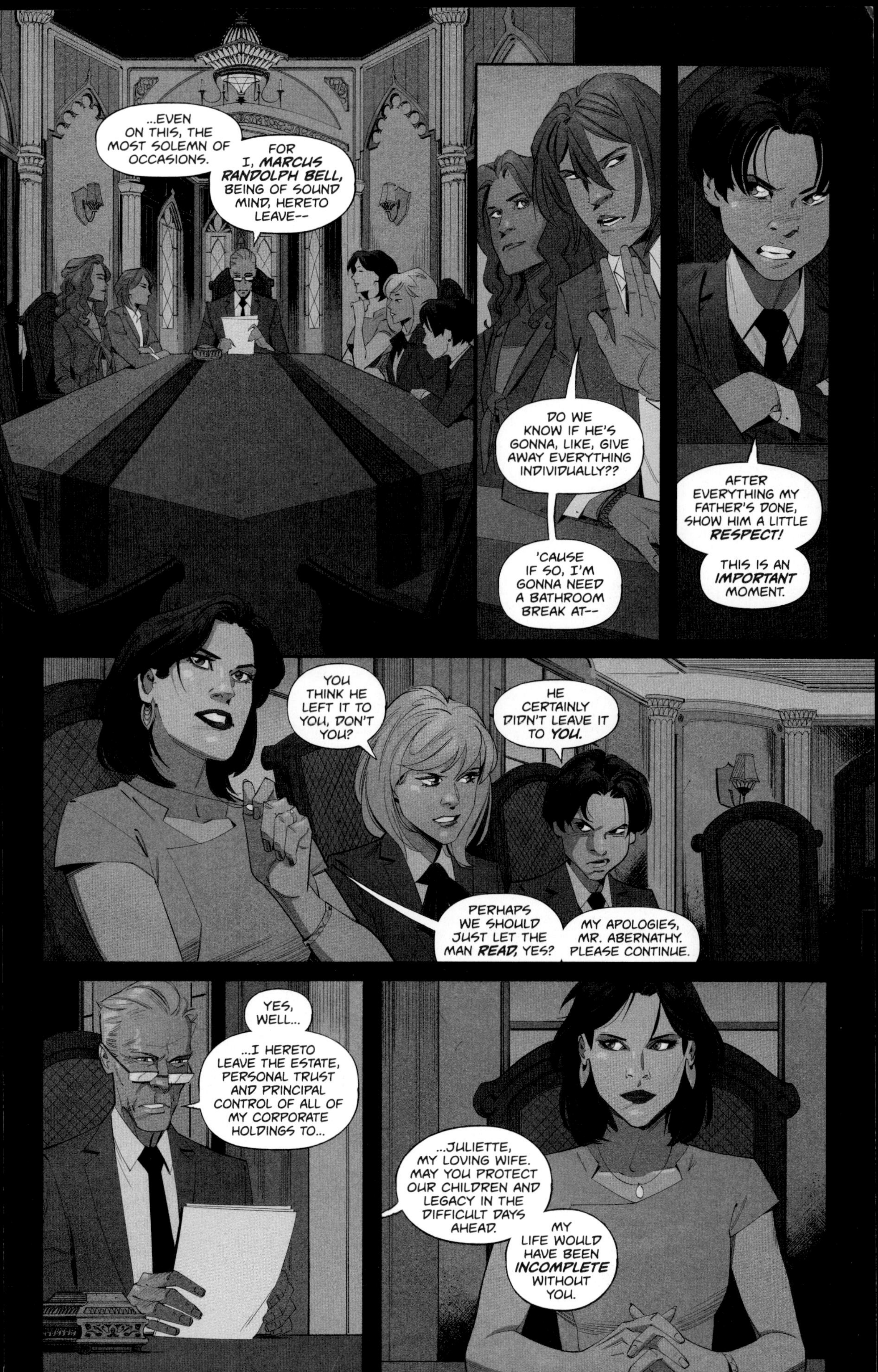
...EVEN ON THIS, THE MOST SOLEMN OF OCCASIONS.
FOR I, MARCUS RANDOLPH BELL, BEING OF SOUND MIND, HERETO LEAVE--
DO WE KNOW IF HE'S GONNA, LIKE, GIVE AWAY EVERYTHING INDIVIDUALLY??
'CAUSE IF SO, I'M GONNA NEED A BATHROOM BREAK AT--
AFTER EVERYTHING MY FATHER'S DONE, SHOW HIM A LITTLE RESPECT!
THIS IS AN IMPORTANT MOMENT.
YOU THINK HE LEFT IT TO YOU, DON'T YOU?
HE CERTAINLY DIDN'T LEAVE IT TO YOU.
PERHAPS WE SHOULD JUST LET THE MAN READ, YES?
MY APOLOGIES, MR. ABERNATHY. PLEASE CONTINUE.
YES, WELL...
...I HERETO LEAVE THE ESTATE, PERSONAL TRUST AND PRINCIPAL CONTROL OF ALL OF MY CORPORATE HOLDINGS TO...
...JULIETTE, MY LOVING WIFE. MAY YOU PROTECT OUR CHILDREN AND LEGACY IN THE DIFFICULT DAYS AHEAD.
MY LIFE WOULD HAVE BEEN INCOMPLETE WITHOUT YOU.

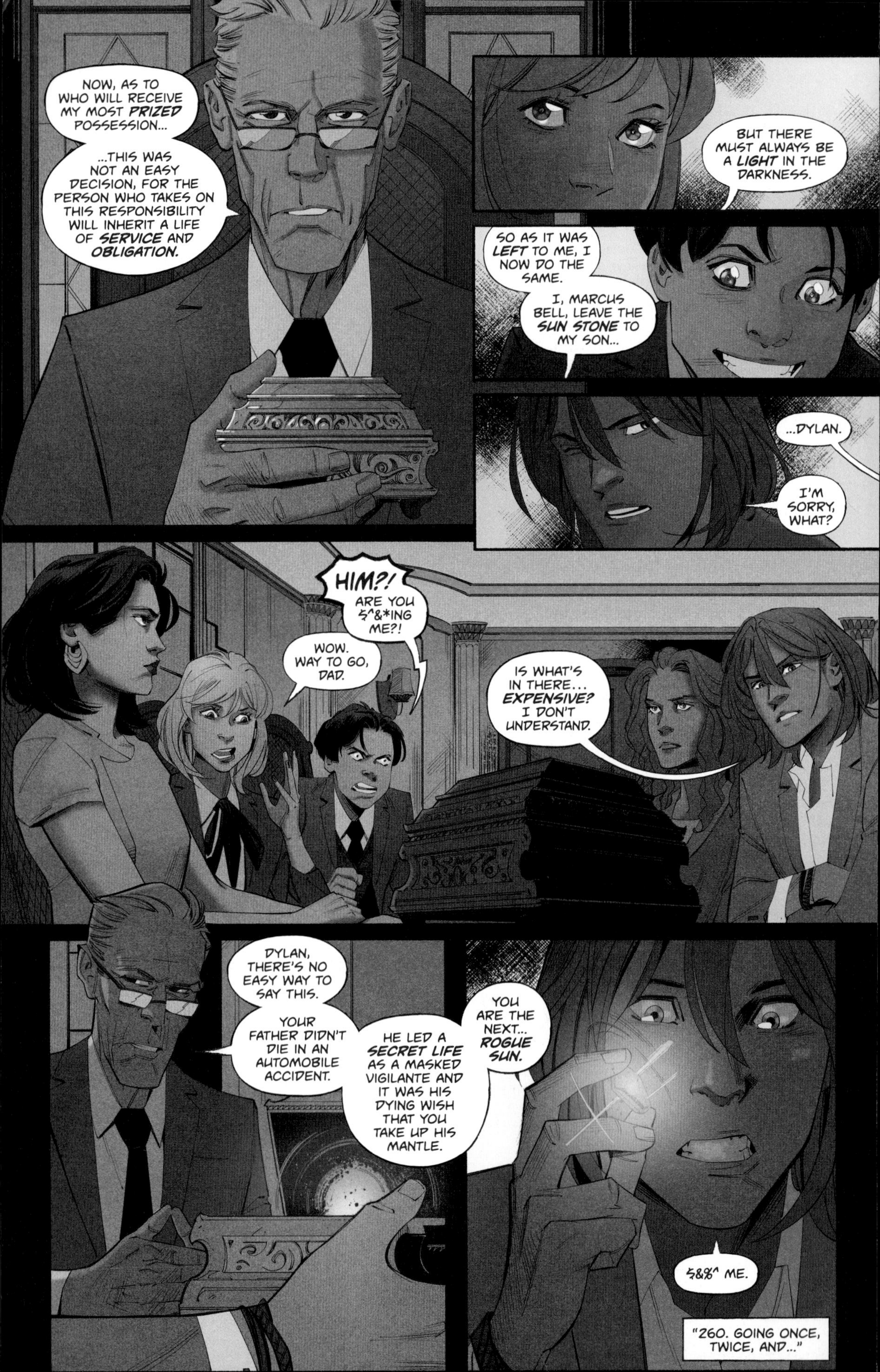
NOW, AS TO WHO WILL RECEIVE MY MOST PRIZED POSSESSION...
...THIS WAS NOT AN EASY DECISION, FOR THE PERSON WHO TAKES ON THIS RESPONSIBILITY WILL INHERIT A LIFE OF SERVICE AND OBLIGATION.
BUT THERE MUST ALWAYS BE A LIGHT IN THE DARKNESS.
SO AS IT WAS LEFT TO ME, I NOW DO THE SAME.
I, MARCUS BELL, LEAVE THE SUN STONE TO MY SON...
...DYLAN.
I'M SORRY, WHAT?
HIM?!
ARE YOU %^&*ING ME?!
WOW. WAY TO GO, DAD.
IS WHAT'S IN THERE... EXPENSIVE? I DON'T UNDERSTAND.
DYLAN, THERE'S NO EASY WAY TO SAY THIS.
YOUR FATHER DIDN'T DIE IN AN AUTOMOBILE ACCIDENT.
HE LED A SECRET LIFE AS A MASKED VIGILANTE AND IT WAS HIS DYING WISH THAT YOU TAKE UP HIS MANTLE.
YOU ARE THE NEXT... ROGUE SUN.
%&%^ ME.
"260. GOING ONCE, TWICE, AND..."

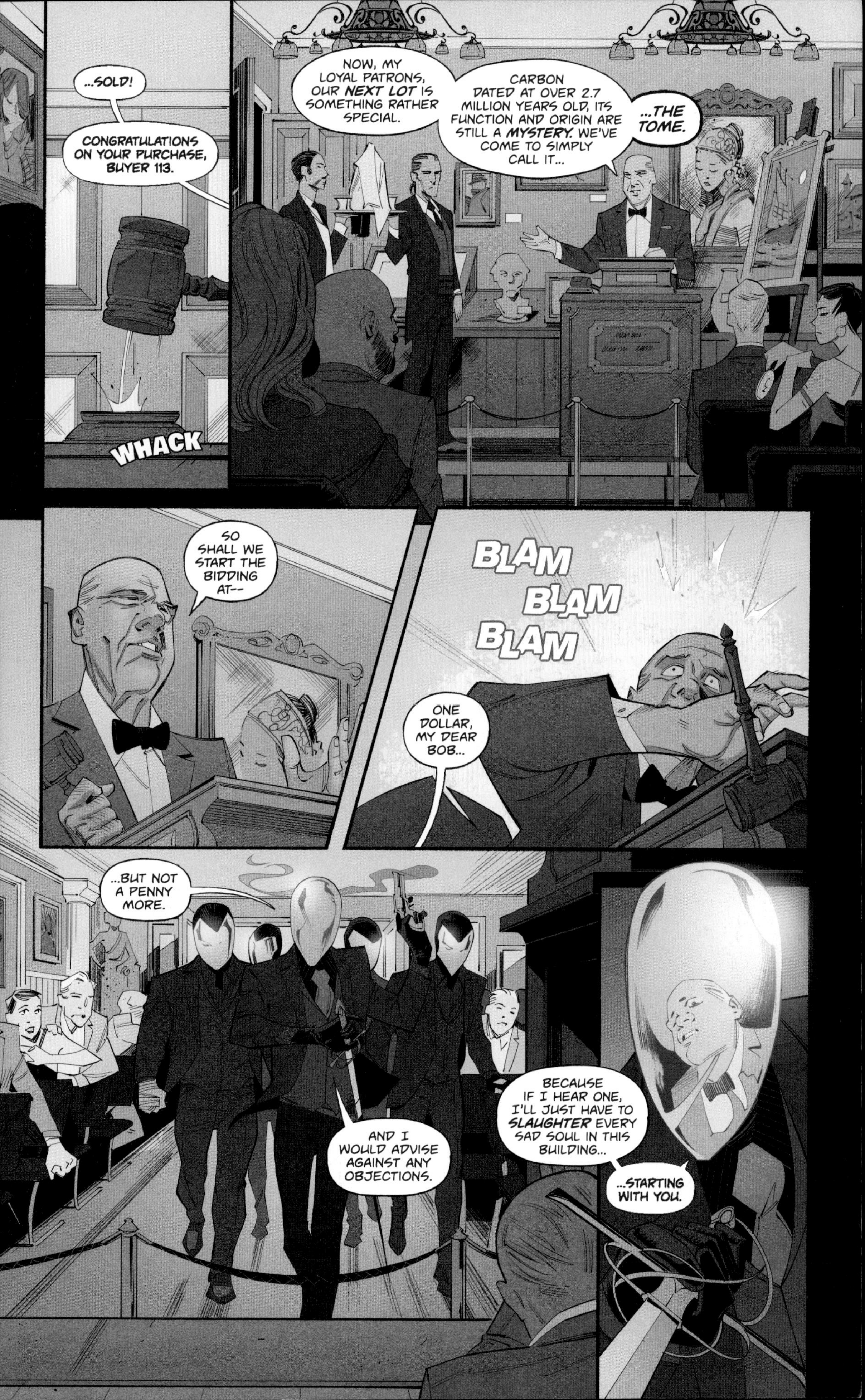
...SOLD!
CONGRATULATIONS ON YOUR PURCHASE, BUYER 113.
WHACK
NOW, MY LOYAL PATRONS, OUR NEXT LOT IS SOMETHING RATHER SPECIAL.
CARBON DATED AT OVER 2.7 MILLION YEARS OLD, ITS FUNCTION AND ORIGIN ARE STILL A MYSTERY. WE'VE COME TO SIMPLY CALL IT...
...THE TOME.
SO SHALL WE START THE BIDDING AT--
BLAM
BLAM
BLAM
ONE DOLLAR, MY DEAR BOB...
...BUT NOT A PENNY MORE.
AND I WOULD ADVISE AGAINST ANY OBJECTIONS.
BECAUSE IF I HEAR ONE, I'LL JUST HAVE TO SLAUGHTER EVERY SAD SOUL IN THIS BUILDING...
...STARTING WITH YOU.

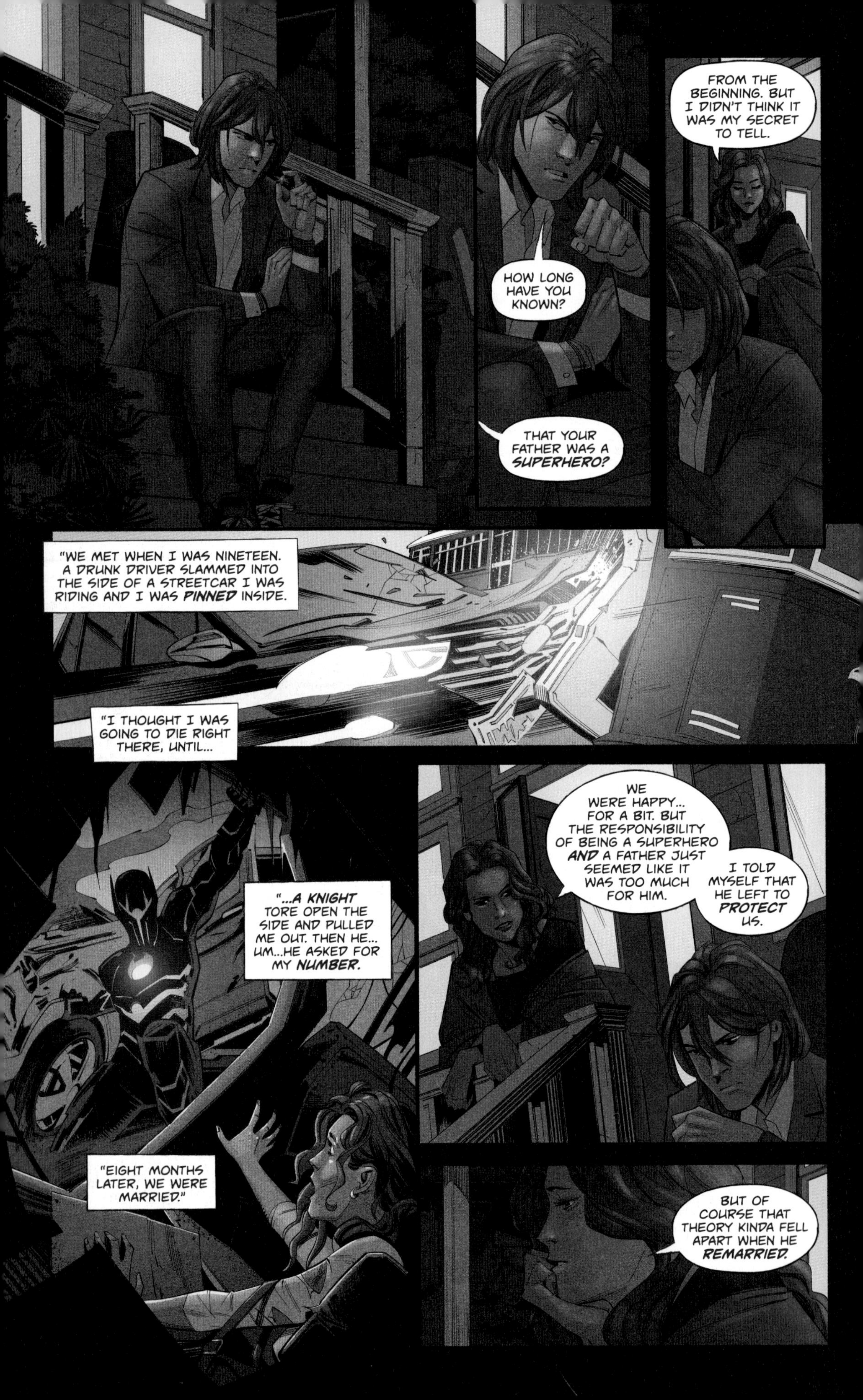
HOW LONG HAVE YOU KNOWN?
THAT YOUR FATHER WAS A SUPERHERO?
FROM THE BEGINNING. BUT I DIDN'T THINK IT WAS MY SECRET TO TELL.
"WE MET WHEN I WAS NINETEEN. A DRUNK DRIVER SLAMMED INTO THE SIDE OF A STREETCAR I WAS RIDING AND I WAS PINNED INSIDE.
"I THOUGHT I WAS GOING TO DIE RIGHT THERE, UNTIL...
"...A KNIGHT TORE OPEN THE SIDE AND PULLED ME OUT. THEN HE... UM...HE ASKED FOR MY NUMBER.
"EIGHT MONTHS LATER, WE WERE MARRIED."
WE WERE HAPPY... FOR A BIT. BUT THE RESPONSIBILITY OF BEING A SUPERHERO AND A FATHER JUST SEEMED LIKE IT WAS TOO MUCH FOR HIM.
I TOLD MYSELF THAT HE LEFT TO PROTECT US.
BUT OF COURSE THAT THEORY KINDA FELL APART WHEN HE REMARRIED.

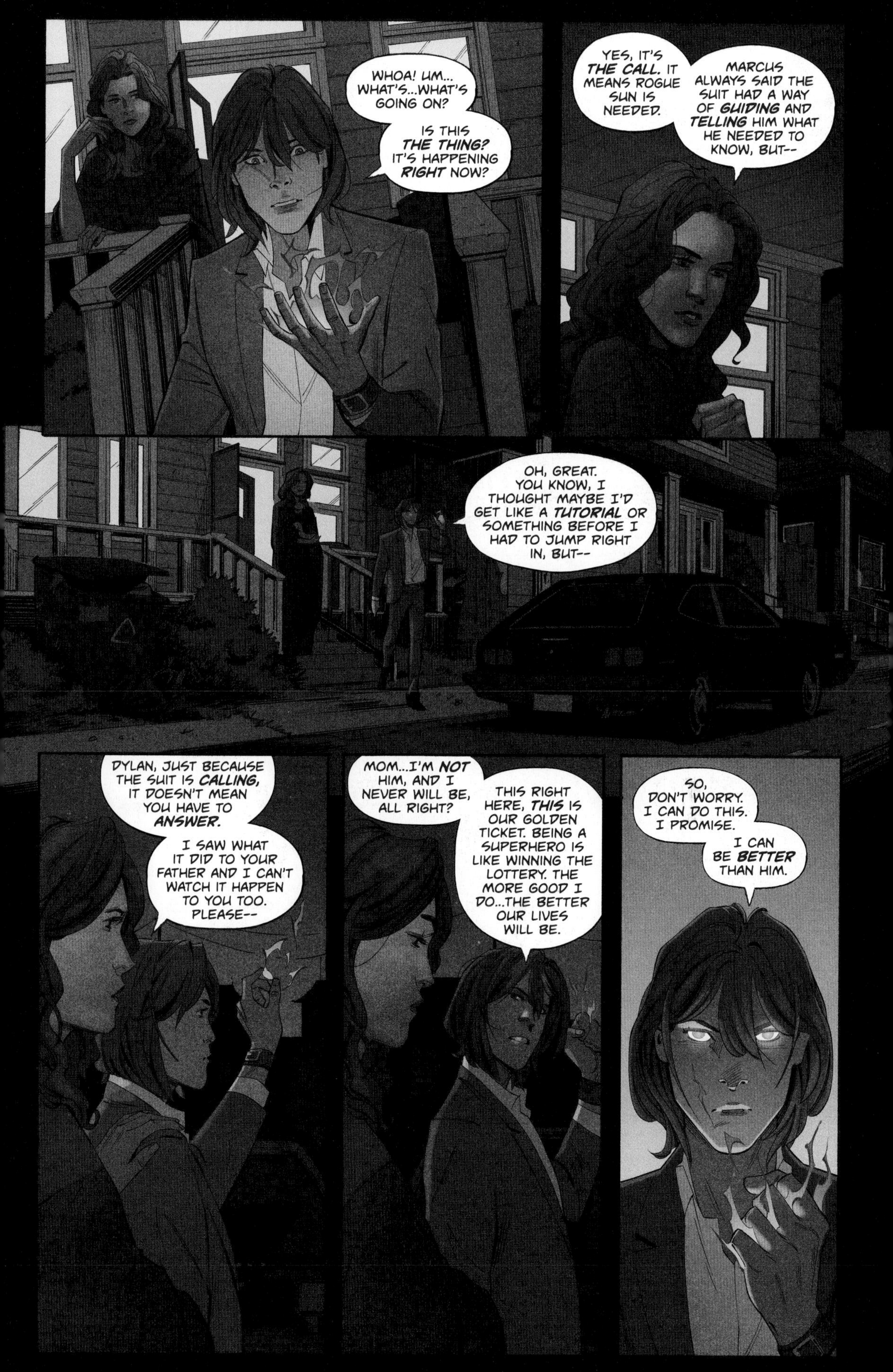
WHOA! UM... WHAT'S...WHAT'S GOING ON?
IS THIS THE THING? IT'S HAPPENING RIGHT NOW?
YES, IT'S THE CALL. IT MEANS ROGUE SUN IS NEEDED.
MARCUS ALWAYS SAID THE SUIT HAD A WAY OF GUIDING AND TELLING HIM WHAT HE NEEDED TO KNOW, BUT--
OH, GREAT. YOU KNOW, I THOUGHT MAYBE I'D GET LIKE A TUTORIAL OR SOMETHING BEFORE I HAD TO JUMP RIGHT IN, BUT--
DYLAN, JUST BECAUSE THE SUIT IS CALLING, IT DOESN'T MEAN YOU HAVE TO ANSWER.
I SAW WHAT IT DID TO YOUR FATHER AND I CAN'T WATCH IT HAPPEN TO YOU TOO. PLEASE--
MOM...I'M NOT HIM, AND I NEVER WILL BE, ALL RIGHT?
THIS RIGHT HERE, THIS IS OUR GOLDEN TICKET. BEING A SUPERHERO IS LIKE WINNING THE LOTTERY. THE MORE GOOD I DO...THE BETTER OUR LIVES WILL BE.
SO, DON'T WORRY. I CAN DO THIS. I PROMISE.
I CAN BE BETTER THAN HIM.

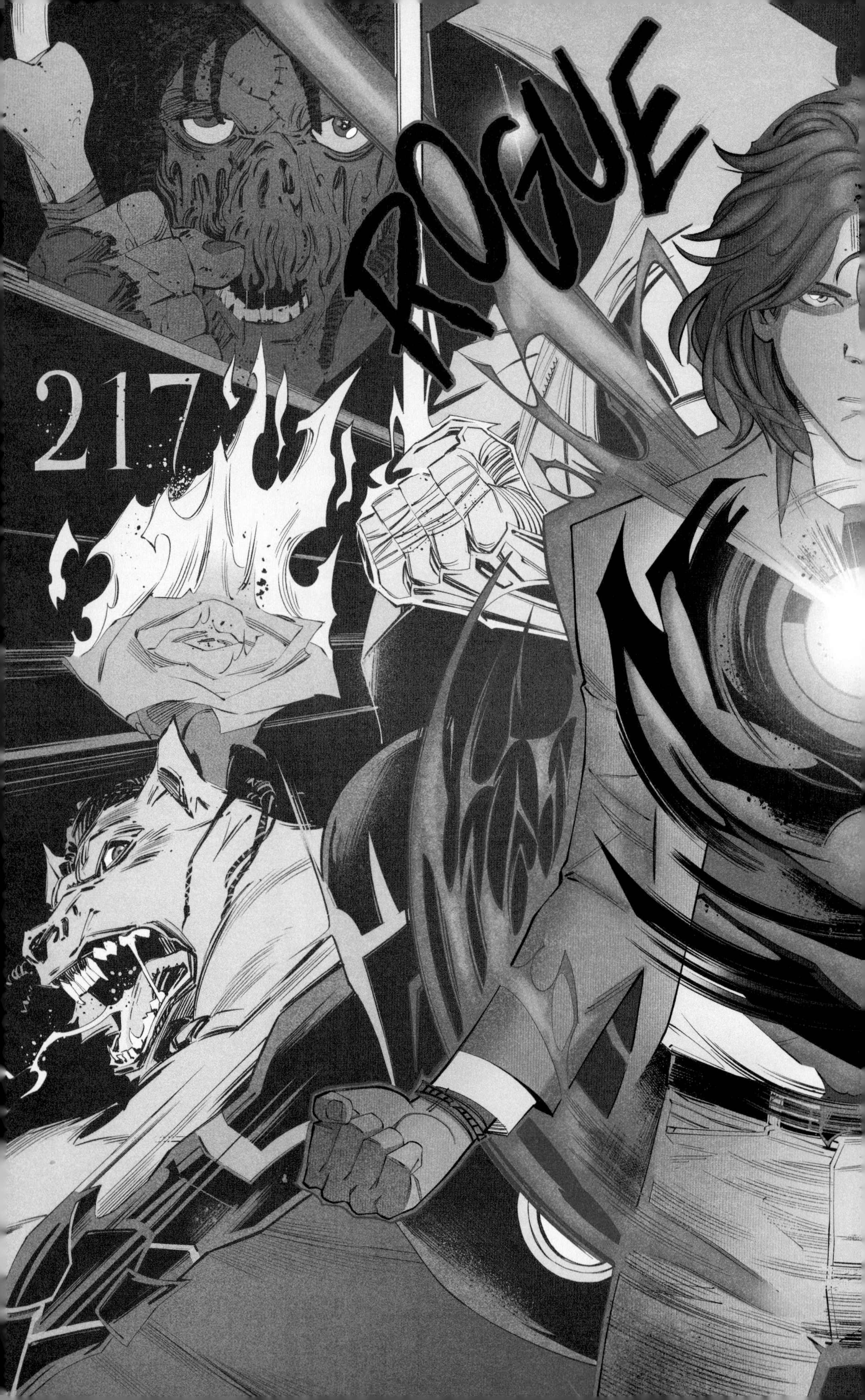
217
ROGUE

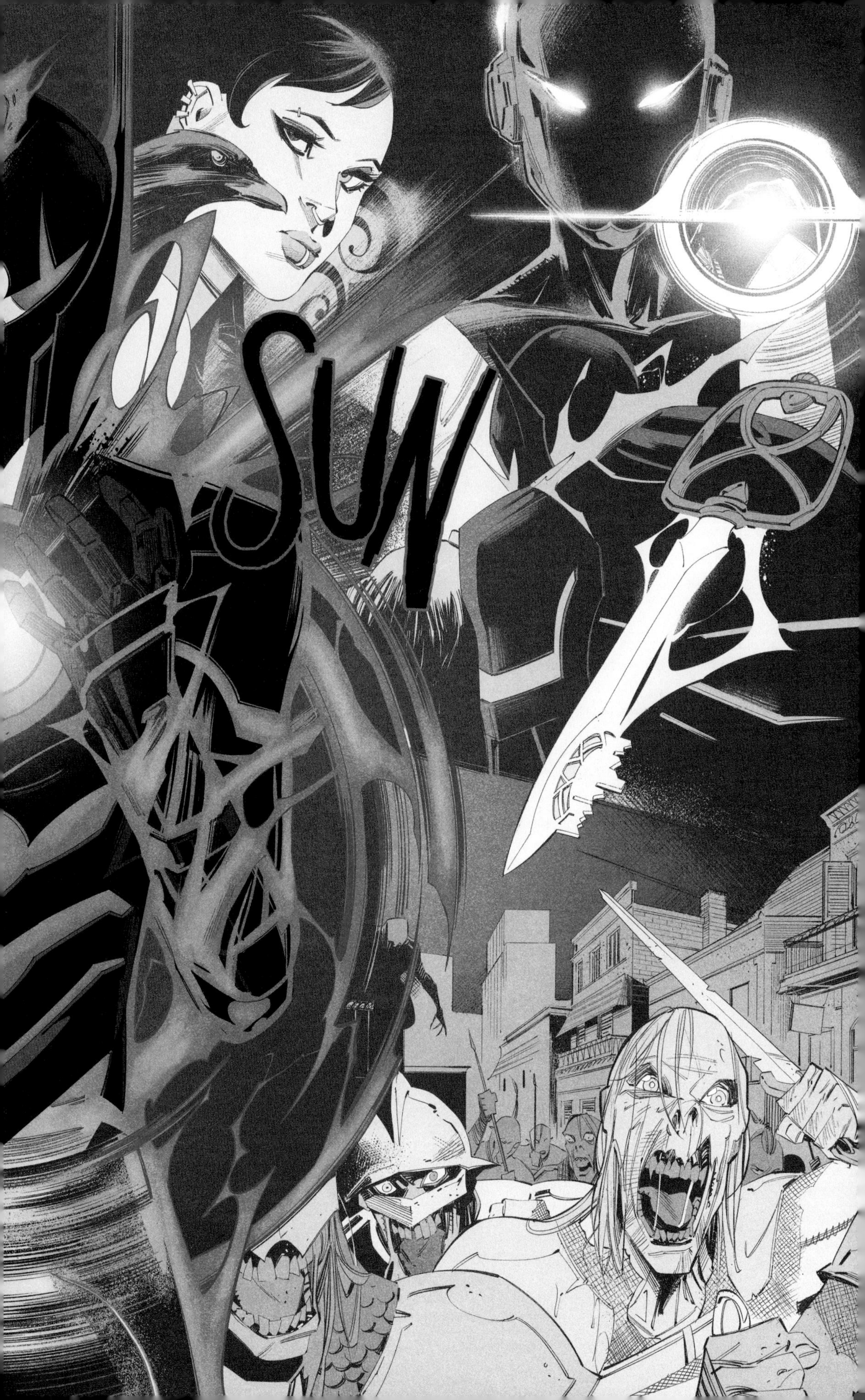
SUW

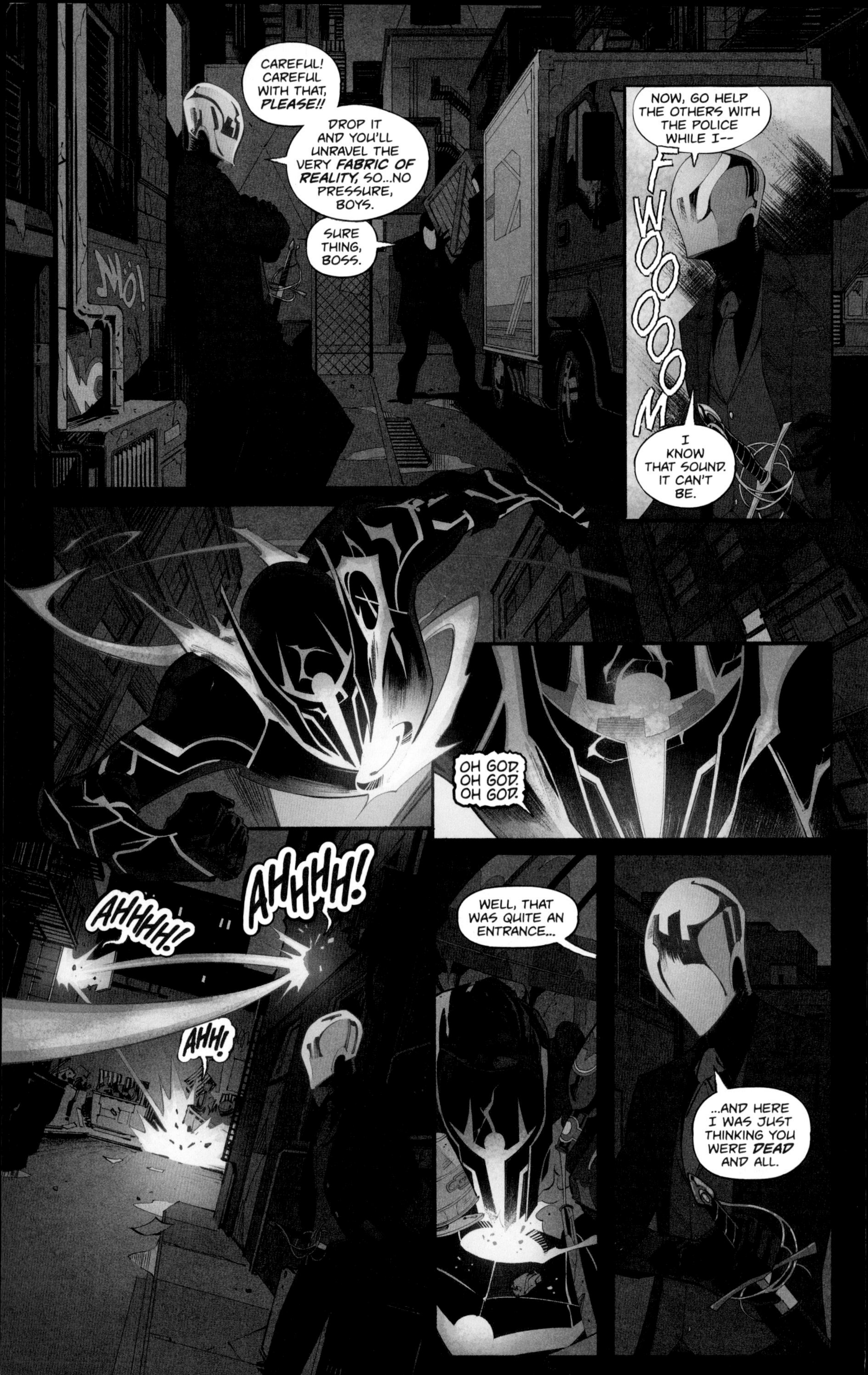
CAREFUL! CAREFUL WITH THAT, PLEASE!!
DROP IT AND YOU'LL UNRAVEL THE VERY FABRIC OF REALITY, SO...NO PRESSURE, BOYS.
SURE THING, BOSS.
NOW, GO HELP THE OTHERS WITH THE POLICE WHILE I--
FWOOOOOM
I KNOW THAT SOUND. IT CAN'T BE.
OH GOD. OH GOD. OH GOD.
AHHHH!
AHHHH!
AHH!
WELL, THAT WAS QUITE AN ENTRANCE...
...AND HERE I WAS JUST THINKING YOU WERE DEAD AND ALL.

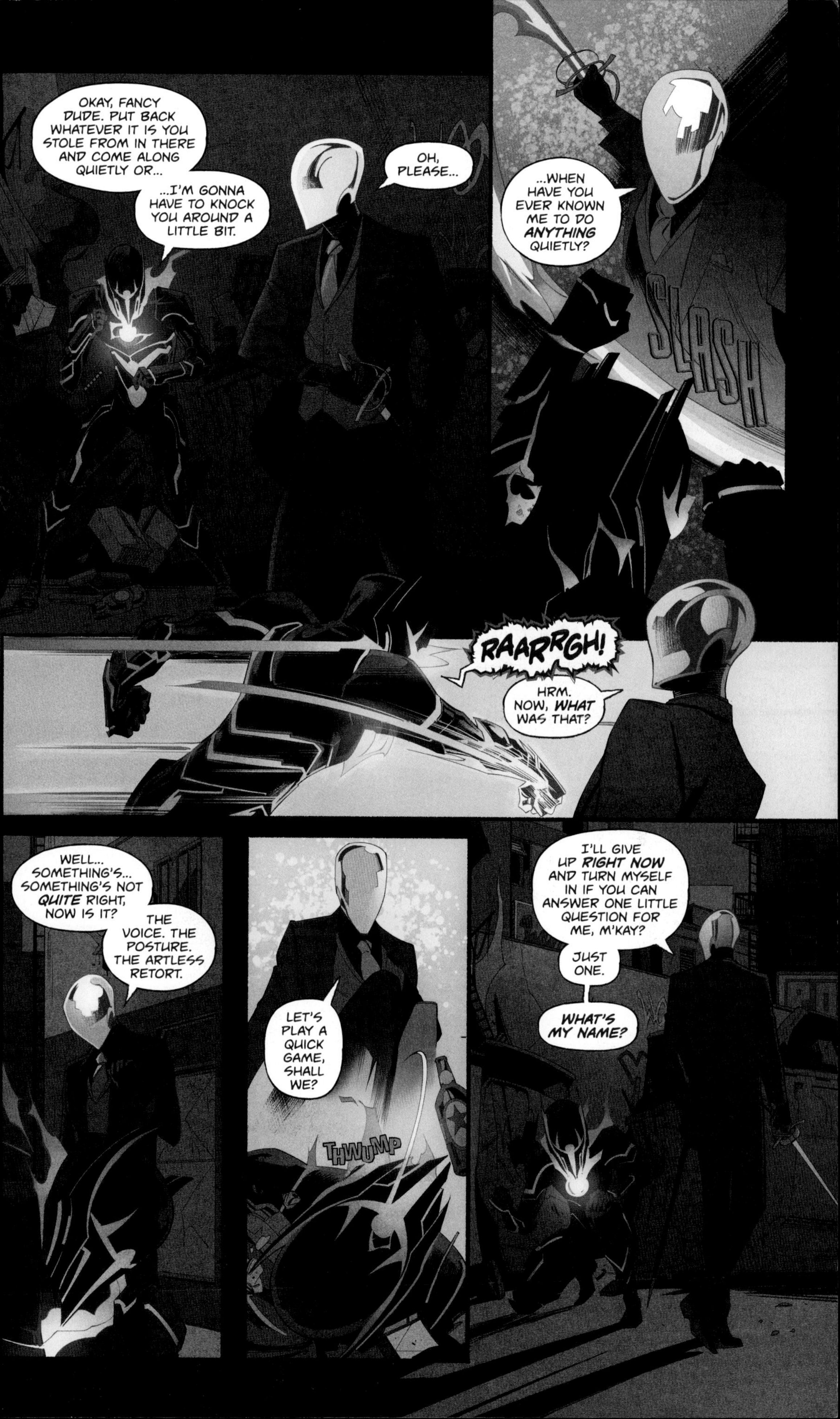
OKAY, FANCY DUDE. PUT BACK WHATEVER IT IS YOU STOLE FROM IN THERE AND COME ALONG QUIETLY OR...
...I'M GONNA HAVE TO KNOCK YOU AROUND A LITTLE BIT.
OH, PLEASE...
...WHEN HAVE YOU EVER KNOWN ME TO DO ANYTHING QUIETLY?
SLASH
RAARRGH!
HRM. NOW, WHAT WAS THAT?
WELL... SOMETHING'S... SOMETHING'S NOT QUITE RIGHT, NOW IS IT?
THE VOICE. THE POSTURE. THE ARTLESS RETORT.
LET'S PLAY A QUICK GAME, SHALL WE?
THWUMP
I'LL GIVE UP RIGHT NOW AND TURN MYSELF IN IF YOU CAN ANSWER ONE LITTLE QUESTION FOR ME, M'KAY?
JUST ONE.
WHAT'S MY NAME?

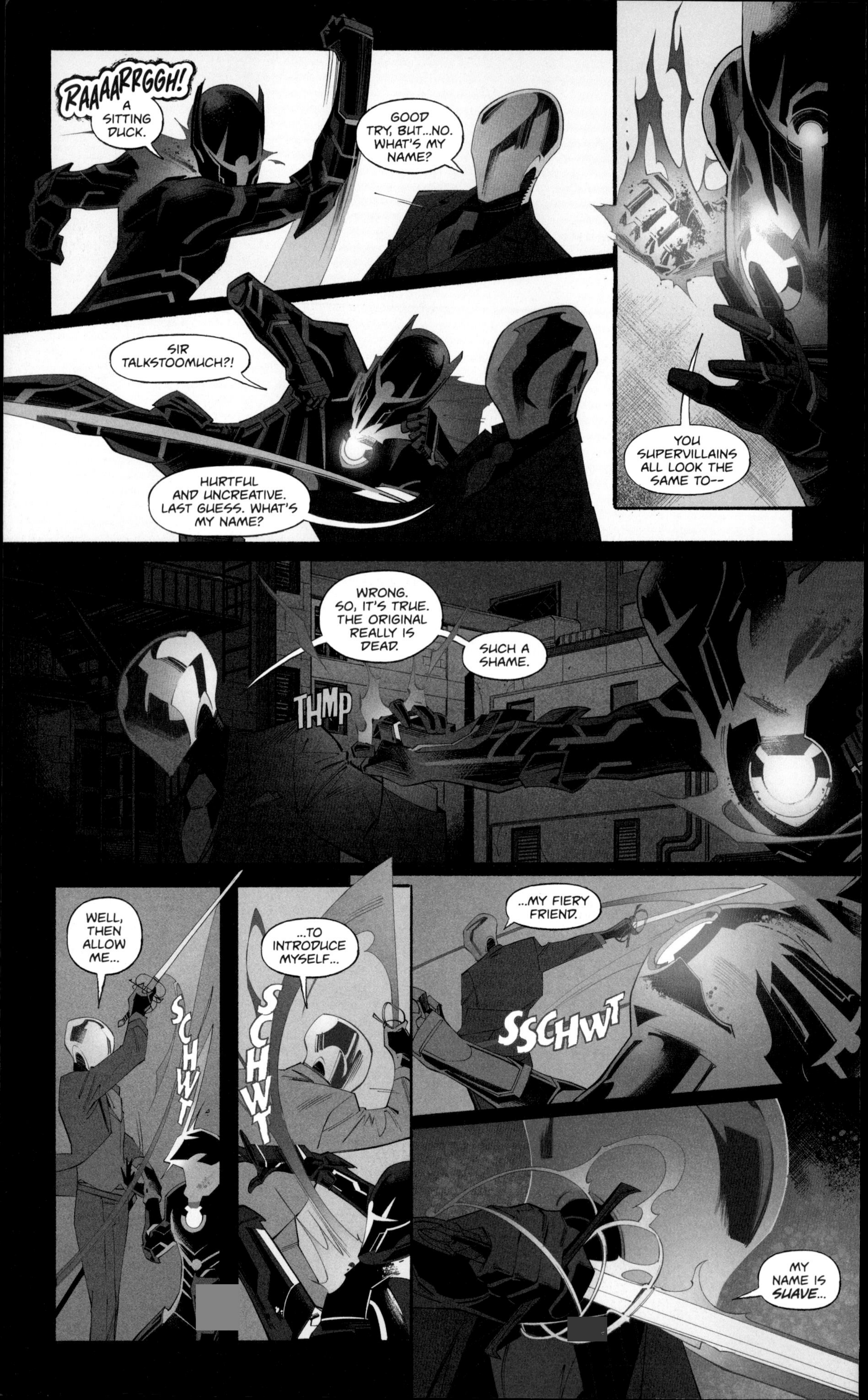
RAAAARRGGH!
A SITTING DUCK.
GOOD TRY, BUT...NO. WHAT'S MY NAME?
SIR TALKSTOOMUCH?!
HURTFUL AND UNCREATIVE. LAST GUESS. WHAT'S MY NAME?
YOU SUPERVILLAINS ALL LOOK THE SAME TO--
WRONG. SO, IT'S TRUE. THE ORIGINAL REALLY IS DEAD.
SUCH A SHAME.
THMP
WELL, THEN ALLOW ME...
SCHWT
...TO INTRODUCE MYSELF...
SCHWT
...MY FIERY FRIEND.
SSCHWT
MY NAME IS SUAVE...

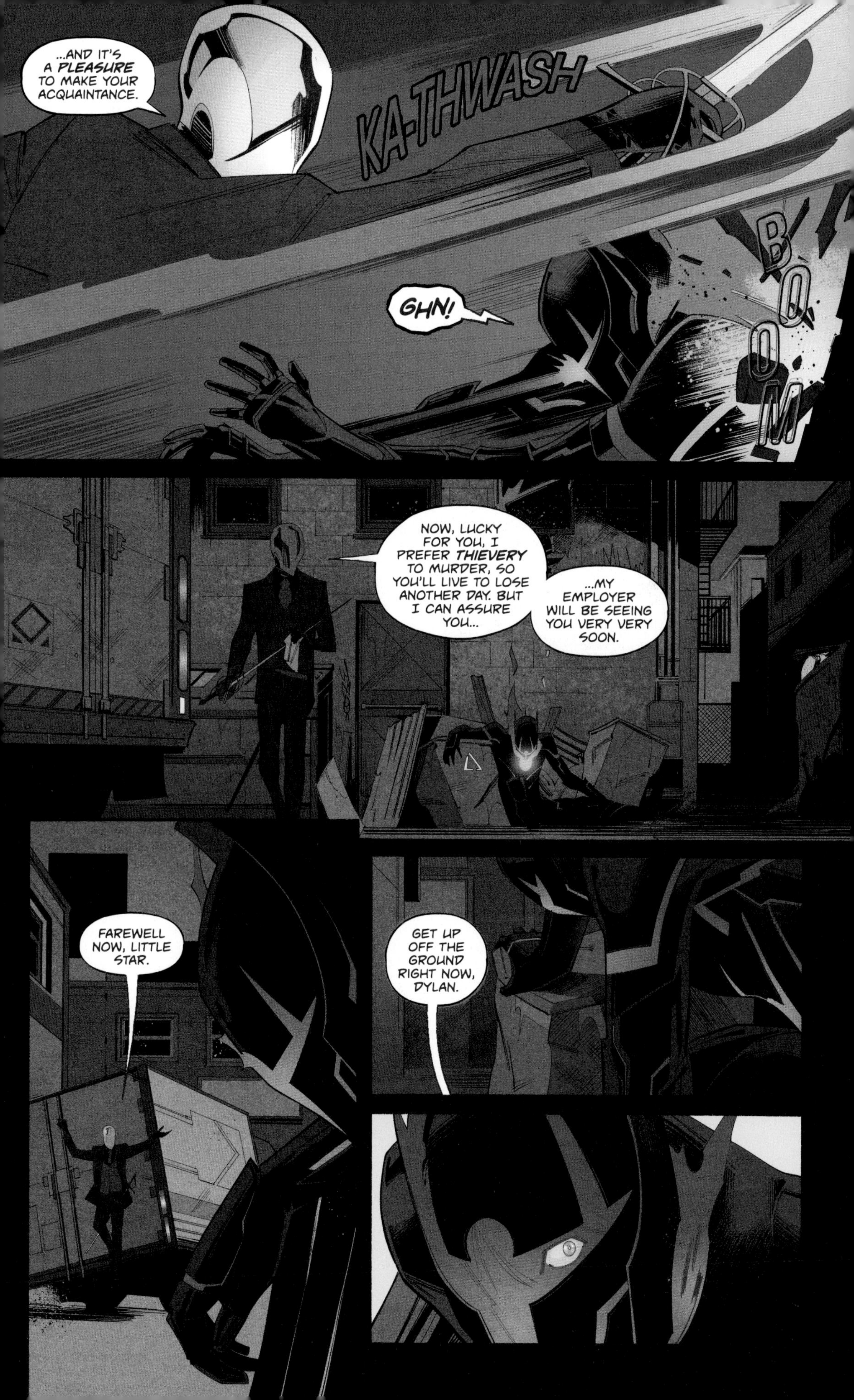
...AND IT'S A PLEASURE TO MAKE YOUR ACQUAINTANCE.
KA-THWASH
GHN!
BOOM
NOW, LUCKY FOR YOU, I PREFER THIEVERY TO MURDER, SO YOU'LL LIVE TO LOSE ANOTHER DAY. BUT I CAN ASSURE YOU...
...MY EMPLOYER WILL BE SEEING YOU VERY VERY SOON.
FAREWELL NOW, LITTLE STAR.
GET UP OFF THE GROUND RIGHT NOW, DYLAN.

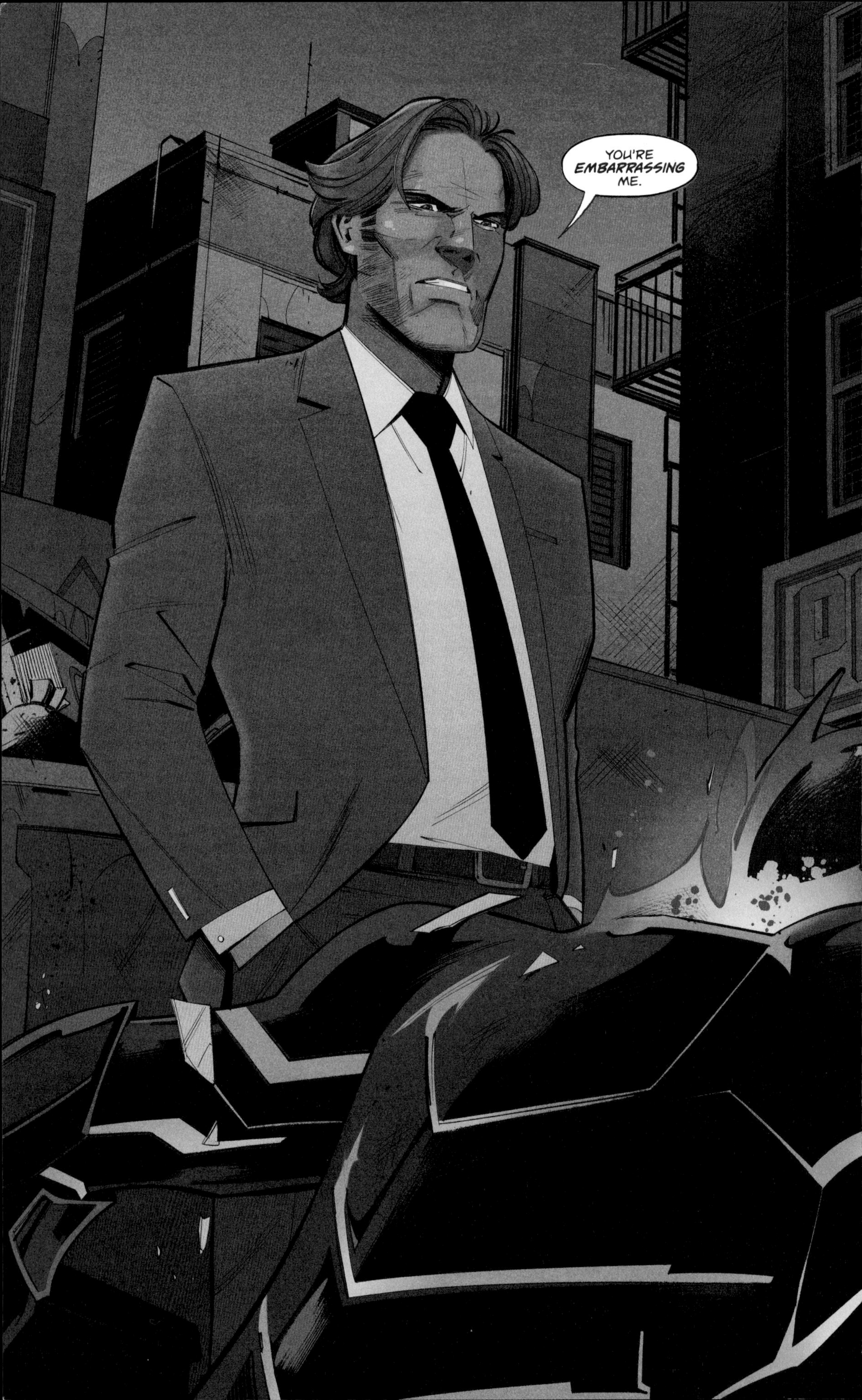
YOU'RE EMBARRASSING ME.

Chapter Two
Hunter's Moon

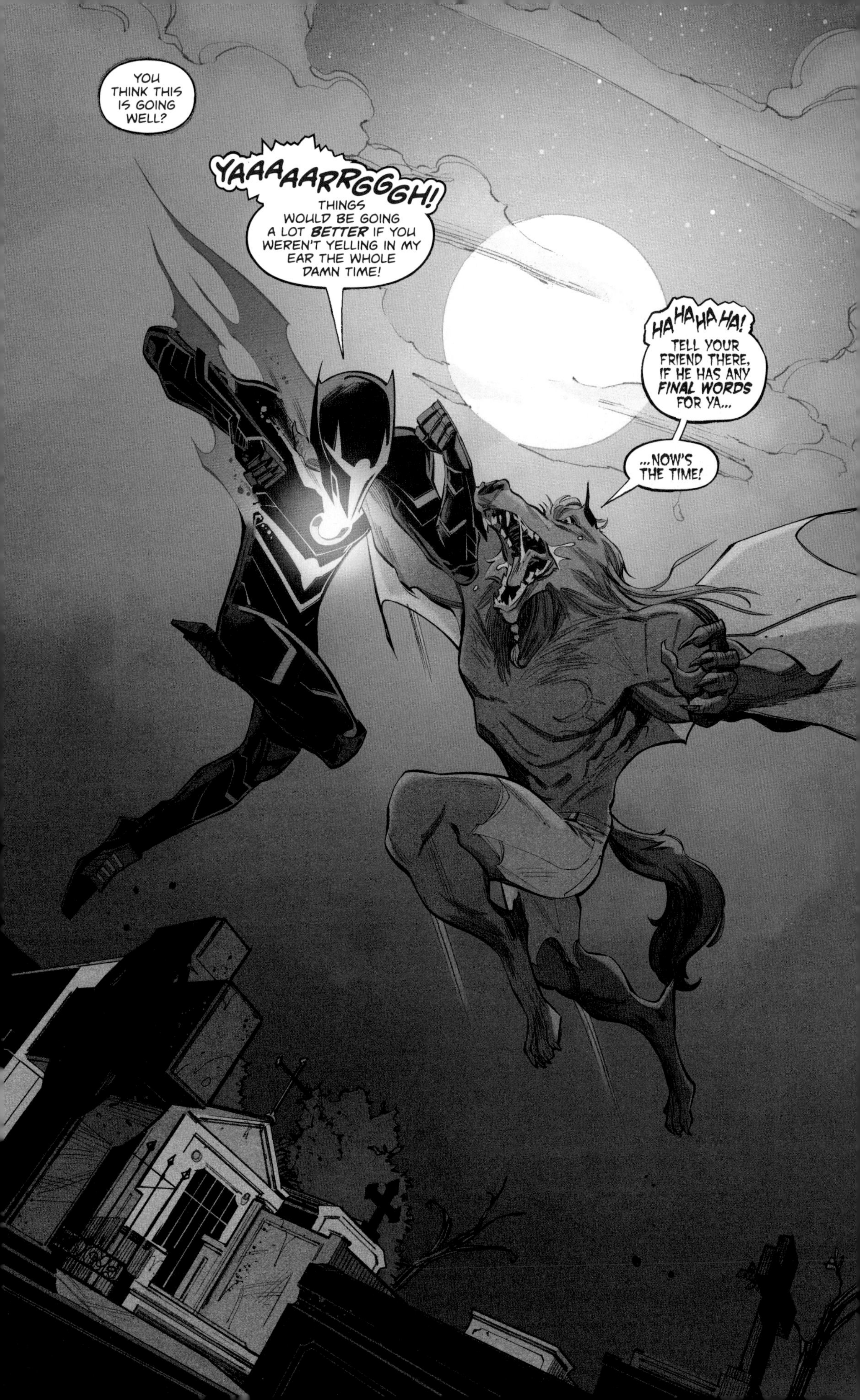
YOU THINK THIS IS GOING WELL?
YAAAAARRGGGH!
THINGS WOULD BE GOING A LOT BETTER IF YOU WEREN'T YELLING IN MY EAR THE WHOLE DAMN TIME!
HAHAHAHA!
TELL YOUR FRIEND THERE, IF HE HAS ANY FINAL WORDS FOR YA...
...NOW'S THE TIME!

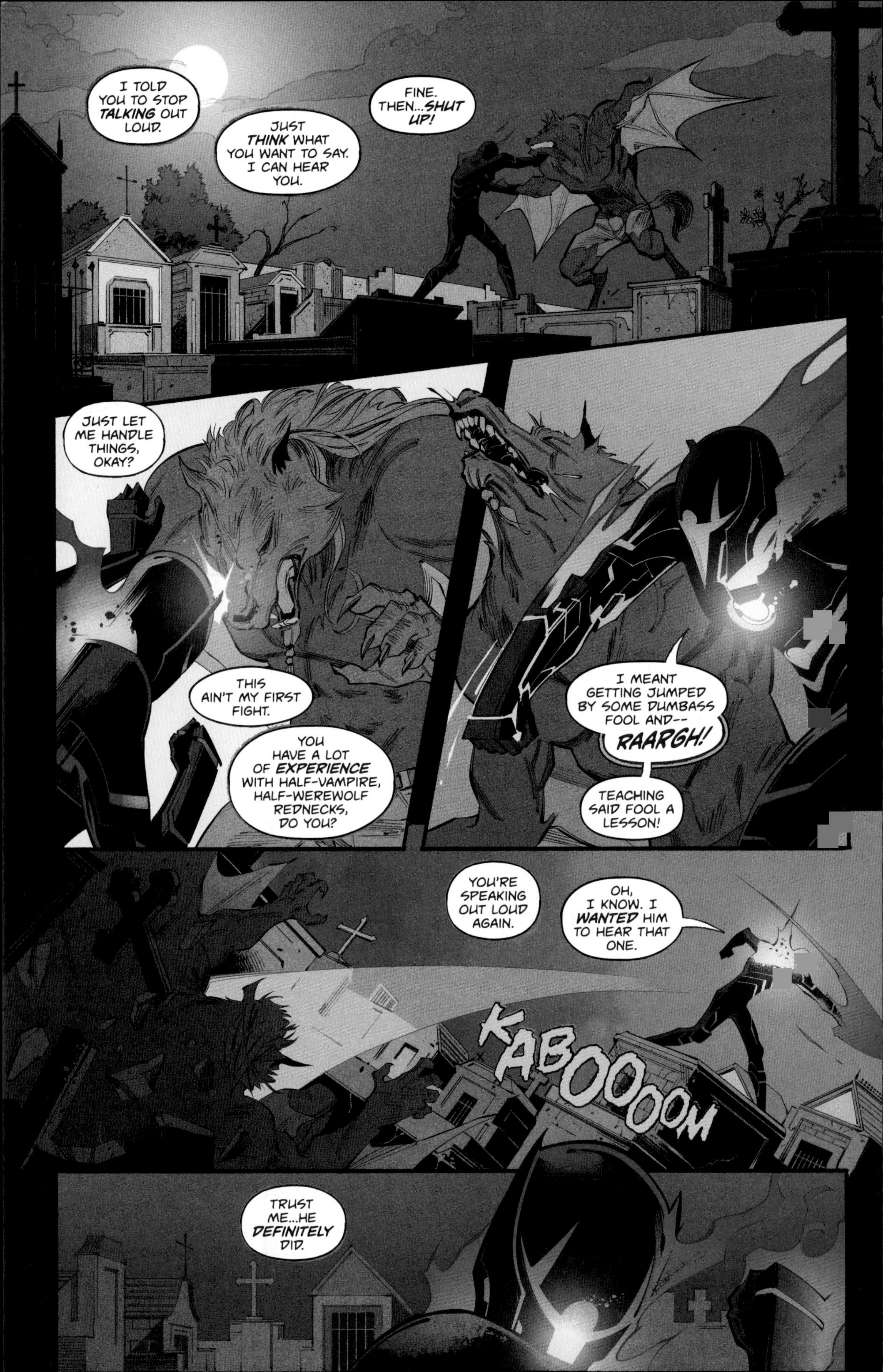
I TOLD YOU TO STOP TALKING OUT LOUD.
JUST THINK WHAT YOU WANT TO SAY. I CAN HEAR YOU.
FINE. THEN...SHUT UP!
JUST LET ME HANDLE THINGS, OKAY?
THIS AIN'T MY FIRST FIGHT.
YOU HAVE A LOT OF EXPERIENCE WITH HALF-VAMPIRE, HALF-WEREWOLF REDNECKS, DO YOU?
I MEANT GETTING JUMPED BY SOME DUMBASS FOOL AND--
RAARGH!
TEACHING SAID FOOL A LESSON!
YOU'RE SPEAKING OUT LOUD AGAIN.
OH, I KNOW. I WANTED HIM TO HEAR THAT ONE.
KABOOOOOM
TRUST ME...HE DEFINITELY DID.

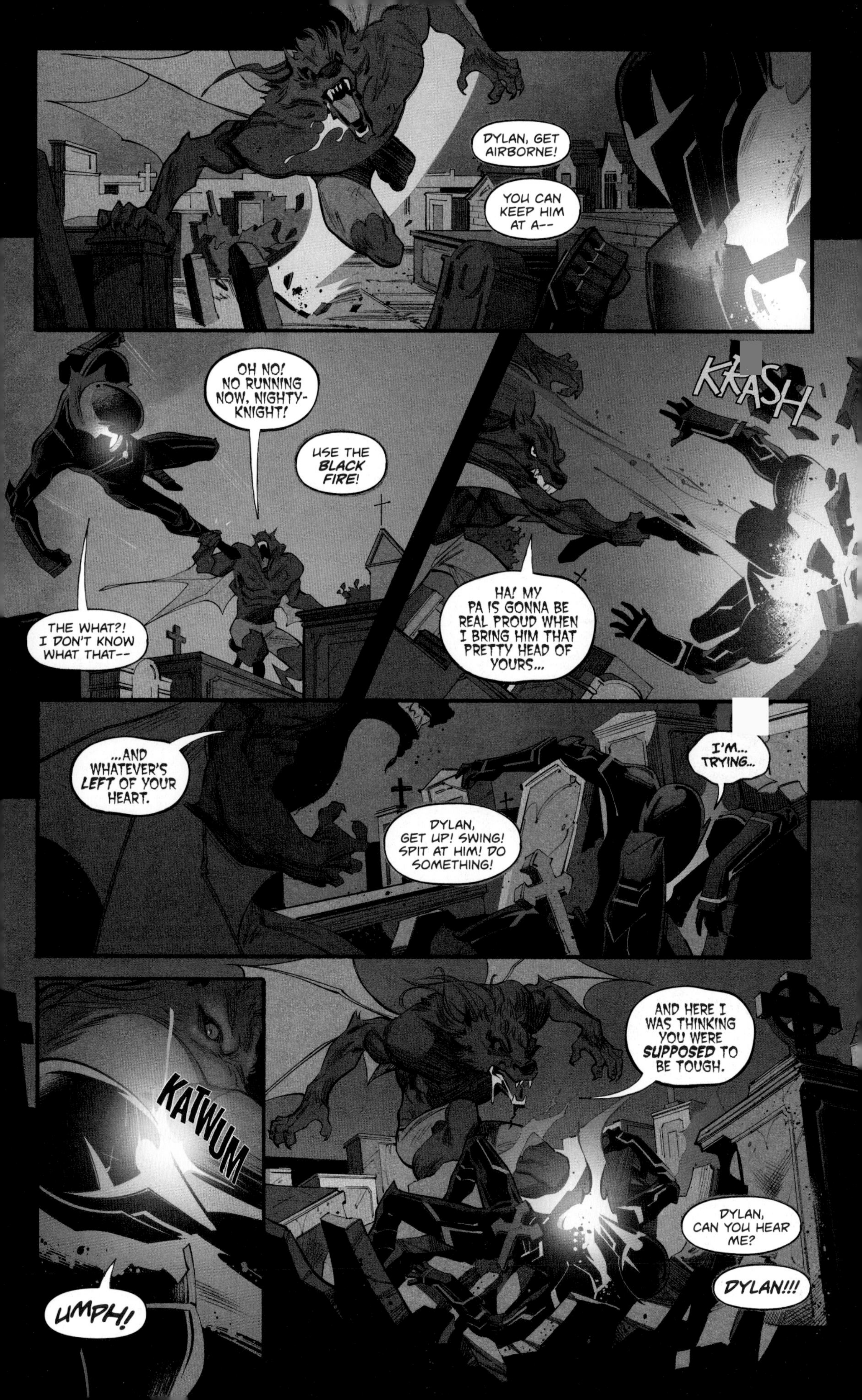
DYLAN, GET AIRBORNE!
YOU CAN KEEP HIM AT A--
OH NO! NO RUNNING NOW, NIGHTY-KNIGHT!
USE THE *BLACK FIRE*!
THE WHAT?! I DON'T KNOW WHAT THAT--
KRASH
HA! MY PA IS GONNA BE REAL PROUD WHEN I BRING HIM THAT PRETTY HEAD OF YOURS...
...AND WHATEVER'S *LEFT* OF YOUR HEART.
DYLAN, GET UP! SWING! SPIT AT HIM! DO SOMETHING!
I'M... TRYING...
KATWUM
UMPH!
AND HERE I WAS THINKING YOU WERE *SUPPOSED* TO BE TOUGH.
DYLAN, CAN YOU HEAR ME?
DYLAN!!!

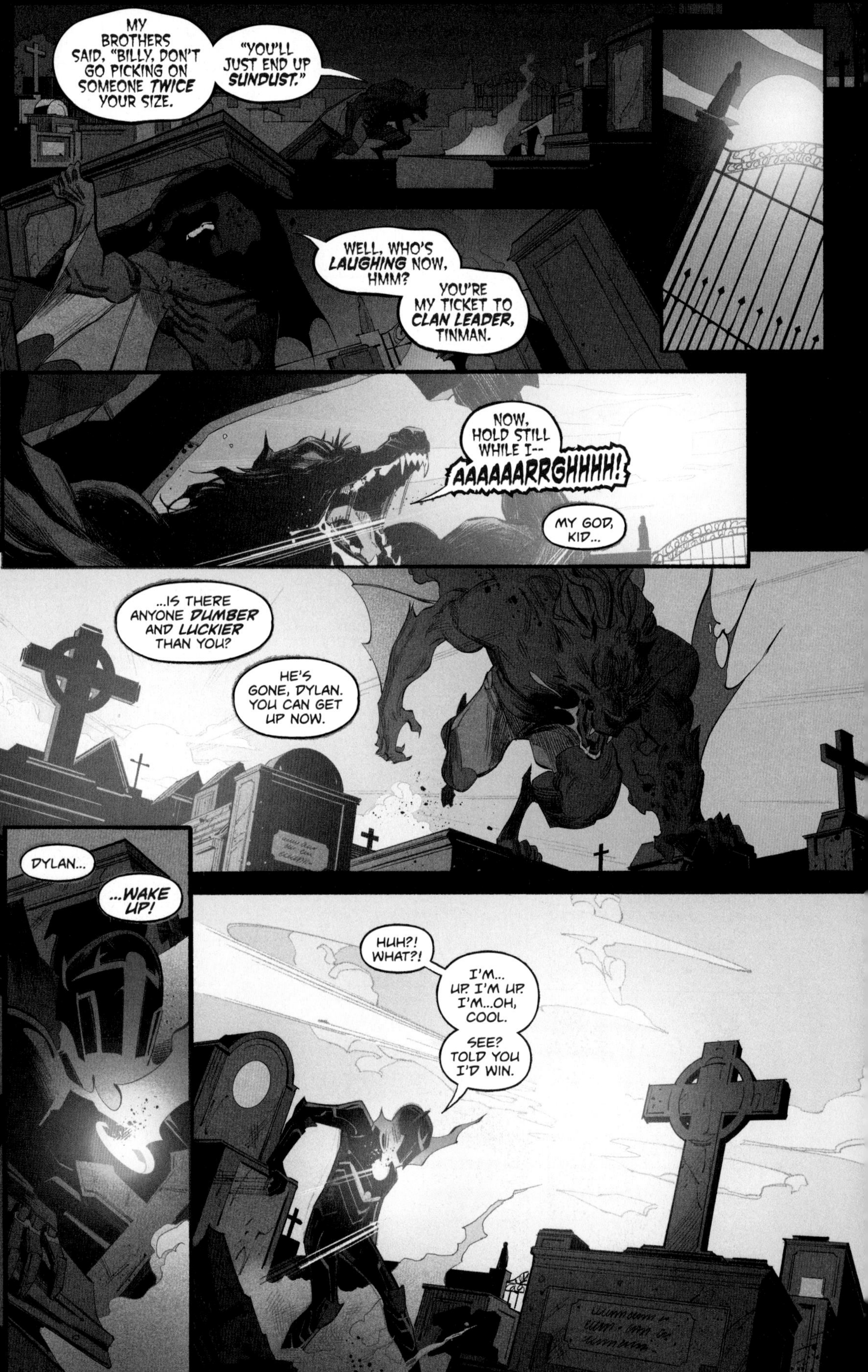
MY BROTHERS SAID, "BILLY, DON'T GO PICKING ON SOMEONE *TWICE* YOUR SIZE.
"YOU'LL JUST END UP *SUNDUST*."
WELL, WHO'S *LAUGHING* NOW, HMM?
YOU'RE MY TICKET TO *CLAN LEADER*, TINMAN.
NOW, HOLD STILL WHILE I--
AAAAAARRGHHHH!
MY GOD, KID...
...IS THERE ANYONE *DUMBER* AND *LUCKIER* THAN YOU?
HE'S GONE, DYLAN. YOU CAN GET UP NOW.
DYLAN...
...WAKE UP!
HUH?! WHAT?!
I'M... UP. I'M UP. I'M...OH, COOL.
SEE? TOLD YOU I'D WIN.

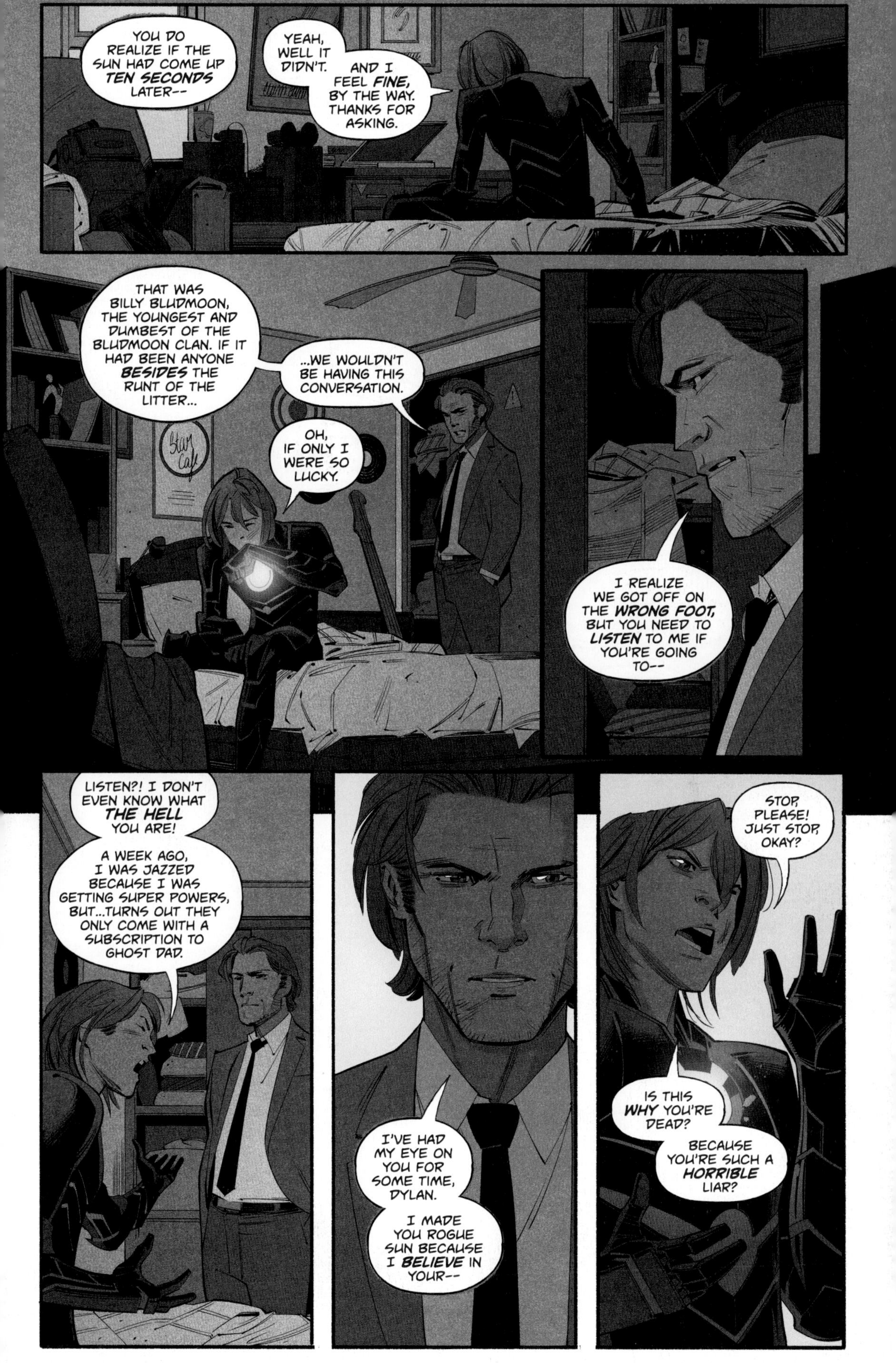
YOU DO REALIZE IF THE SUN HAD COME UP TEN SECONDS LATER--
YEAH, WELL IT DIDN'T.
AND I FEEL FINE, BY THE WAY. THANKS FOR ASKING.
THAT WAS BILLY BLUDMOON, THE YOUNGEST AND DUMBEST OF THE BLUDMOON CLAN. IF IT HAD BEEN ANYONE BESIDES THE RUNT OF THE LITTER...
...WE WOULDN'T BE HAVING THIS CONVERSATION.
OH, IF ONLY I WERE SO LUCKY.
I REALIZE WE GOT OFF ON THE WRONG FOOT, BUT YOU NEED TO LISTEN TO ME IF YOU'RE GOING TO--
LISTEN?! I DON'T EVEN KNOW WHAT THE HELL YOU ARE!
A WEEK AGO, I WAS JAZZED BECAUSE I WAS GETTING SUPER POWERS, BUT...TURNS OUT THEY ONLY COME WITH A SUBSCRIPTION TO GHOST DAD.
I'VE HAD MY EYE ON YOU FOR SOME TIME, DYLAN.
I MADE YOU ROGUE SUN BECAUSE I BELIEVE IN YOUR--
STOP, PLEASE! JUST STOP, OKAY?
IS THIS WHY YOU'RE DEAD?
BECAUSE YOU'RE SUCH A HORRIBLE LIAR?

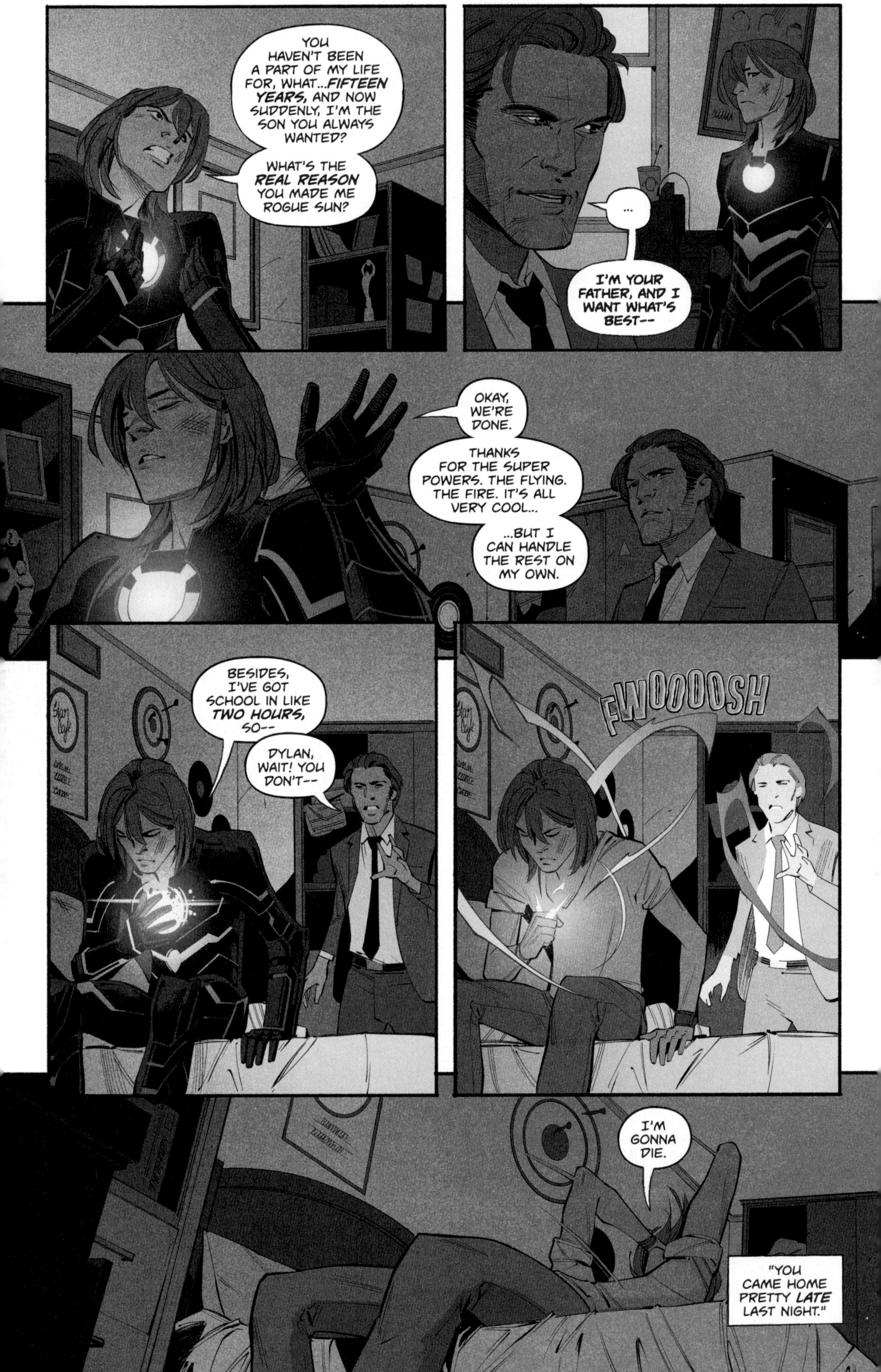

YOU HAVEN'T BEEN A PART OF MY LIFE FOR, WHAT...FIFTEEN YEARS, AND NOW SUDDENLY, I'M THE SON YOU ALWAYS WANTED?
WHAT'S THE REAL REASON YOU MADE ME ROGUE SUN?
...
I'M YOUR FATHER, AND I WANT WHAT'S BEST--
OKAY, WE'RE DONE.
THANKS FOR THE SUPER POWERS. THE FLYING. THE FIRE. IT'S ALL VERY COOL...
...BUT I CAN HANDLE THE REST ON MY OWN.
BESIDES, I'VE GOT SCHOOL IN LIKE TWO HOURS, SO--
DYLAN, WAIT! YOU DON'T--
FWOOOOOSH
I'M GONNA DIE.
"YOU CAME HOME PRETTY LATE LAST NIGHT."

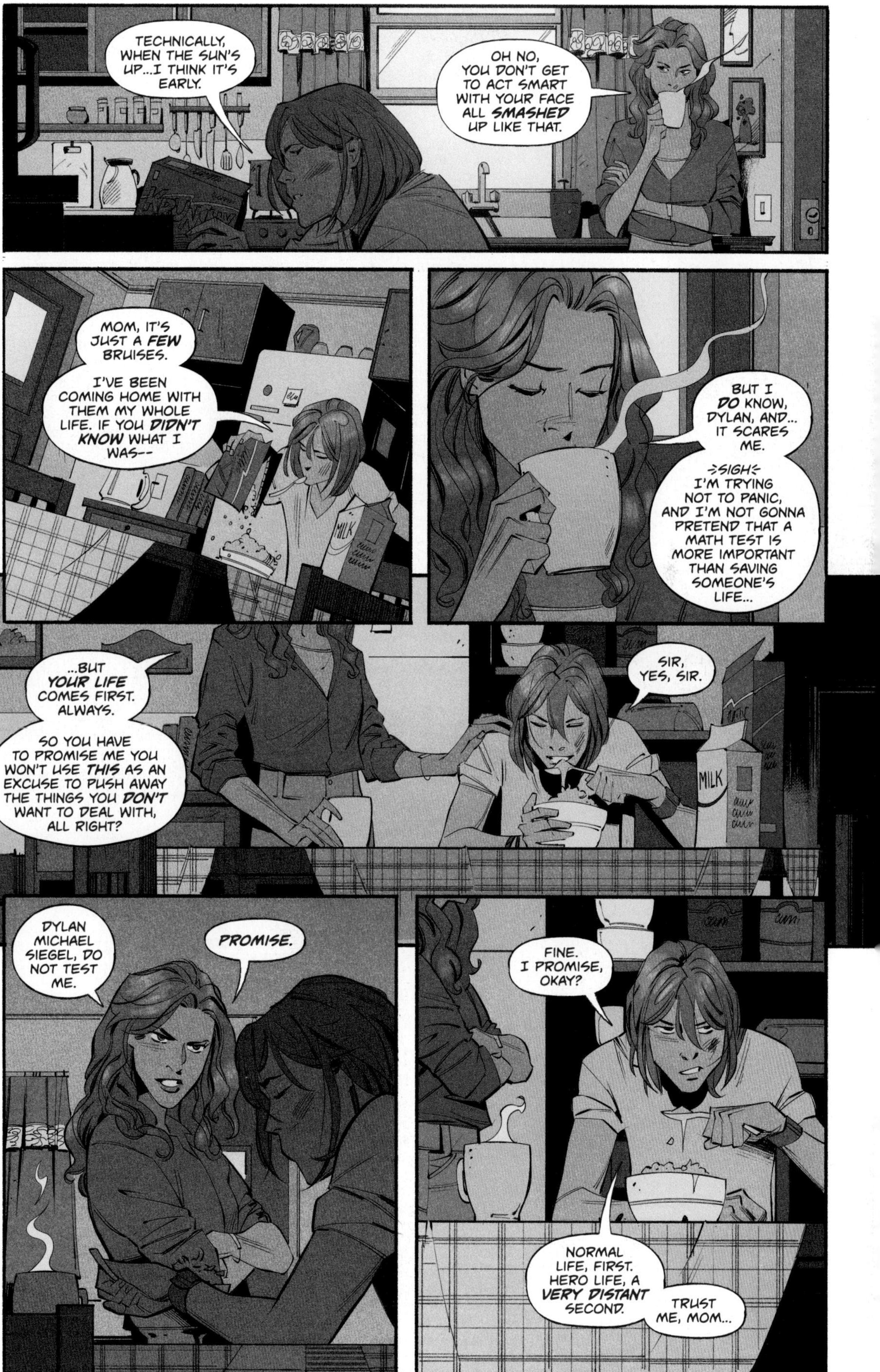
TECHNICALLY, WHEN THE SUN'S UP...I THINK IT'S EARLY.
OH NO, YOU DON'T GET TO ACT SMART WITH YOUR FACE ALL SMASHED UP LIKE THAT.
MOM, IT'S JUST A FEW BRUISES.
I'VE BEEN COMING HOME WITH THEM MY WHOLE LIFE. IF YOU DIDN'T KNOW WHAT I WAS--
BUT I DO KNOW, DYLAN, AND... IT SCARES ME.
SIGH
I'M TRYING NOT TO PANIC, AND I'M NOT GONNA PRETEND THAT A MATH TEST IS MORE IMPORTANT THAN SAVING SOMEONE'S LIFE...
...BUT YOUR LIFE COMES FIRST. ALWAYS.
SO YOU HAVE TO PROMISE ME YOU WON'T USE THIS AS AN EXCUSE TO PUSH AWAY THE THINGS YOU DON'T WANT TO DEAL WITH, ALL RIGHT?
SIR, YES, SIR.
MILK
DYLAN MICHAEL SIEGEL, DO NOT TEST ME.
PROMISE.
FINE. I PROMISE, OKAY?
NORMAL LIFE, FIRST. HERO LIFE, A VERY DISTANT SECOND.
TRUST ME, MOM...

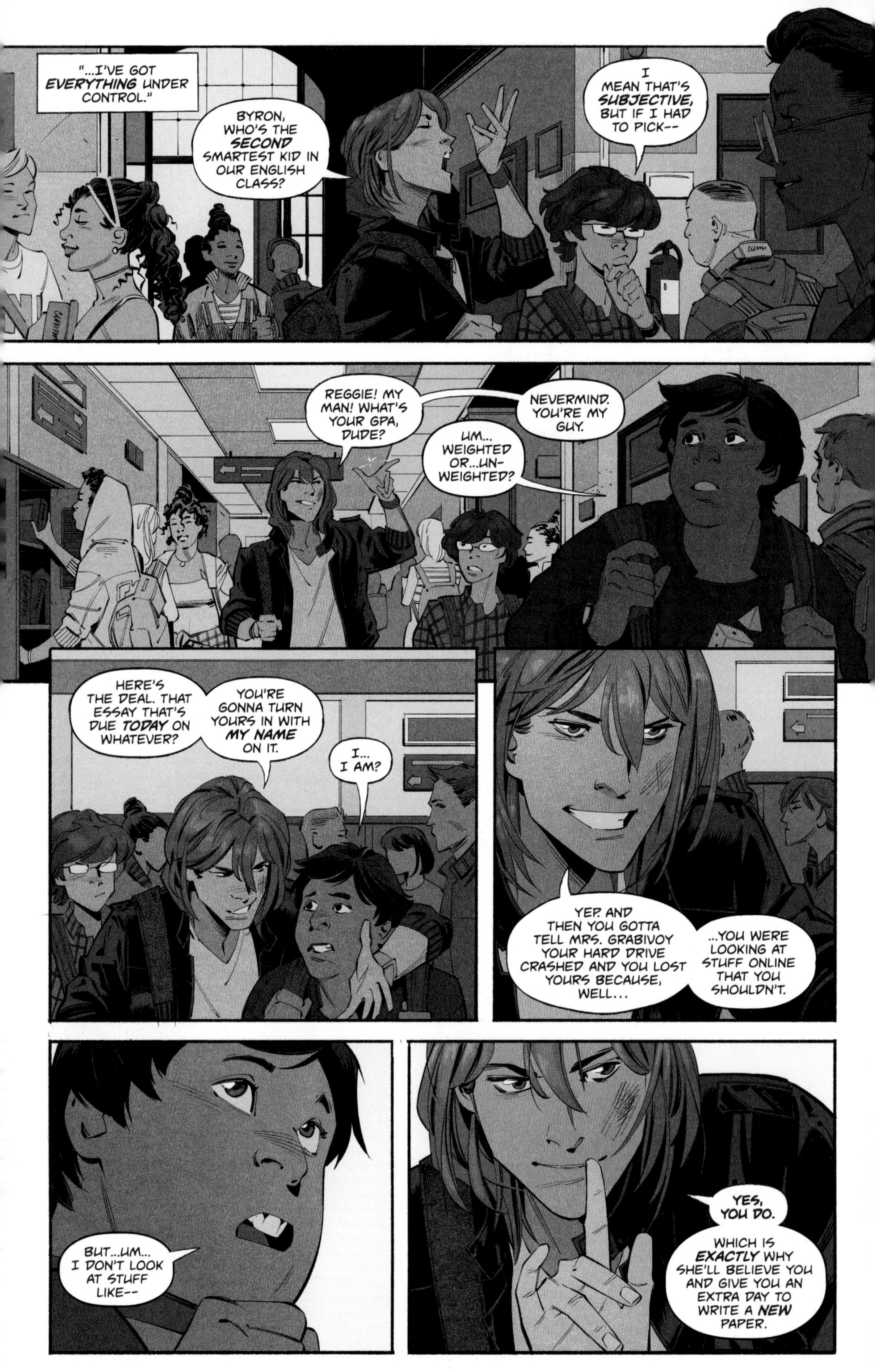
"...I'VE GOT EVERYTHING UNDER CONTROL."
BYRON, WHO'S THE SECOND SMARTEST KID IN OUR ENGLISH CLASS?
I MEAN THAT'S SUBJECTIVE, BUT IF I HAD TO PICK--
REGGIE! MY MAN! WHAT'S YOUR GPA, DUDE?
UM... WEIGHTED OR...UN-WEIGHTED?
NEVERMIND. YOU'RE MY GUY.
HERE'S THE DEAL. THAT ESSAY THAT'S DUE TODAY ON WHATEVER?
YOU'RE GONNA TURN YOURS IN WITH MY NAME ON IT.
I... I AM?
YEP. AND THEN YOU GOTTA TELL MRS. GRABIVOY YOUR HARD DRIVE CRASHED AND YOU LOST YOURS BECAUSE, WELL...
...YOU WERE LOOKING AT STUFF ONLINE THAT YOU SHOULDN'T.
BUT...UM... I DON'T LOOK AT STUFF LIKE--
YES, YOU DO.
WHICH IS EXACTLY WHY SHE'LL BELIEVE YOU AND GIVE YOU AN EXTRA DAY TO WRITE A NEW PAPER.

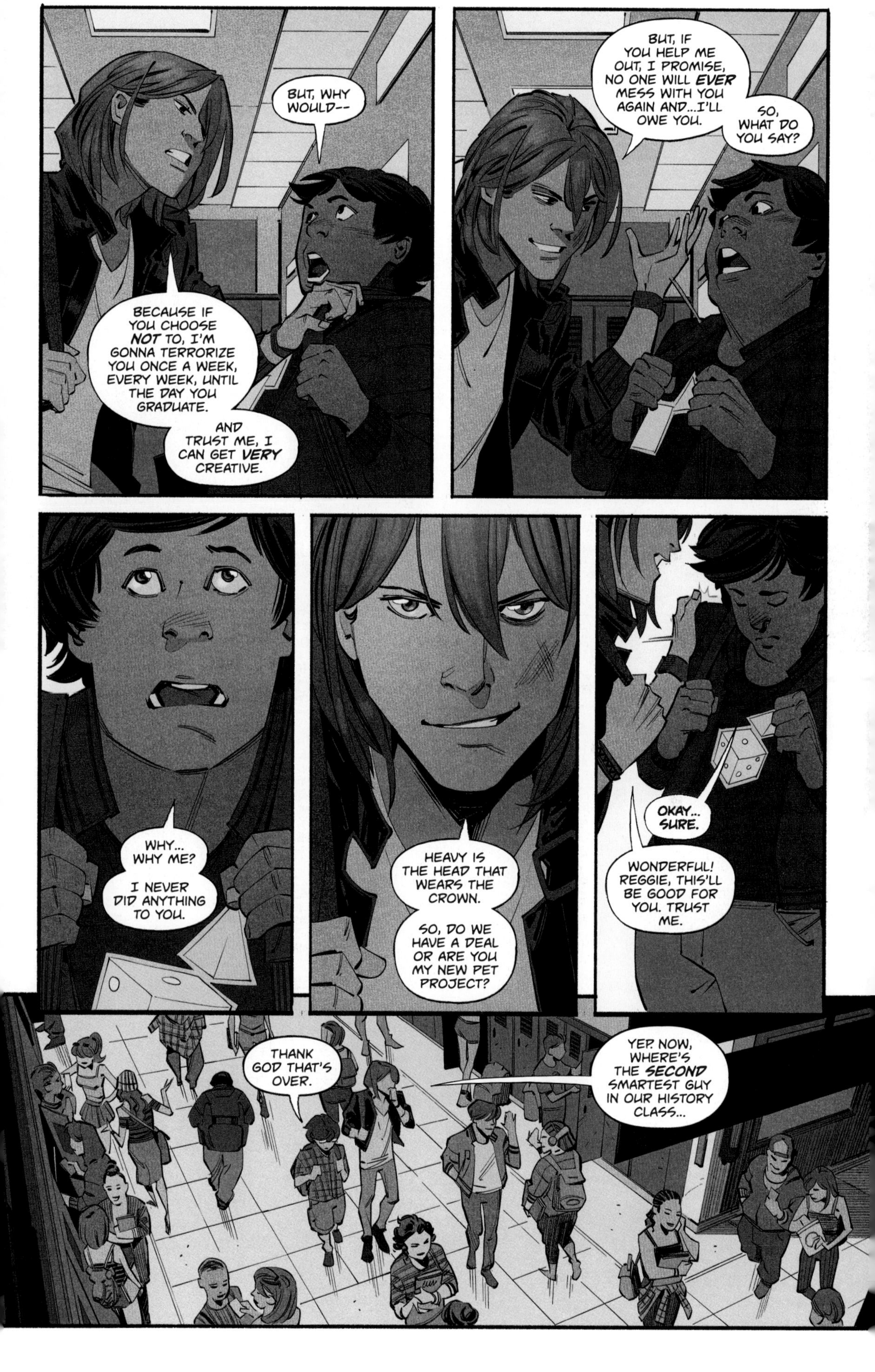
BUT, WHY WOULD--
BECAUSE IF YOU CHOOSE NOT TO, I'M GONNA TERRORIZE YOU ONCE A WEEK, EVERY WEEK, UNTIL THE DAY YOU GRADUATE.
AND TRUST ME, I CAN GET VERY CREATIVE.
BUT, IF YOU HELP ME OUT, I PROMISE, NO ONE WILL EVER MESS WITH YOU AGAIN AND...I'LL OWE YOU.
SO, WHAT DO YOU SAY?
WHY... WHY ME?
I NEVER DID ANYTHING TO YOU.
HEAVY IS THE HEAD THAT WEARS THE CROWN.
SO, DO WE HAVE A DEAL OR ARE YOU MY NEW PET PROJECT?
OKAY... SURE.
WONDERFUL! REGGIE, THIS'LL BE GOOD FOR YOU. TRUST ME.
THANK GOD THAT'S OVER.
YEP. NOW, WHERE'S THE SECOND SMARTEST GUY IN OUR HISTORY CLASS...

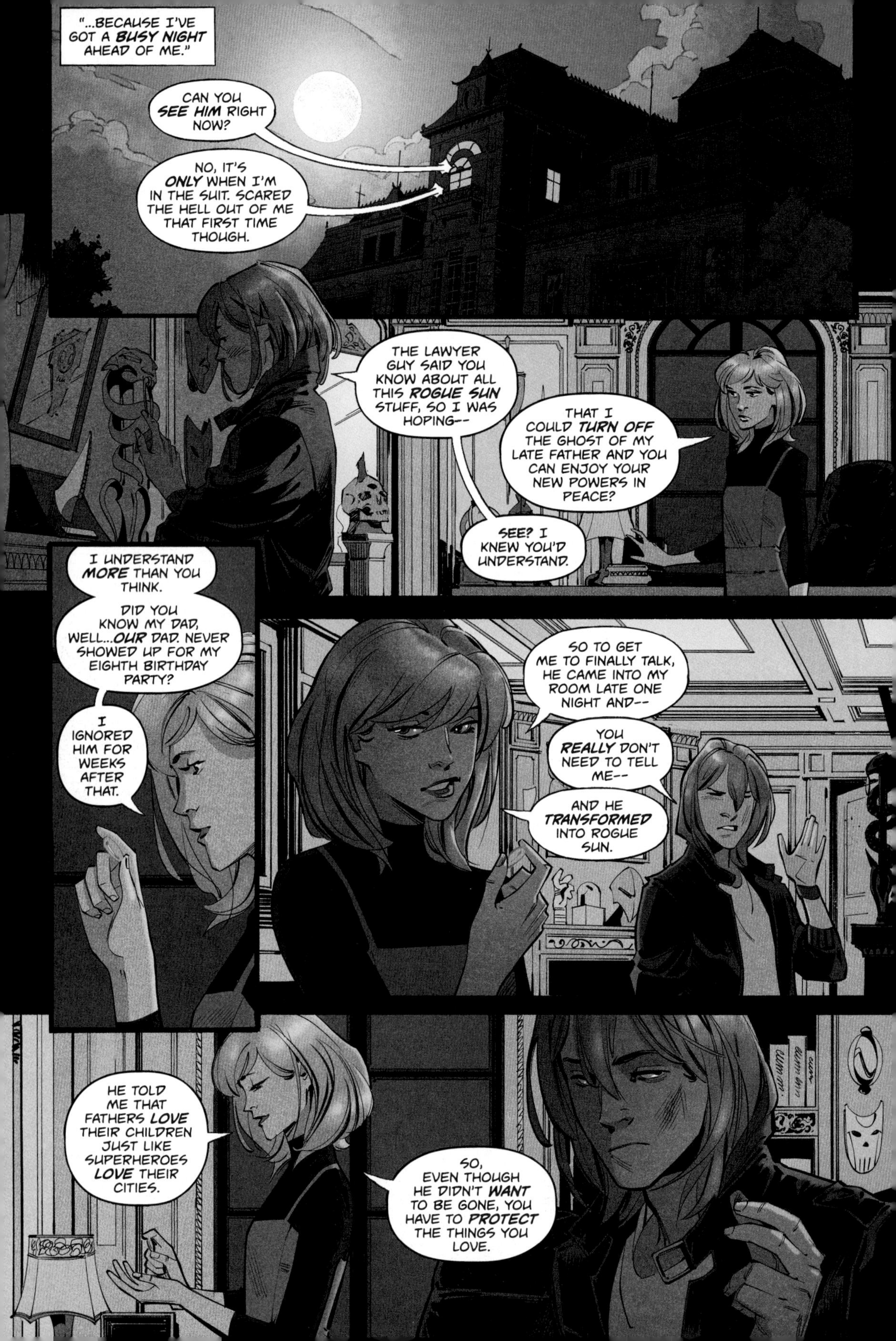
"...BECAUSE I'VE GOT A BUSY NIGHT AHEAD OF ME."
CAN YOU SEE HIM RIGHT NOW?
NO, IT'S ONLY WHEN I'M IN THE SUIT. SCARED THE HELL OUT OF ME THAT FIRST TIME THOUGH.
THE LAWYER GUY SAID YOU KNOW ABOUT ALL THIS ROGUE SUN STUFF, SO I WAS HOPING--
THAT I COULD TURN OFF THE GHOST OF MY LATE FATHER AND YOU CAN ENJOY YOUR NEW POWERS IN PEACE?
SEE? I KNEW YOU'D UNDERSTAND.
I UNDERSTAND MORE THAN YOU THINK.
DID YOU KNOW MY DAD, WELL...OUR DAD. NEVER SHOWED UP FOR MY EIGHTH BIRTHDAY PARTY?
I IGNORED HIM FOR WEEKS AFTER THAT.
SO TO GET ME TO FINALLY TALK, HE CAME INTO MY ROOM LATE ONE NIGHT AND--
YOU REALLY DON'T NEED TO TELL ME--
AND HE TRANSFORMED INTO ROGUE SUN.
HE TOLD ME THAT FATHERS LOVE THEIR CHILDREN JUST LIKE SUPERHEROES LOVE THEIR CITIES.
SO, EVEN THOUGH HE DIDN'T WANT TO BE GONE, YOU HAVE TO PROTECT THE THINGS YOU LOVE.

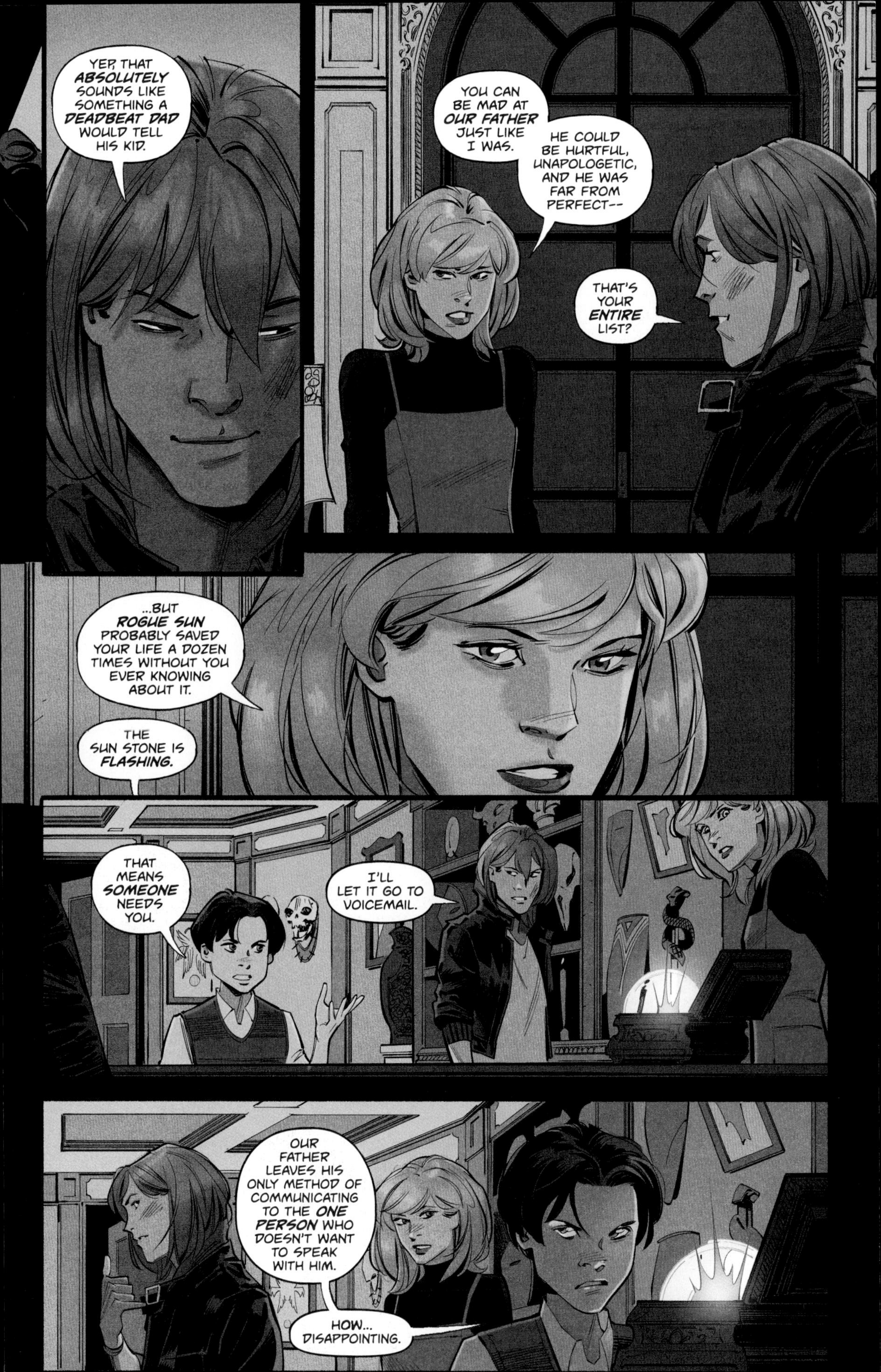
YEP, THAT ABSOLUTELY SOUNDS LIKE SOMETHING A DEADBEAT DAD WOULD TELL HIS KID.
YOU CAN BE MAD AT OUR FATHER JUST LIKE I WAS.
HE COULD BE HURTFUL, UNAPOLOGETIC, AND HE WAS FAR FROM PERFECT--
THAT'S YOUR ENTIRE LIST?
...BUT ROGUE SUN PROBABLY SAVED YOUR LIFE A DOZEN TIMES WITHOUT YOU EVER KNOWING ABOUT IT.
THE SUN STONE IS FLASHING.
THAT MEANS SOMEONE NEEDS YOU.
I'LL LET IT GO TO VOICEMAIL.
OUR FATHER LEAVES HIS ONLY METHOD OF COMMUNICATING TO THE ONE PERSON WHO DOESN'T WANT TO SPEAK WITH HIM.
HOW... DISAPPOINTING.

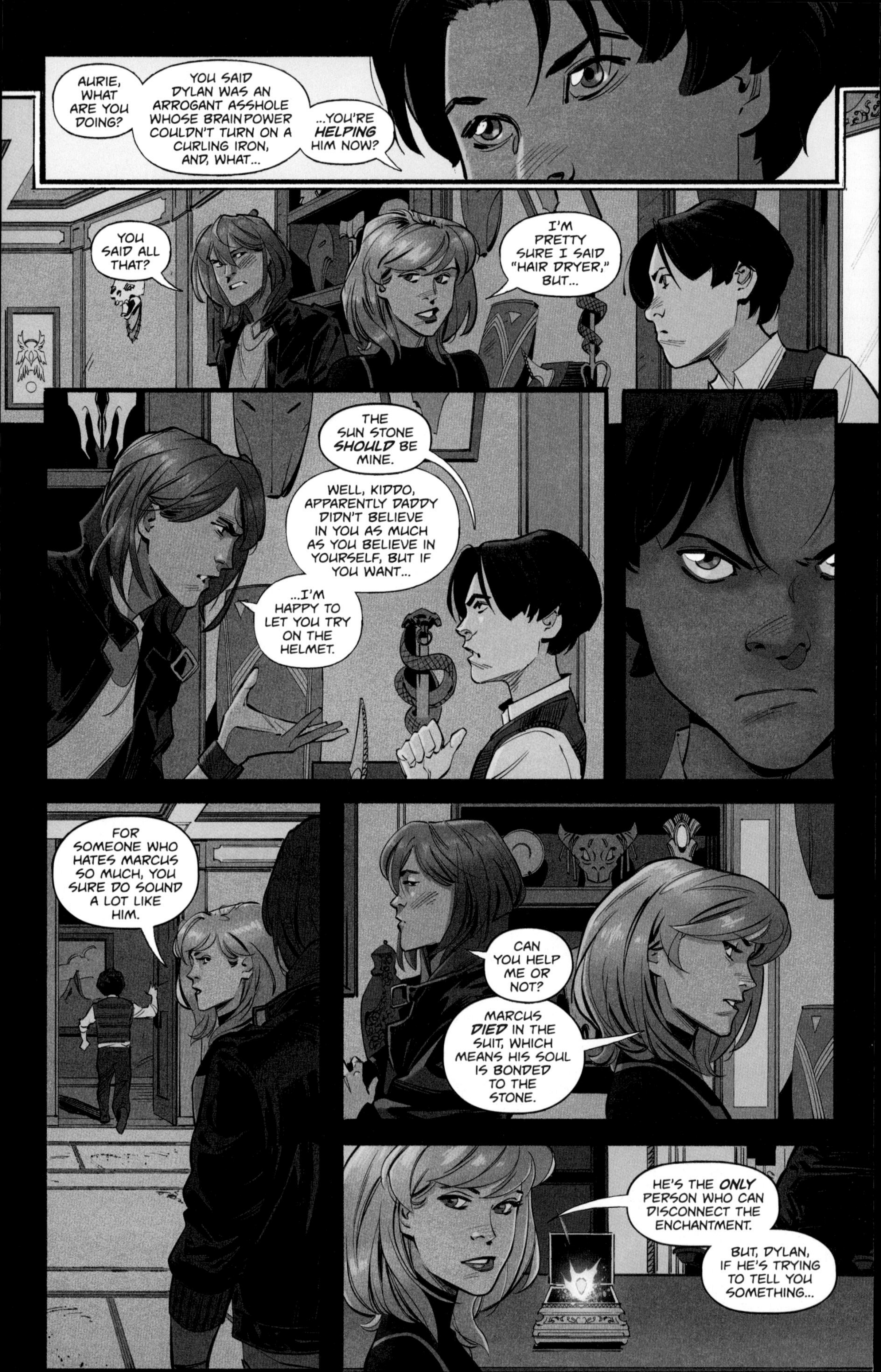
AURIE, WHAT ARE YOU DOING?
YOU SAID DYLAN WAS AN ARROGANT ASSHOLE WHOSE BRAINPOWER COULDN'T TURN ON A CURLING IRON, AND, WHAT...
...YOU'RE HELPING HIM NOW?
YOU SAID ALL THAT?
I'M PRETTY SURE I SAID "HAIR DRYER," BUT...
THE SUN STONE SHOULD BE MINE.
WELL, KIDDO, APPARENTLY DADDY DIDN'T BELIEVE IN YOU AS MUCH AS YOU BELIEVE IN YOURSELF, BUT IF YOU WANT...
...I'M HAPPY TO LET YOU TRY ON THE HELMET.
FOR SOMEONE WHO HATES MARCUS SO MUCH, YOU SURE DO SOUND A LOT LIKE HIM.
CAN YOU HELP ME OR NOT?
MARCUS DIED IN THE SUIT, WHICH MEANS HIS SOUL IS BONDED TO THE STONE.
HE'S THE ONLY PERSON WHO CAN DISCONNECT THE ENCHANTMENT.
BUT, DYLAN, IF HE'S TRYING TO TELL YOU SOMETHING...

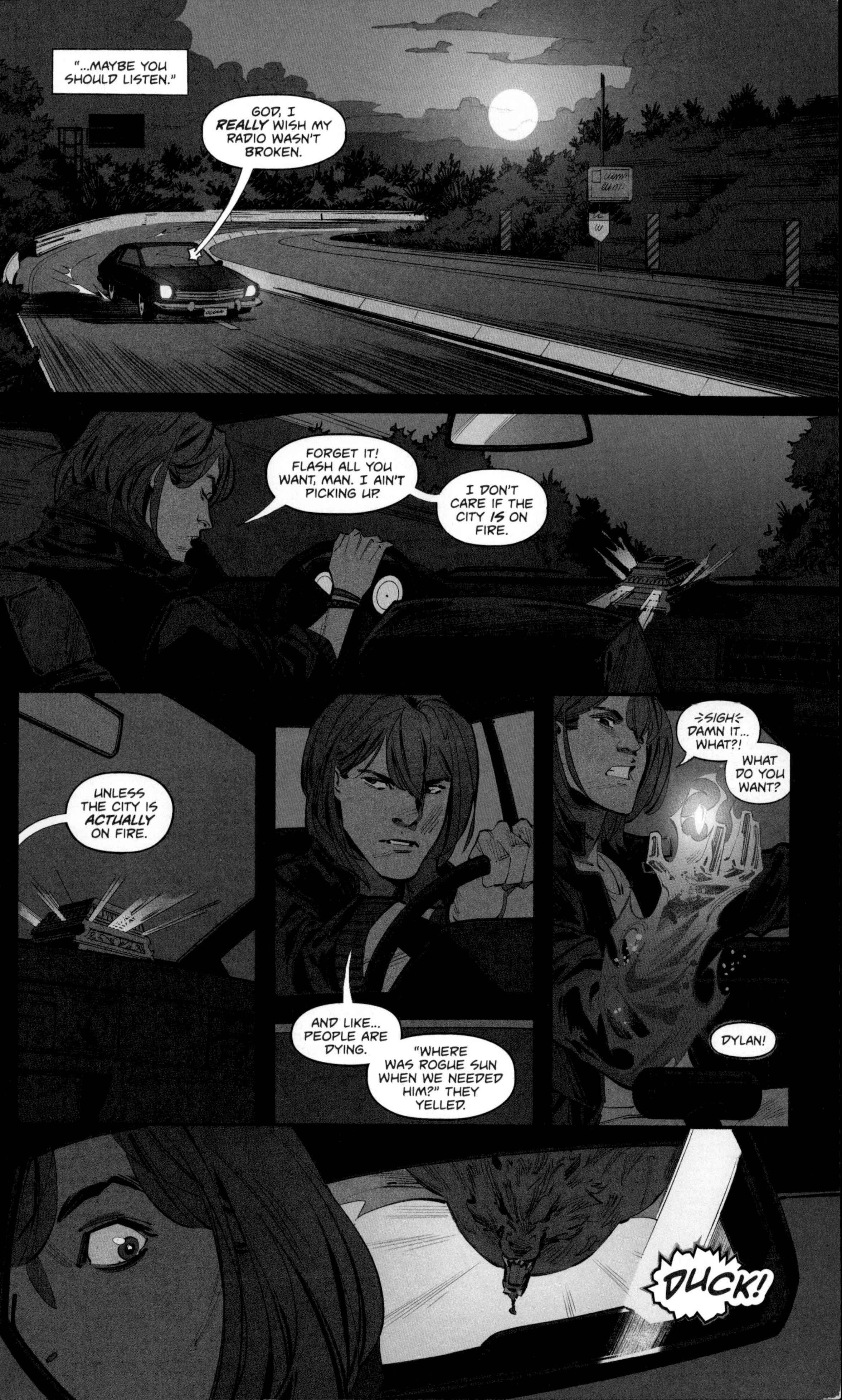

"...MAYBE YOU SHOULD LISTEN."
GOD, I *REALLY* WISH MY RADIO WASN'T BROKEN.
FORGET IT! FLASH ALL YOU WANT, MAN. I AIN'T PICKING UP.
I DON'T CARE IF THE CITY *IS* ON FIRE.
UNLESS THE CITY IS *ACTUALLY* ON FIRE.
AND LIKE... PEOPLE ARE DYING.
"WHERE WAS ROGUE SUN WHEN WE NEEDED HIM?" THEY YELLED.
SIGH
DAMN IT... WHAT?!
WHAT DO YOU WANT?
DYLAN!
DUCK!

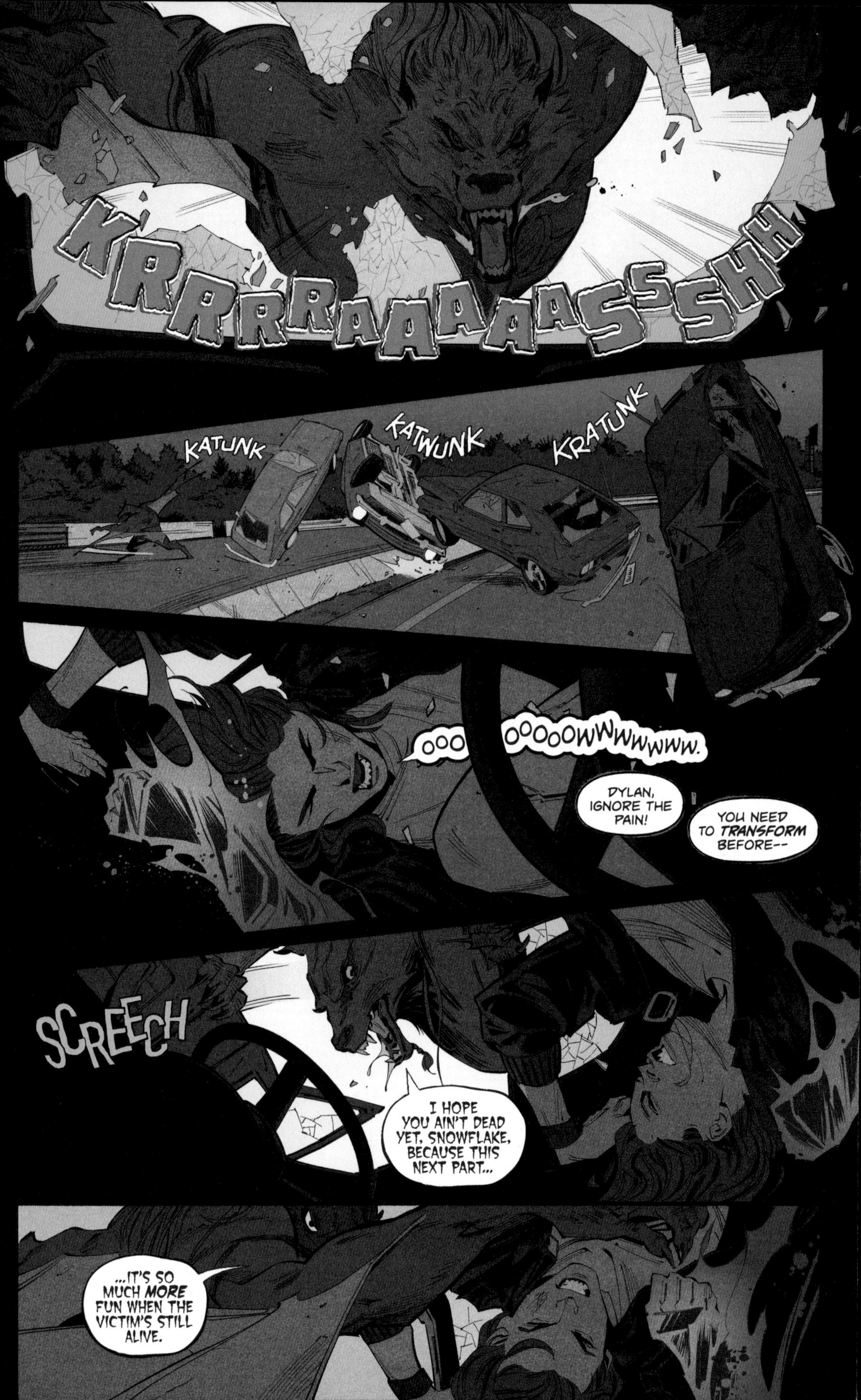
KRRRRAAAASSSHH
KATUNK
KATWUNK
KRATUNK
OOOOOOOOWWWWWWW.
DYLAN, IGNORE THE PAIN!
YOU NEED TO *TRANSFORM* BEFORE--
SCREECH
I HOPE YOU AIN'T DEAD YET, SNOWFLAKE, BECAUSE THIS NEXT PART...
...IT'S SO MUCH *MORE* FUN WHEN THE VICTIM'S STILL ALIVE.

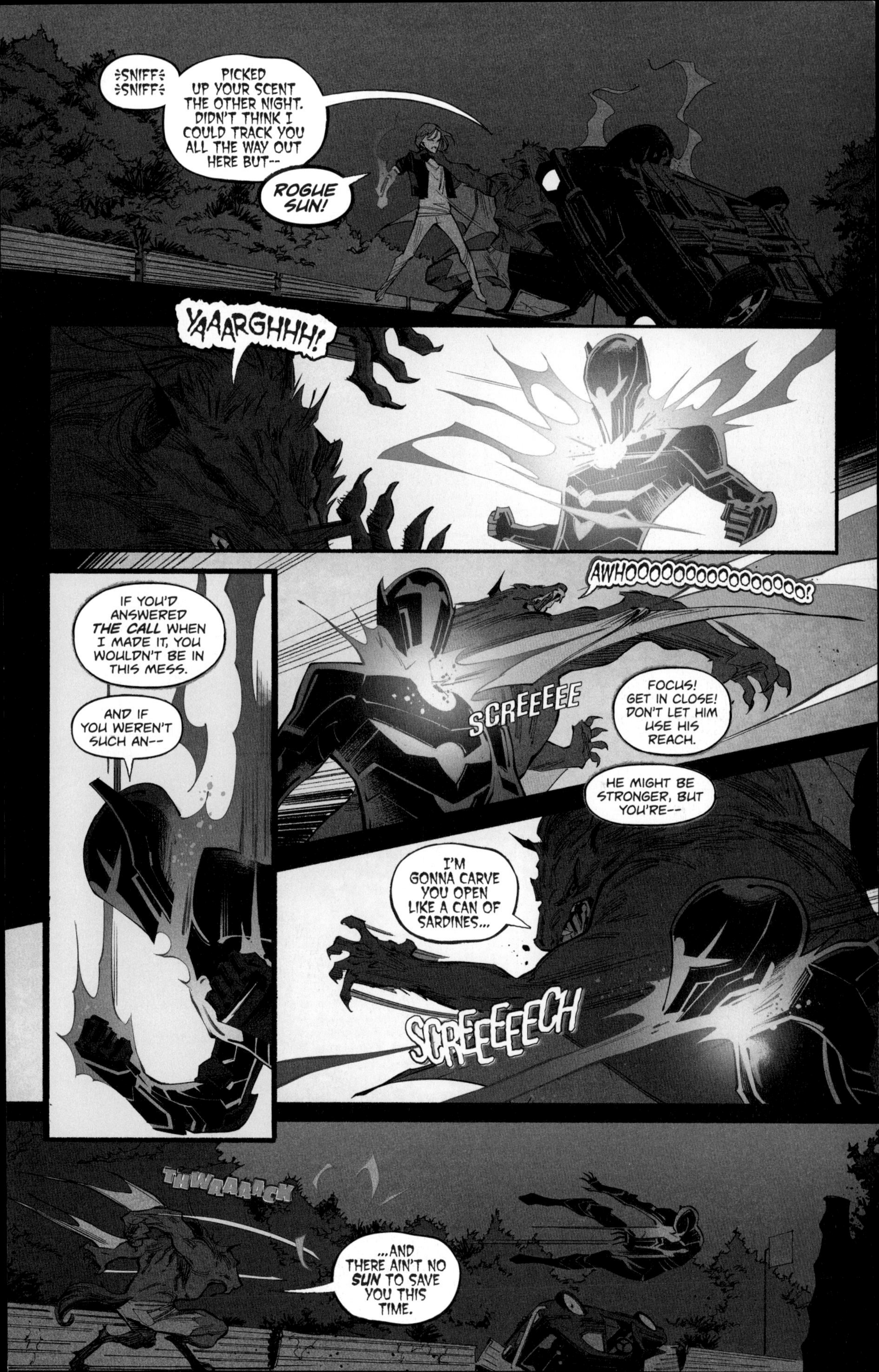

SNIFF SNIFF
PICKED UP YOUR SCENT THE OTHER NIGHT. DIDN'T THINK I COULD TRACK YOU ALL THE WAY OUT HERE BUT--
ROGUE SUN!
YAAARGHHH!
AWHOOOOOOOOOOOOOOOOO!
IF YOU'D ANSWERED THE CALL WHEN I MADE IT, YOU WOULDN'T BE IN THIS MESS.
AND IF YOU WEREN'T SUCH AN--
SCREEEEE
FOCUS! GET IN CLOSE! DON'T LET HIM USE HIS REACH.
HE MIGHT BE STRONGER, BUT YOU'RE--
I'M GONNA CARVE YOU OPEN LIKE A CAN OF SARDINES...
SCREEEEECH
THWAAAACK
...AND THERE AIN'T NO SUN TO SAVE YOU THIS TIME.

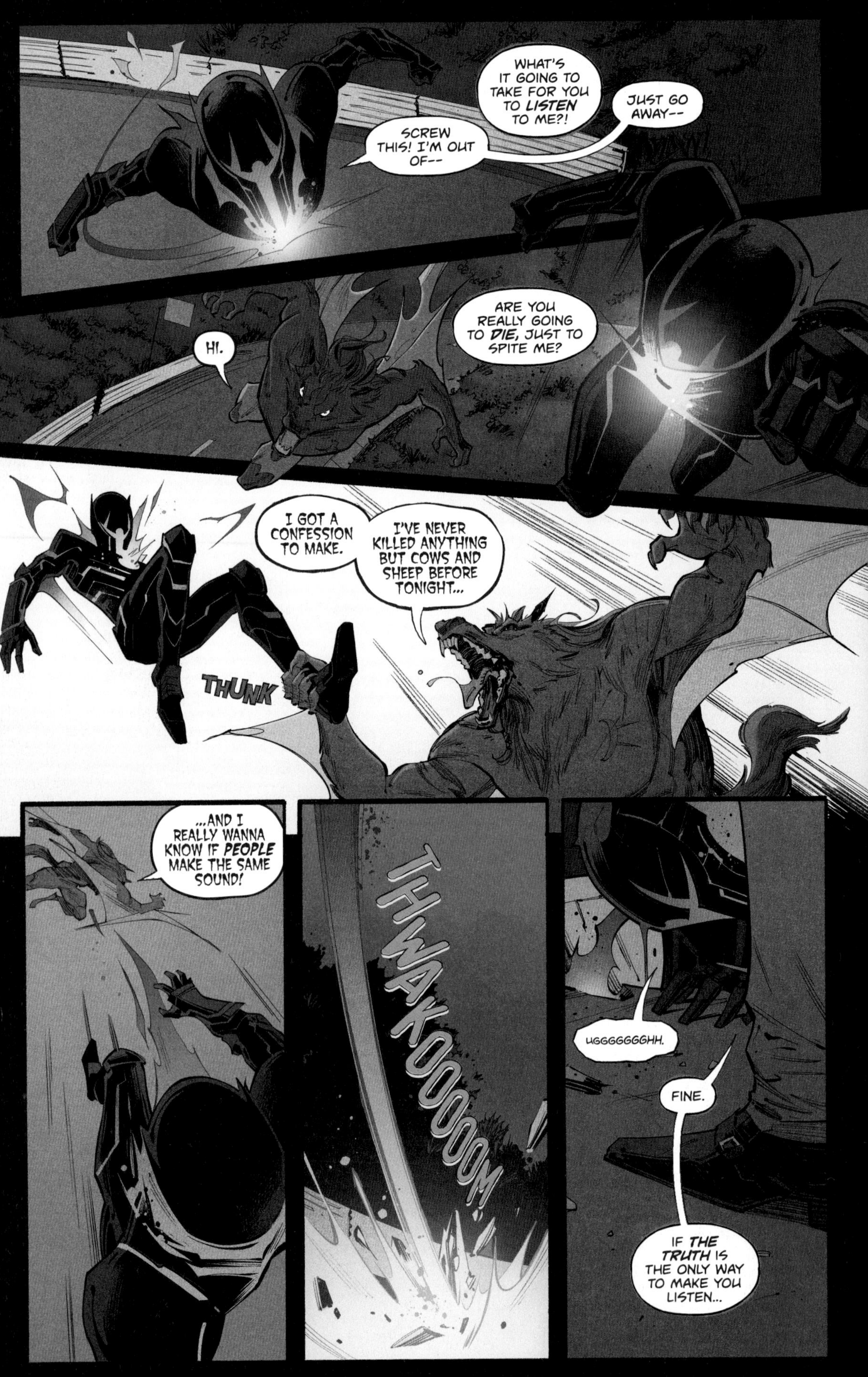
WHAT'S IT GOING TO TAKE FOR YOU TO LISTEN TO ME?!
SCREW THIS! I'M OUT OF--
JUST GO AWAY--
HI.
ARE YOU REALLY GOING TO DIE, JUST TO SPITE ME?
I GOT A CONFESSION TO MAKE.
I'VE NEVER KILLED ANYTHING BUT COWS AND SHEEP BEFORE TONIGHT...
THUNK
...AND I REALLY WANNA KNOW IF PEOPLE MAKE THE SAME SOUND!
THWAKOOOOOM
UGGGGGGGHH.
FINE.
IF THE TRUTH IS THE ONLY WAY TO MAKE YOU LISTEN...

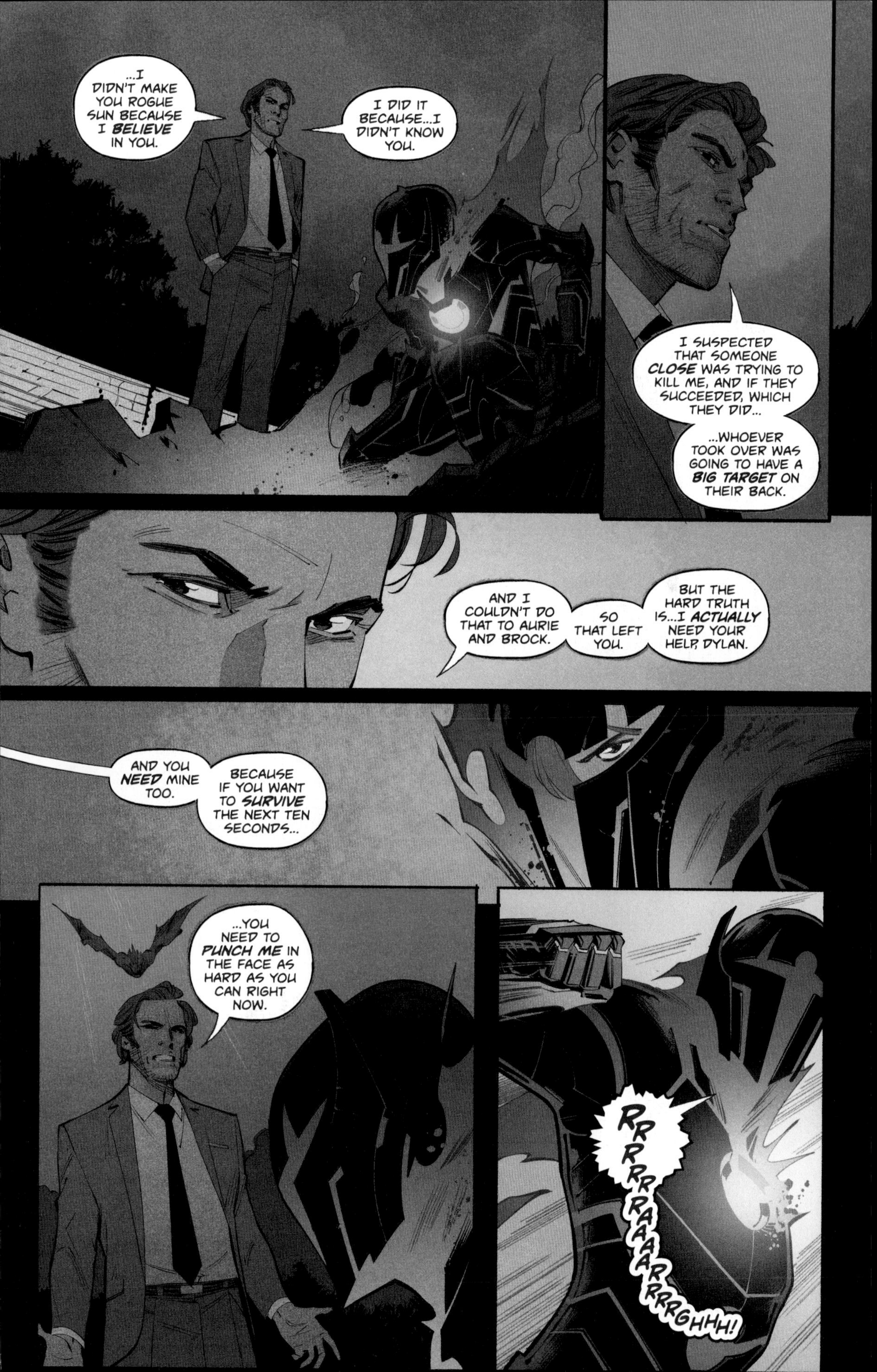
...I DIDN'T MAKE YOU ROGUE SUN BECAUSE I BELIEVE IN YOU.
I DID IT BECAUSE...I DIDN'T KNOW YOU.
I SUSPECTED THAT SOMEONE CLOSE WAS TRYING TO KILL ME, AND IF THEY SUCCEEDED, WHICH THEY DID...
...WHOEVER TOOK OVER WAS GOING TO HAVE A BIG TARGET ON THEIR BACK.
AND I COULDN'T DO THAT TO AURIE AND BROCK.
SO THAT LEFT YOU.
BUT THE HARD TRUTH IS...I ACTUALLY NEED YOUR HELP, DYLAN.
AND YOU NEED MINE TOO.
BECAUSE IF YOU WANT TO SURVIVE THE NEXT TEN SECONDS...
...YOU NEED TO PUNCH ME IN THE FACE AS HARD AS YOU CAN RIGHT NOW.
RRRRRAAARRRGHHH!

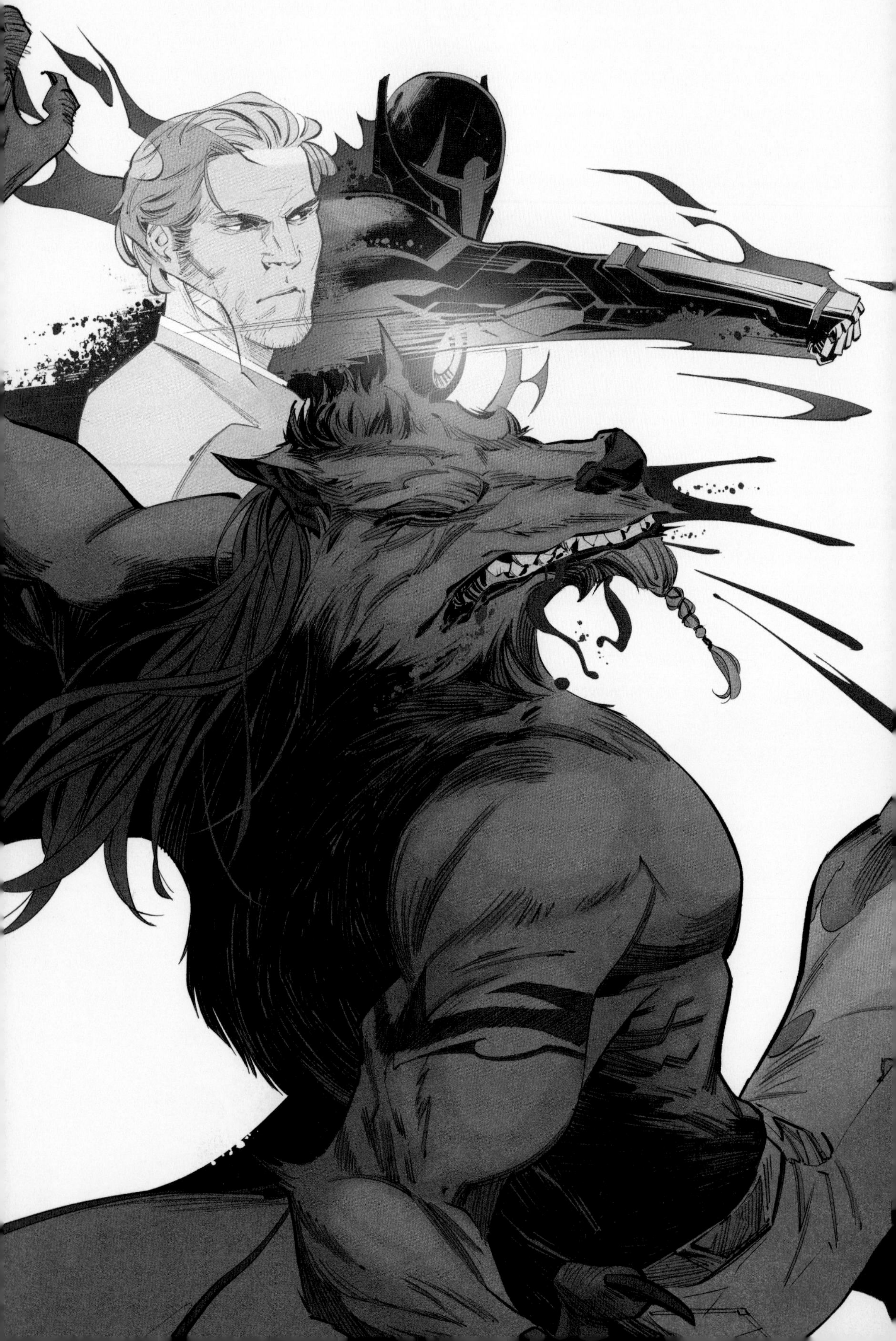

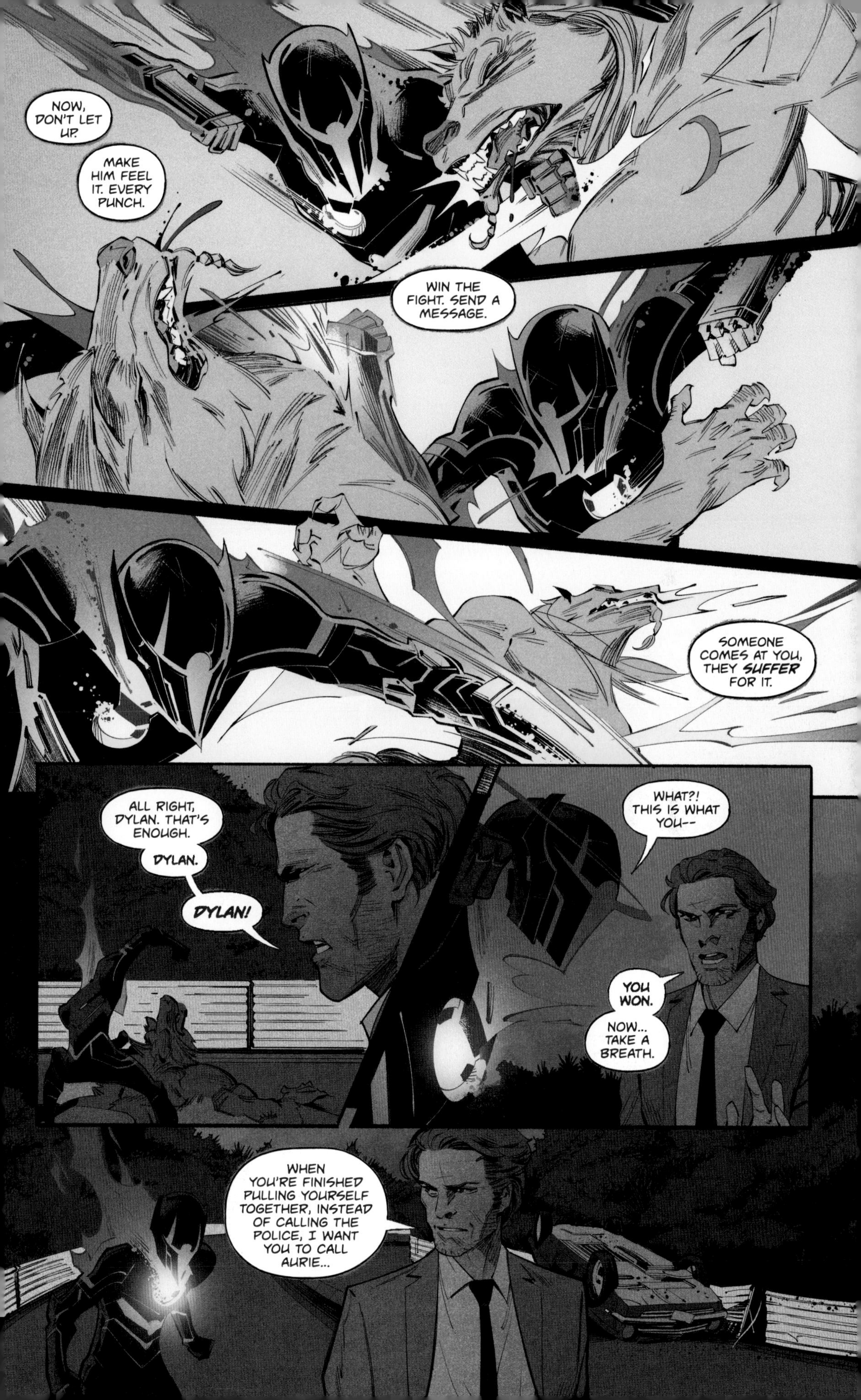
NOW, DON'T LET UP.
MAKE HIM FEEL IT. EVERY PUNCH.
WIN THE FIGHT. SEND A MESSAGE.
SOMEONE COMES AT YOU, THEY SUFFER FOR IT.
ALL RIGHT, DYLAN. THAT'S ENOUGH.
DYLAN.
DYLAN!
WHAT?! THIS IS WHAT YOU--
YOU WON.
NOW... TAKE A BREATH.
WHEN YOU'RE FINISHED PULLING YOURSELF TOGETHER, INSTEAD OF CALLING THE POLICE, I WANT YOU TO CALL AURIE...

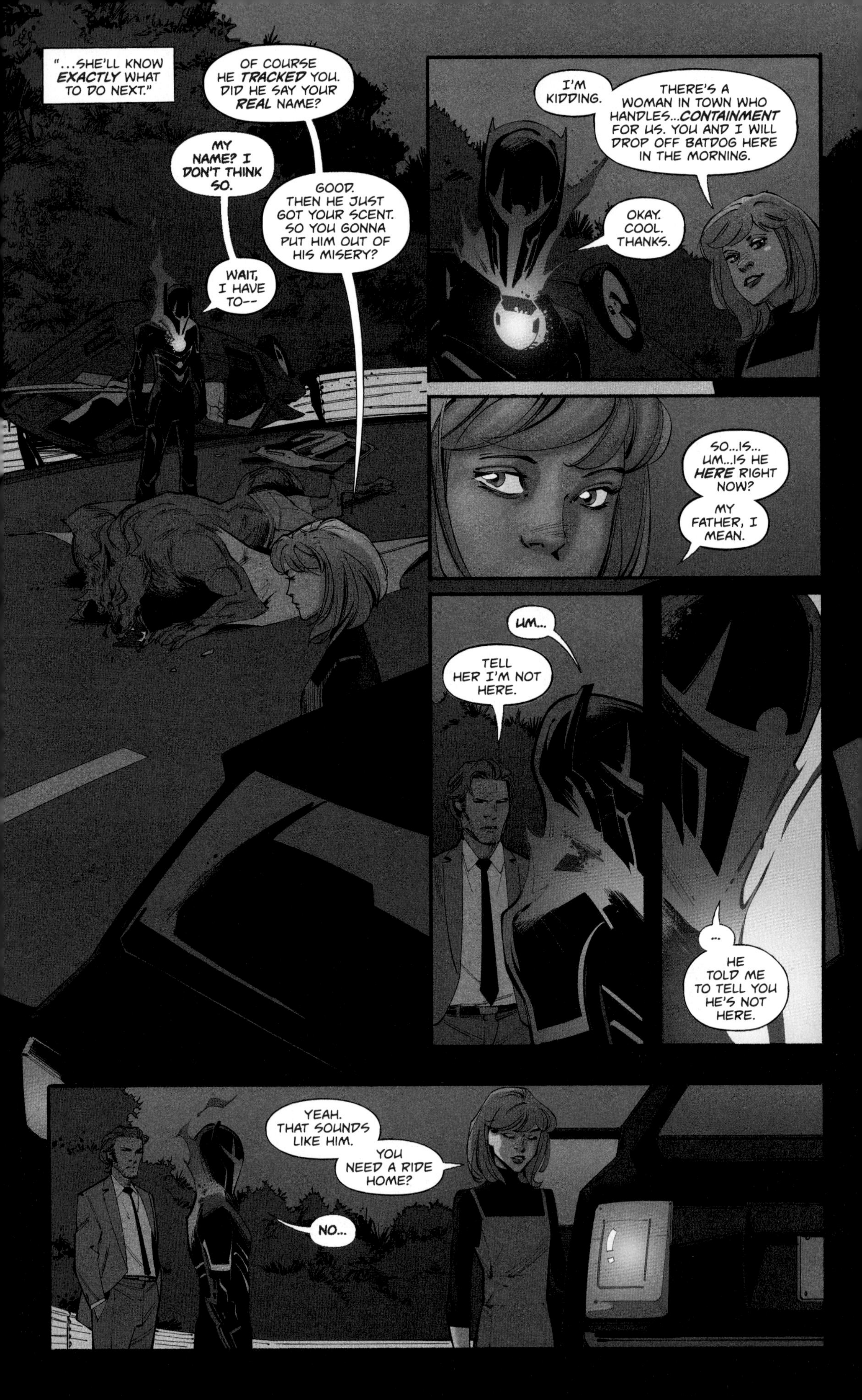
"...SHE'LL KNOW EXACTLY WHAT TO DO NEXT."
OF COURSE HE TRACKED YOU. DID HE SAY YOUR REAL NAME?
MY NAME? I DON'T THINK SO.
GOOD. THEN HE JUST GOT YOUR SCENT. SO YOU GONNA PUT HIM OUT OF HIS MISERY?
WAIT, I HAVE TO--
I'M KIDDING.
THERE'S A WOMAN IN TOWN WHO HANDLES...CONTAINMENT FOR US. YOU AND I WILL DROP OFF BATDOG HERE IN THE MORNING.
OKAY. COOL. THANKS.
SO...IS... UM...IS HE HERE RIGHT NOW?
MY FATHER, I MEAN.
UM...
TELL HER I'M NOT HERE.
...
HE TOLD ME TO TELL YOU HE'S NOT HERE.
YEAH. THAT SOUNDS LIKE HIM.
YOU NEED A RIDE HOME?
NO...

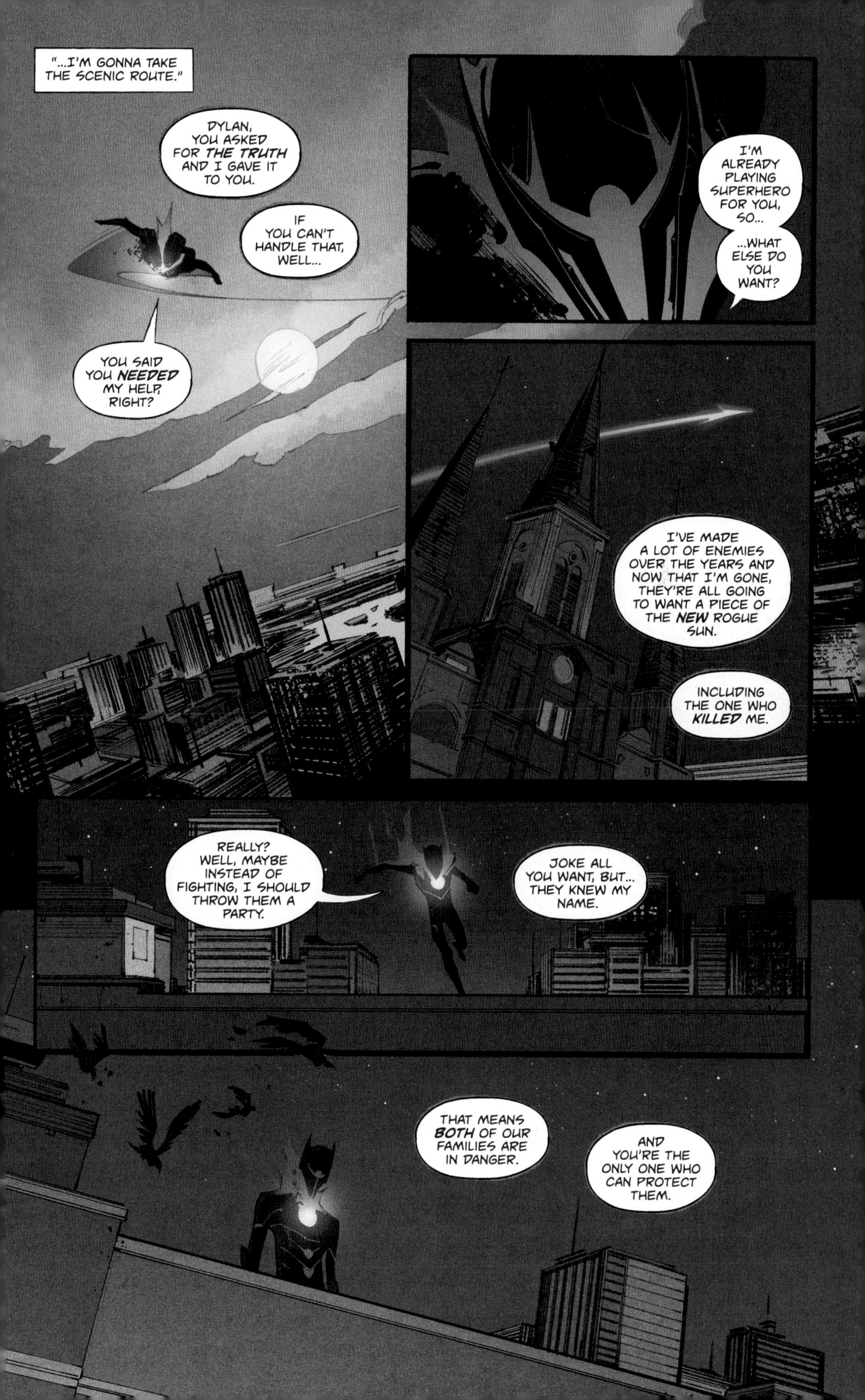
"...I'M GONNA TAKE THE SCENIC ROUTE."
DYLAN, YOU ASKED FOR *THE TRUTH* AND I GAVE IT TO YOU.
IF YOU CAN'T HANDLE THAT, WELL...
YOU SAID YOU *NEEDED* MY HELP, RIGHT?
I'M ALREADY PLAYING SUPERHERO FOR YOU, SO...
...WHAT ELSE DO YOU WANT?
I'VE MADE A LOT OF ENEMIES OVER THE YEARS AND NOW THAT I'M GONE, THEY'RE ALL GOING TO WANT A PIECE OF THE *NEW* ROGUE SUN.
INCLUDING THE ONE WHO *KILLED* ME.
REALLY? WELL, MAYBE INSTEAD OF FIGHTING, I SHOULD THROW THEM A PARTY.
JOKE ALL YOU WANT, BUT... THEY KNEW MY NAME.
THAT MEANS *BOTH* OF OUR FAMILIES ARE IN DANGER.
AND YOU'RE THE ONLY ONE WHO CAN PROTECT THEM.

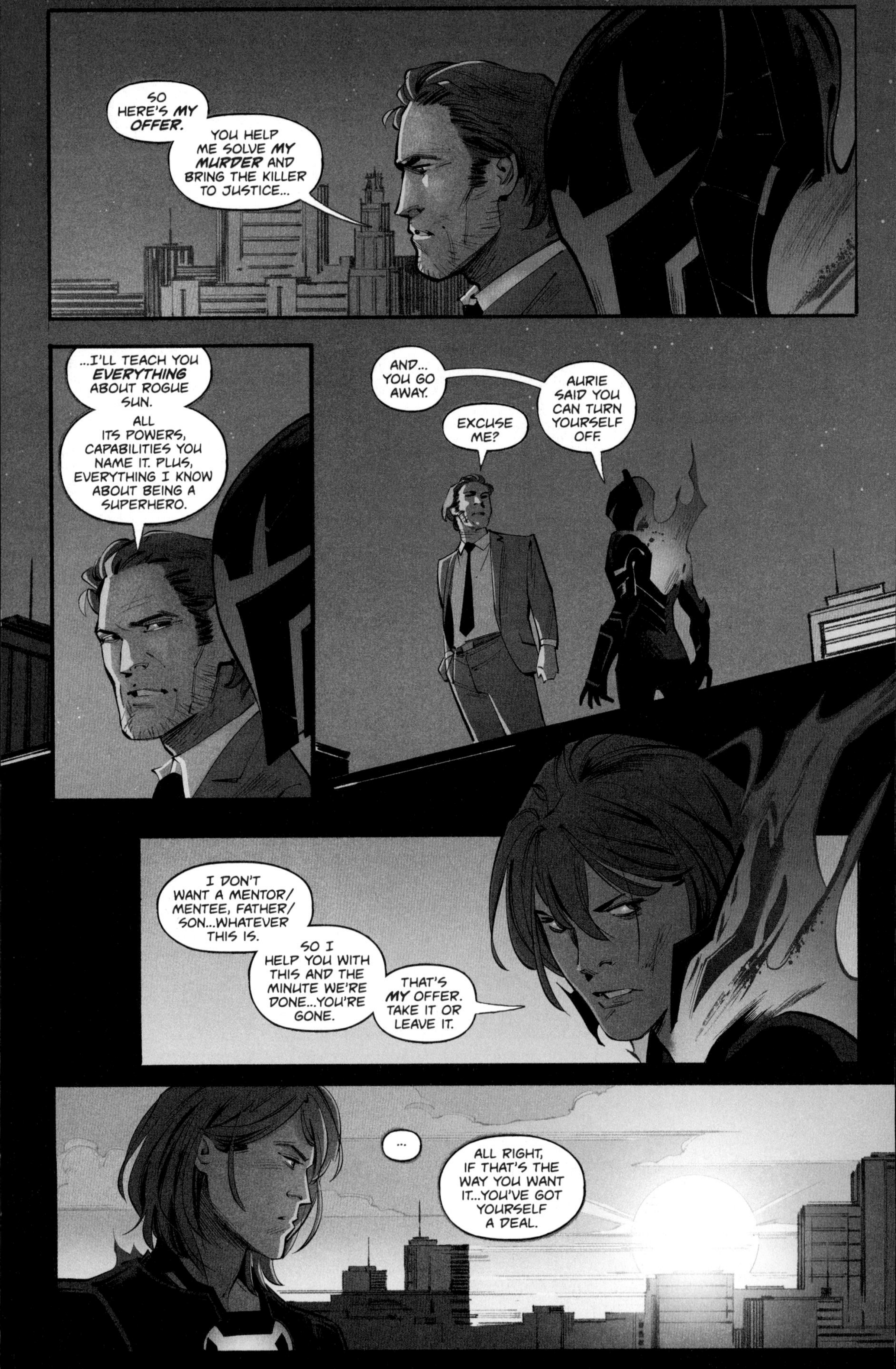
SO HERE'S MY OFFER.
YOU HELP ME SOLVE MY MURDER AND BRING THE KILLER TO JUSTICE...
...I'LL TEACH YOU EVERYTHING ABOUT ROGUE SUN.
ALL ITS POWERS, CAPABILITIES YOU NAME IT. PLUS, EVERYTHING I KNOW ABOUT BEING A SUPERHERO.
EXCUSE ME?
AURIE SAID YOU CAN TURN YOURSELF OFF.
AND... YOU GO AWAY.
I DON'T WANT A MENTOR/ MENTEE, FATHER/ SON...WHATEVER THIS IS.
SO I HELP YOU WITH THIS AND THE MINUTE WE'RE DONE...YOU'RE GONE.
THAT'S MY OFFER. TAKE IT OR LEAVE IT.
...
ALL RIGHT, IF THAT'S THE WAY YOU WANT IT...YOU'VE GOT YOURSELF A DEAL.

Interlude
A Taste of Home

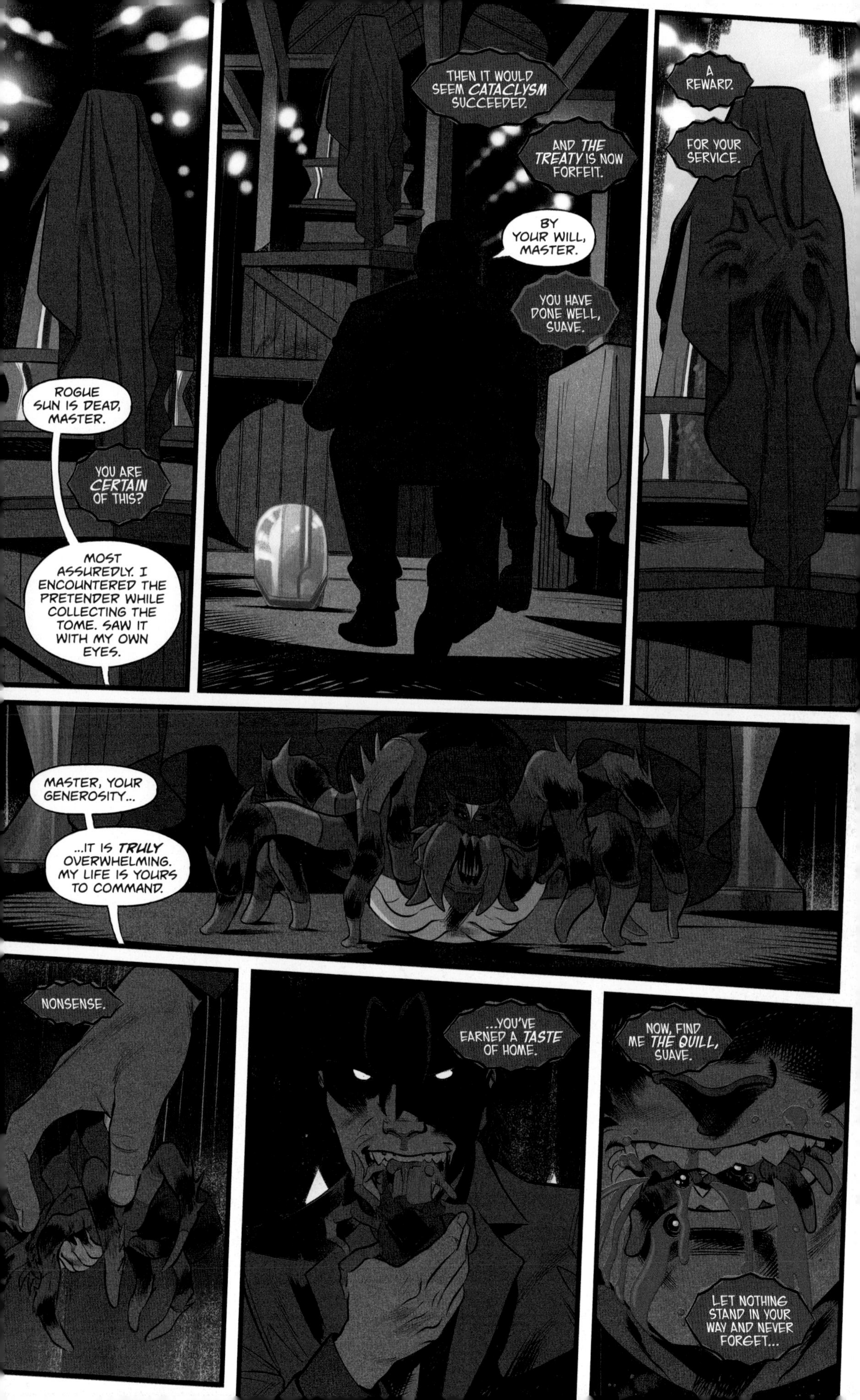
ROGUE SUN IS DEAD, MASTER.
YOU ARE *CERTAIN* OF THIS?
MOST ASSUREDLY. I ENCOUNTERED THE PRETENDER WHILE COLLECTING THE TOME. SAW IT WITH MY OWN EYES.
THEN IT WOULD SEEM *CATACLYSM* SUCCEEDED.
AND *THE TREATY* IS NOW FORFEIT.
BY YOUR WILL, MASTER.
YOU HAVE DONE WELL, SUAVE.
A REWARD.
FOR YOUR SERVICE.
MASTER, YOUR GENEROSITY...
...IT IS *TRULY* OVERWHELMING. MY LIFE IS YOURS TO COMMAND.
NONSENSE.
...YOU'VE EARNED A *TASTE* OF HOME.
NOW, FIND ME *THE QUILL,* SUAVE.
LET NOTHING STAND IN YOUR WAY AND NEVER FORGET...

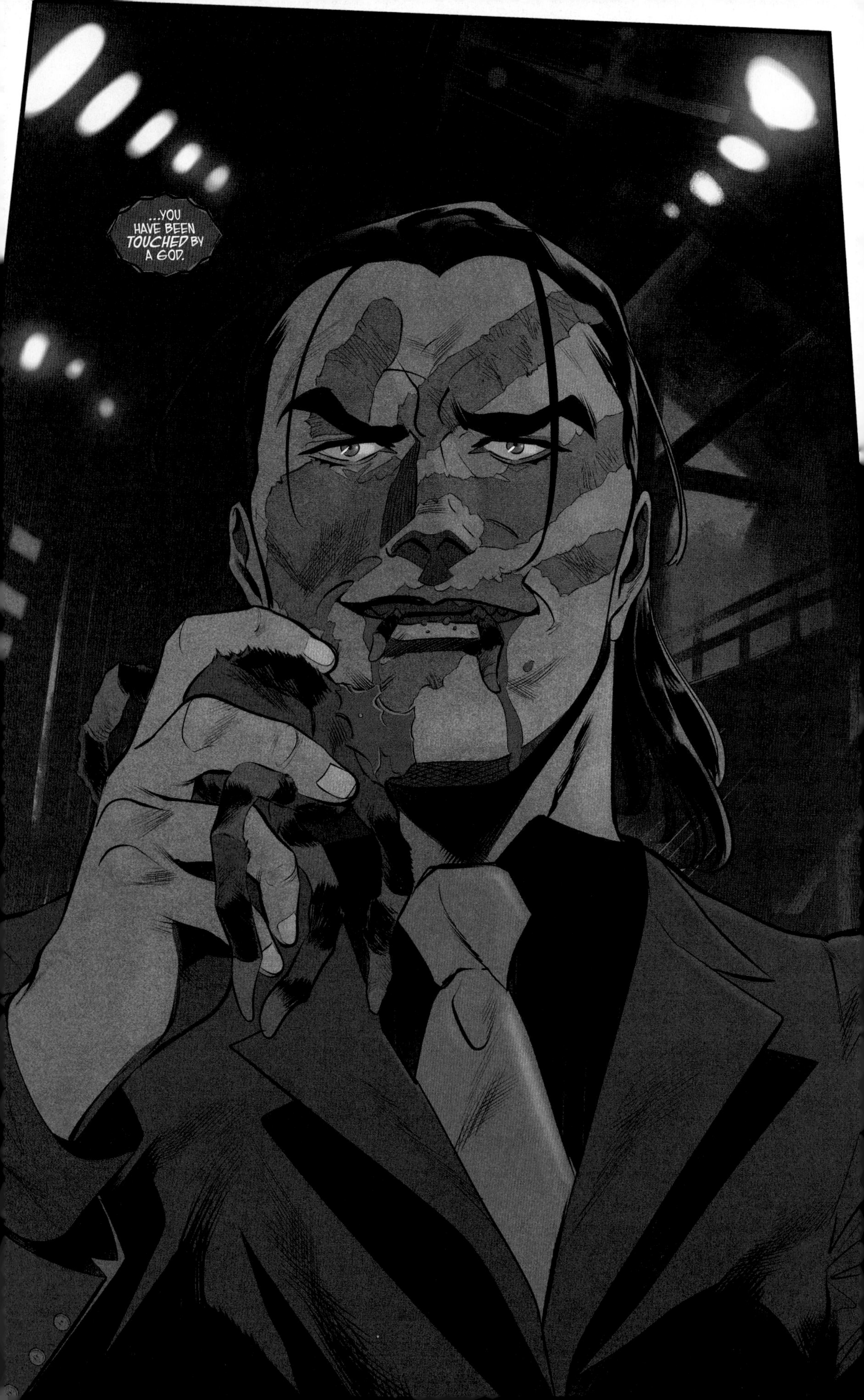
...YOU HAVE BEEN TOUCHED BY A GOD.

Chapter Three
The Crystal Menagerie

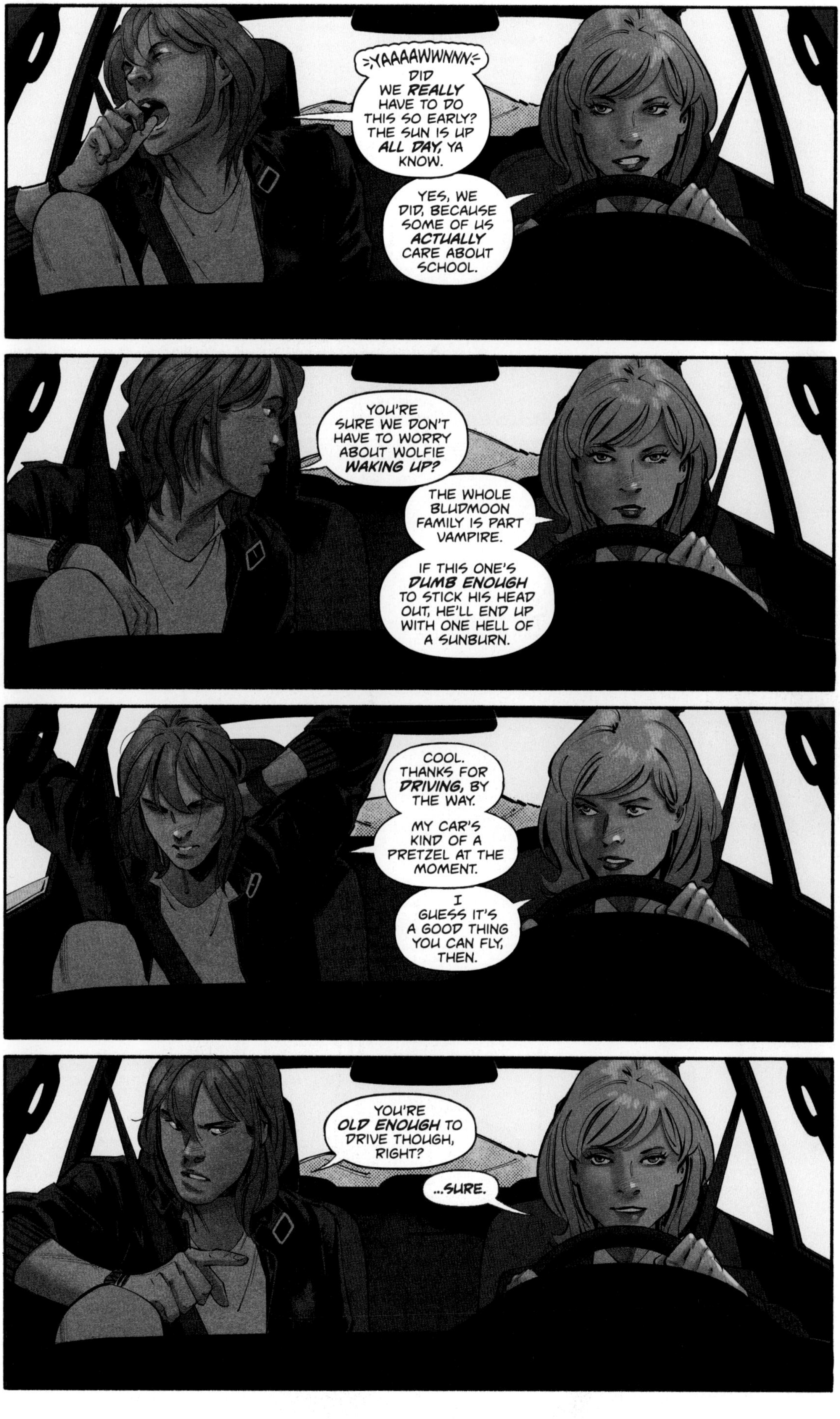

YAAAAWWNNN
DID WE REALLY HAVE TO DO THIS SO EARLY? THE SUN IS UP ALL DAY, YA KNOW.
YES, WE DID, BECAUSE SOME OF US ACTUALLY CARE ABOUT SCHOOL.
YOU'RE SURE WE DON'T HAVE TO WORRY ABOUT WOLFIE WAKING UP?
THE WHOLE BLUDMOON FAMILY IS PART VAMPIRE.
IF THIS ONE'S DUMB ENOUGH TO STICK HIS HEAD OUT, HE'LL END UP WITH ONE HELL OF A SUNBURN.
COOL. THANKS FOR DRIVING, BY THE WAY.
MY CAR'S KIND OF A PRETZEL AT THE MOMENT.
I GUESS IT'S A GOOD THING YOU CAN FLY, THEN.
YOU'RE OLD ENOUGH TO DRIVE THOUGH, RIGHT?
...SURE.

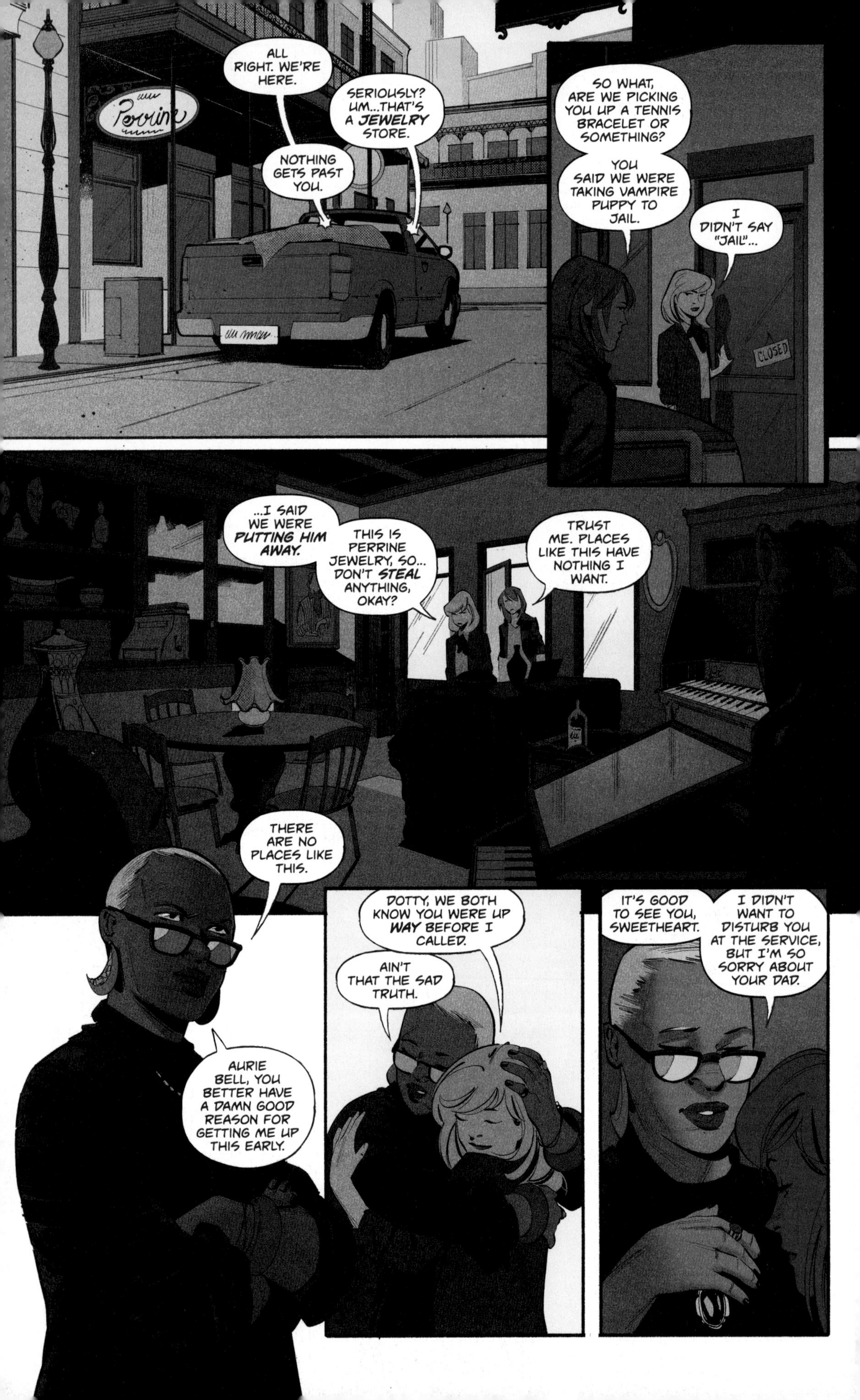
Perrine
ALL RIGHT. WE'RE HERE.
SERIOUSLY? UM...THAT'S A JEWELRY STORE.
NOTHING GETS PAST YOU.
SO WHAT, ARE WE PICKING YOU UP A TENNIS BRACELET OR SOMETHING?
YOU SAID WE WERE TAKING VAMPIRE PUPPY TO JAIL.
I DIDN'T SAY "JAIL"...
CLOSED
...I SAID WE WERE PUTTING HIM AWAY.
THIS IS PERRINE JEWELRY, SO... DON'T STEAL ANYTHING, OKAY?
TRUST ME. PLACES LIKE THIS HAVE NOTHING I WANT.
THERE ARE NO PLACES LIKE THIS.
AURIE BELL, YOU BETTER HAVE A DAMN GOOD REASON FOR GETTING ME UP THIS EARLY.
DOTTY, WE BOTH KNOW YOU WERE UP WAY BEFORE I CALLED.
AIN'T THAT THE SAD TRUTH.
IT'S GOOD TO SEE YOU, SWEETHEART.
I DIDN'T WANT TO DISTURB YOU AT THE SERVICE, BUT I'M SO SORRY ABOUT YOUR DAD.

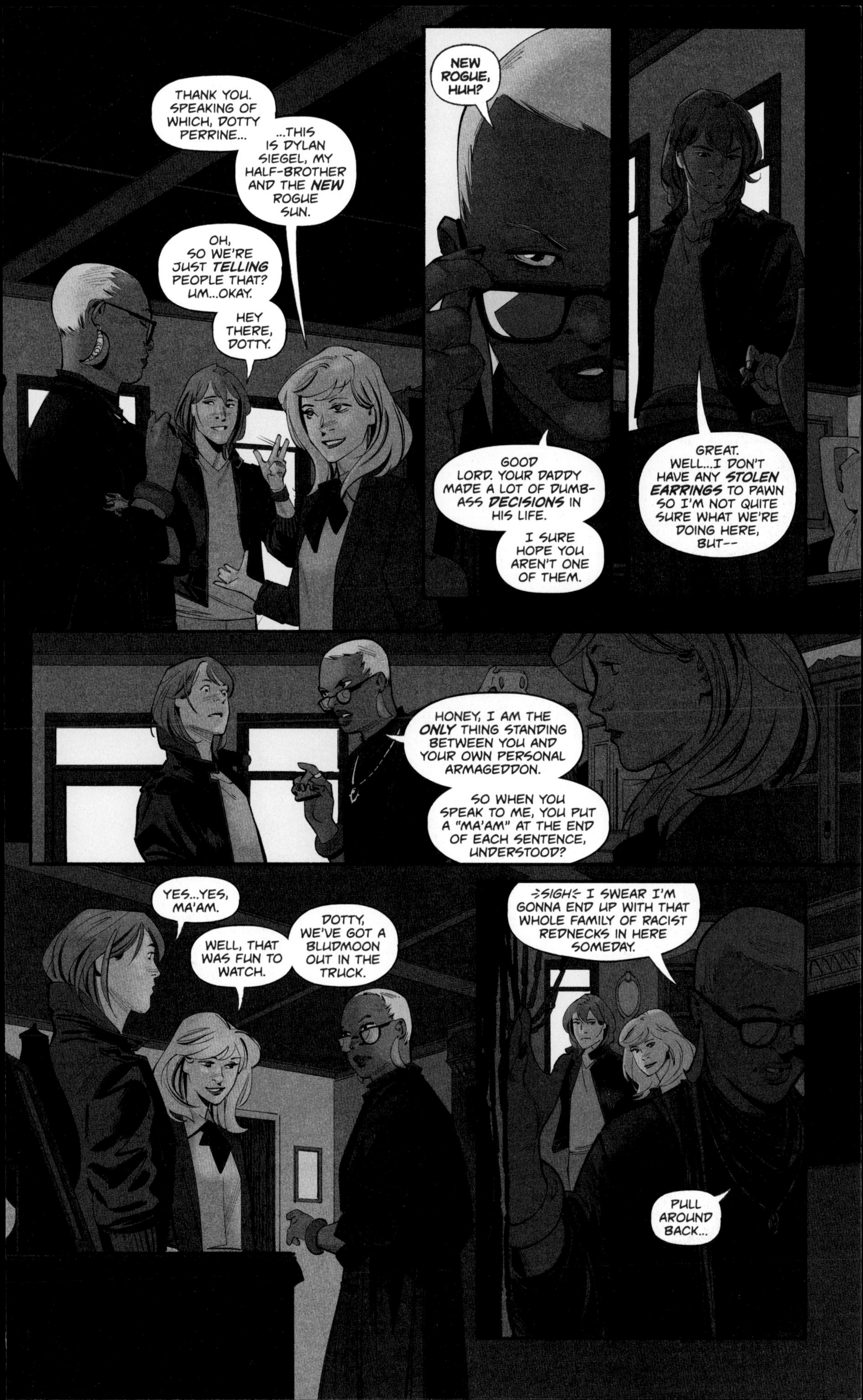
THANK YOU. SPEAKING OF WHICH, DOTTY PERRINE...
...THIS IS DYLAN SIEGEL, MY HALF-BROTHER AND THE NEW ROGUE SUN.
OH, SO WE'RE JUST TELLING PEOPLE THAT? UM...OKAY.
HEY THERE, DOTTY.
NEW ROGUE, HUH?
GOOD LORD. YOUR DADDY MADE A LOT OF DUMB-ASS DECISIONS IN HIS LIFE.
I SURE HOPE YOU AREN'T ONE OF THEM.
GREAT. WELL...I DON'T HAVE ANY STOLEN EARRINGS TO PAWN SO I'M NOT QUITE SURE WHAT WE'RE DOING HERE, BUT--
HONEY, I AM THE ONLY THING STANDING BETWEEN YOU AND YOUR OWN PERSONAL ARMAGEDDON.
SO WHEN YOU SPEAK TO ME, YOU PUT A "MA'AM" AT THE END OF EACH SENTENCE, UNDERSTOOD?
YES...YES, MA'AM.
WELL, THAT WAS FUN TO WATCH.
DOTTY, WE'VE GOT A BLUDMOON OUT IN THE TRUCK.
SIGH I SWEAR I'M GONNA END UP WITH THAT WHOLE FAMILY OF RACIST REDNECKS IN HERE SOMEDAY.
PULL AROUND BACK...

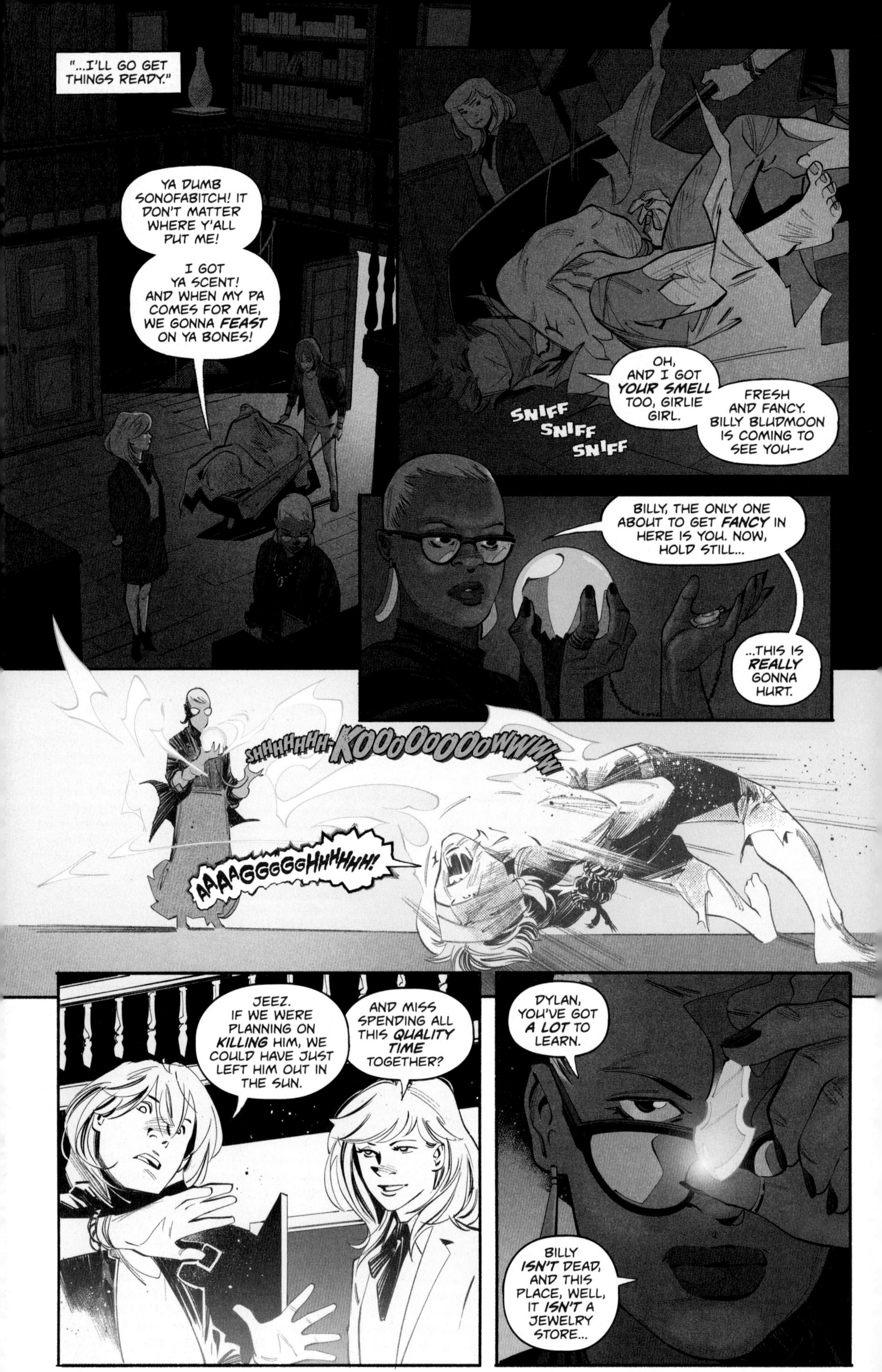
"...I'LL GO GET THINGS READY."
YA DUMB SONOFABITCH! IT DON'T MATTER WHERE Y'ALL PUT ME!
I GOT YA SCENT! AND WHEN MY PA COMES FOR ME, WE GONNA FEAST ON YA BONES!
SNIFF SNIFF SNIFF
OH, AND I GOT YOUR SMELL TOO, GIRLIE GIRL.
FRESH AND FANCY. BILLY BLUDMOON IS COMING TO SEE YOU--
BILLY, THE ONLY ONE ABOUT TO GET FANCY IN HERE IS YOU. NOW, HOLD STILL...
...THIS IS REALLY GONNA HURT.
SHHHHHHH-KOOOOOOOOOWWWW
AAAAGGGGGHHHHHH!
JEEZ. IF WE WERE PLANNING ON KILLING HIM, WE COULD HAVE JUST LEFT HIM OUT IN THE SUN.
AND MISS SPENDING ALL THIS QUALITY TIME TOGETHER?
DYLAN, YOU'VE GOT A LOT TO LEARN.
BILLY ISN'T DEAD, AND THIS PLACE, WELL, IT ISN'T A JEWELRY STORE...

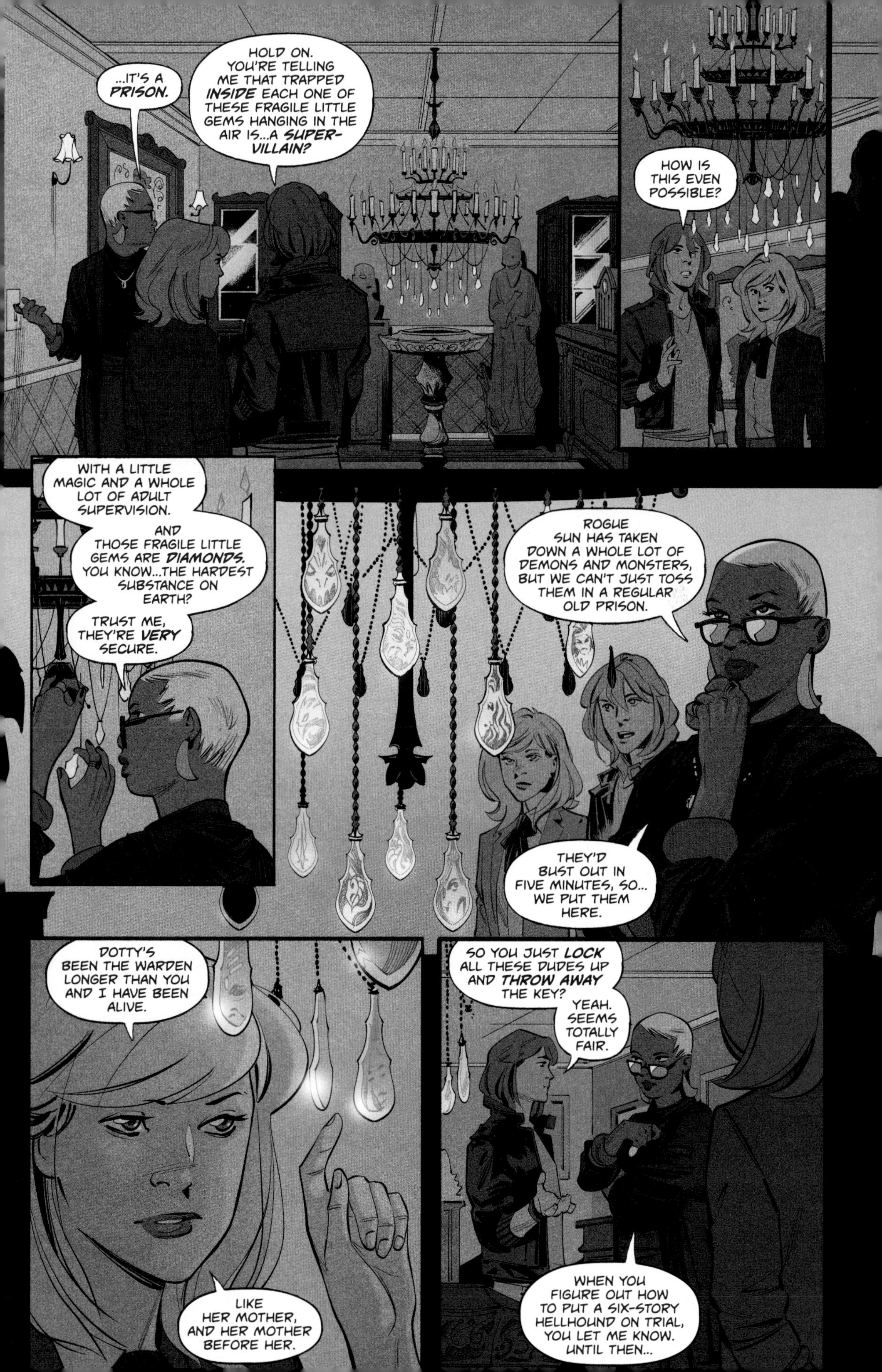
...IT'S A PRISON.
HOLD ON. YOU'RE TELLING ME THAT TRAPPED INSIDE EACH ONE OF THESE FRAGILE LITTLE GEMS HANGING IN THE AIR IS...A SUPER-VILLAIN?
HOW IS THIS EVEN POSSIBLE?
WITH A LITTLE MAGIC AND A WHOLE LOT OF ADULT SUPERVISION.
AND THOSE FRAGILE LITTLE GEMS ARE DIAMONDS. YOU KNOW...THE HARDEST SUBSTANCE ON EARTH?
TRUST ME, THEY'RE VERY SECURE.
ROGUE SUN HAS TAKEN DOWN A WHOLE LOT OF DEMONS AND MONSTERS, BUT WE CAN'T JUST TOSS THEM IN A REGULAR OLD PRISON.
THEY'D BUST OUT IN FIVE MINUTES, SO... WE PUT THEM HERE.
DOTTY'S BEEN THE WARDEN LONGER THAN YOU AND I HAVE BEEN ALIVE.
LIKE HER MOTHER, AND HER MOTHER BEFORE HER.
SO YOU JUST LOCK ALL THESE DUDES UP AND THROW AWAY THE KEY?
YEAH. SEEMS TOTALLY FAIR.
WHEN YOU FIGURE OUT HOW TO PUT A SIX-STORY HELLHOUND ON TRIAL, YOU LET ME KNOW. UNTIL THEN...

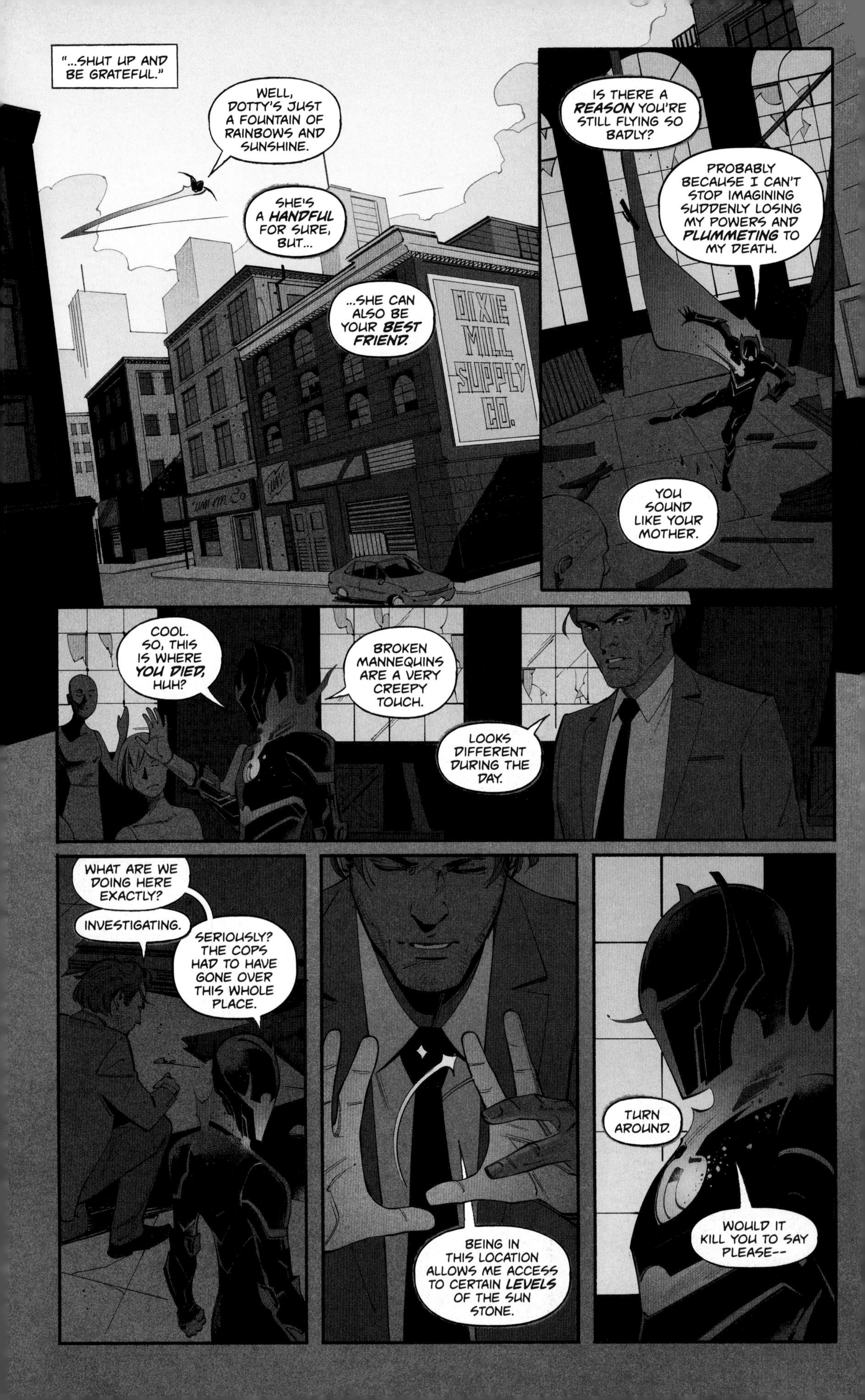
"...SHUT UP AND BE GRATEFUL."
WELL, DOTTY'S JUST A FOUNTAIN OF RAINBOWS AND SUNSHINE.
SHE'S A HANDFUL FOR SURE, BUT...
...SHE CAN ALSO BE YOUR BEST FRIEND.
DIXIE MILL SUPPLY CO.
IS THERE A REASON YOU'RE STILL FLYING SO BADLY?
PROBABLY BECAUSE I CAN'T STOP IMAGINING SUDDENLY LOSING MY POWERS AND PLUMMETING TO MY DEATH.
YOU SOUND LIKE YOUR MOTHER.
COOL. SO, THIS IS WHERE YOU DIED, HUH?
BROKEN MANNEQUINS ARE A VERY CREEPY TOUCH.
LOOKS DIFFERENT DURING THE DAY.
WHAT ARE WE DOING HERE EXACTLY?
INVESTIGATING.
SERIOUSLY? THE COPS HAD TO HAVE GONE OVER THIS WHOLE PLACE.
BEING IN THIS LOCATION ALLOWS ME ACCESS TO CERTAIN LEVELS OF THE SUN STONE.
TURN AROUND.
WOULD IT KILL YOU TO SAY PLEASE--

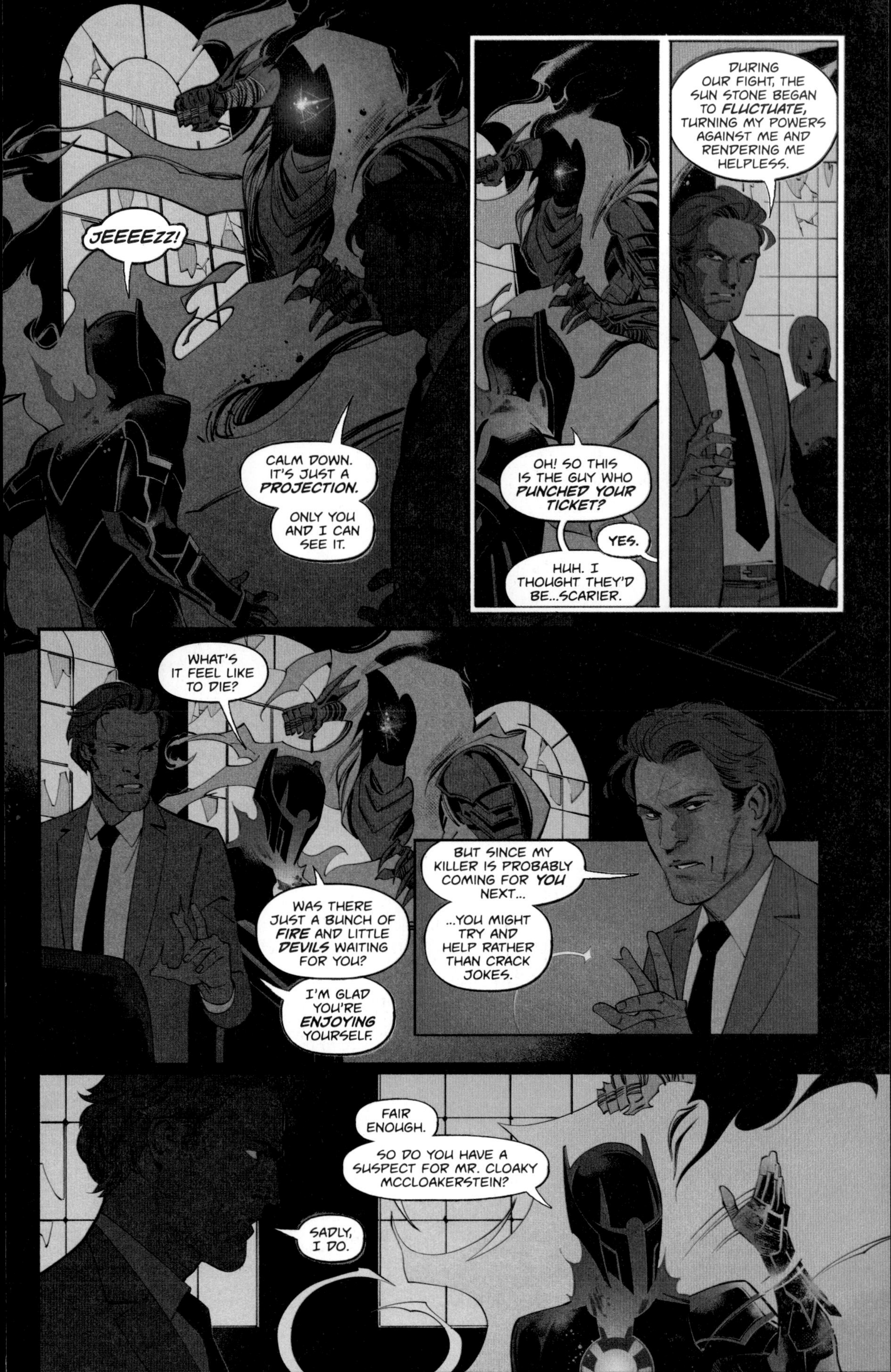
JEEEEZZ!
CALM DOWN. IT'S JUST A PROJECTION.
ONLY YOU AND I CAN SEE IT.
DURING OUR FIGHT, THE SUN STONE BEGAN TO FLUCTUATE, TURNING MY POWERS AGAINST ME AND RENDERING ME HELPLESS.
OH! SO THIS IS THE GUY WHO PUNCHED YOUR TICKET?
YES.
HUH. I THOUGHT THEY'D BE...SCARIER.
WHAT'S IT FEEL LIKE TO DIE?
WAS THERE JUST A BUNCH OF FIRE AND LITTLE DEVILS WAITING FOR YOU?
I'M GLAD YOU'RE ENJOYING YOURSELF.
BUT SINCE MY KILLER IS PROBABLY COMING FOR YOU NEXT...
...YOU MIGHT TRY AND HELP RATHER THAN CRACK JOKES.
FAIR ENOUGH.
SO DO YOU HAVE A SUSPECT FOR MR. CLOAKY MCCLOAKERSTEIN?
SADLY, I DO.

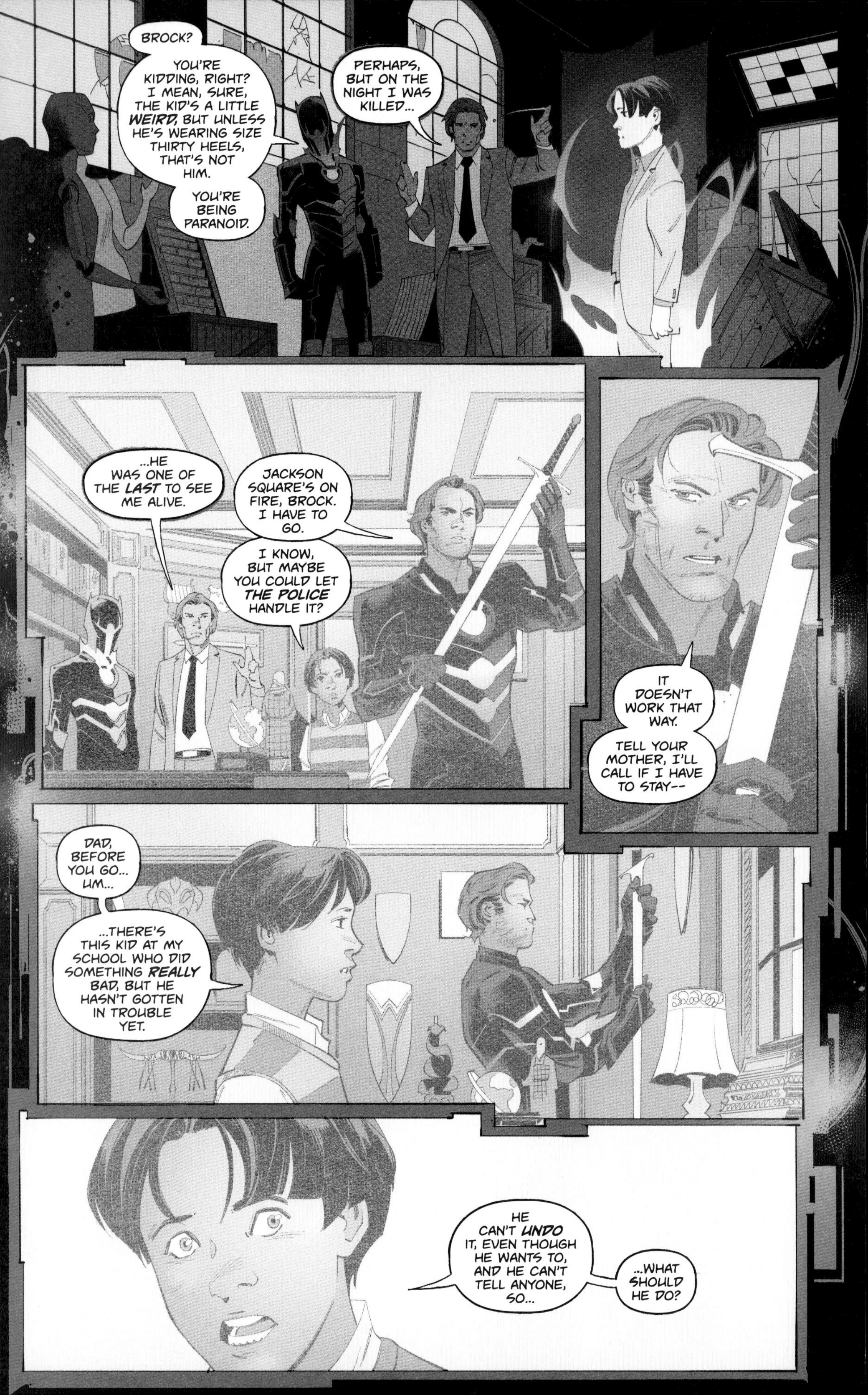
BROCK?
YOU'RE KIDDING, RIGHT? I MEAN, SURE, THE KID'S A LITTLE WEIRD, BUT UNLESS HE'S WEARING SIZE THIRTY HEELS, THAT'S NOT HIM.
YOU'RE BEING PARANOID.
PERHAPS, BUT ON THE NIGHT I WAS KILLED...
...HE WAS ONE OF THE LAST TO SEE ME ALIVE.
JACKSON SQUARE'S ON FIRE, BROCK. I HAVE TO GO.
I KNOW, BUT MAYBE YOU COULD LET THE POLICE HANDLE IT?
IT DOESN'T WORK THAT WAY.
TELL YOUR MOTHER, I'LL CALL IF I HAVE TO STAY--
DAD, BEFORE YOU GO... UM...
...THERE'S THIS KID AT MY SCHOOL WHO DID SOMETHING REALLY BAD, BUT HE HASN'T GOTTEN IN TROUBLE YET.
HE CAN'T UNDO IT, EVEN THOUGH HE WANTS TO, AND HE CAN'T TELL ANYONE, SO...
...WHAT SHOULD HE DO?

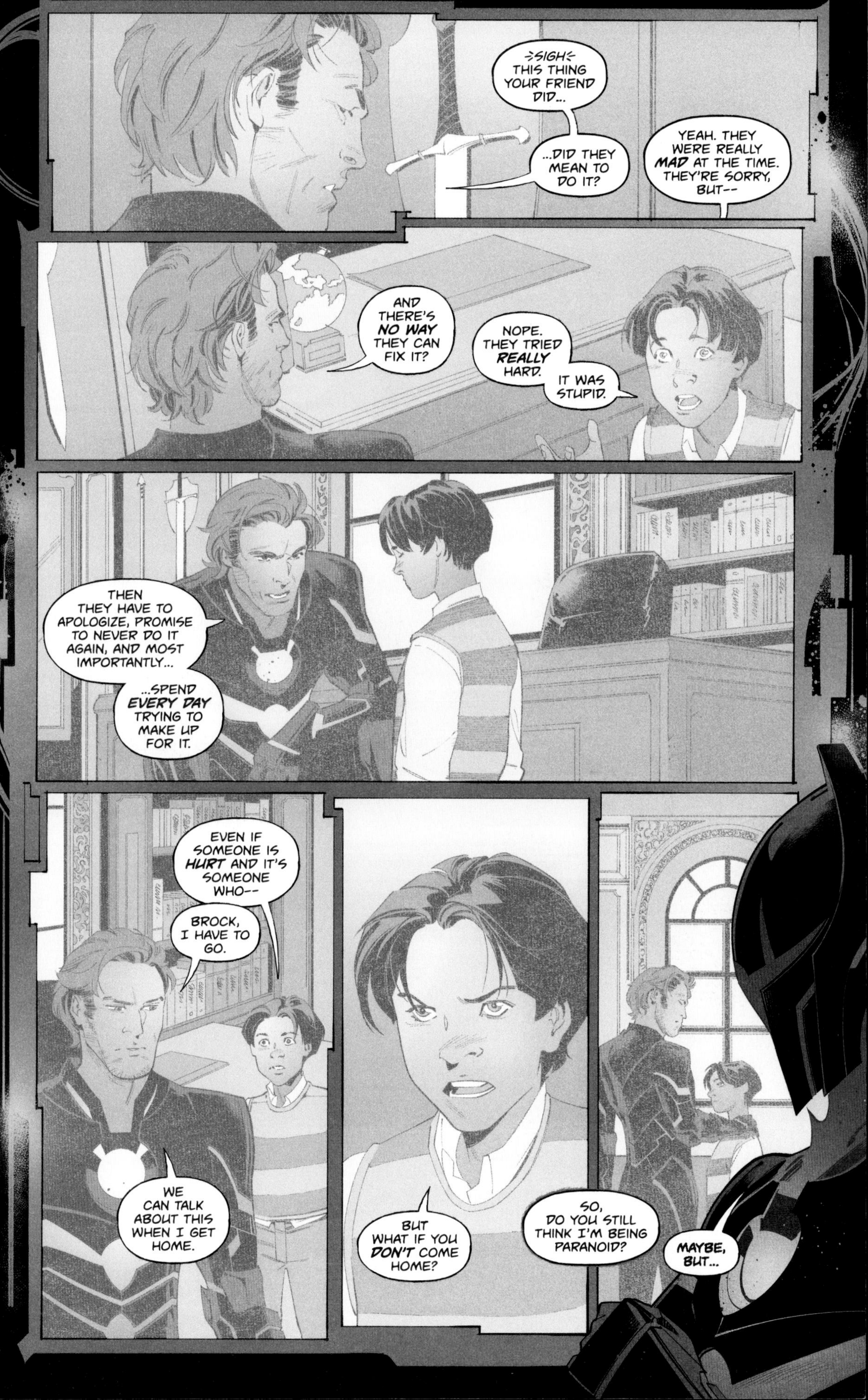

≈SIGH≈ THIS THING YOUR FRIEND DID...
...DID THEY MEAN TO DO IT?
YEAH. THEY WERE REALLY **MAD** AT THE TIME. THEY'RE SORRY, BUT--
AND THERE'S **NO WAY** THEY CAN FIX IT?
NOPE. THEY TRIED **REALLY** HARD.
IT WAS STUPID.
THEN THEY HAVE TO APOLOGIZE, PROMISE TO NEVER DO IT AGAIN, AND MOST IMPORTANTLY...
...SPEND **EVERY DAY** TRYING TO MAKE UP FOR IT.
EVEN IF SOMEONE IS **HURT** AND IT'S SOMEONE WHO--
BROCK, I HAVE TO GO.
WE CAN TALK ABOUT THIS WHEN I GET HOME.
BUT WHAT IF YOU **DON'T** COME HOME?
SO, DO YOU STILL THINK I'M BEING PARANOID?
MAYBE, BUT...

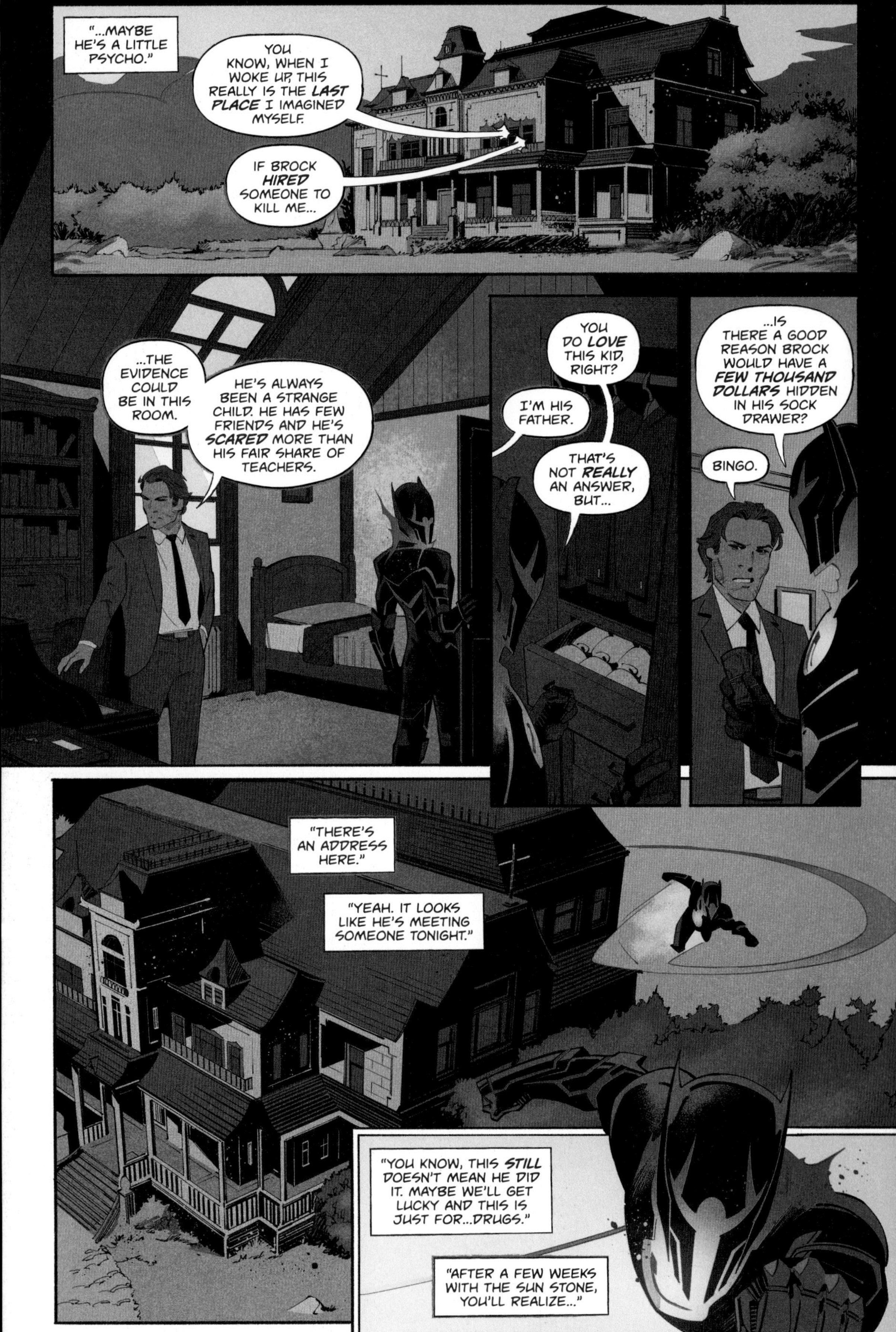
"...MAYBE HE'S A LITTLE PSYCHO."
YOU KNOW, WHEN I WOKE UP, THIS REALLY IS THE LAST PLACE I IMAGINED MYSELF.
IF BROCK HIRED SOMEONE TO KILL ME...
...THE EVIDENCE COULD BE IN THIS ROOM.
HE'S ALWAYS BEEN A STRANGE CHILD. HE HAS FEW FRIENDS AND HE'S SCARED MORE THAN HIS FAIR SHARE OF TEACHERS.
YOU DO LOVE THIS KID, RIGHT?
I'M HIS FATHER.
THAT'S NOT REALLY AN ANSWER, BUT...
...IS THERE A GOOD REASON BROCK WOULD HAVE A FEW THOUSAND DOLLARS HIDDEN IN HIS SOCK DRAWER?
BINGO.
"THERE'S AN ADDRESS HERE."
"YEAH. IT LOOKS LIKE HE'S MEETING SOMEONE TONIGHT."
"YOU KNOW, THIS STILL DOESN'T MEAN HE DID IT. MAYBE WE'LL GET LUCKY AND THIS IS JUST FOR...DRUGS."
"AFTER A FEW WEEKS WITH THE SUN STONE, YOU'LL REALIZE..."

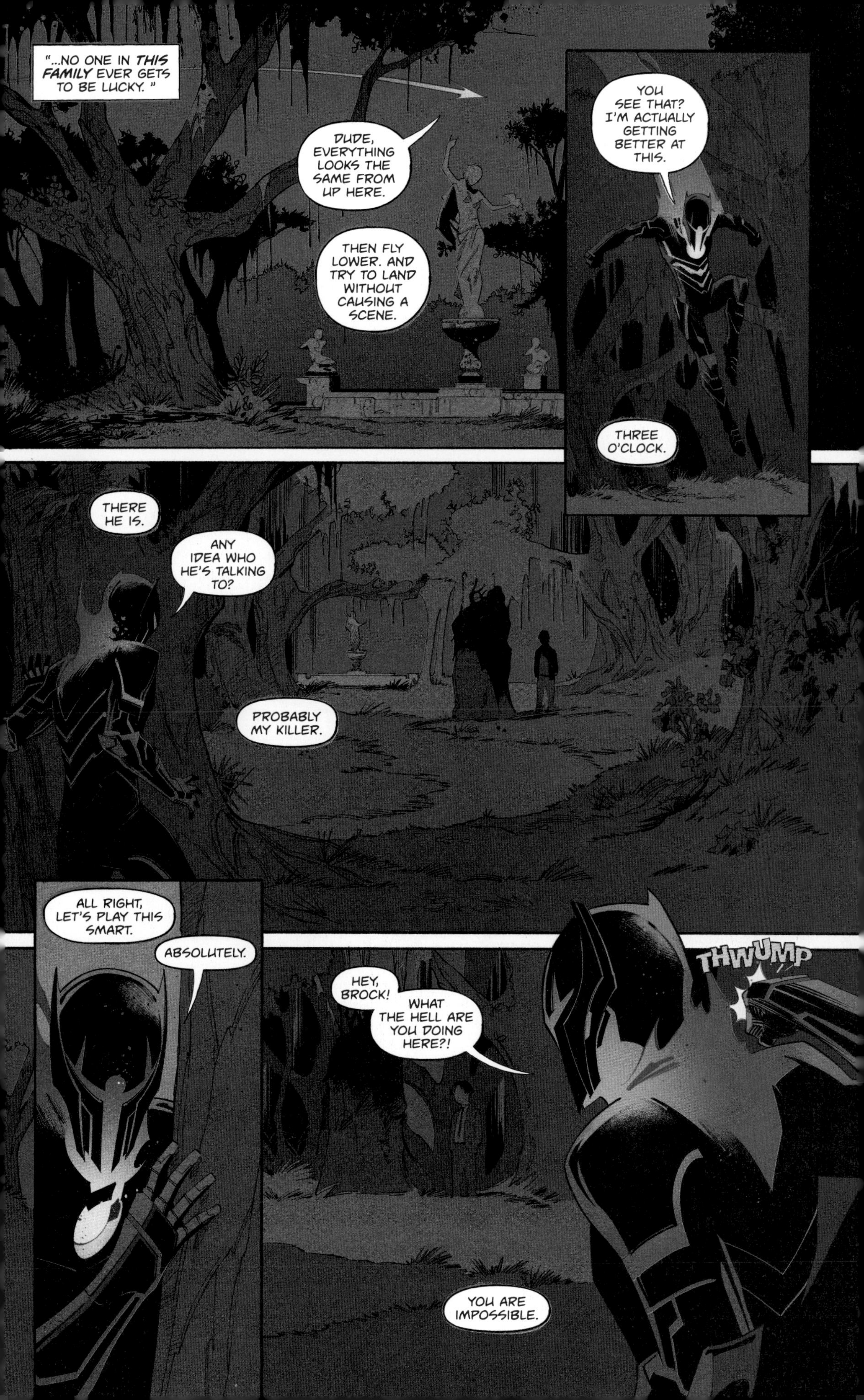
"...NO ONE IN THIS FAMILY EVER GETS TO BE LUCKY."
DUDE, EVERYTHING LOOKS THE SAME FROM UP HERE.
THEN FLY LOWER. AND TRY TO LAND WITHOUT CAUSING A SCENE.
YOU SEE THAT? I'M ACTUALLY GETTING BETTER AT THIS.
THREE O'CLOCK.
THERE HE IS.
ANY IDEA WHO HE'S TALKING TO?
PROBABLY MY KILLER.
ALL RIGHT, LET'S PLAY THIS SMART.
ABSOLUTELY.
HEY, BROCK!
WHAT THE HELL ARE YOU DOING HERE?!
THWUMP
YOU ARE IMPOSSIBLE.

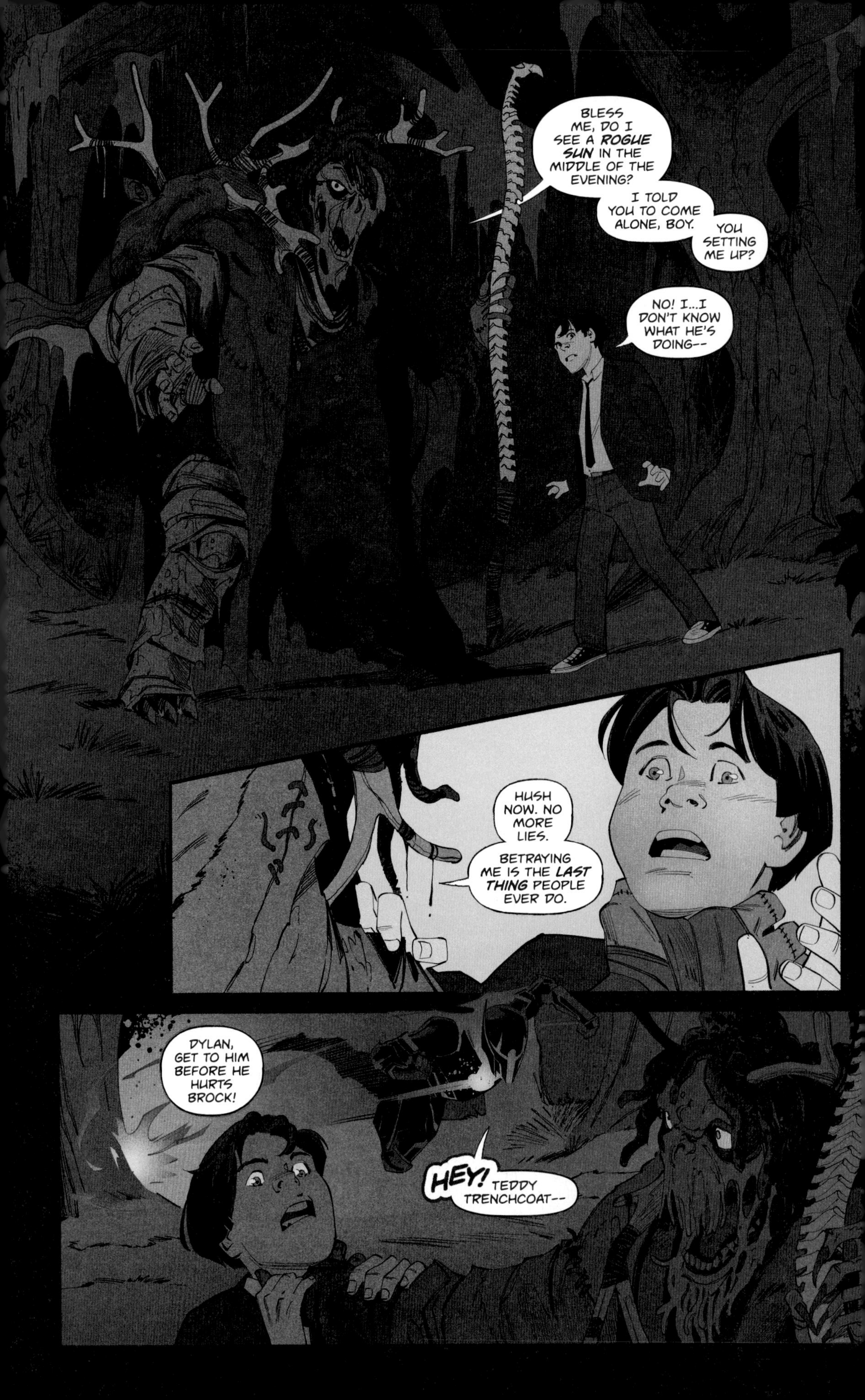
BLESS ME, DO I SEE A ROGUE SUN IN THE MIDDLE OF THE EVENING?
I TOLD YOU TO COME ALONE, BOY.
YOU SETTING ME UP?
NO! I...I DON'T KNOW WHAT HE'S DOING--
HUSH NOW. NO MORE LIES.
BETRAYING ME IS THE LAST THING PEOPLE EVER DO.
DYLAN, GET TO HIM BEFORE HE HURTS BROCK!
HEY! TEDDY TRENCHCOAT--

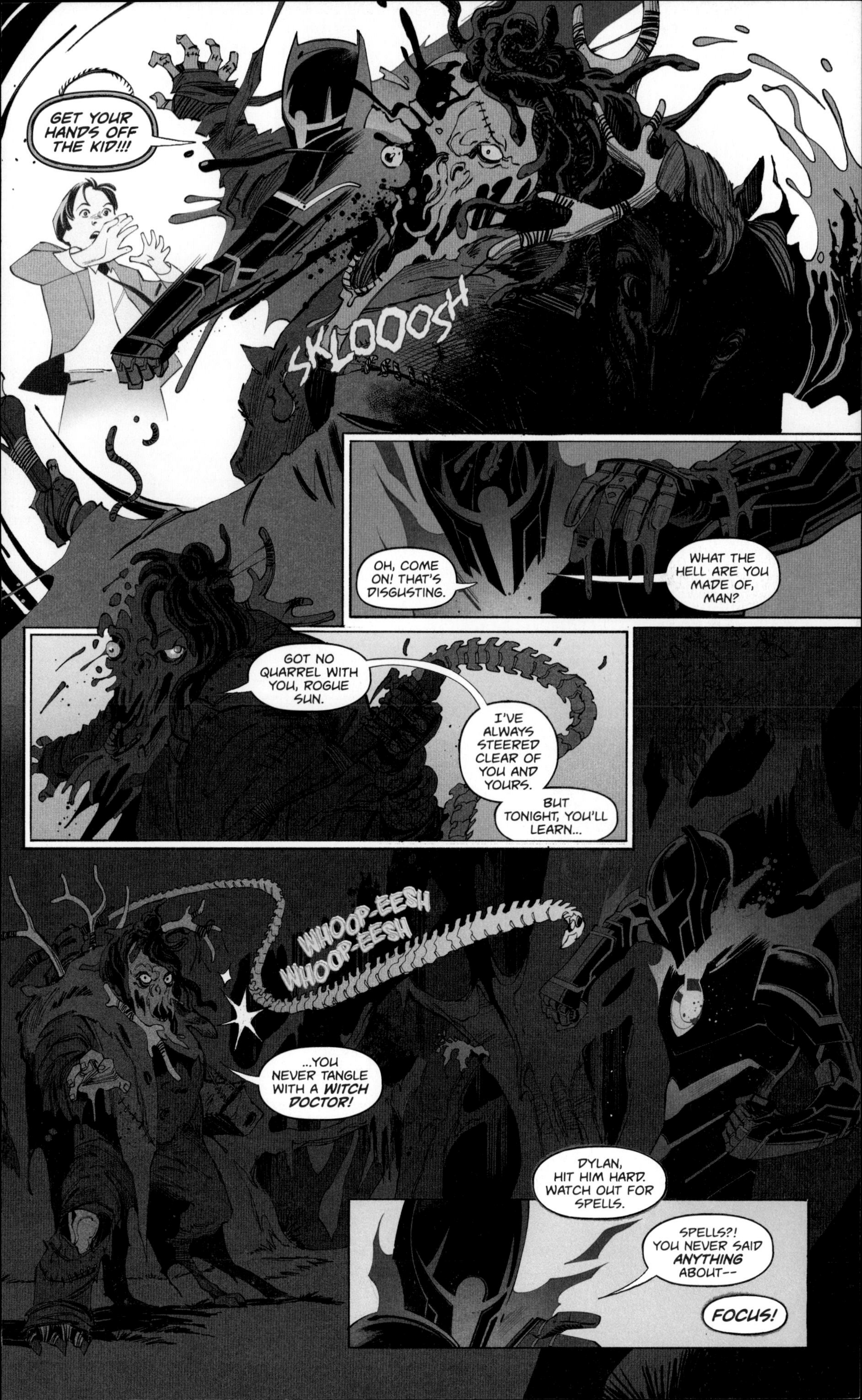
GET YOUR HANDS OFF THE KID!!!
SKLOOOSH
OH, COME ON! THAT'S DISGUSTING.
WHAT THE HELL ARE YOU MADE OF, MAN?
GOT NO QUARREL WITH YOU, ROGUE SUN.
I'VE ALWAYS STEERED CLEAR OF YOU AND YOURS.
BUT TONIGHT, YOU'LL LEARN...
WHOOP-EESH WHOOP-EESH
...YOU NEVER TANGLE WITH A WITCH DOCTOR!
DYLAN, HIT HIM HARD. WATCH OUT FOR SPELLS.
SPELLS?! YOU NEVER SAID ANYTHING ABOUT--
FOCUS!

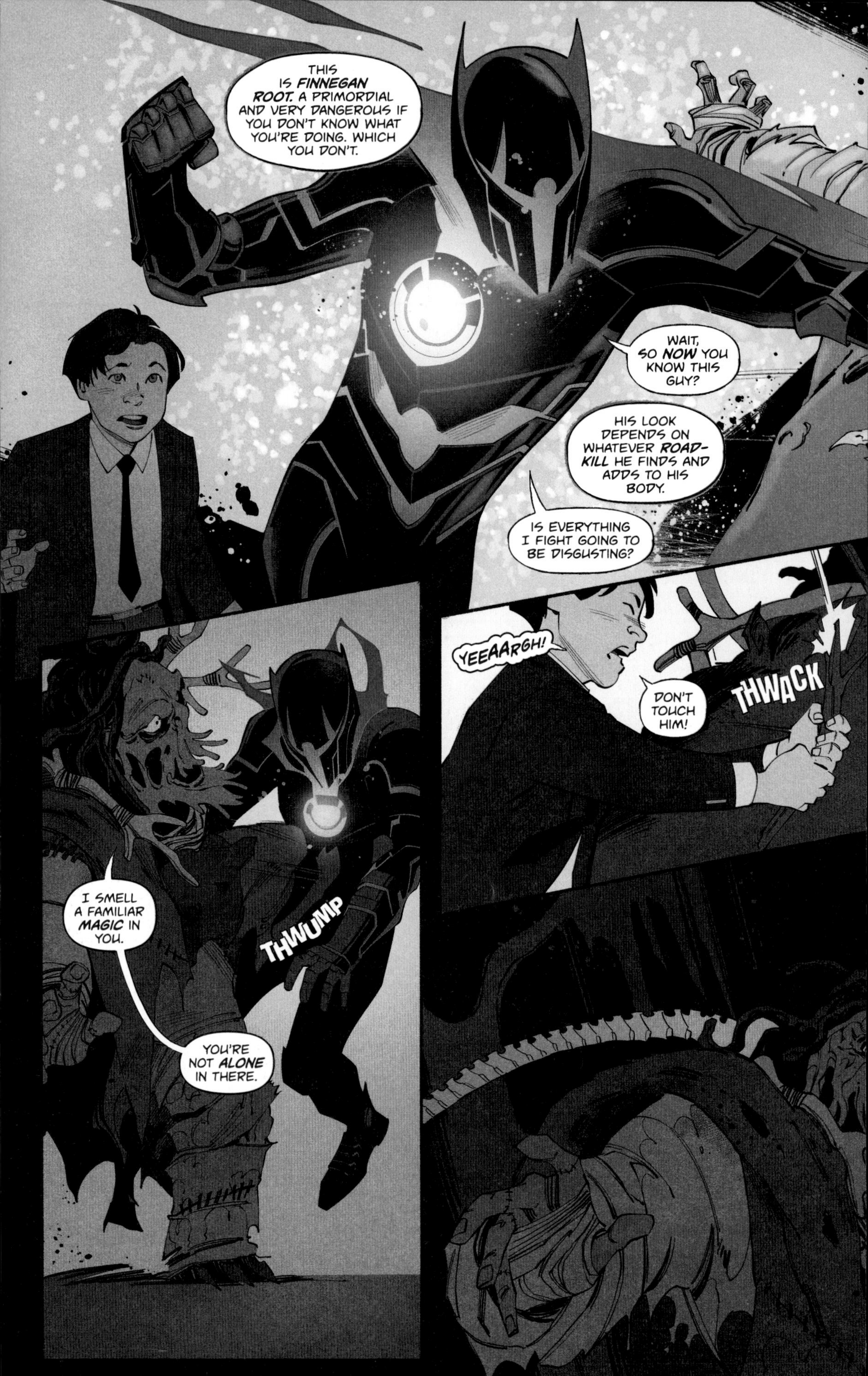
THIS IS FINNEGAN ROOT. A PRIMORDIAL AND VERY DANGEROUS IF YOU DON'T KNOW WHAT YOU'RE DOING. WHICH YOU DON'T.
WAIT, SO NOW YOU KNOW THIS GUY?
HIS LOOK DEPENDS ON WHATEVER ROAD-KILL HE FINDS AND ADDS TO HIS BODY.
IS EVERYTHING I FIGHT GOING TO BE DISGUSTING?
I SMELL A FAMILIAR MAGIC IN YOU.
THWUMP
YOU'RE NOT ALONE IN THERE.
YEEAAARGH!
DON'T TOUCH HIM!
THWACK

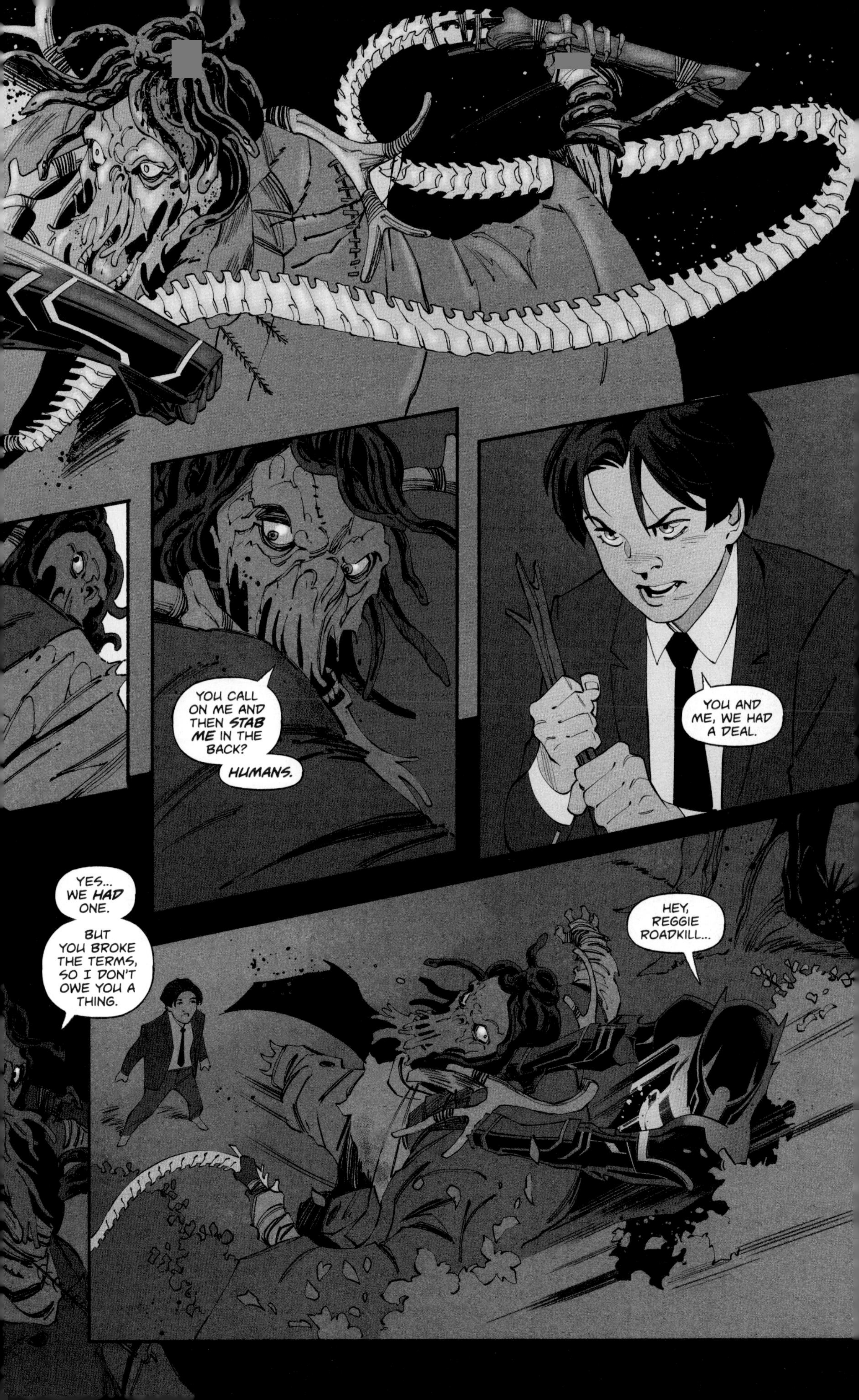
YOU CALL ON ME AND THEN STAB ME IN THE BACK?
HUMANS.
YOU AND ME, WE HAD A DEAL.
YES... WE HAD ONE.
BUT YOU BROKE THE TERMS, SO I DON'T OWE YOU A THING.
HEY, REGGIE ROADKILL...

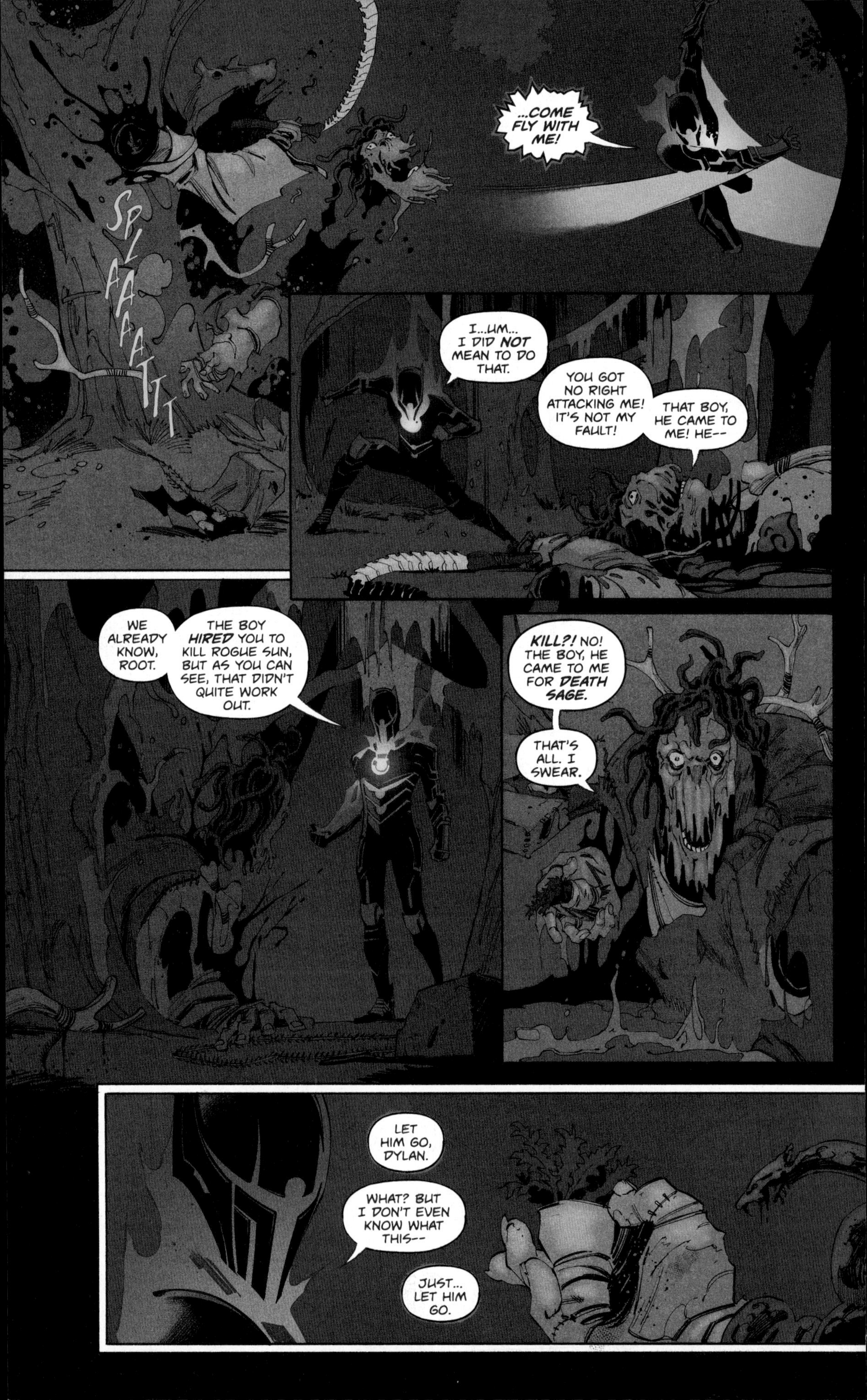
SPLAAAATTT
...COME FLY WITH ME!
I...UM... I DID NOT MEAN TO DO THAT.
YOU GOT NO RIGHT ATTACKING ME! IT'S NOT MY FAULT!
THAT BOY, HE CAME TO ME! HE--
WE ALREADY KNOW, ROOT.
THE BOY HIRED YOU TO KILL ROGUE SUN, BUT AS YOU CAN SEE, THAT DIDN'T QUITE WORK OUT.
KILL?! NO! THE BOY, HE CAME TO ME FOR DEATH SAGE.
THAT'S ALL. I SWEAR.
LET HIM GO, DYLAN.
WHAT? BUT I DON'T EVEN KNOW WHAT THIS--
JUST... LET HIM GO.

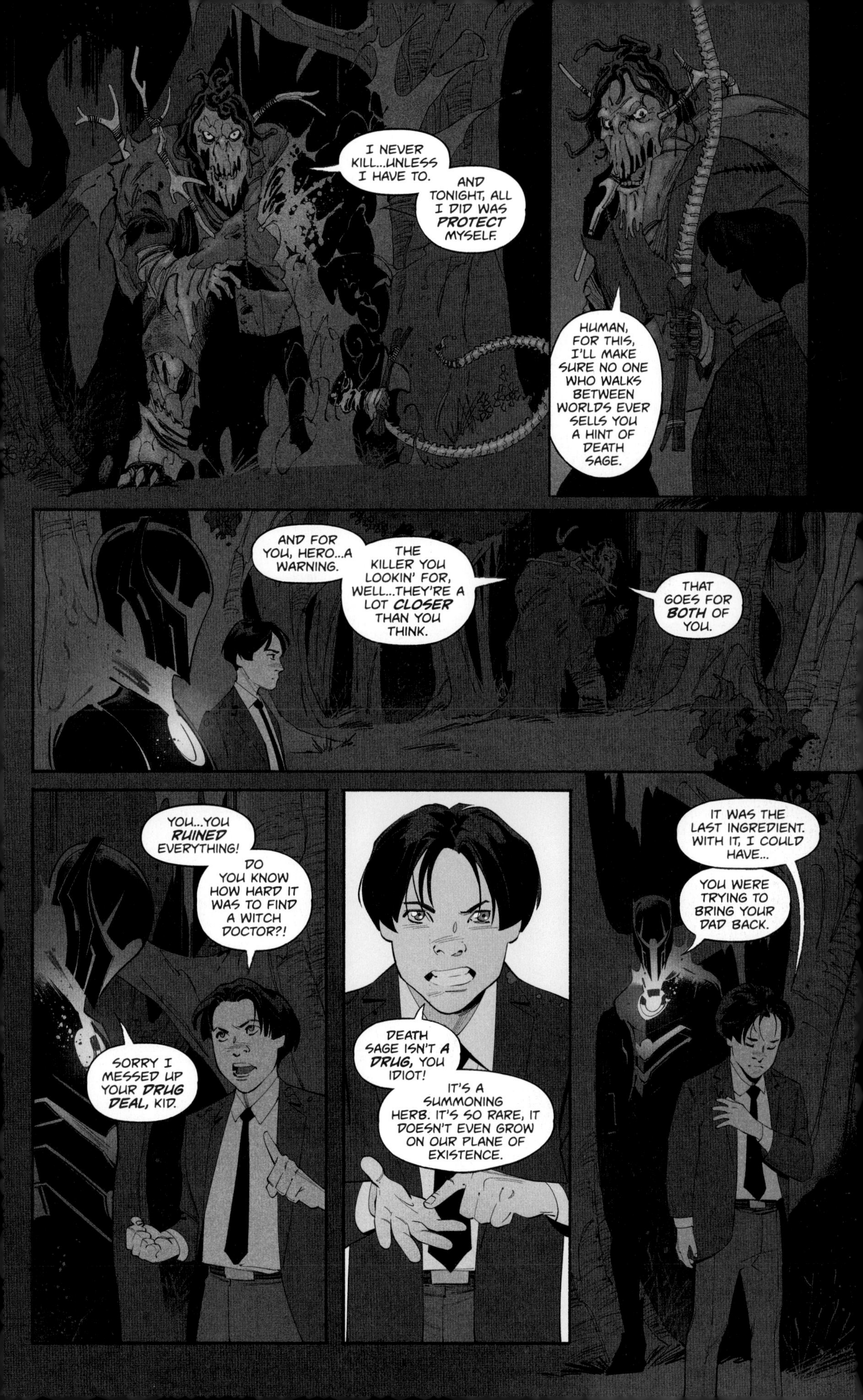
I NEVER KILL...UNLESS I HAVE TO.
AND TONIGHT, ALL I DID WAS PROTECT MYSELF.
HUMAN, FOR THIS, I'LL MAKE SURE NO ONE WHO WALKS BETWEEN WORLDS EVER SELLS YOU A HINT OF DEATH SAGE.
AND FOR YOU, HERO...A WARNING.
THE KILLER YOU LOOKIN' FOR, WELL...THEY'RE A LOT CLOSER THAN YOU THINK.
THAT GOES FOR BOTH OF YOU.
YOU...YOU RUINED EVERYTHING!
DO YOU KNOW HOW HARD IT WAS TO FIND A WITCH DOCTOR?!
SORRY I MESSED UP YOUR DRUG DEAL, KID.
DEATH SAGE ISN'T A DRUG, YOU IDIOT!
IT'S A SUMMONING HERB. IT'S SO RARE, IT DOESN'T EVEN GROW ON OUR PLANE OF EXISTENCE.
IT WAS THE LAST INGREDIENT. WITH IT, I COULD HAVE...
YOU WERE TRYING TO BRING YOUR DAD BACK.

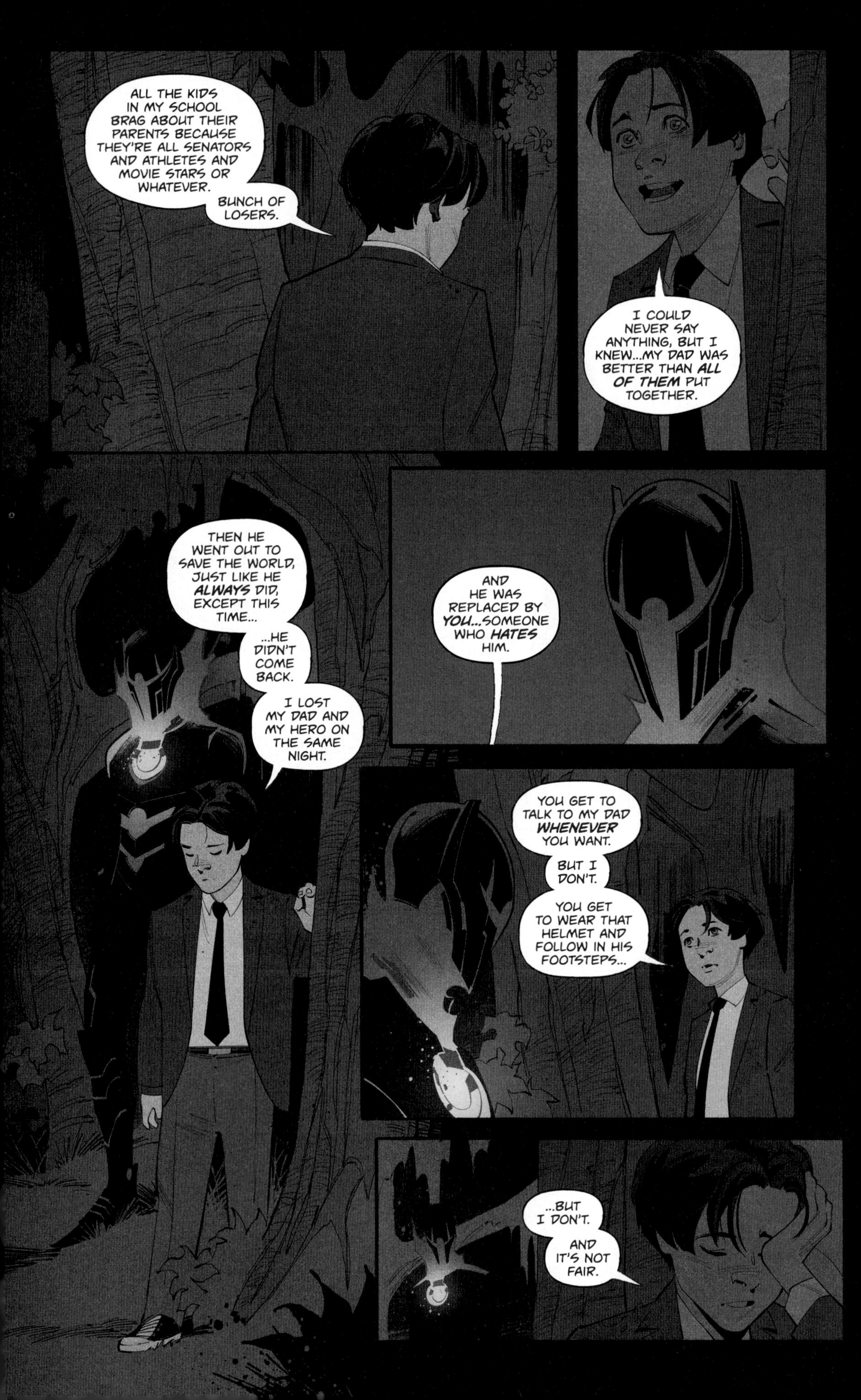
ALL THE KIDS IN MY SCHOOL BRAG ABOUT THEIR PARENTS BECAUSE THEY'RE ALL SENATORS AND ATHLETES AND MOVIE STARS OR WHATEVER.
BUNCH OF LOSERS.
I COULD NEVER SAY ANYTHING, BUT I KNEW...MY DAD WAS BETTER THAN ALL OF THEM PUT TOGETHER.
THEN HE WENT OUT TO SAVE THE WORLD, JUST LIKE HE ALWAYS DID, EXCEPT THIS TIME...
...HE DIDN'T COME BACK.
I LOST MY DAD AND MY HERO ON THE SAME NIGHT.
AND HE WAS REPLACED BY YOU...SOMEONE WHO HATES HIM.
YOU GET TO TALK TO MY DAD WHENEVER YOU WANT.
BUT I DON'T.
YOU GET TO WEAR THAT HELMET AND FOLLOW IN HIS FOOTSTEPS...
...BUT I DON'T.
AND IT'S NOT FAIR.

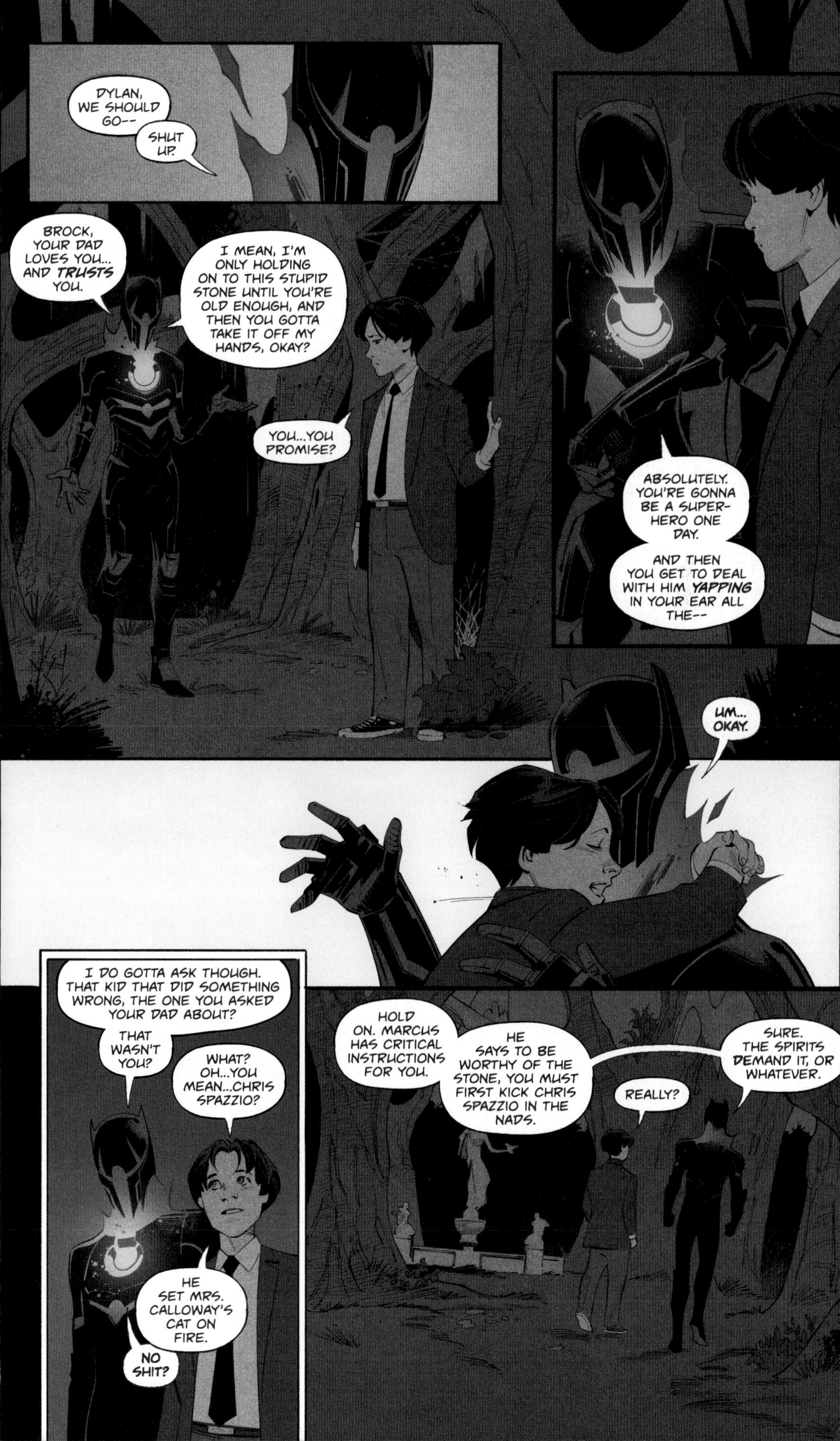
DYLAN, WE SHOULD GO--
SHUT UP.
BROCK, YOUR DAD LOVES YOU... AND TRUSTS YOU.
I MEAN, I'M ONLY HOLDING ON TO THIS STUPID STONE UNTIL YOU'RE OLD ENOUGH, AND THEN YOU GOTTA TAKE IT OFF MY HANDS, OKAY?
YOU...YOU PROMISE?
ABSOLUTELY. YOU'RE GONNA BE A SUPER-HERO ONE DAY.
AND THEN YOU GET TO DEAL WITH HIM YAPPING IN YOUR EAR ALL THE--
UM... OKAY.
I DO GOTTA ASK THOUGH. THAT KID THAT DID SOMETHING WRONG, THE ONE YOU ASKED YOUR DAD ABOUT?
THAT WASN'T YOU?
WHAT? OH...YOU MEAN...CHRIS SPAZZIO?
HE SET MRS. CALLOWAY'S CAT ON FIRE.
NO SHIT?
HOLD ON. MARCUS HAS CRITICAL INSTRUCTIONS FOR YOU.
HE SAYS TO BE WORTHY OF THE STONE, YOU MUST FIRST KICK CHRIS SPAZZIO IN THE NADS.
REALLY?
SURE. THE SPIRITS DEMAND IT, OR WHATEVER.

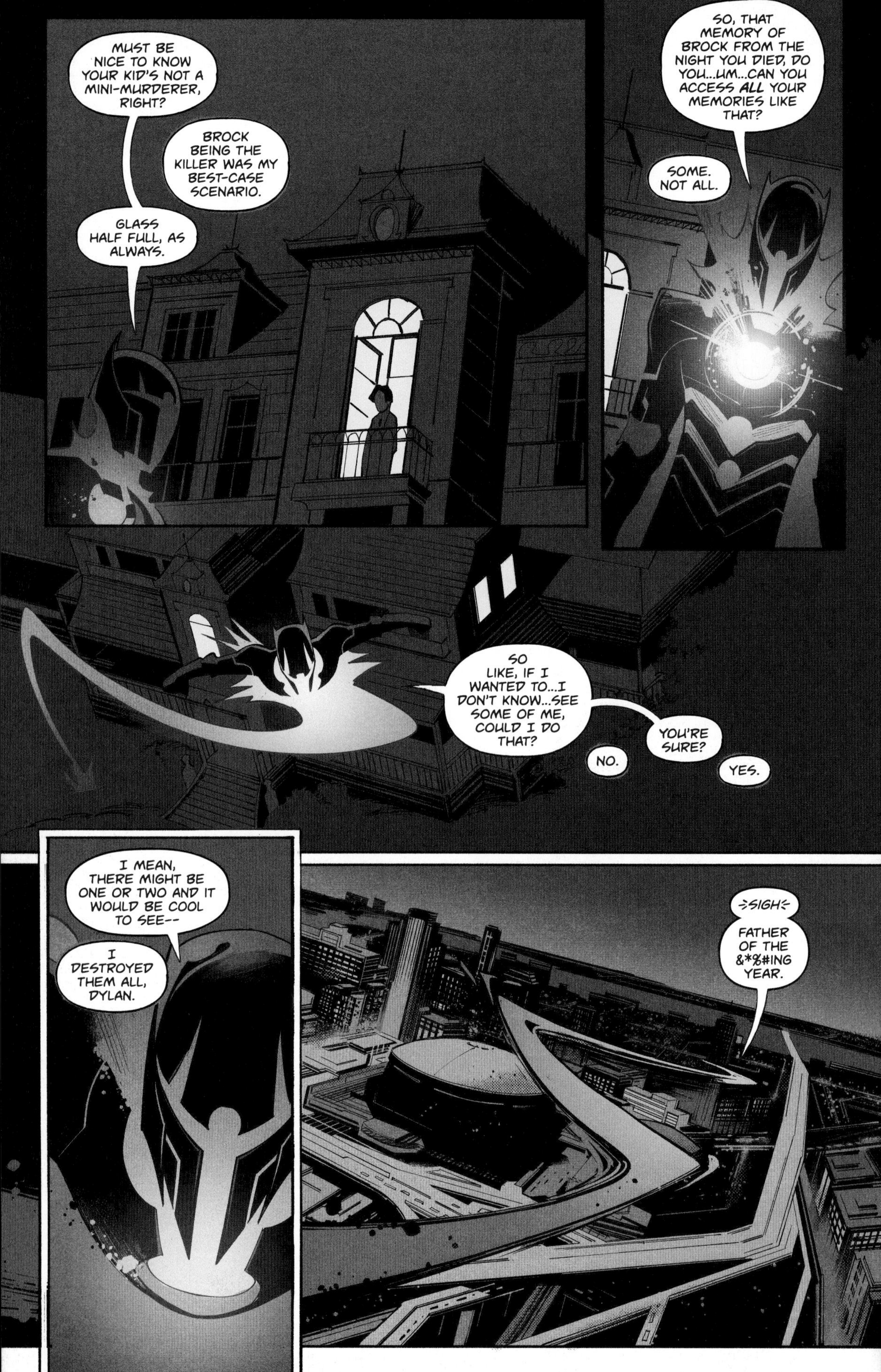
MUST BE NICE TO KNOW YOUR KID'S NOT A MINI-MURDERER, RIGHT?
BROCK BEING THE KILLER WAS MY BEST-CASE SCENARIO.
GLASS HALF FULL, AS ALWAYS.
SO, THAT MEMORY OF BROCK FROM THE NIGHT YOU DIED, DO YOU...UM...CAN YOU ACCESS ALL YOUR MEMORIES LIKE THAT?
SOME. NOT ALL.
SO LIKE, IF I WANTED TO...I DON'T KNOW...SEE SOME OF ME, COULD I DO THAT?
NO.
YOU'RE SURE?
YES.
I MEAN, THERE MIGHT BE ONE OR TWO AND IT WOULD BE COOL TO SEE--
I DESTROYED THEM ALL, DYLAN.
SIGH
FATHER OF THE &*%#ING YEAR.

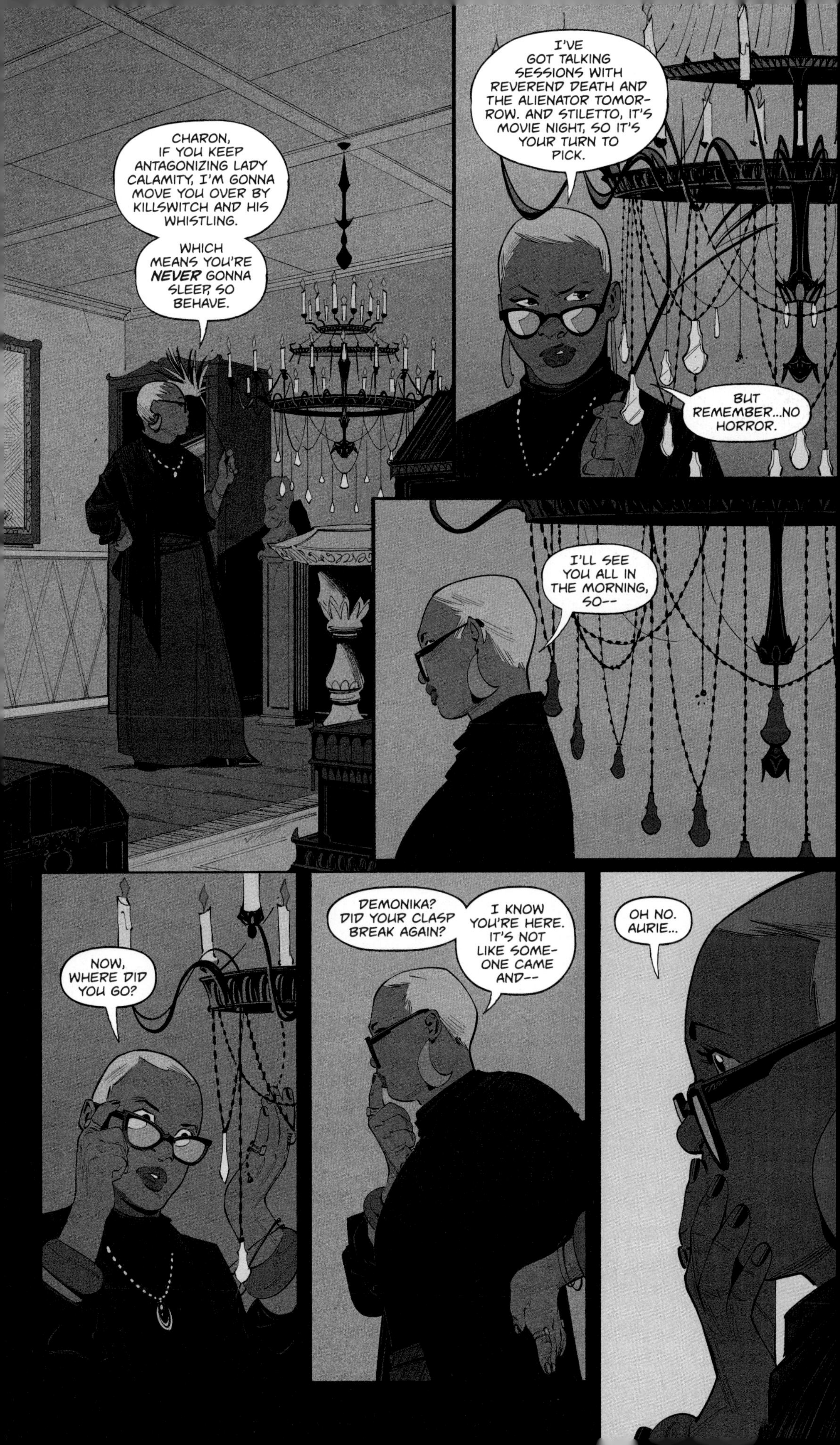
CHARON, IF YOU KEEP ANTAGONIZING LADY CALAMITY, I'M GONNA MOVE YOU OVER BY KILLSWITCH AND HIS WHISTLING.
WHICH MEANS YOU'RE ***NEVER*** GONNA SLEEP, SO BEHAVE.
I'VE GOT TALKING SESSIONS WITH REVEREND DEATH AND THE ALIENATOR TOMOR-ROW. AND STILETTO, IT'S MOVIE NIGHT, SO IT'S YOUR TURN TO PICK.
BUT REMEMBER...NO HORROR.
I'LL SEE YOU ALL IN THE MORNING, SO--
NOW, WHERE DID YOU GO?
DEMONIKA? DID YOUR CLASP BREAK AGAIN?
I KNOW YOU'RE HERE. IT'S NOT LIKE SOME-ONE CAME AND--
OH NO. AURIE...

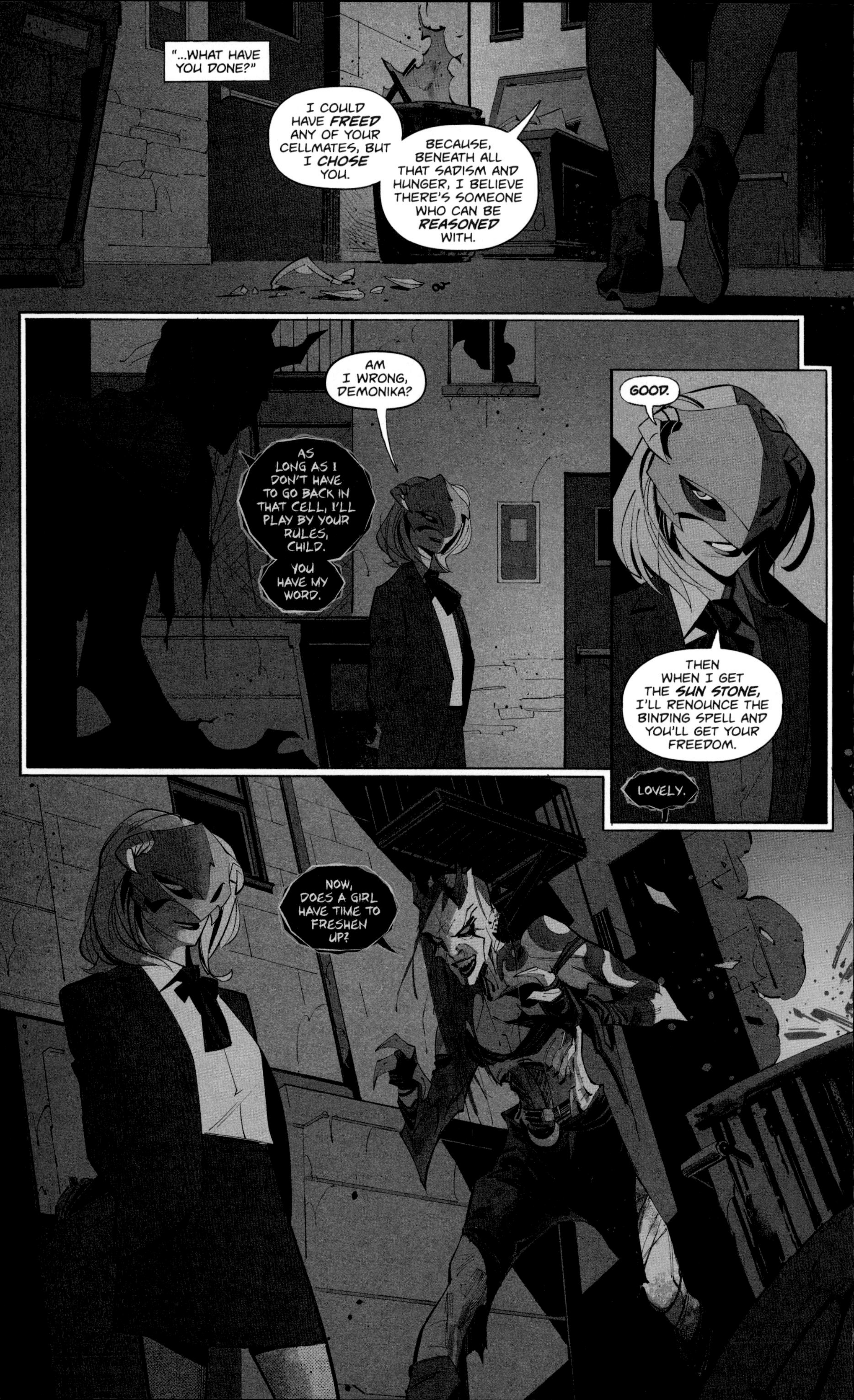
"...WHAT HAVE YOU DONE?"
I COULD HAVE FREED ANY OF YOUR CELLMATES, BUT I CHOSE YOU.
BECAUSE, BENEATH ALL THAT SADISM AND HUNGER, I BELIEVE THERE'S SOMEONE WHO CAN BE REASONED WITH.
AM I WRONG, DEMONIKA?
AS LONG AS I DON'T HAVE TO GO BACK IN THAT CELL, I'LL PLAY BY YOUR RULES, CHILD.
YOU HAVE MY WORD.
GOOD.
THEN WHEN I GET THE SUN STONE, I'LL RENOUNCE THE BINDING SPELL AND YOU'LL GET YOUR FREEDOM.
LOVELY.
NOW, DOES A GIRL HAVE TIME TO FRESHEN UP?

Interlude
No Exit

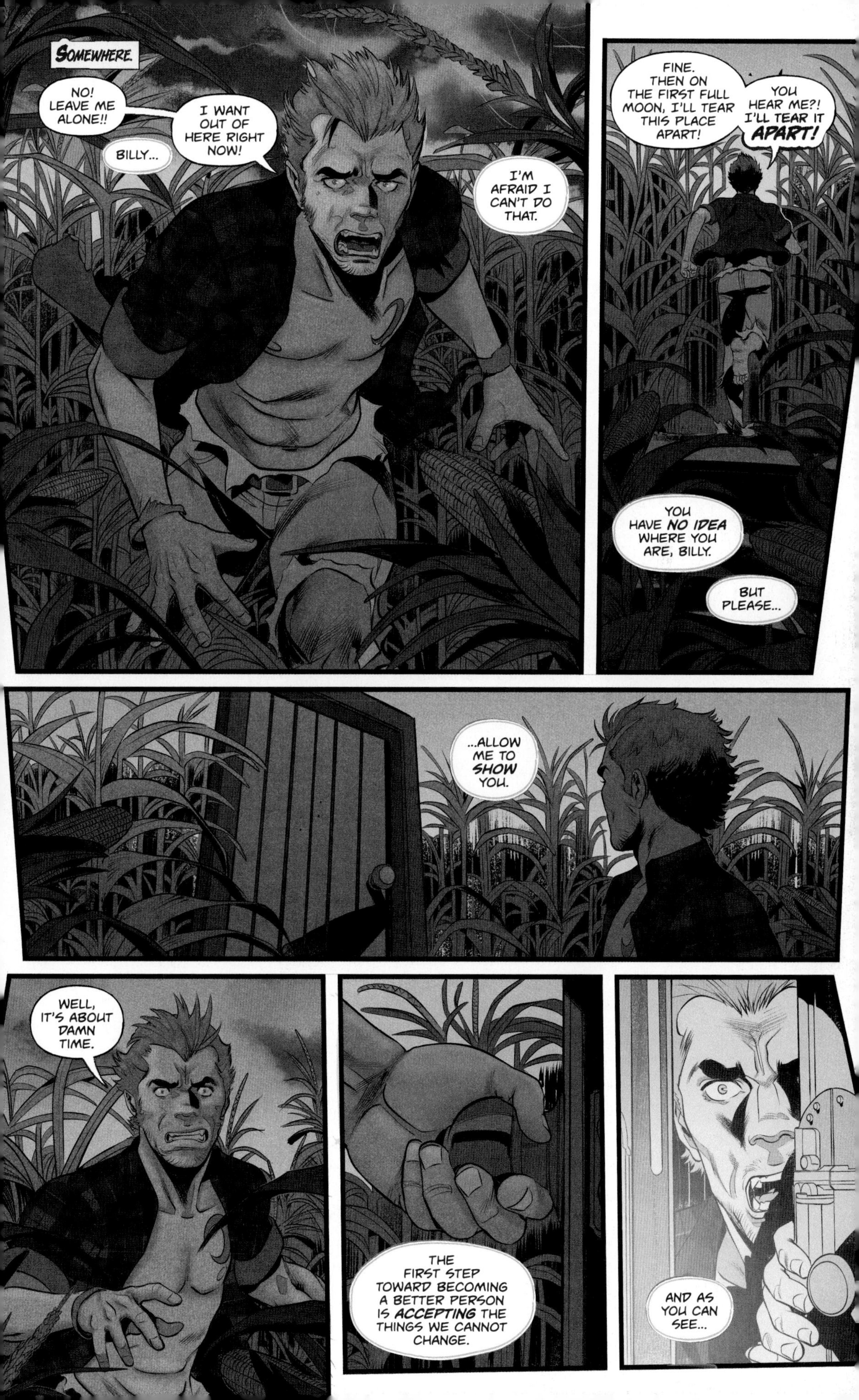
SOMEWHERE.
NO! LEAVE ME ALONE!!
I WANT OUT OF HERE RIGHT NOW!
BILLY...
I'M AFRAID I CAN'T DO THAT.
FINE. THEN ON THE FIRST FULL MOON, I'LL TEAR THIS PLACE APART!
YOU HEAR ME?! I'LL TEAR IT APART!
YOU HAVE NO IDEA WHERE YOU ARE, BILLY.
BUT PLEASE...
...ALLOW ME TO SHOW YOU.
WELL, IT'S ABOUT DAMN TIME.
THE FIRST STEP TOWARD BECOMING A BETTER PERSON IS ACCEPTING THE THINGS WE CANNOT CHANGE.
AND AS YOU CAN SEE...

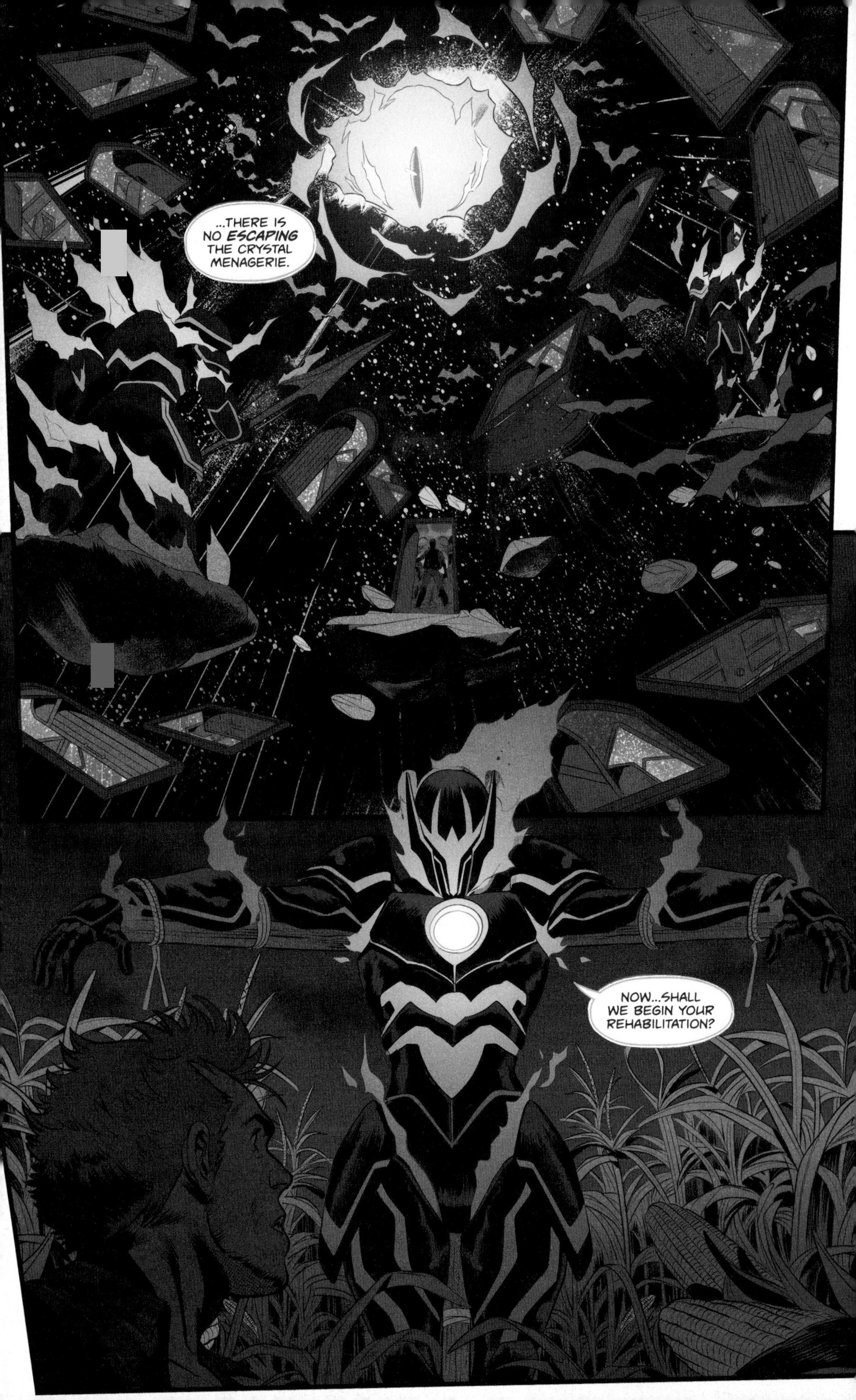
...THERE IS NO ESCAPING THE CRYSTAL MENAGERIE.
NOW...SHALL WE BEGIN YOUR REHABILITATION?

Chapter Four
A Sour Note

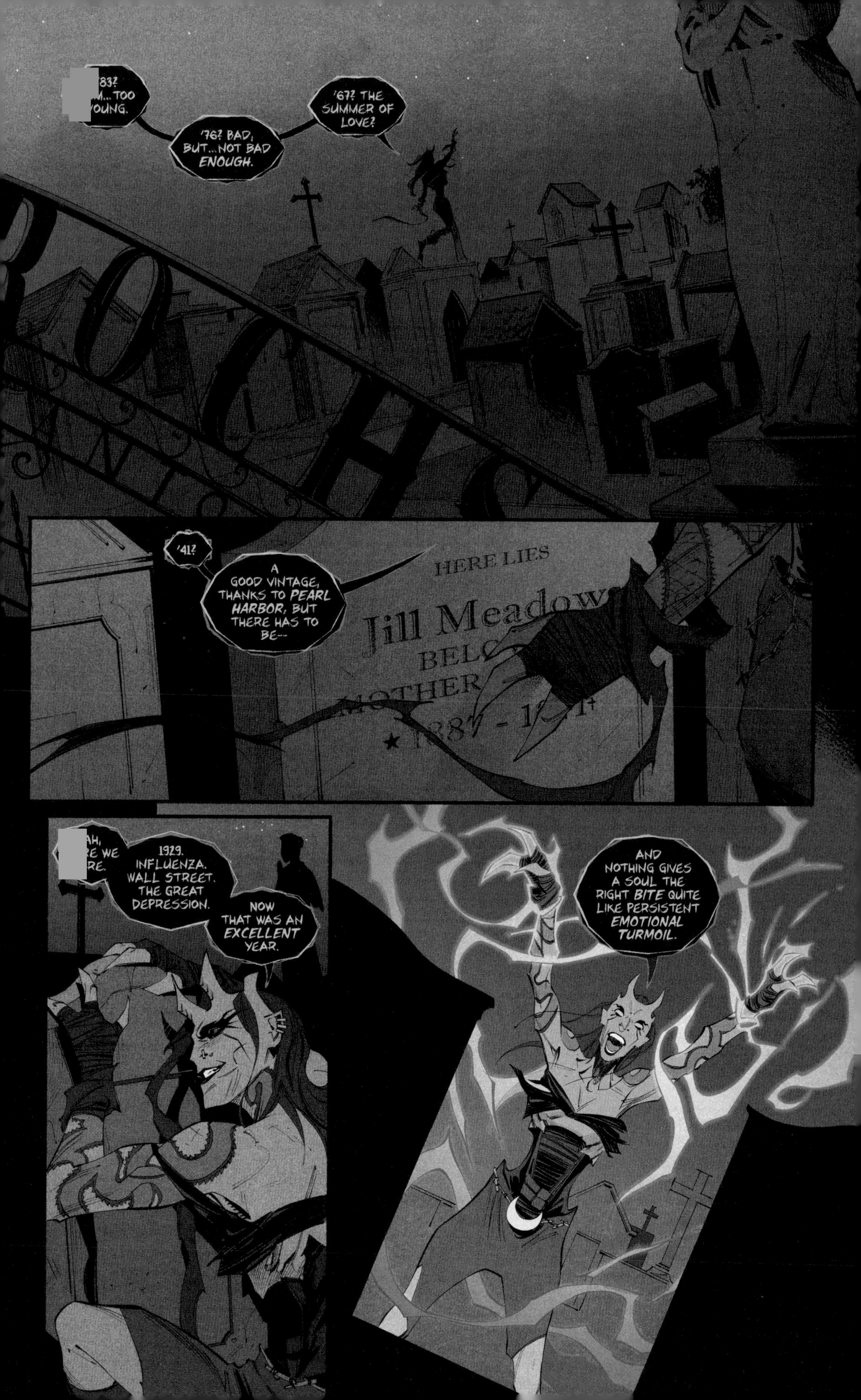

[redacted]83? [redacted]M... TOO [redacted]YOUNG.
'76? BAD, BUT...NOT BAD ENOUGH.
'67? THE SUMMER OF LOVE?
'41?
A GOOD VINTAGE, THANKS TO PEARL HARBOR, BUT THERE HAS TO BE--
HERE LIES
Jill Meadow
MOTHER
[redacted]AH, [redacted]RE WE [redacted]RE.
1929. INFLUENZA. WALL STREET. THE GREAT DEPRESSION.
NOW THAT WAS AN EXCELLENT YEAR.
AND NOTHING GIVES A SOUL THE RIGHT BITE QUITE LIKE PERSISTENT EMOTIONAL TURMOIL.

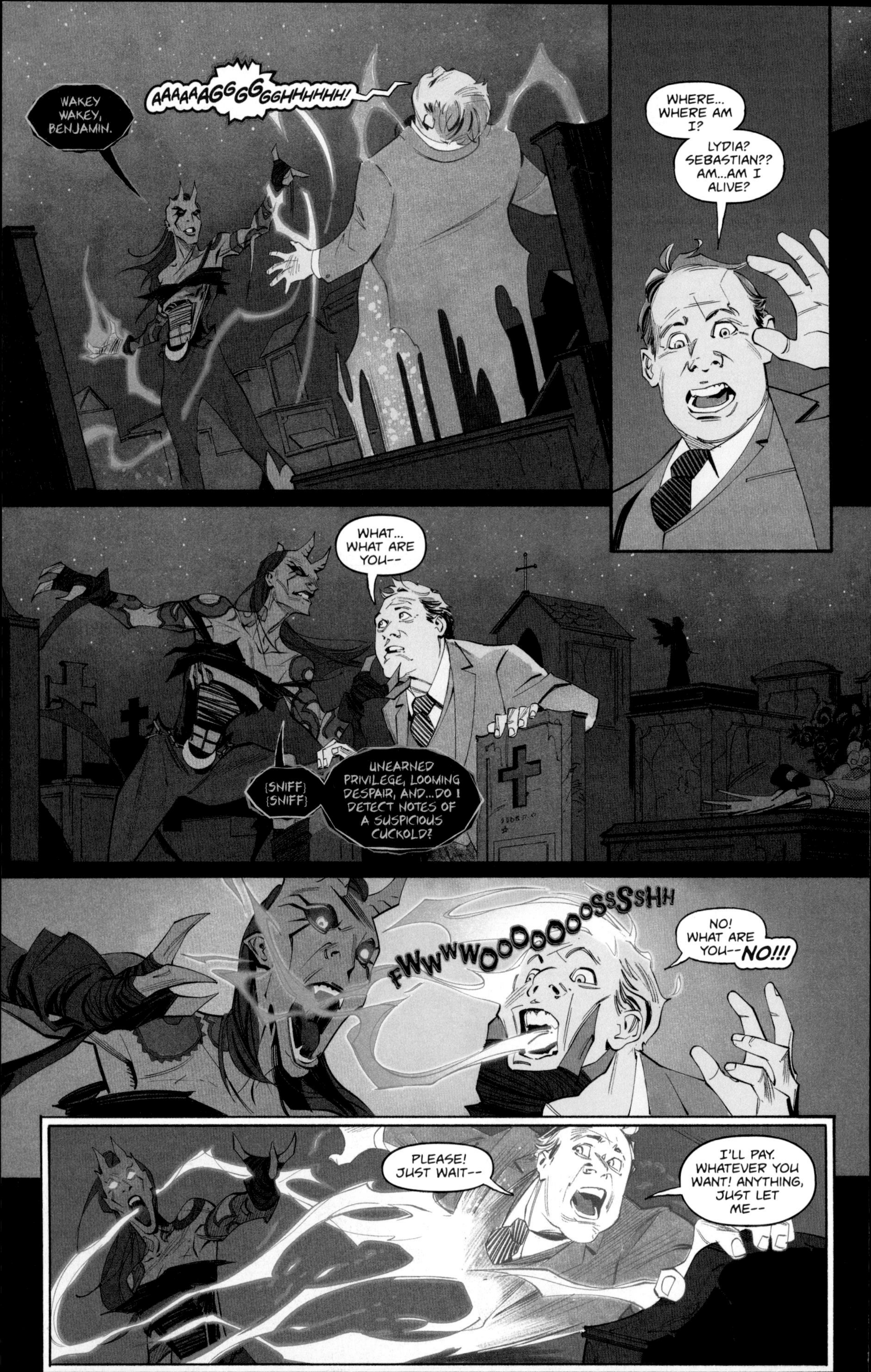
WAKEY WAKEY, BENJAMIN.
AAAAAAGGGGGGHHHHHHH!
WHERE... WHERE AM I?
LYDIA? SEBASTIAN?? AM...AM I ALIVE?
WHAT... WHAT ARE YOU--
{SNIFF} {SNIFF}
UNEARNED PRIVILEGE, LOOMING DESPAIR, AND...DO I DETECT NOTES OF A SUSPICIOUS CUCKOLD?
FWWWWOOOOOOOOSSSSHH
NO! WHAT ARE YOU--NO!!!
PLEASE! JUST WAIT--
I'LL PAY. WHATEVER YOU WANT! ANYTHING, JUST LET ME--

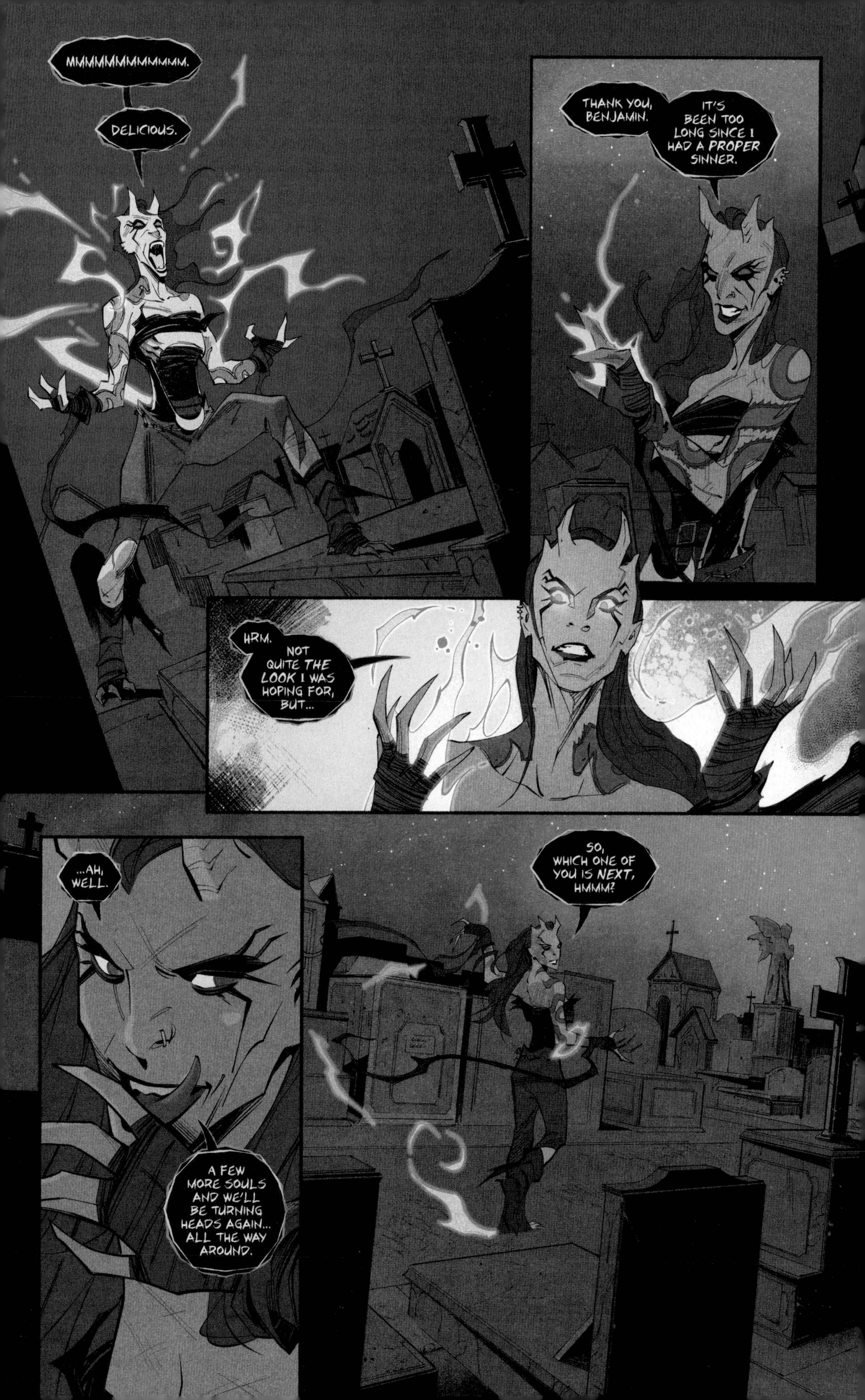
MMMMMMMMMMMM.
DELICIOUS.
THANK YOU, BENJAMIN.
IT'S BEEN TOO LONG SINCE I HAD A PROPER SINNER.
HRM.
NOT QUITE THE LOOK I WAS HOPING FOR, BUT...
...AH, WELL.
A FEW MORE SOULS AND WE'LL BE TURNING HEADS AGAIN... ALL THE WAY AROUND.
SO, WHICH ONE OF YOU IS NEXT, HMMM?

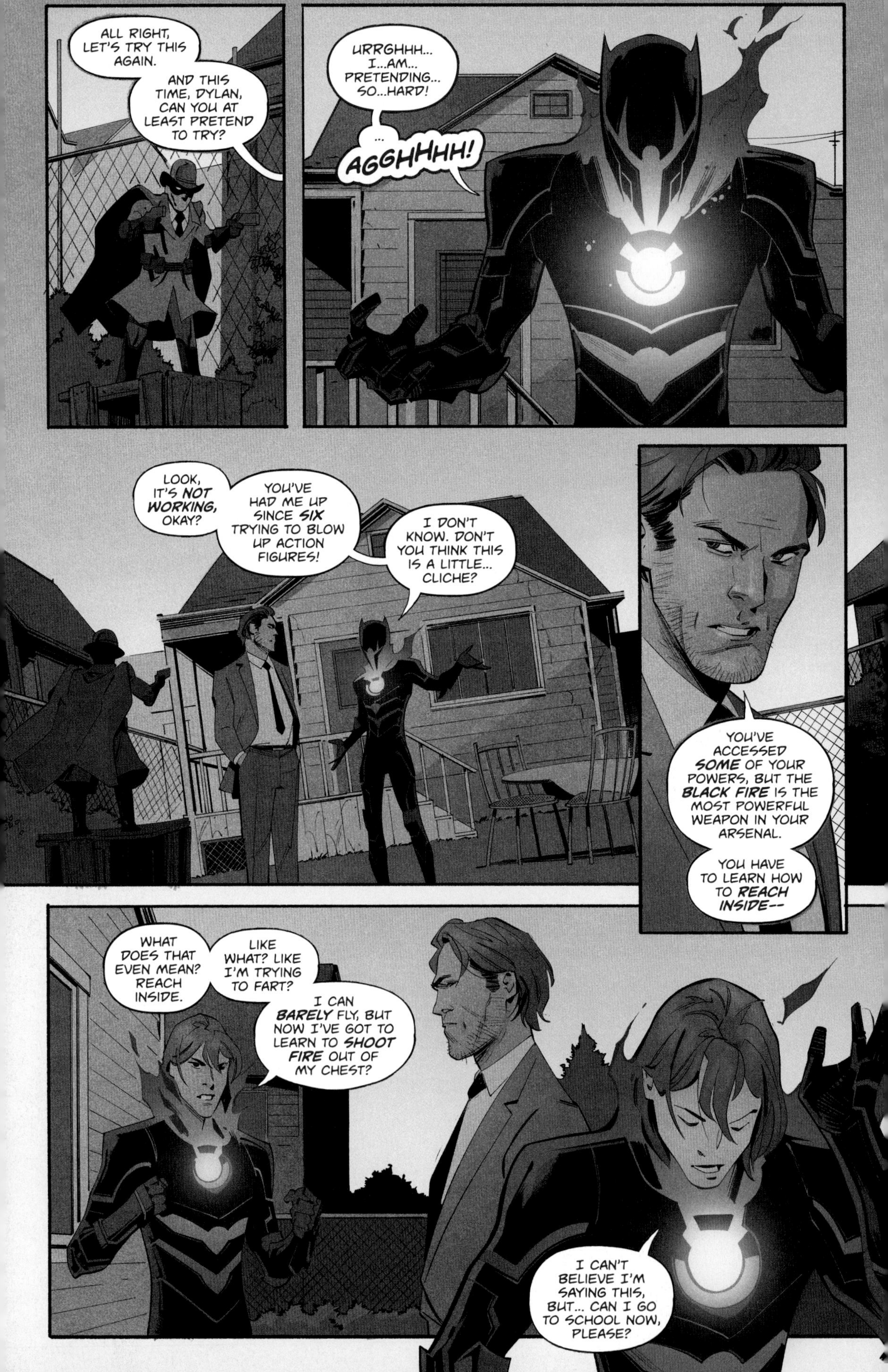
ALL RIGHT, LET'S TRY THIS AGAIN.
AND THIS TIME, DYLAN, CAN YOU AT LEAST PRETEND TO TRY?
URRGHHH... I...AM... PRETENDING... SO...HARD!
...
AGGHHHH!
LOOK, IT'S NOT WORKING, OKAY?
YOU'VE HAD ME UP SINCE SIX TRYING TO BLOW UP ACTION FIGURES!
I DON'T KNOW. DON'T YOU THINK THIS IS A LITTLE... CLICHE?
YOU'VE ACCESSED SOME OF YOUR POWERS, BUT THE BLACK FIRE IS THE MOST POWERFUL WEAPON IN YOUR ARSENAL.
YOU HAVE TO LEARN HOW TO REACH INSIDE--
WHAT DOES THAT EVEN MEAN? REACH INSIDE.
LIKE WHAT? LIKE I'M TRYING TO FART?
I CAN BARELY FLY, BUT NOW I'VE GOT TO LEARN TO SHOOT FIRE OUT OF MY CHEST?
I CAN'T BELIEVE I'M SAYING THIS, BUT... CAN I GO TO SCHOOL NOW, PLEASE?

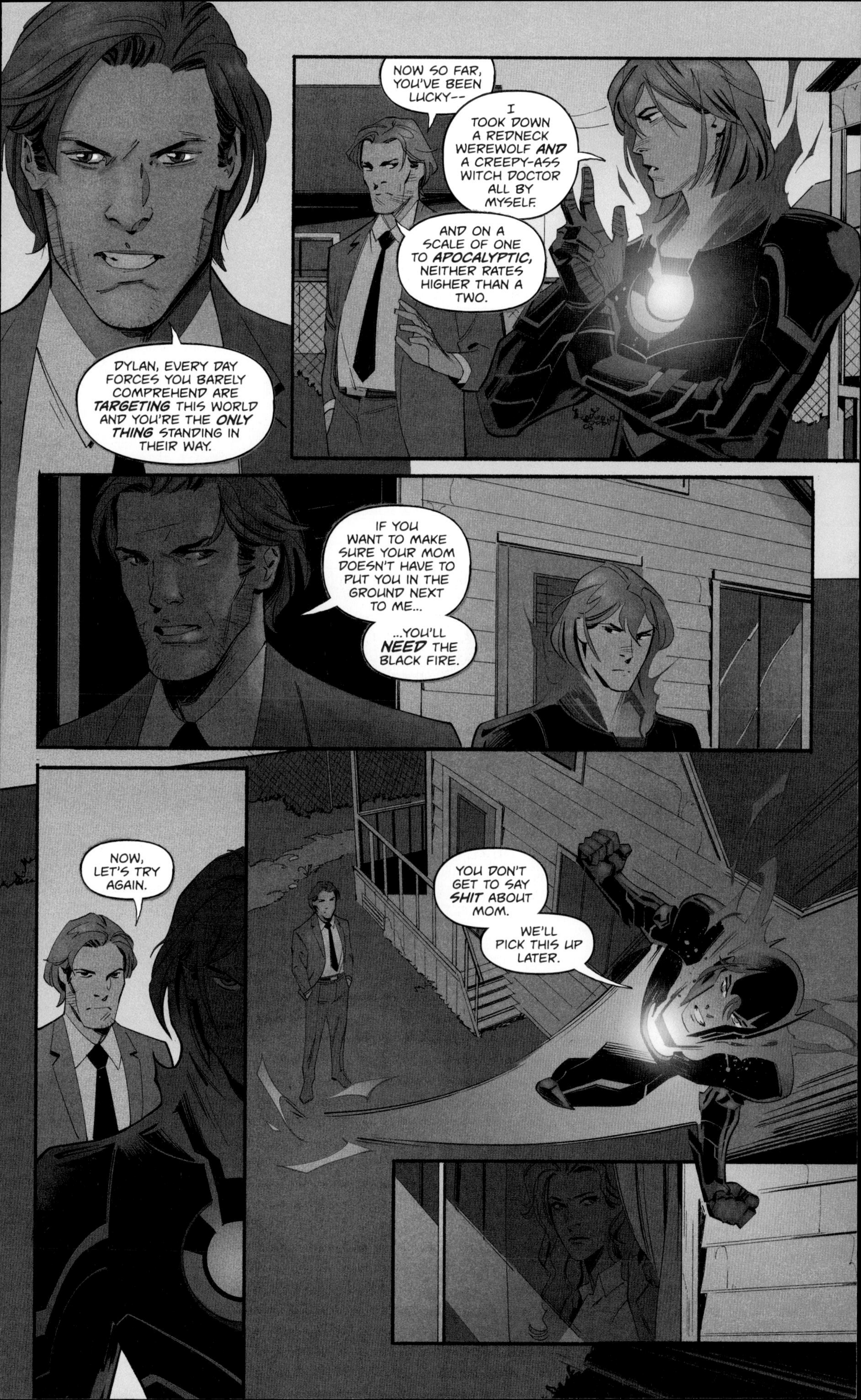
NOW SO FAR, YOU'VE BEEN LUCKY--
I TOOK DOWN A REDNECK WEREWOLF AND A CREEPY-ASS WITCH DOCTOR ALL BY MYSELF.
AND ON A SCALE OF ONE TO APOCALYPTIC, NEITHER RATES HIGHER THAN A TWO.
DYLAN, EVERY DAY FORCES YOU BARELY COMPREHEND ARE TARGETING THIS WORLD AND YOU'RE THE ONLY THING STANDING IN THEIR WAY.
IF YOU WANT TO MAKE SURE YOUR MOM DOESN'T HAVE TO PUT YOU IN THE GROUND NEXT TO ME...
...YOU'LL NEED THE BLACK FIRE.
NOW, LET'S TRY AGAIN.
YOU DON'T GET TO SAY SHIT ABOUT MOM.
WE'LL PICK THIS UP LATER.

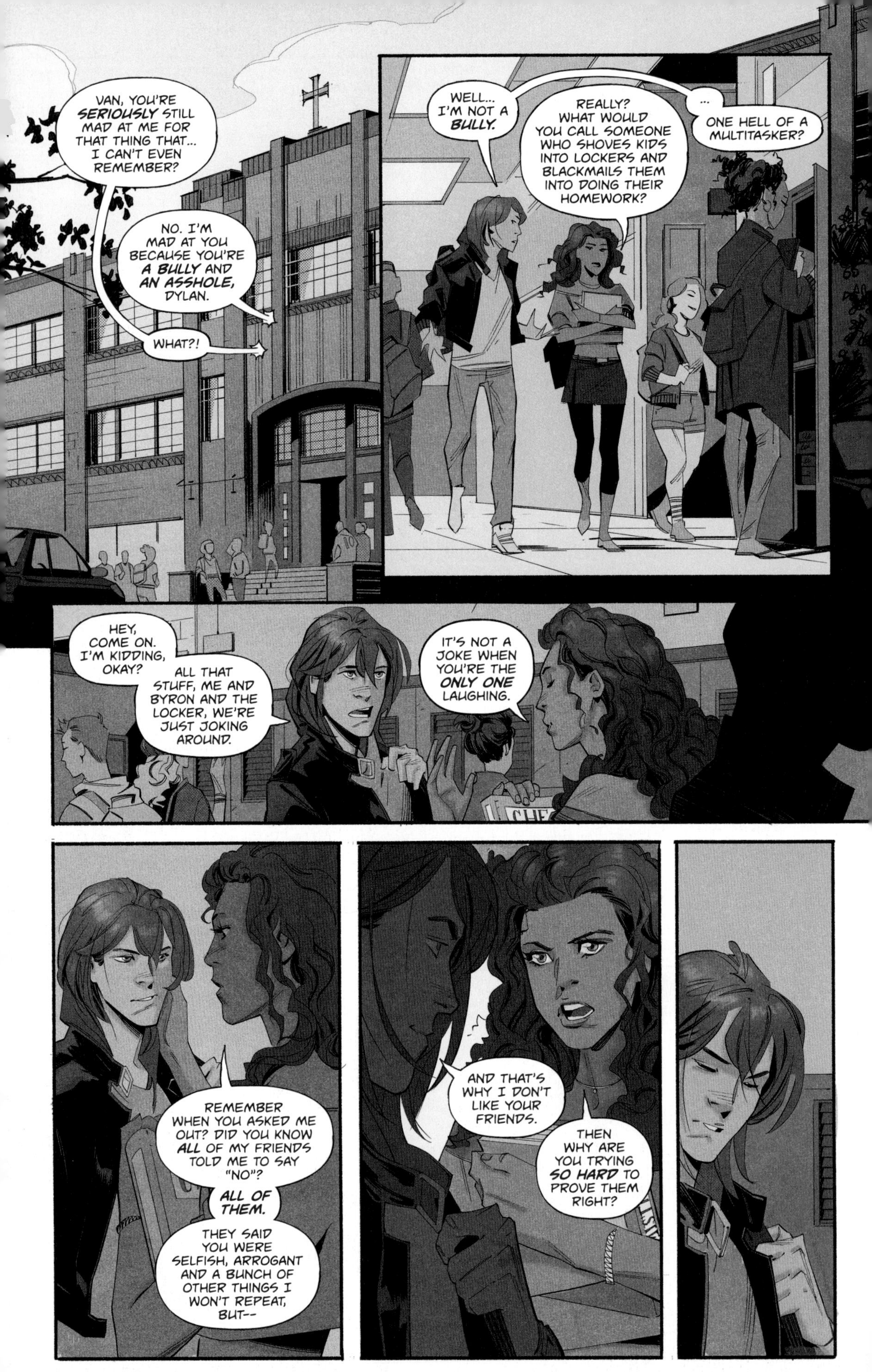

VAN, YOU'RE SERIOUSLY STILL MAD AT ME FOR THAT THING THAT... I CAN'T EVEN REMEMBER?
NO. I'M MAD AT YOU BECAUSE YOU'RE A BULLY AND AN ASSHOLE, DYLAN.
WHAT?!
WELL... I'M NOT A BULLY.
REALLY? WHAT WOULD YOU CALL SOMEONE WHO SHOVES KIDS INTO LOCKERS AND BLACKMAILS THEM INTO DOING THEIR HOMEWORK?
...
ONE HELL OF A MULTITASKER?
HEY, COME ON. I'M KIDDING, OKAY?
ALL THAT STUFF, ME AND BYRON AND THE LOCKER, WE'RE JUST JOKING AROUND.
IT'S NOT A JOKE WHEN YOU'RE THE ONLY ONE LAUGHING.
REMEMBER WHEN YOU ASKED ME OUT? DID YOU KNOW ALL OF MY FRIENDS TOLD ME TO SAY "NO"?
ALL OF THEM.
THEY SAID YOU WERE SELFISH, ARROGANT AND A BUNCH OF OTHER THINGS I WON'T REPEAT, BUT--
AND THAT'S WHY I DON'T LIKE YOUR FRIENDS.
THEN WHY ARE YOU TRYING SO HARD TO PROVE THEM RIGHT?

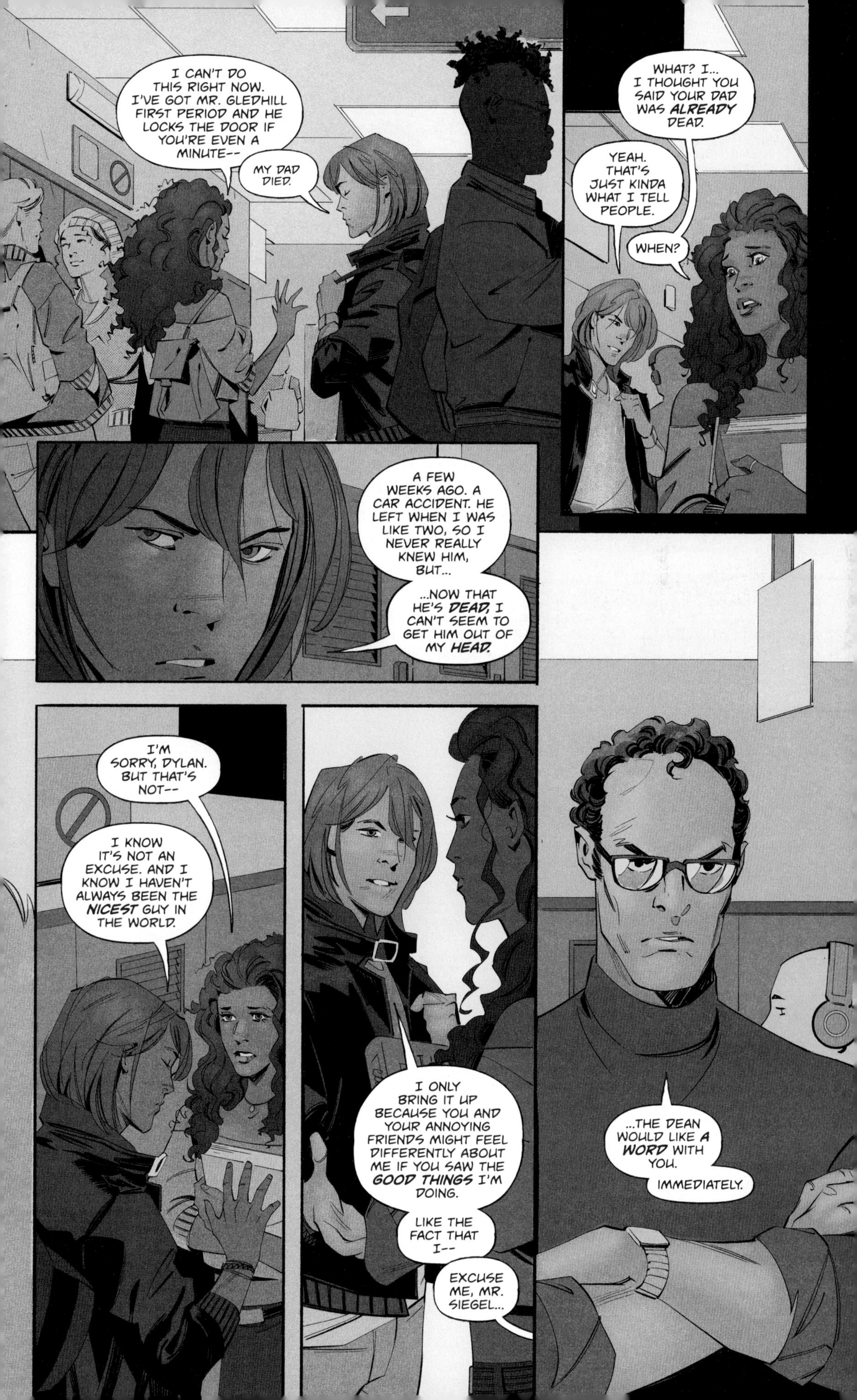

I CAN'T DO THIS RIGHT NOW. I'VE GOT MR. GLEDHILL FIRST PERIOD AND HE LOCKS THE DOOR IF YOU'RE EVEN A MINUTE--
MY DAD DIED.
WHAT? I... I THOUGHT YOU SAID YOUR DAD WAS ALREADY DEAD.
YEAH. THAT'S JUST KINDA WHAT I TELL PEOPLE.
WHEN?
A FEW WEEKS AGO. A CAR ACCIDENT. HE LEFT WHEN I WAS LIKE TWO, SO I NEVER REALLY KNEW HIM, BUT...
...NOW THAT HE'S DEAD, I CAN'T SEEM TO GET HIM OUT OF MY HEAD.
I'M SORRY, DYLAN. BUT THAT'S NOT--
I KNOW IT'S NOT AN EXCUSE. AND I KNOW I HAVEN'T ALWAYS BEEN THE NICEST GUY IN THE WORLD.
I ONLY BRING IT UP BECAUSE YOU AND YOUR ANNOYING FRIENDS MIGHT FEEL DIFFERENTLY ABOUT ME IF YOU SAW THE GOOD THINGS I'M DOING.
LIKE THE FACT THAT I--
EXCUSE ME, MR. SIEGEL...
...THE DEAN WOULD LIKE A WORD WITH YOU.
IMMEDIATELY.

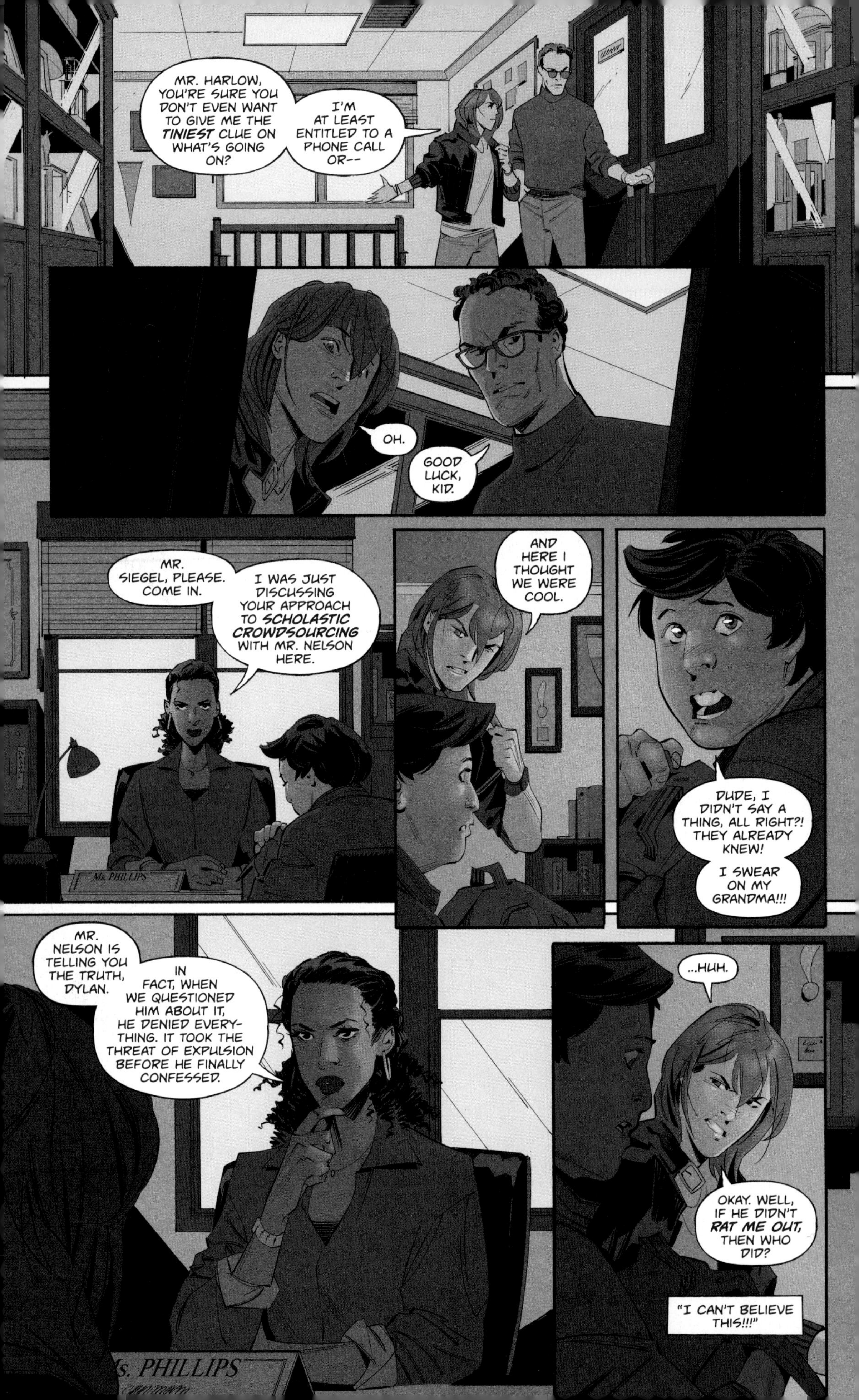
MR. HARLOW, YOU'RE SURE YOU DON'T EVEN WANT TO GIVE ME THE TINIEST CLUE ON WHAT'S GOING ON?
I'M AT LEAST ENTITLED TO A PHONE CALL OR--
OH.
GOOD LUCK, KID.
MR. SIEGEL, PLEASE. COME IN.
I WAS JUST DISCUSSING YOUR APPROACH TO SCHOLASTIC CROWDSOURCING WITH MR. NELSON HERE.
Ms. PHILLIPS
AND HERE I THOUGHT WE WERE COOL.
DUDE, I DIDN'T SAY A THING, ALL RIGHT?! THEY ALREADY KNEW!
I SWEAR ON MY GRANDMA!!!
MR. NELSON IS TELLING YOU THE TRUTH, DYLAN.
IN FACT, WHEN WE QUESTIONED HIM ABOUT IT, HE DENIED EVERYTHING. IT TOOK THE THREAT OF EXPULSION BEFORE HE FINALLY CONFESSED.
...HUH.
OKAY. WELL, IF HE DIDN'T RAT ME OUT, THEN WHO DID?
"I CAN'T BELIEVE THIS!!!"
Ms. PHILLIPS

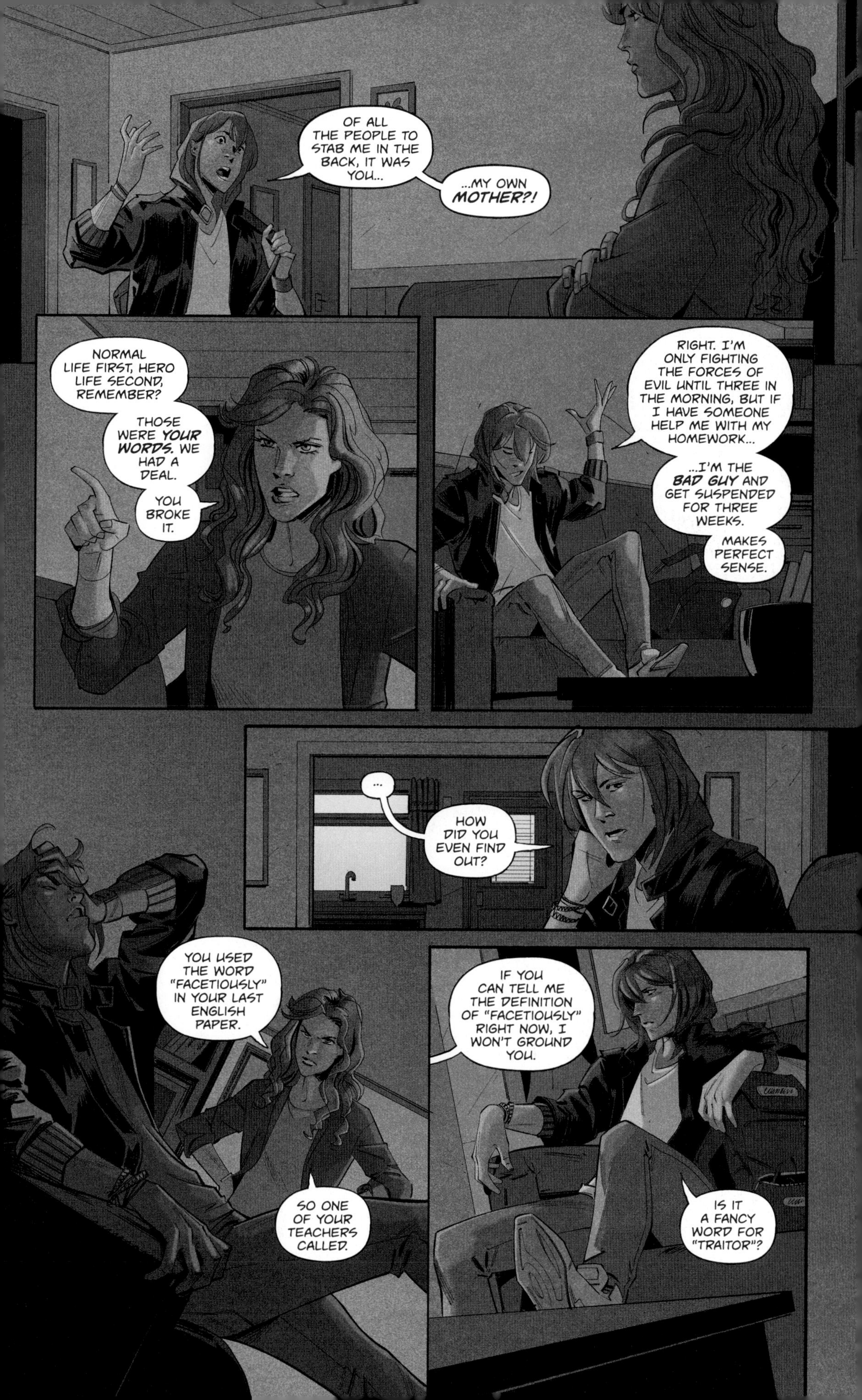
OF ALL THE PEOPLE TO STAB ME IN THE BACK, IT WAS YOU...
...MY OWN MOTHER?!
NORMAL LIFE FIRST, HERO LIFE SECOND, REMEMBER?
THOSE WERE YOUR WORDS. WE HAD A DEAL.
YOU BROKE IT.
RIGHT. I'M ONLY FIGHTING THE FORCES OF EVIL UNTIL THREE IN THE MORNING, BUT IF I HAVE SOMEONE HELP ME WITH MY HOMEWORK...
...I'M THE BAD GUY AND GET SUSPENDED FOR THREE WEEKS.
MAKES PERFECT SENSE.
...
HOW DID YOU EVEN FIND OUT?
YOU USED THE WORD "FACETIOUSLY" IN YOUR LAST ENGLISH PAPER.
SO ONE OF YOUR TEACHERS CALLED.
IF YOU CAN TELL ME THE DEFINITION OF "FACETIOUSLY" RIGHT NOW, I WON'T GROUND YOU.
IS IT A FANCY WORD FOR "TRAITOR"?

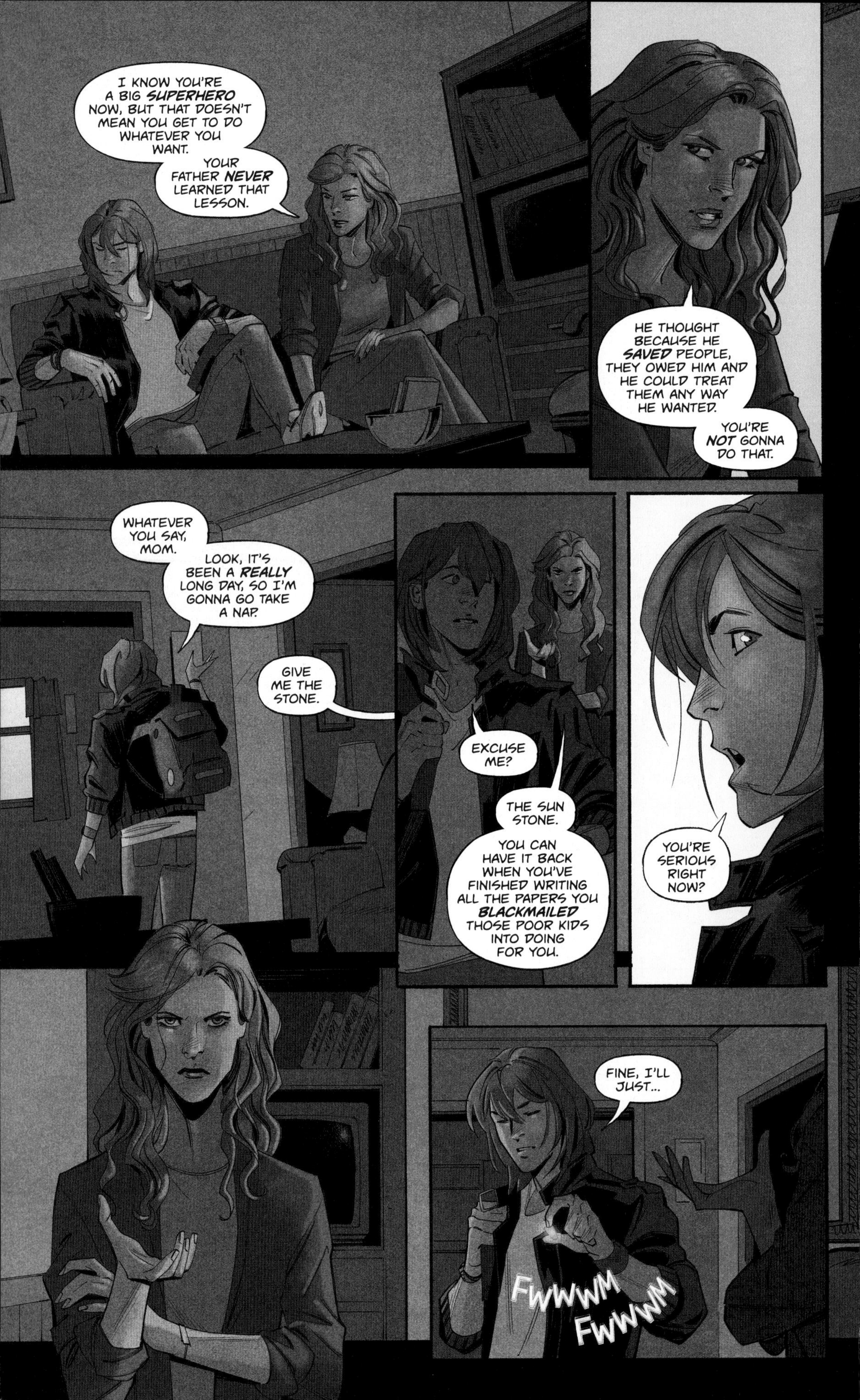
I KNOW YOU'RE A BIG SUPERHERO NOW, BUT THAT DOESN'T MEAN YOU GET TO DO WHATEVER YOU WANT.
YOUR FATHER NEVER LEARNED THAT LESSON.
HE THOUGHT BECAUSE HE SAVED PEOPLE, THEY OWED HIM AND HE COULD TREAT THEM ANY WAY HE WANTED.
YOU'RE NOT GONNA DO THAT.
WHATEVER YOU SAY, MOM.
LOOK, IT'S BEEN A REALLY LONG DAY, SO I'M GONNA GO TAKE A NAP.
GIVE ME THE STONE.
EXCUSE ME?
THE SUN STONE.
YOU CAN HAVE IT BACK WHEN YOU'VE FINISHED WRITING ALL THE PAPERS YOU BLACKMAILED THOSE POOR KIDS INTO DOING FOR YOU.
YOU'RE SERIOUS RIGHT NOW?
FINE, I'LL JUST...
FWWWM
FWWWM

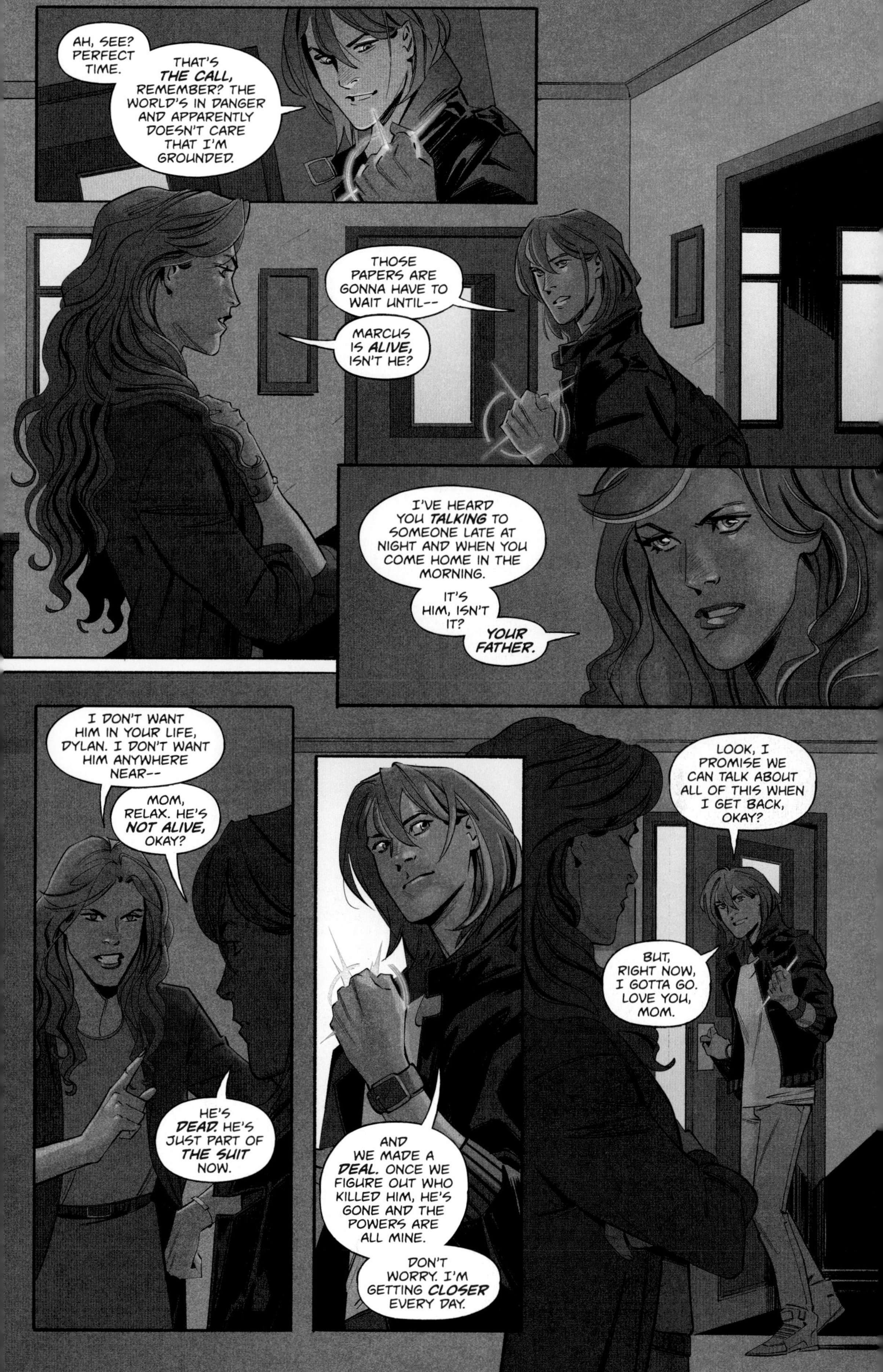
AH, SEE? PERFECT TIME.
THAT'S **THE CALL,** REMEMBER? THE WORLD'S IN DANGER AND APPARENTLY DOESN'T CARE THAT I'M GROUNDED.
THOSE PAPERS ARE GONNA HAVE TO WAIT UNTIL--
MARCUS IS **ALIVE,** ISN'T HE?
I'VE HEARD YOU **TALKING** TO SOMEONE LATE AT NIGHT AND WHEN YOU COME HOME IN THE MORNING.
IT'S HIM, ISN'T IT?
YOUR FATHER.
I DON'T WANT HIM IN YOUR LIFE, DYLAN. I DON'T WANT HIM ANYWHERE NEAR--
MOM, RELAX. HE'S **NOT ALIVE,** OKAY?
HE'S **DEAD.** HE'S JUST PART OF **THE SUIT** NOW.
AND WE MADE A **DEAL.** ONCE WE FIGURE OUT WHO KILLED HIM, HE'S GONE AND THE POWERS ARE ALL MINE.
DON'T WORRY. I'M GETTING **CLOSER** EVERY DAY.
LOOK, I PROMISE WE CAN TALK ABOUT ALL OF THIS WHEN I GET BACK, OKAY?
BUT, RIGHT NOW, I GOTTA GO. LOVE YOU, MOM.

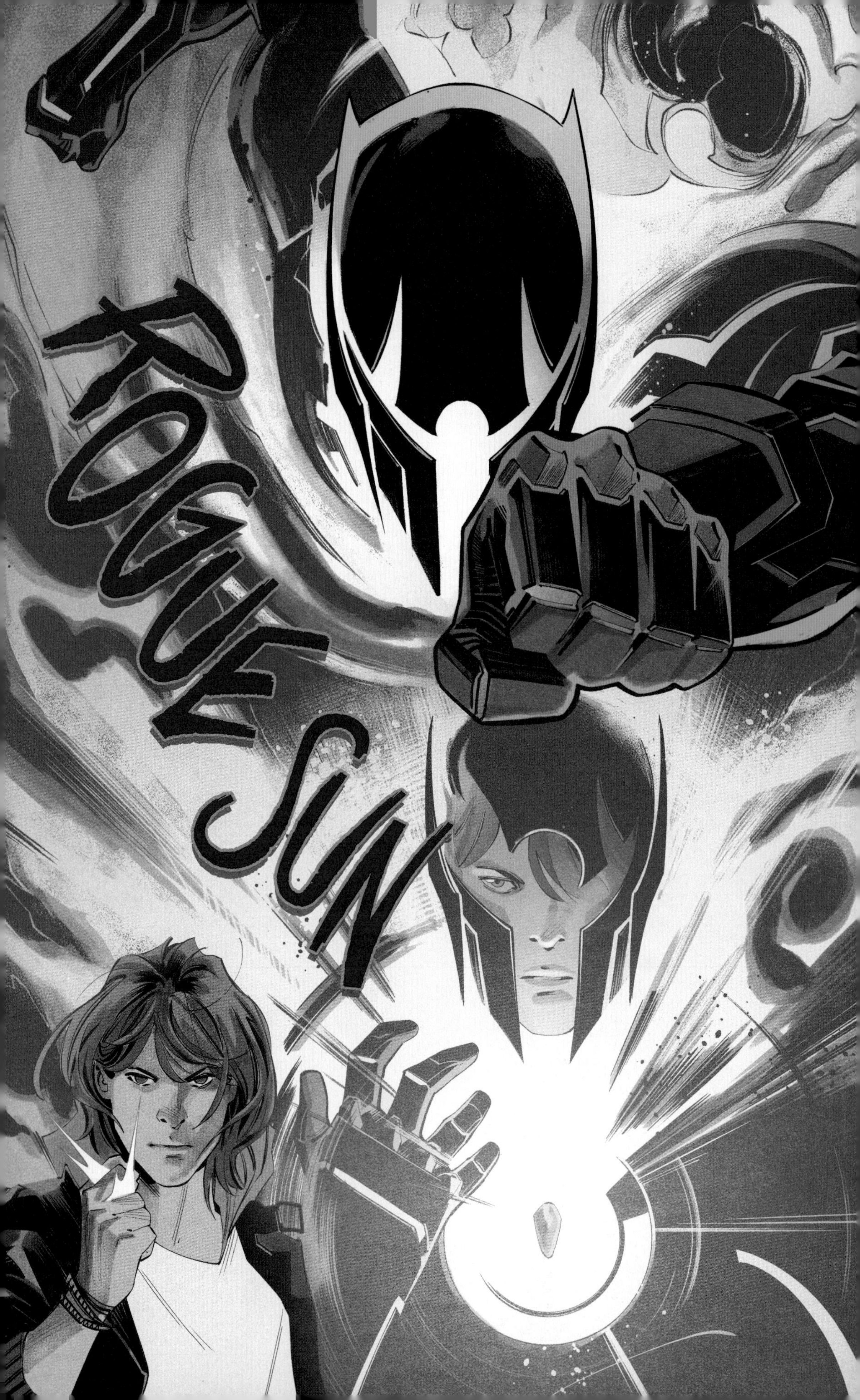

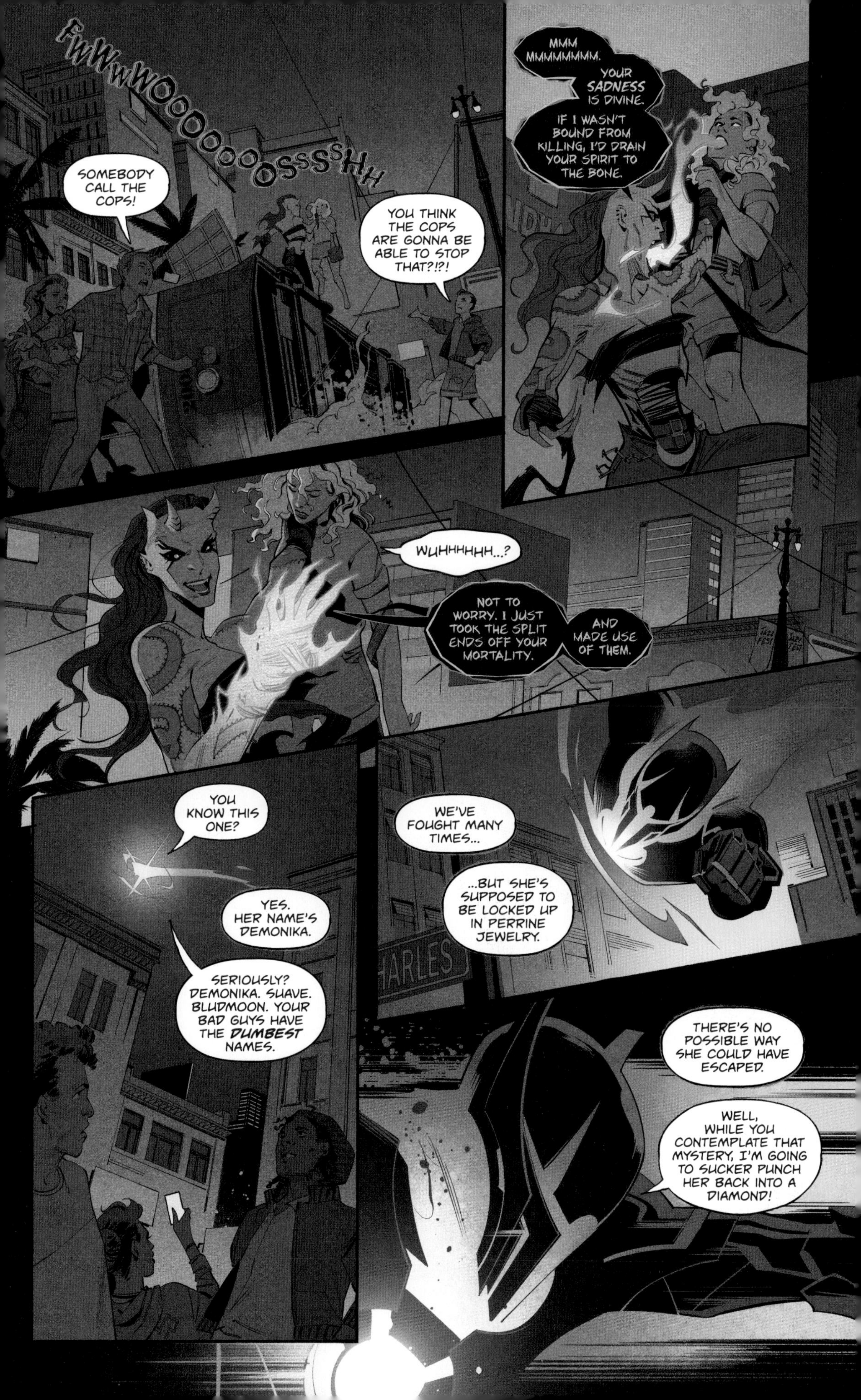
FWWWWOOOOOOOOSSSSHH
SOMEBODY CALL THE COPS!
YOU THINK THE COPS ARE GONNA BE ABLE TO STOP THAT?!?!
MMM MMMMMMMM.
YOUR SADNESS IS DIVINE.
IF I WASN'T BOUND FROM KILLING, I'D DRAIN YOUR SPIRIT TO THE BONE.
WUHHHHHH...?
NOT TO WORRY. I JUST TOOK THE SPLIT ENDS OFF YOUR MORTALITY.
AND MADE USE OF THEM.
YOU KNOW THIS ONE?
YES. HER NAME'S DEMONIKA.
SERIOUSLY? DEMONIKA. SUAVE. BLUDMOON. YOUR BAD GUYS HAVE THE DUMBEST NAMES.
WE'VE FOUGHT MANY TIMES...
...BUT SHE'S SUPPOSED TO BE LOCKED UP IN PERRINE JEWELRY.
THERE'S NO POSSIBLE WAY SHE COULD HAVE ESCAPED.
WELL, WHILE YOU CONTEMPLATE THAT MYSTERY, I'M GOING TO SUCKER PUNCH HER BACK INTO A DIAMOND!

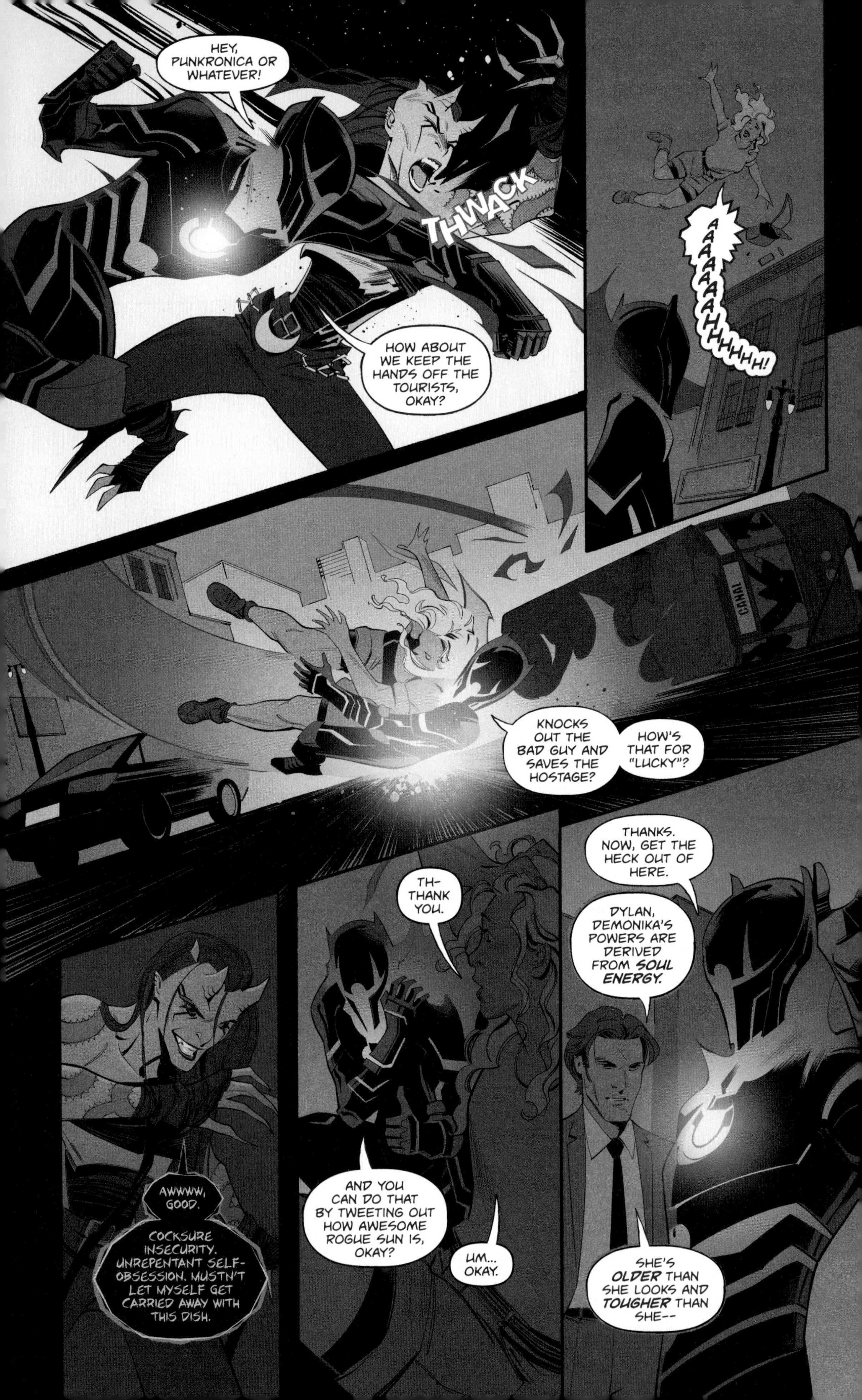

HEY, PUNKRONICA OR WHATEVER!
THWACK
HOW ABOUT WE KEEP THE HANDS OFF THE TOURISTS, OKAY?
AAAAAAAHHHHHH!
CANAL
KNOCKS OUT THE BAD GUY AND SAVES THE HOSTAGE?
HOW'S THAT FOR "LUCKY"?
AWWWW, GOOD.
COCKSURE INSECURITY. UNREPENTANT SELF-OBSESSION. MUSTN'T LET MYSELF GET CARRIED AWAY WITH THIS DISH.
TH-THANK YOU.
AND YOU CAN DO THAT BY TWEETING OUT HOW AWESOME ROGUE SUN IS, OKAY?
UM... OKAY.
THANKS. NOW, GET THE HECK OUT OF HERE.
DYLAN, DEMONIKA'S POWERS ARE DERIVED FROM SOUL ENERGY.
SHE'S OLDER THAN SHE LOOKS AND TOUGHER THAN SHE--

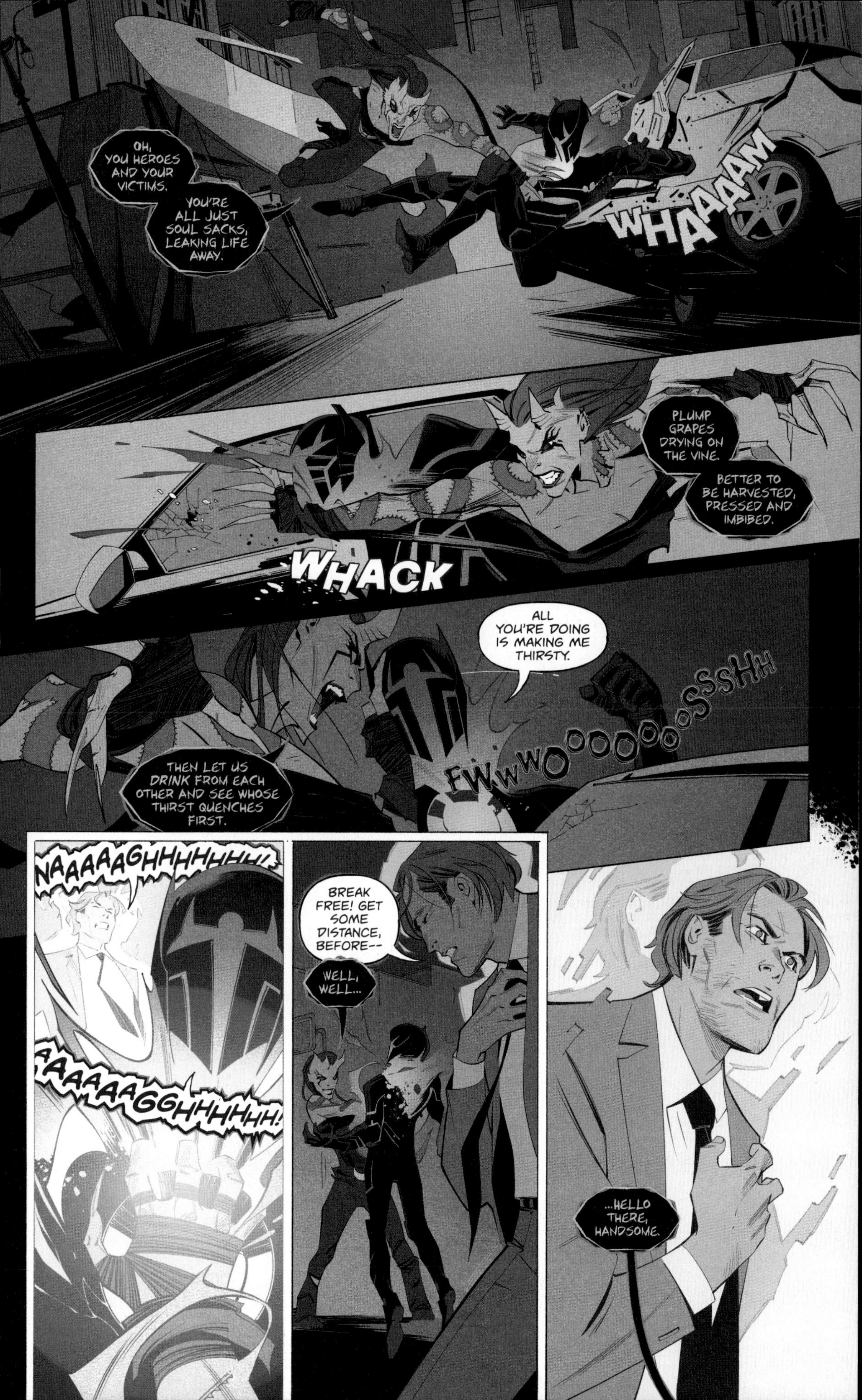
OH, YOU HEROES AND YOUR VICTIMS.
YOU'RE ALL JUST SOUL SACKS, LEAKING LIFE AWAY.
WHAAAAM
PLUMP GRAPES DRYING ON THE VINE.
BETTER TO BE HARVESTED, PRESSED AND IMBIBED.
WHACK
ALL YOU'RE DOING IS MAKING ME THIRSTY.
THEN LET US DRINK FROM EACH OTHER AND SEE WHOSE THIRST QUENCHES FIRST.
FWWWOOOOOOOOSSSHH
NAAAAAGHHHHHHH!
AAAAAAAGGHHHHHH!
BREAK FREE! GET SOME DISTANCE, BEFORE--
WELL, WELL...
...HELLO THERE, HANDSOME.

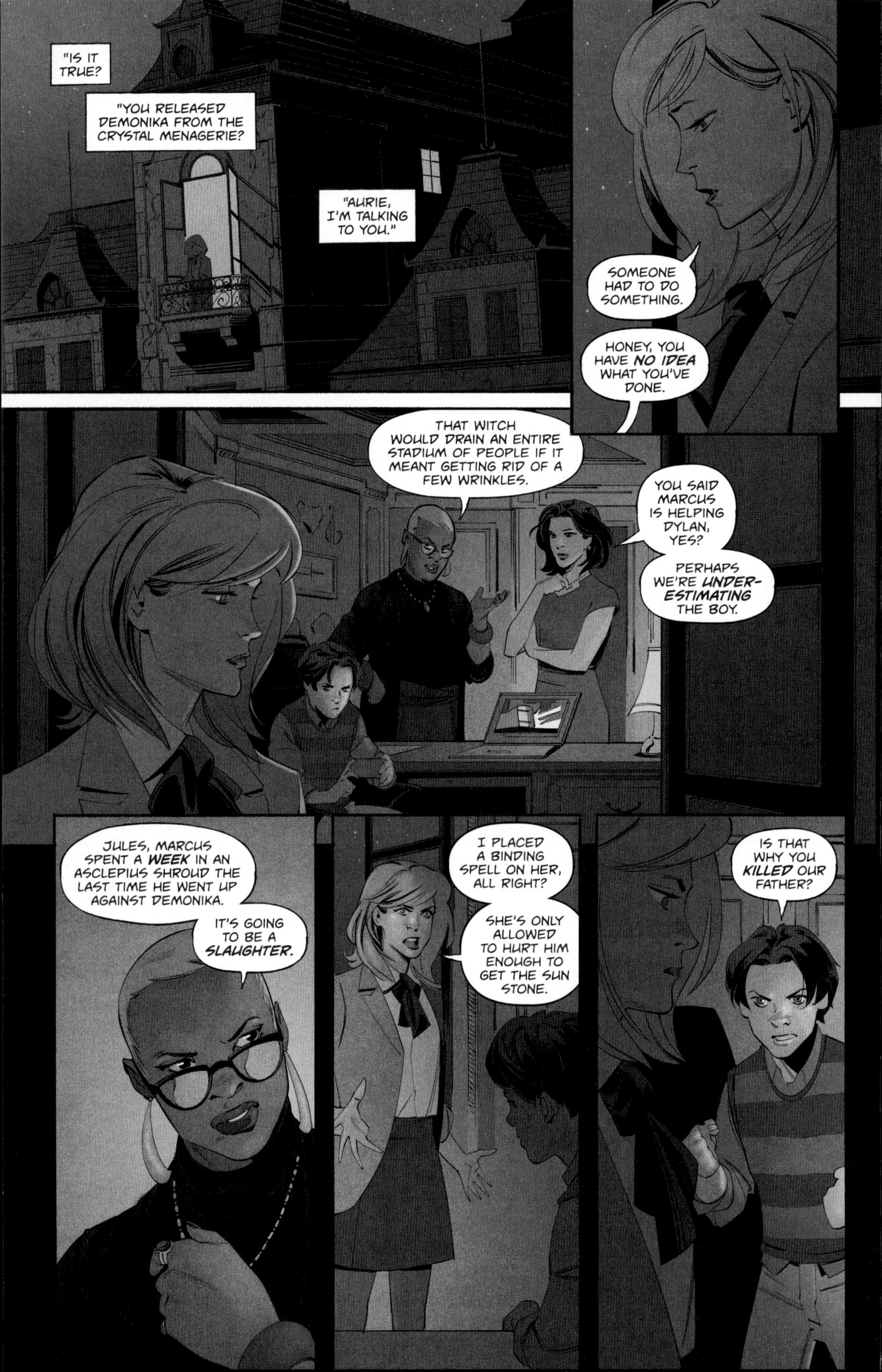
"IS IT TRUE?
"YOU RELEASED DEMONIKA FROM THE CRYSTAL MENAGERIE?
"AURIE, I'M TALKING TO YOU."
SOMEONE HAD TO DO SOMETHING.
HONEY, YOU HAVE NO IDEA WHAT YOU'VE DONE.
THAT WITCH WOULD DRAIN AN ENTIRE STADIUM OF PEOPLE IF IT MEANT GETTING RID OF A FEW WRINKLES.
YOU SAID MARCUS IS HELPING DYLAN, YES?
PERHAPS WE'RE UNDER-ESTIMATING THE BOY.
JULES, MARCUS SPENT A WEEK IN AN ASCLEPIUS SHROUD THE LAST TIME HE WENT UP AGAINST DEMONIKA.
IT'S GOING TO BE A SLAUGHTER.
I PLACED A BINDING SPELL ON HER, ALL RIGHT?
SHE'S ONLY ALLOWED TO HURT HIM ENOUGH TO GET THE SUN STONE.
IS THAT WHY YOU KILLED OUR FATHER?

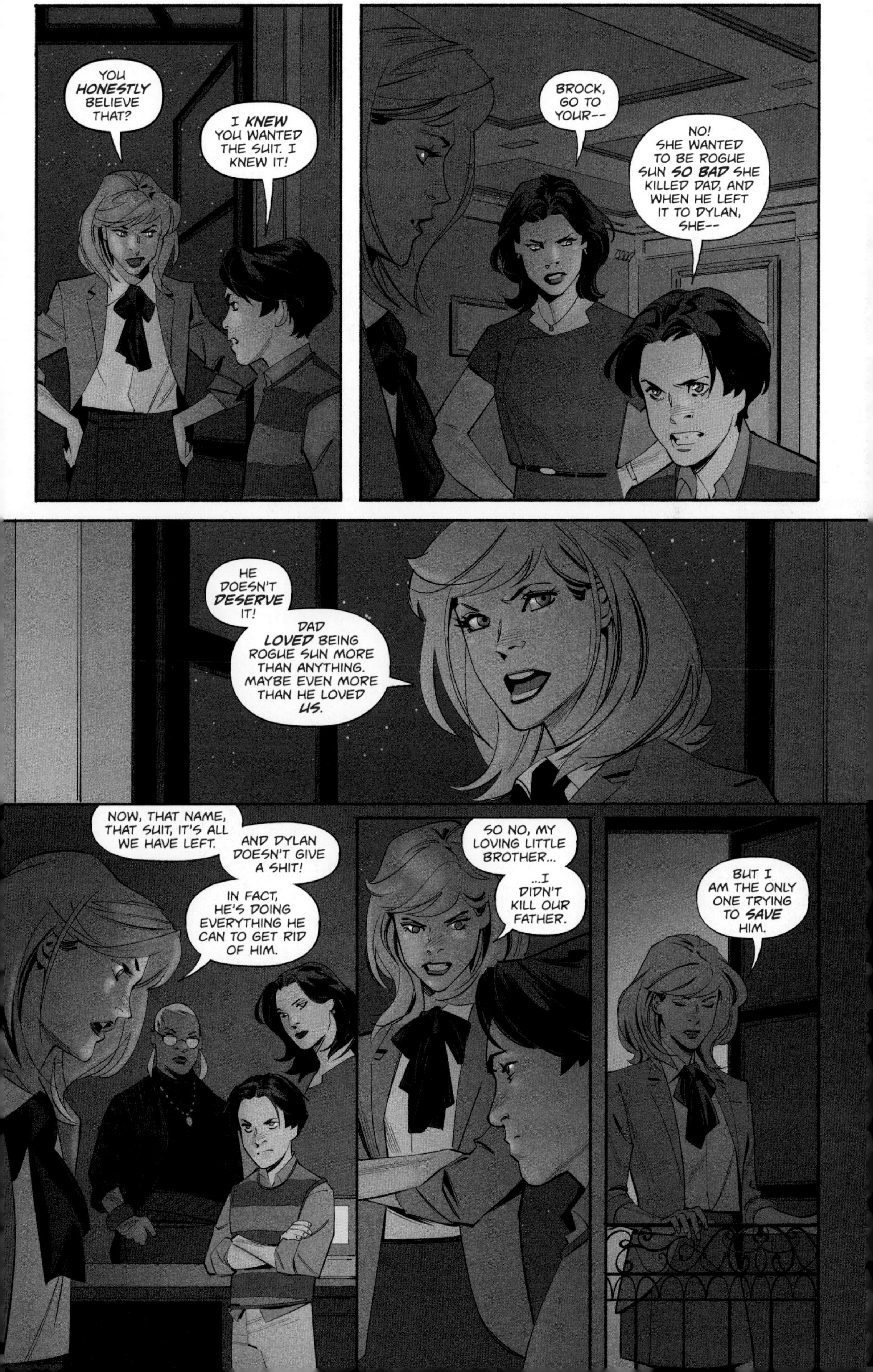
YOU *HONESTLY* BELIEVE THAT?
I *KNEW* YOU WANTED THE SUIT. I KNEW IT!
BROCK, GO TO YOUR--
NO! SHE WANTED TO BE ROGUE SUN *SO BAD* SHE KILLED DAD, AND WHEN HE LEFT IT TO DYLAN, SHE--
HE DOESN'T *DESERVE* IT!
DAD *LOVED* BEING ROGUE SUN MORE THAN ANYTHING. MAYBE EVEN MORE THAN HE LOVED *US*.
NOW, THAT NAME, THAT SUIT, IT'S ALL WE HAVE LEFT.
AND DYLAN DOESN'T GIVE A SHIT!
IN FACT, HE'S DOING EVERYTHING HE CAN TO GET RID OF HIM.
SO NO, MY LOVING LITTLE BROTHER...
...I DIDN'T KILL OUR FATHER.
BUT I AM THE ONLY ONE TRYING TO *SAVE* HIM.

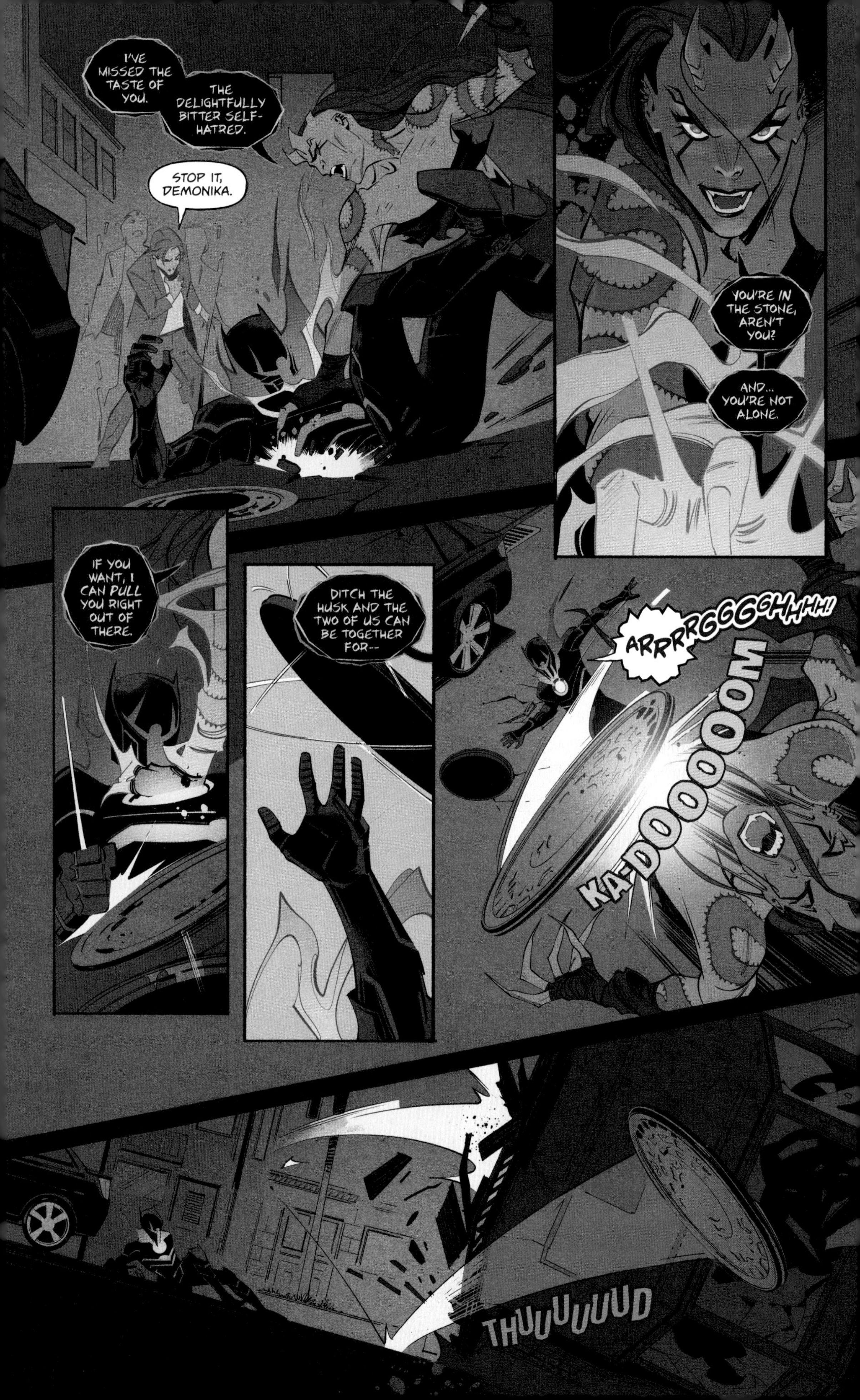
I'VE MISSED THE TASTE OF YOU.
THE DELIGHTFULLY BITTER SELF-HATRED.
STOP IT, DEMONIKA.
YOU'RE IN THE STONE, AREN'T YOU?
AND... YOU'RE NOT ALONE.
IF YOU WANT, I CAN PULL YOU RIGHT OUT OF THERE.
DITCH THE HUSK AND THE TWO OF US CAN BE TOGETHER FOR--
ARRRRGGGGHHHH!
KA-DOOOOOOOM
THUUUUUUD

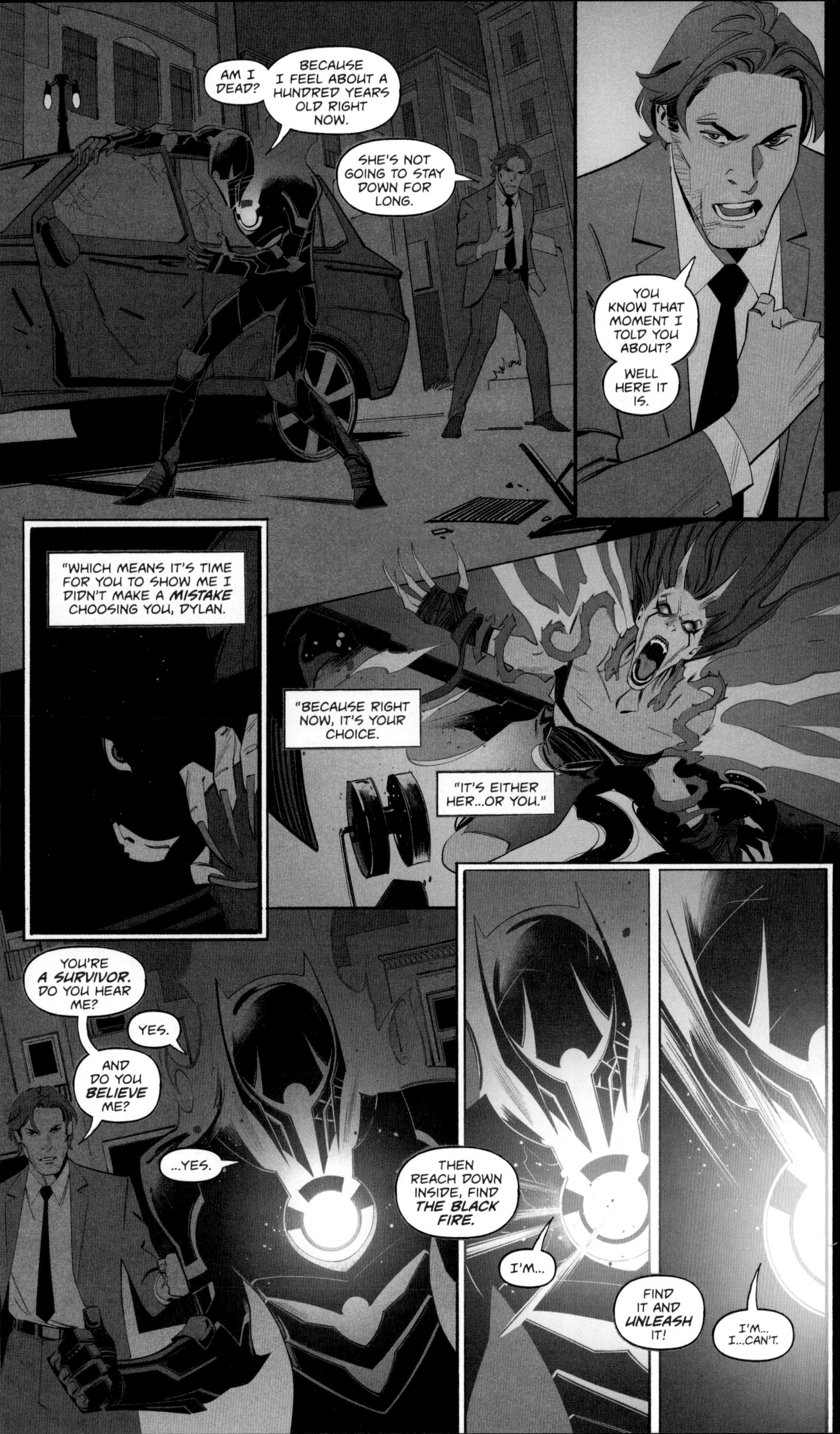
AM I DEAD?
BECAUSE I FEEL ABOUT A HUNDRED YEARS OLD RIGHT NOW.
SHE'S NOT GOING TO STAY DOWN FOR LONG.
YOU KNOW THAT MOMENT I TOLD YOU ABOUT?
WELL HERE IT IS.
"WHICH MEANS IT'S TIME FOR YOU TO SHOW ME I DIDN'T MAKE A *MISTAKE* CHOOSING YOU, DYLAN.
"BECAUSE RIGHT NOW, IT'S YOUR CHOICE.
"IT'S EITHER HER...OR YOU."
YOU'RE *A SURVIVOR.* DO YOU HEAR ME?
YES.
AND DO YOU *BELIEVE* ME?
...YES.
THEN REACH DOWN INSIDE, FIND *THE BLACK FIRE.*
I'M...
FIND IT AND *UNLEASH* IT!
I'M... I...CAN'T.

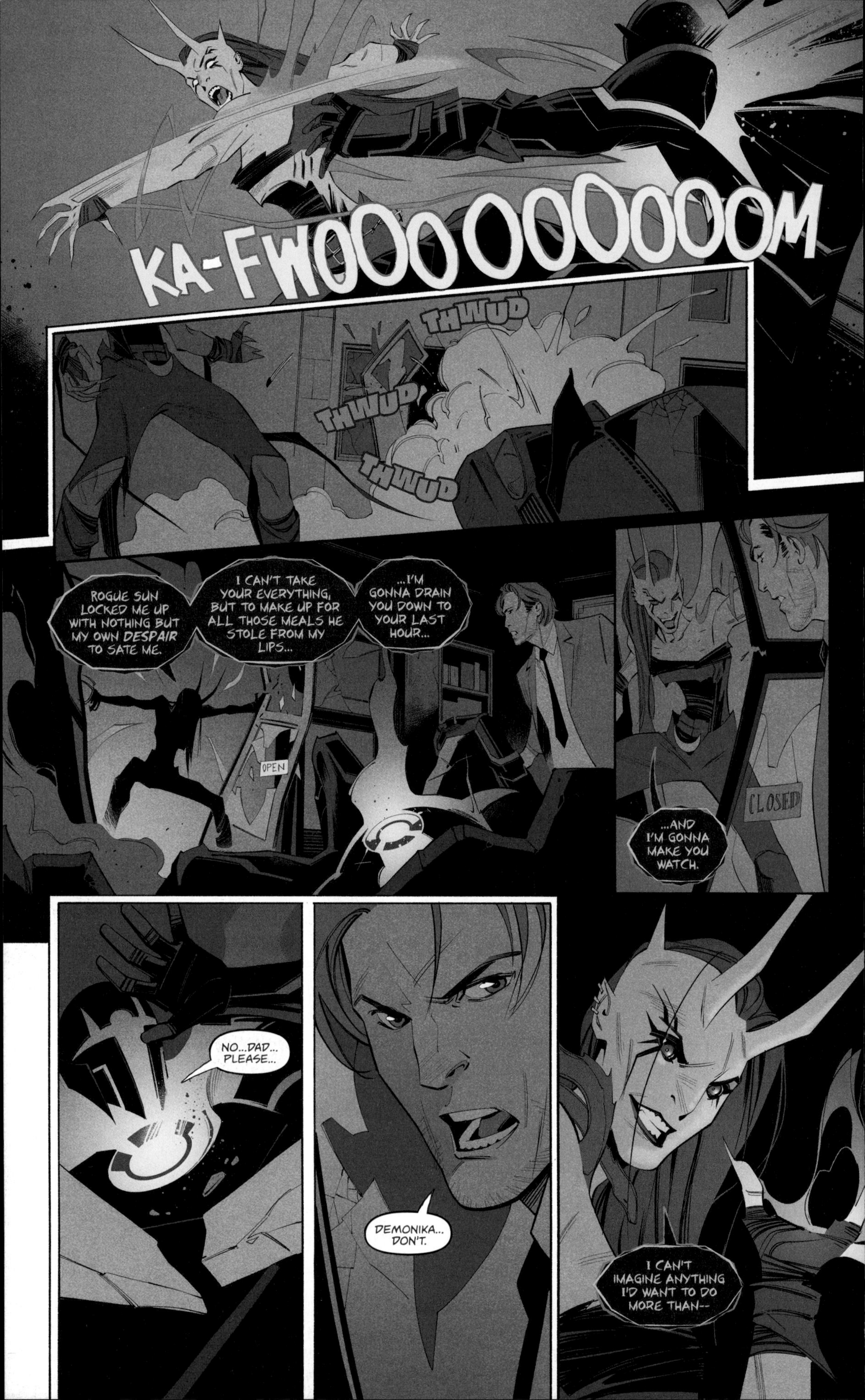
KA-FWOOOOOOOOOM
THWUD
THWUD
THWUD
ROGUE SUN LOCKED ME UP WITH NOTHING BUT MY OWN DESPAIR TO SATE ME.
I CAN'T TAKE YOUR EVERYTHING, BUT TO MAKE UP FOR ALL THOSE MEALS HE STOLE FROM MY LIPS...
...I'M GONNA DRAIN YOU DOWN TO YOUR LAST HOUR...
OPEN
CLOSED
...AND I'M GONNA MAKE YOU WATCH.
NO...DAD... PLEASE...
DEMONIKA... DON'T.
I CAN'T IMAGINE ANYTHING I'D WANT TO DO MORE THAN--

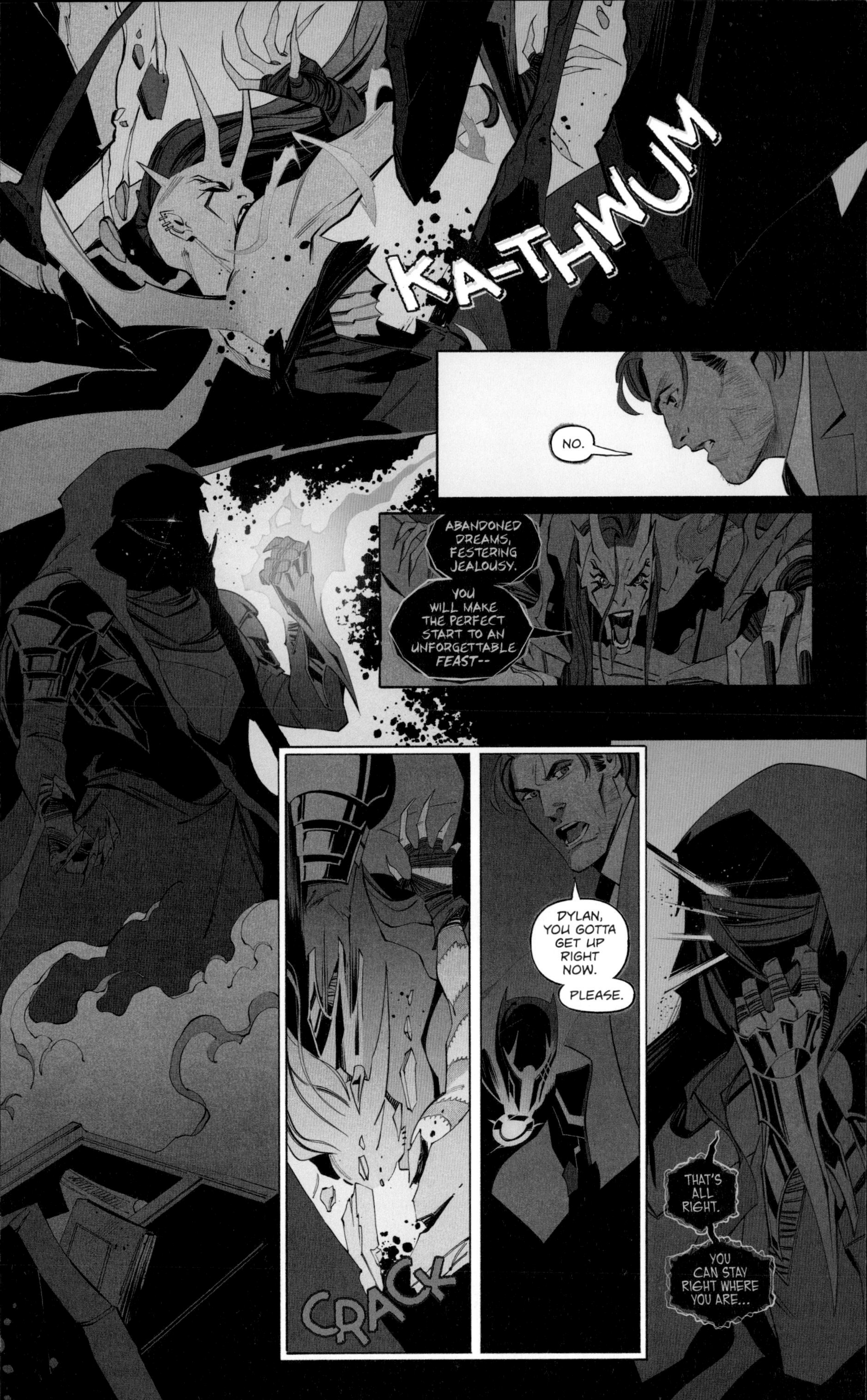
KA-THWUM
NO.
ABANDONED DREAMS, FESTERING JEALOUSY.
YOU WILL MAKE THE PERFECT START TO AN UNFORGETTABLE FEAST--
CRACK
DYLAN, YOU GOTTA GET UP RIGHT NOW.
PLEASE.
THAT'S ALL RIGHT.
YOU CAN STAY RIGHT WHERE YOU ARE...

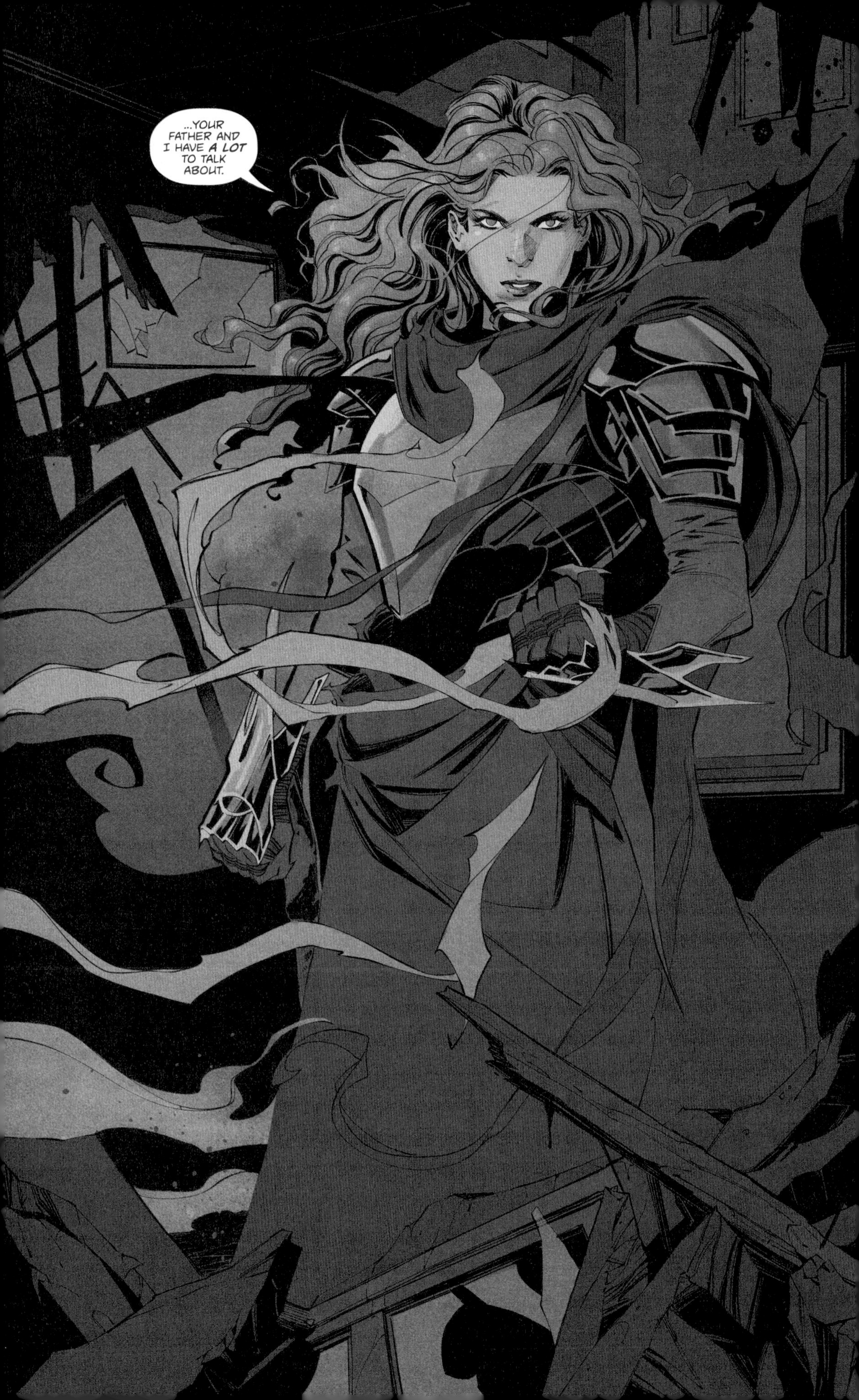
...YOUR FATHER AND I HAVE A LOT TO TALK ABOUT.

Chapter Five
Making a Murderer

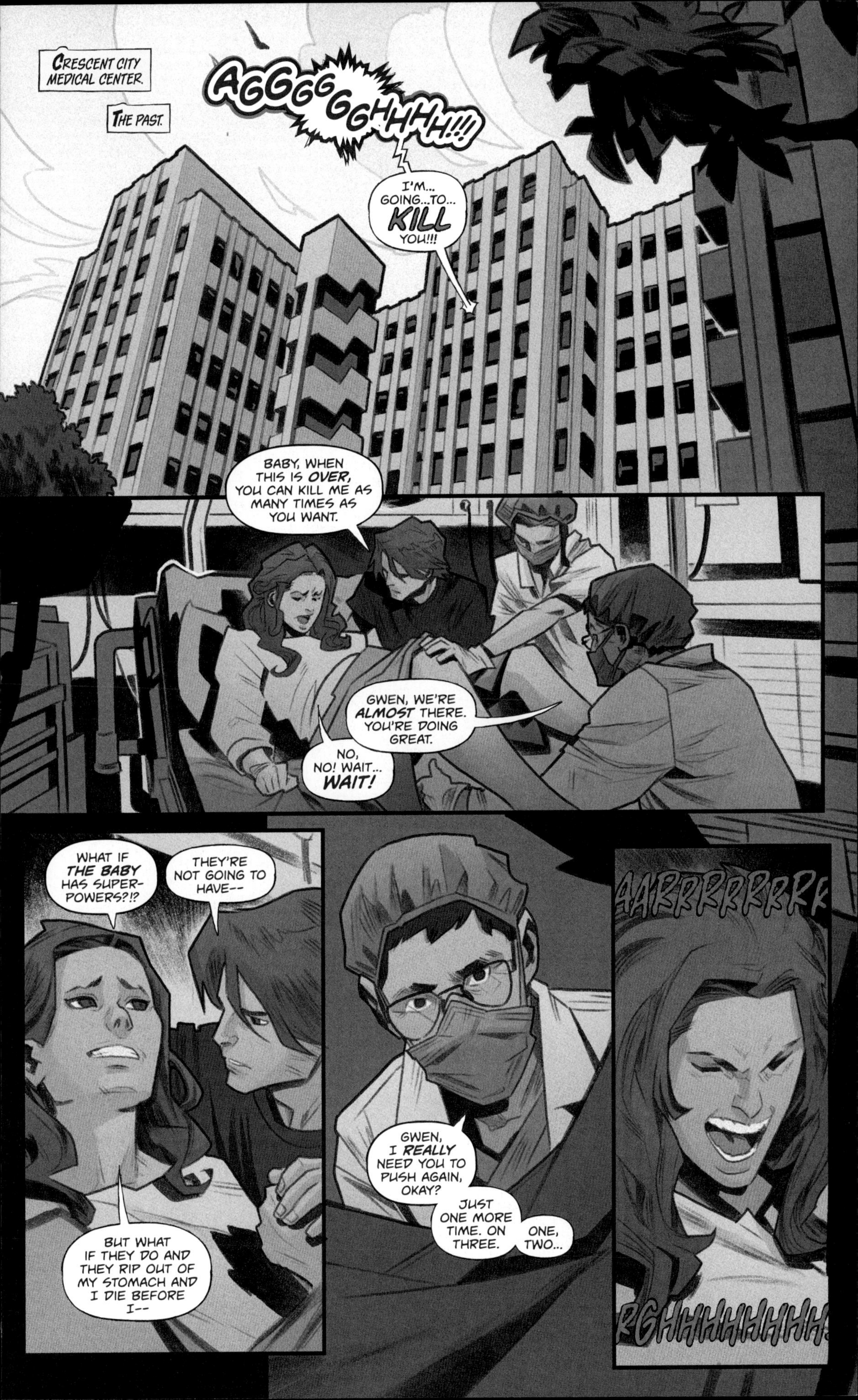
CRESCENT CITY MEDICAL CENTER.
THE PAST.
AGGGGGGHHHH!!!
I'M... GOING...TO... KILL YOU!!!
BABY, WHEN THIS IS OVER, YOU CAN KILL ME AS MANY TIMES AS YOU WANT.
GWEN, WE'RE ALMOST THERE. YOU'RE DOING GREAT.
NO, NO! WAIT... WAIT!
WHAT IF THE BABY HAS SUPER-POWERS?!?
THEY'RE NOT GOING TO HAVE--
BUT WHAT IF THEY DO AND THEY RIP OUT OF MY STOMACH AND I DIE BEFORE I--
GWEN, I REALLY NEED YOU TO PUSH AGAIN, OKAY?
JUST ONE MORE TIME. ON THREE.
ONE, TWO...
AARRRRRRRR
RGHHHHHHHHH

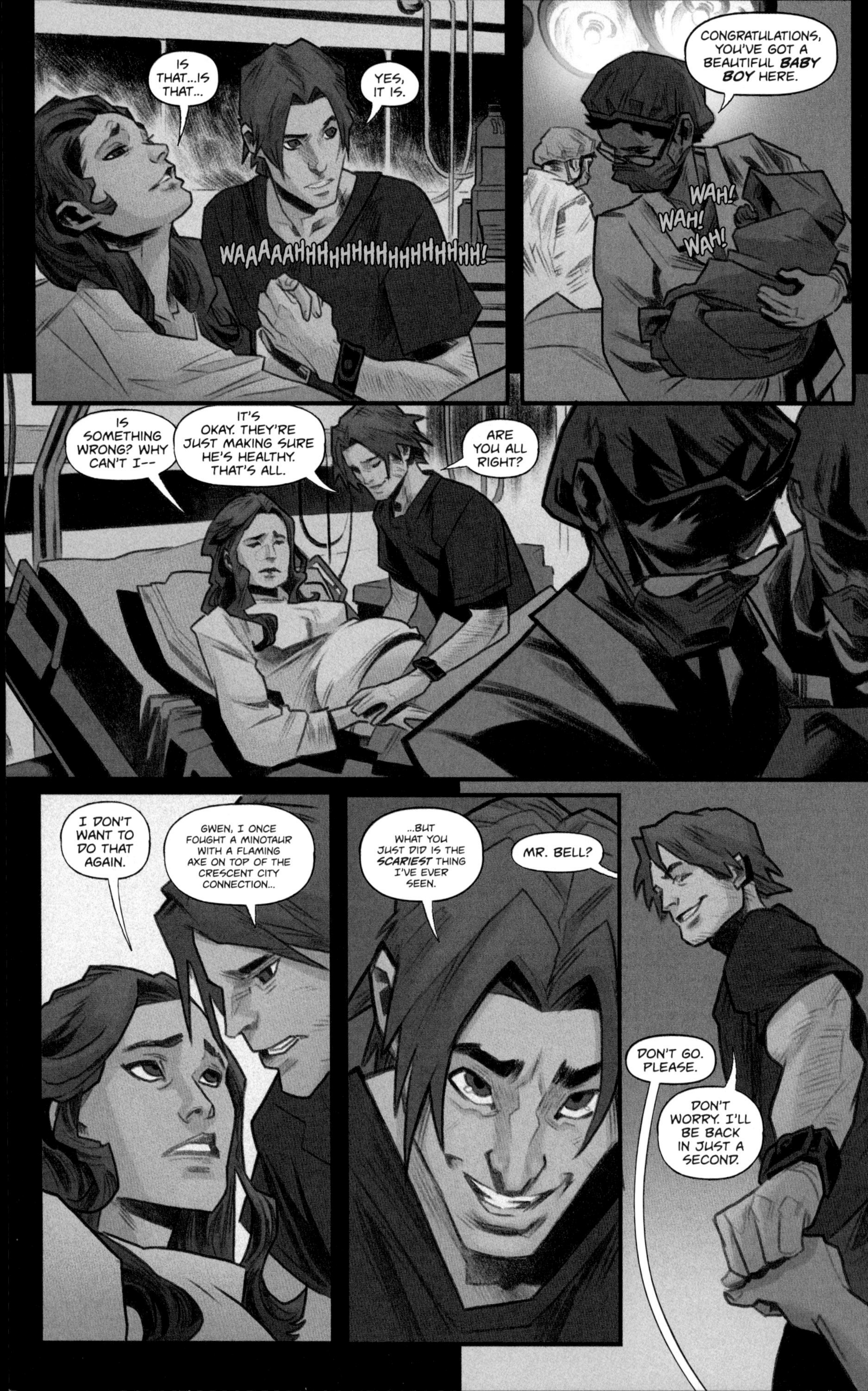
IS THAT...IS THAT...
YES, IT IS.
WAAAAAHHHHHHHHHHHHHHH!
CONGRATULATIONS, YOU'VE GOT A BEAUTIFUL BABY BOY HERE.
WAH! WAH! WAH!
IS SOMETHING WRONG? WHY CAN'T I--
IT'S OKAY. THEY'RE JUST MAKING SURE HE'S HEALTHY. THAT'S ALL.
ARE YOU ALL RIGHT?
I DON'T WANT TO DO THAT AGAIN.
GWEN, I ONCE FOUGHT A MINOTAUR WITH A FLAMING AXE ON TOP OF THE CRESCENT CITY CONNECTION...
...BUT WHAT YOU JUST DID IS THE SCARIEST THING I'VE EVER SEEN.
MR. BELL?
DON'T GO. PLEASE.
DON'T WORRY. I'LL BE BACK IN JUST A SECOND.

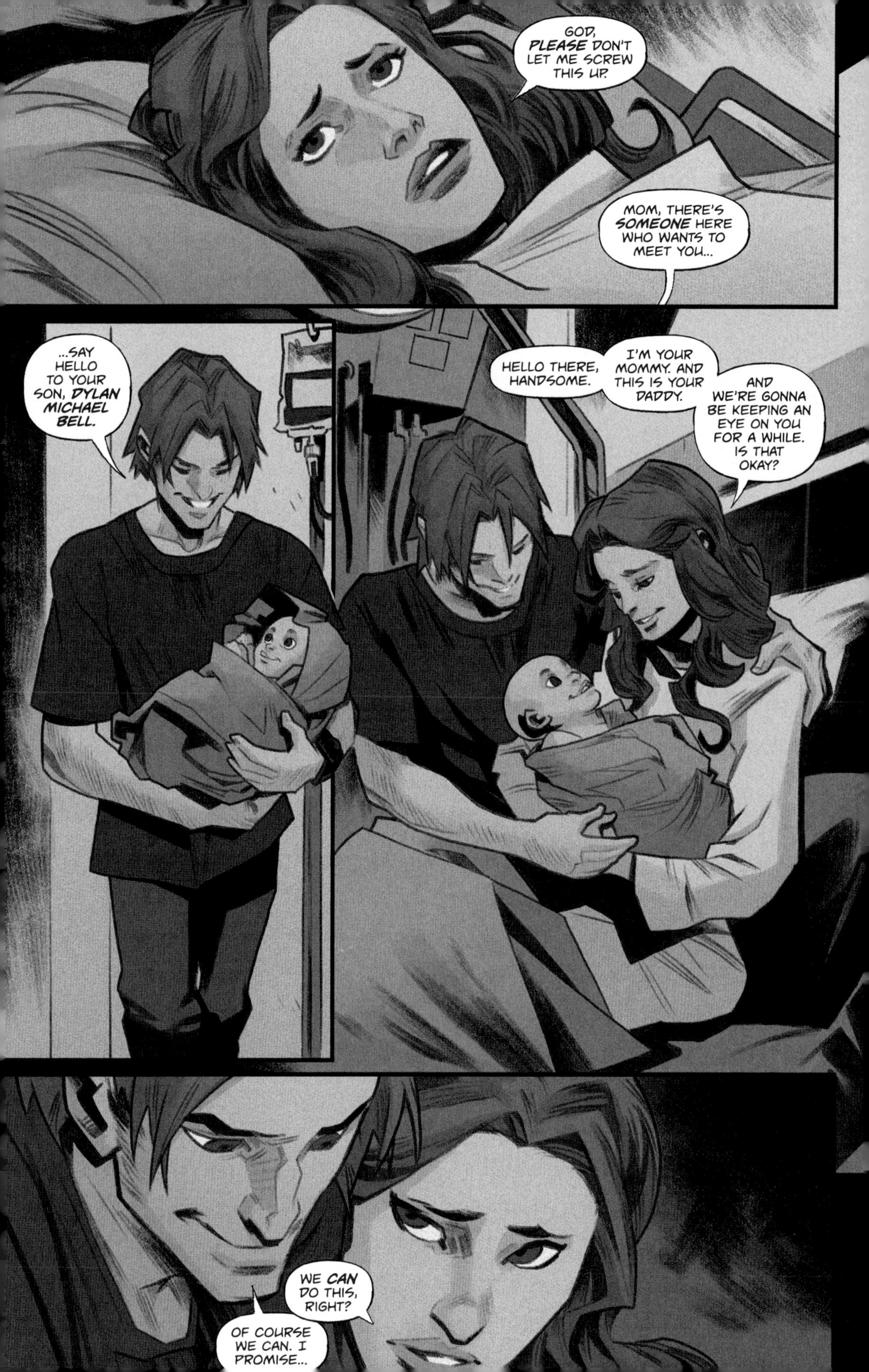
GOD, PLEASE DON'T LET ME SCREW THIS UP.
MOM, THERE'S SOMEONE HERE WHO WANTS TO MEET YOU...
...SAY HELLO TO YOUR SON, DYLAN MICHAEL BELL.
HELLO THERE, HANDSOME.
I'M YOUR MOMMY. AND THIS IS YOUR DADDY.
AND WE'RE GONNA BE KEEPING AN EYE ON YOU FOR A WHILE. IS THAT OKAY?
WE CAN DO THIS, RIGHT?
OF COURSE WE CAN. I PROMISE...

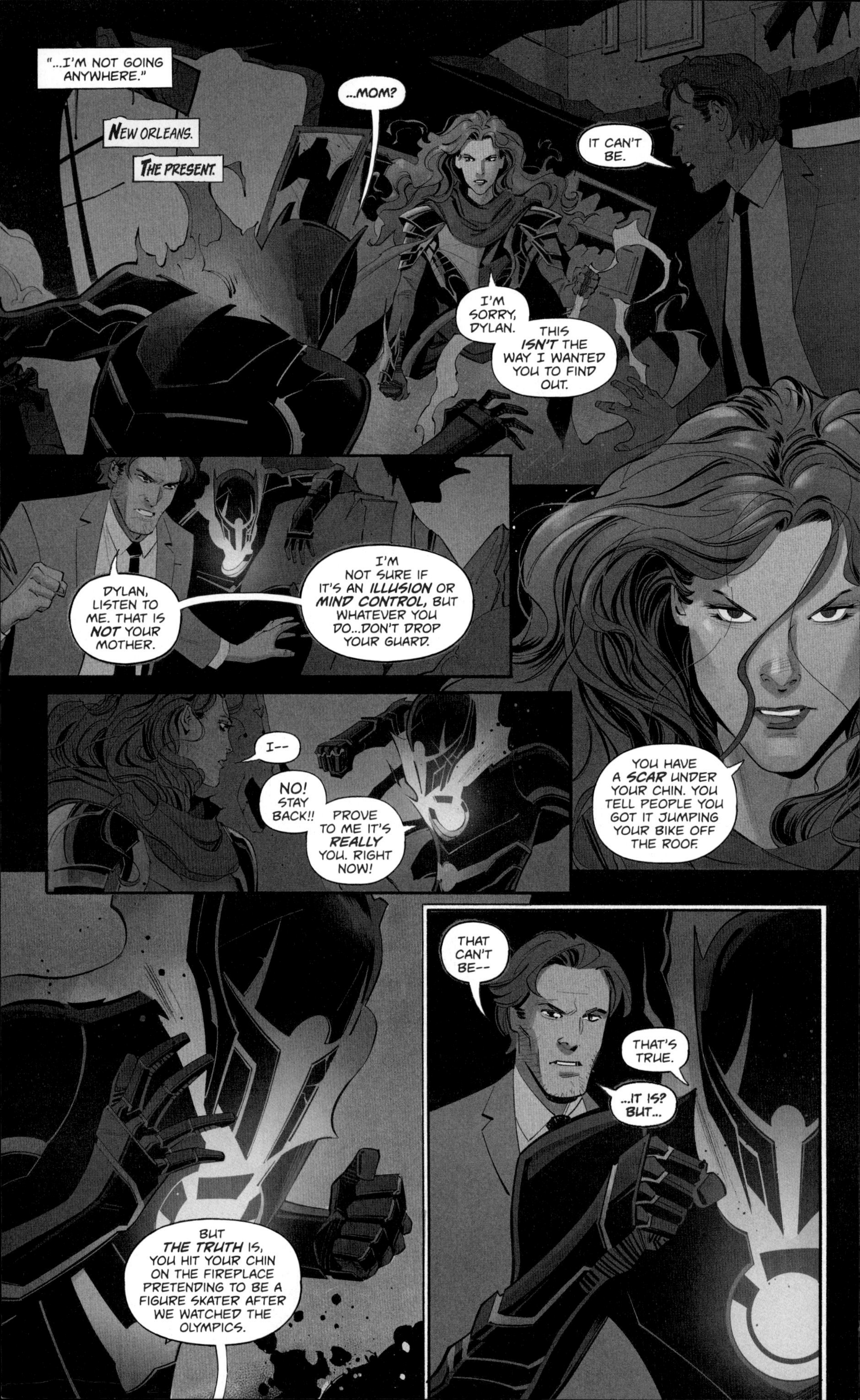
"...I'M NOT GOING ANYWHERE."
NEW ORLEANS.
THE PRESENT.
...MOM?
IT CAN'T BE.
I'M SORRY, DYLAN.
THIS ISN'T THE WAY I WANTED YOU TO FIND OUT.
DYLAN, LISTEN TO ME. THAT IS NOT YOUR MOTHER.
I'M NOT SURE IF IT'S AN ILLUSION OR MIND CONTROL, BUT WHATEVER YOU DO...DON'T DROP YOUR GUARD.
I--
NO! STAY BACK!!
PROVE TO ME IT'S REALLY YOU. RIGHT NOW!
YOU HAVE A SCAR UNDER YOUR CHIN. YOU TELL PEOPLE YOU GOT IT JUMPING YOUR BIKE OFF THE ROOF.
BUT THE TRUTH IS, YOU HIT YOUR CHIN ON THE FIREPLACE PRETENDING TO BE A FIGURE SKATER AFTER WE WATCHED THE OLYMPICS.
THAT CAN'T BE--
THAT'S TRUE.
...IT IS? BUT...

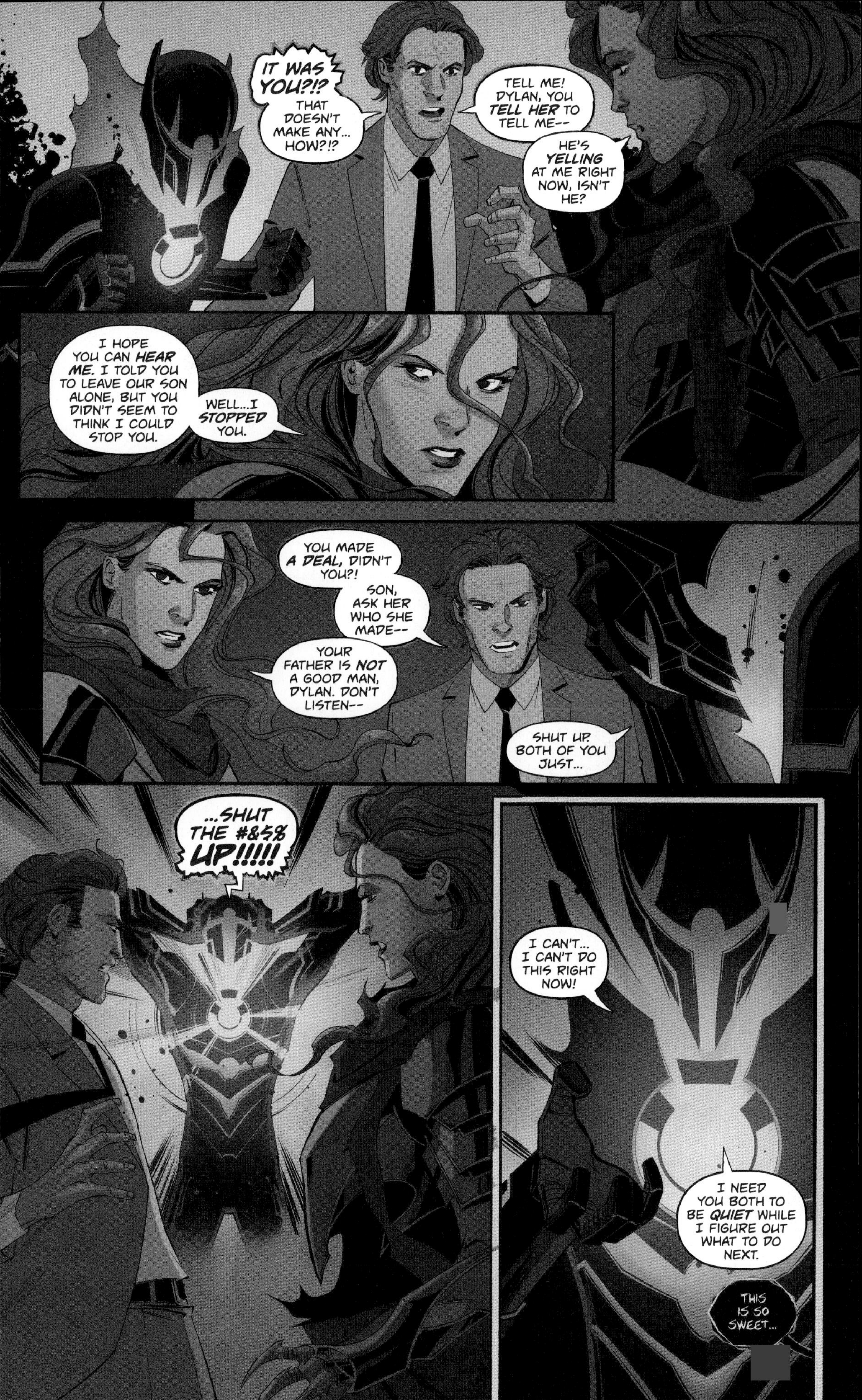
IT WAS YOU?!? THAT DOESN'T MAKE ANY... HOW?!?
TELL ME! DYLAN, YOU TELL HER TO TELL ME--
HE'S YELLING AT ME RIGHT NOW, ISN'T HE?
I HOPE YOU CAN HEAR ME. I TOLD YOU TO LEAVE OUR SON ALONE, BUT YOU DIDN'T SEEM TO THINK I COULD STOP YOU.
WELL...I STOPPED YOU.
YOU MADE A DEAL, DIDN'T YOU?!
SON, ASK HER WHO SHE MADE--
YOUR FATHER IS NOT A GOOD MAN, DYLAN. DON'T LISTEN--
SHUT UP. BOTH OF YOU JUST...
...SHUT THE #&$% UP!!!!!
I CAN'T... I CAN'T DO THIS RIGHT NOW!
I NEED YOU BOTH TO BE QUIET WHILE I FIGURE OUT WHAT TO DO NEXT.
THIS IS SO SWEET...

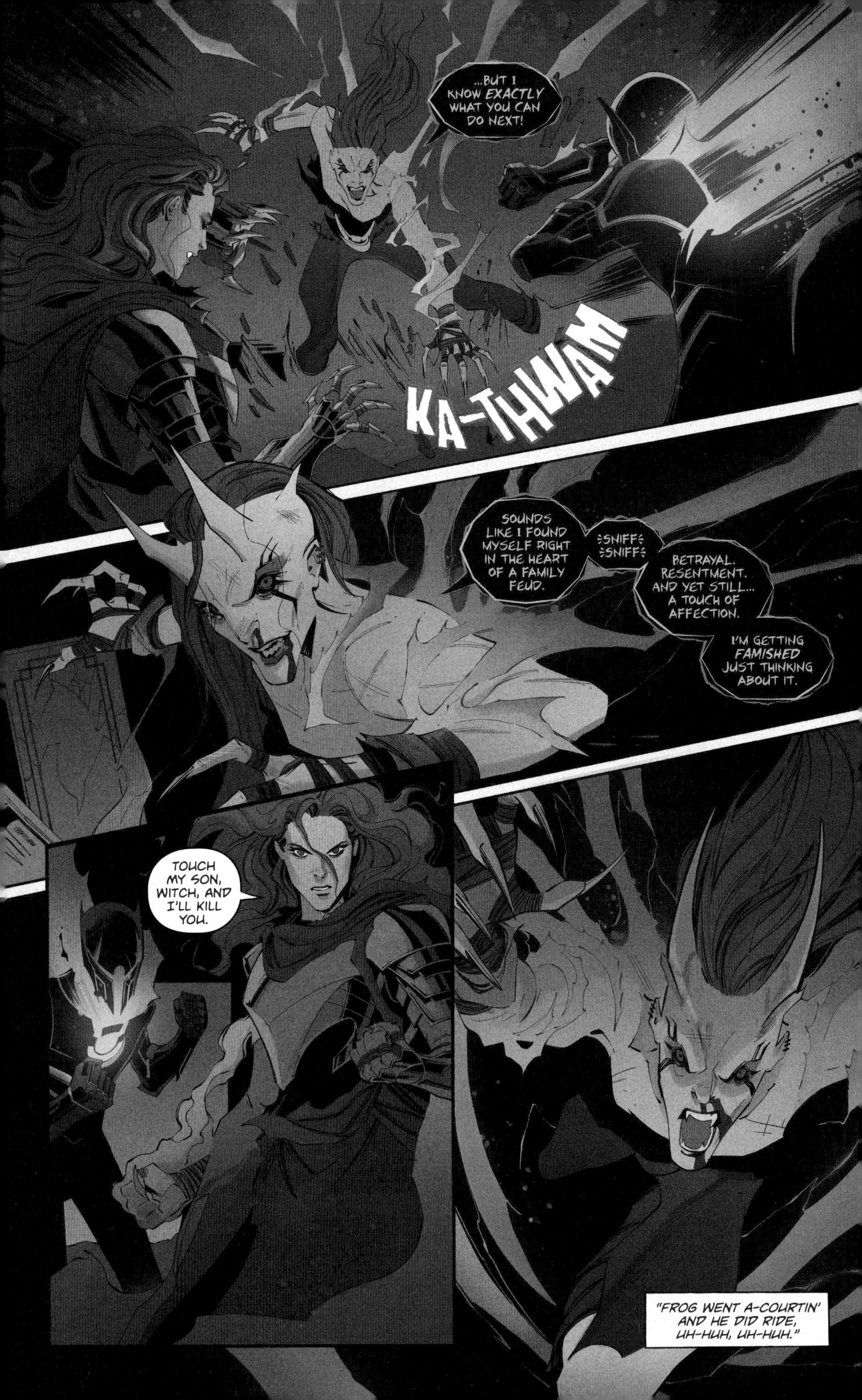
...BUT I KNOW EXACTLY WHAT YOU CAN DO NEXT!
KA-THWAM
SOUNDS LIKE I FOUND MYSELF RIGHT IN THE HEART OF A FAMILY FEUD.
SNIFF SNIFF
BETRAYAL. RESENTMENT. AND YET STILL... A TOUCH OF AFFECTION.
I'M GETTING FAMISHED JUST THINKING ABOUT IT.
TOUCH MY SON, WITCH, AND I'LL KILL YOU.
"FROG WENT A-COURTIN' AND HE DID RIDE, UH-HUH, UH-HUH."

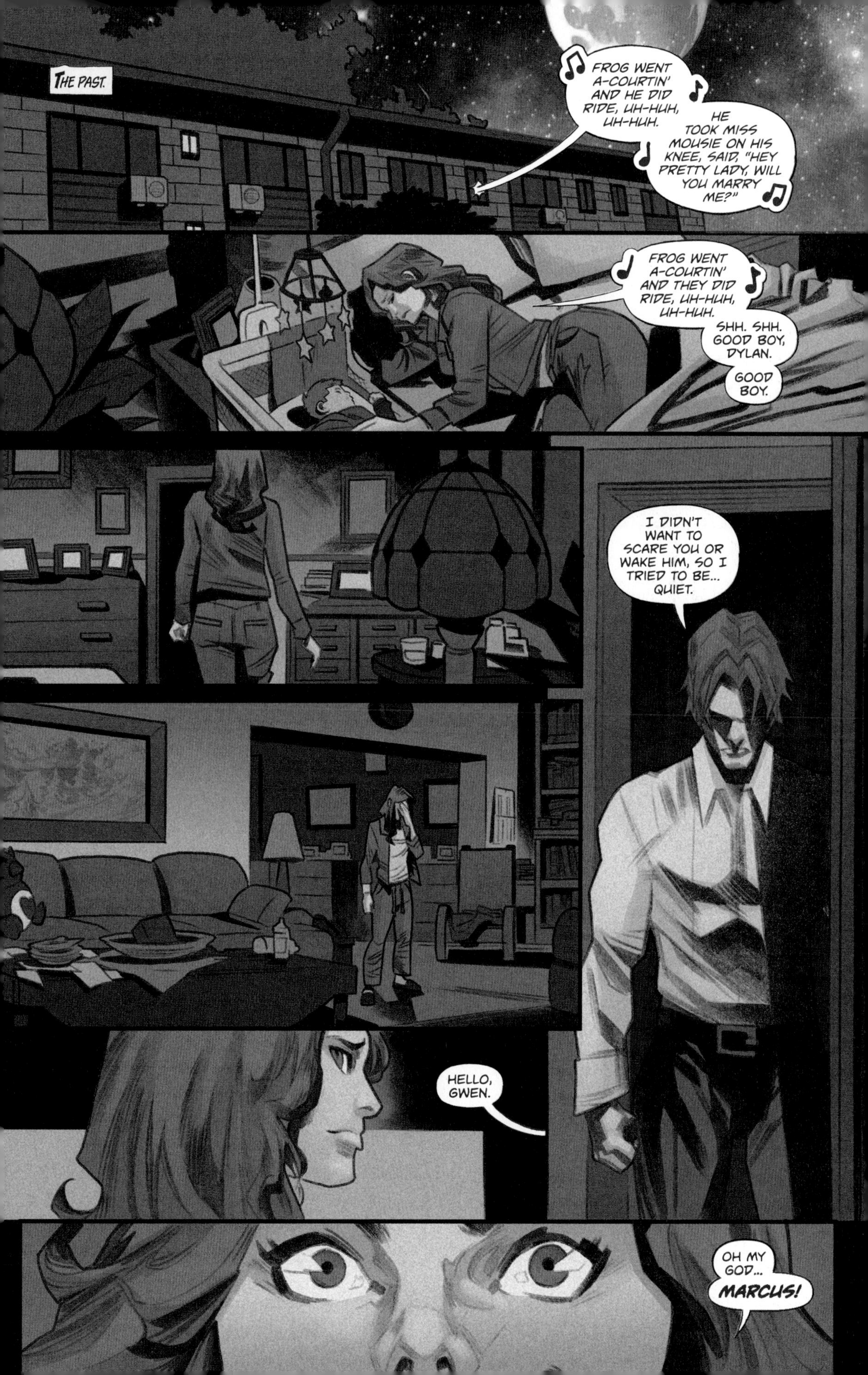
THE PAST.
FROG WENT A-COURTIN' AND HE DID RIDE, UH-HUH, UH-HUH.
HE TOOK MISS MOUSIE ON HIS KNEE, SAID, "HEY PRETTY LADY, WILL YOU MARRY ME?"
FROG WENT A-COURTIN' AND THEY DID RIDE, UH-HUH, UH-HUH.
SHH. SHH. GOOD BOY, DYLAN.
GOOD BOY.
I DIDN'T WANT TO SCARE YOU OR WAKE HIM, SO I TRIED TO BE... QUIET.
HELLO, GWEN.
OH MY GOD... MARCUS!

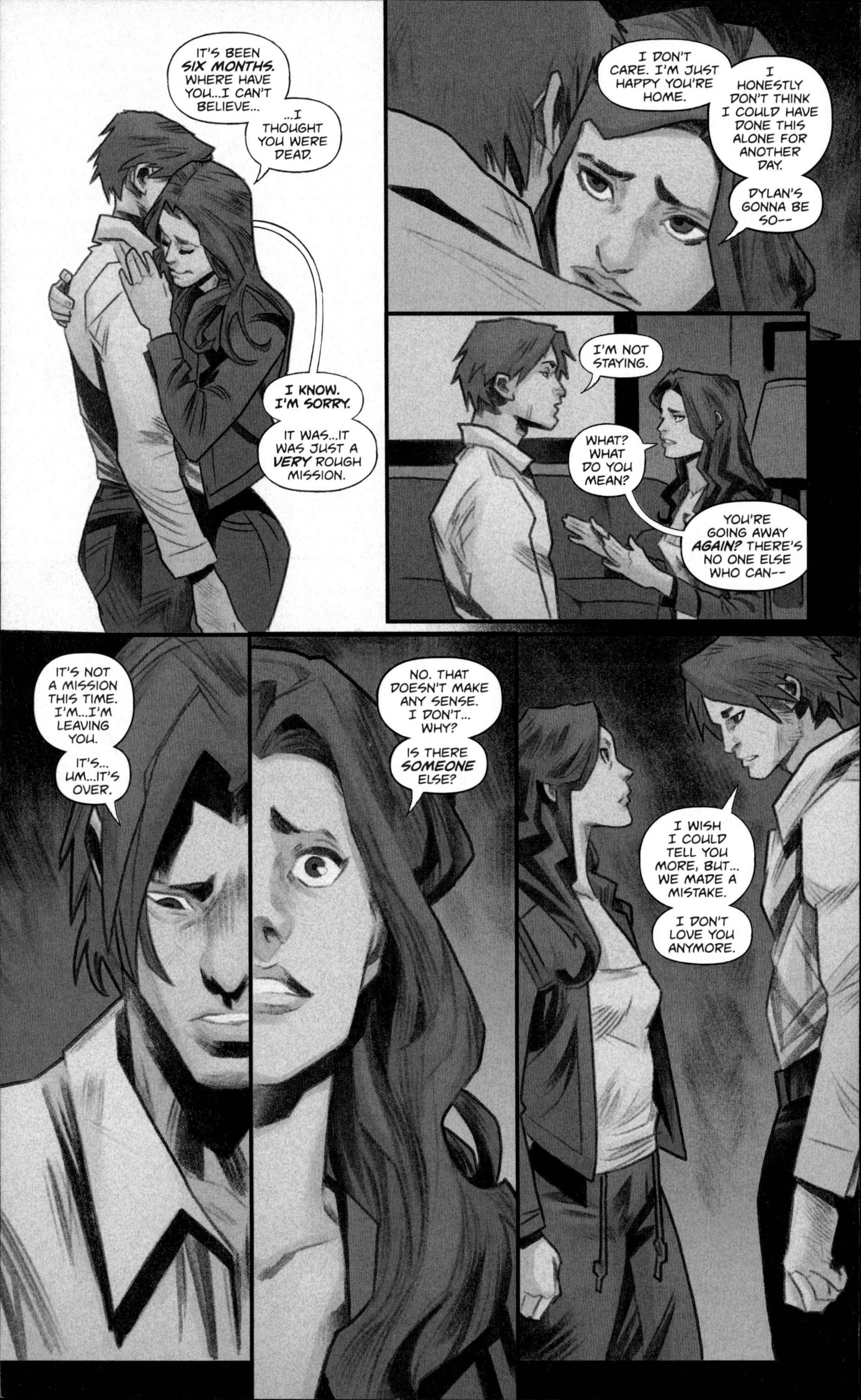
IT'S BEEN SIX MONTHS. WHERE HAVE YOU...I CAN'T BELIEVE...
...I THOUGHT YOU WERE DEAD.
I KNOW. I'M SORRY.
IT WAS...IT WAS JUST A VERY ROUGH MISSION.
I DON'T CARE. I'M JUST HAPPY YOU'RE HOME.
I HONESTLY DON'T THINK I COULD HAVE DONE THIS ALONE FOR ANOTHER DAY.
DYLAN'S GONNA BE SO--
I'M NOT STAYING.
WHAT? WHAT DO YOU MEAN?
YOU'RE GOING AWAY AGAIN? THERE'S NO ONE ELSE WHO CAN--
IT'S NOT A MISSION THIS TIME. I'M...I'M LEAVING YOU.
IT'S... UM...IT'S OVER.
NO. THAT DOESN'T MAKE ANY SENSE. I DON'T... WHY?
IS THERE SOMEONE ELSE?
I WISH I COULD TELL YOU MORE, BUT... WE MADE A MISTAKE.
I DON'T LOVE YOU ANYMORE.

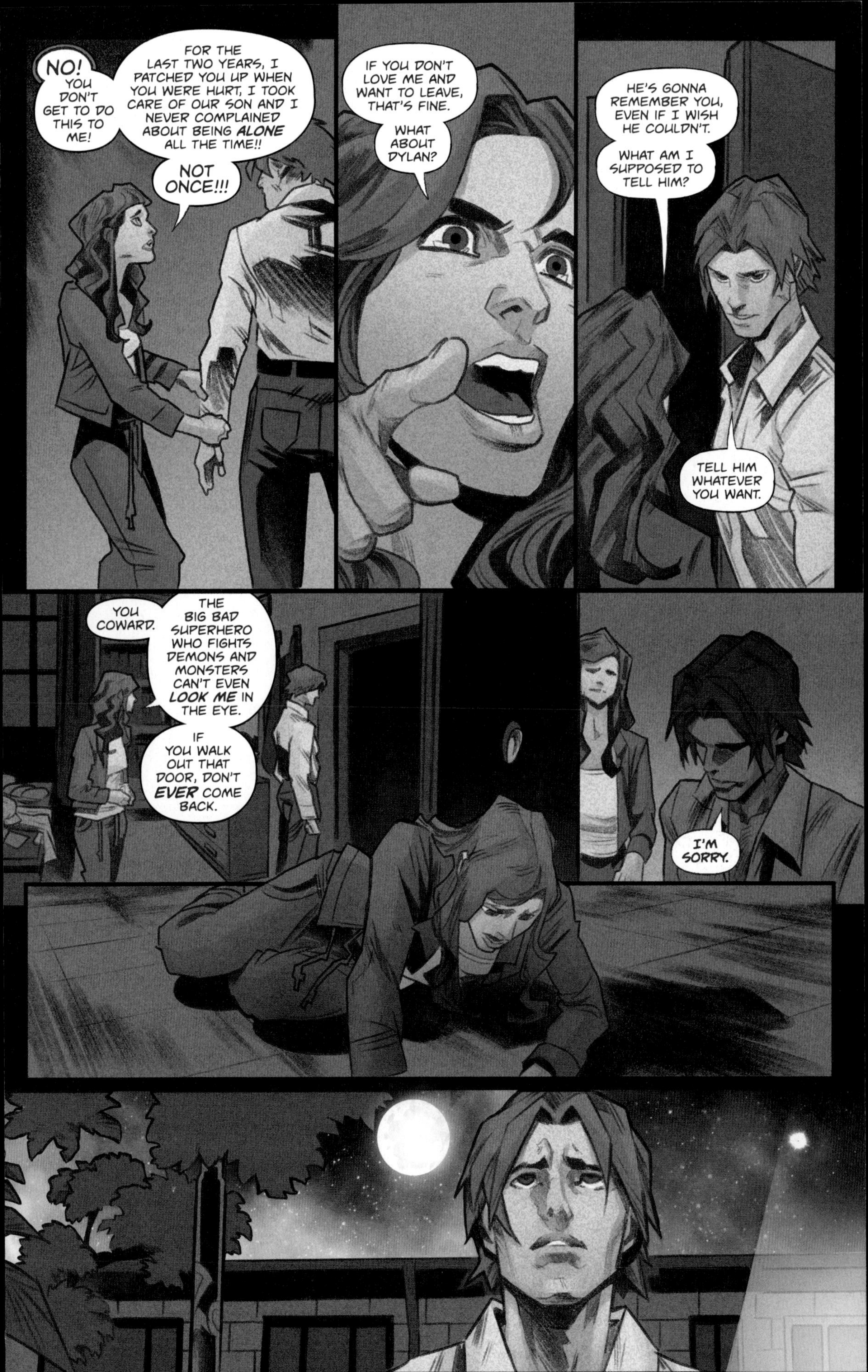
NO! YOU DON'T GET TO DO THIS TO ME!
FOR THE LAST TWO YEARS, I PATCHED YOU UP WHEN YOU WERE HURT, I TOOK CARE OF OUR SON AND I NEVER COMPLAINED ABOUT BEING ALONE ALL THE TIME!!
NOT ONCE!!!
IF YOU DON'T LOVE ME AND WANT TO LEAVE, THAT'S FINE.
WHAT ABOUT DYLAN?
HE'S GONNA REMEMBER YOU, EVEN IF I WISH HE COULDN'T.
WHAT AM I SUPPOSED TO TELL HIM?
TELL HIM WHATEVER YOU WANT.
YOU COWARD.
THE BIG BAD SUPERHERO WHO FIGHTS DEMONS AND MONSTERS CAN'T EVEN LOOK ME IN THE EYE.
IF YOU WALK OUT THAT DOOR, DON'T EVER COME BACK.
I'M SORRY.

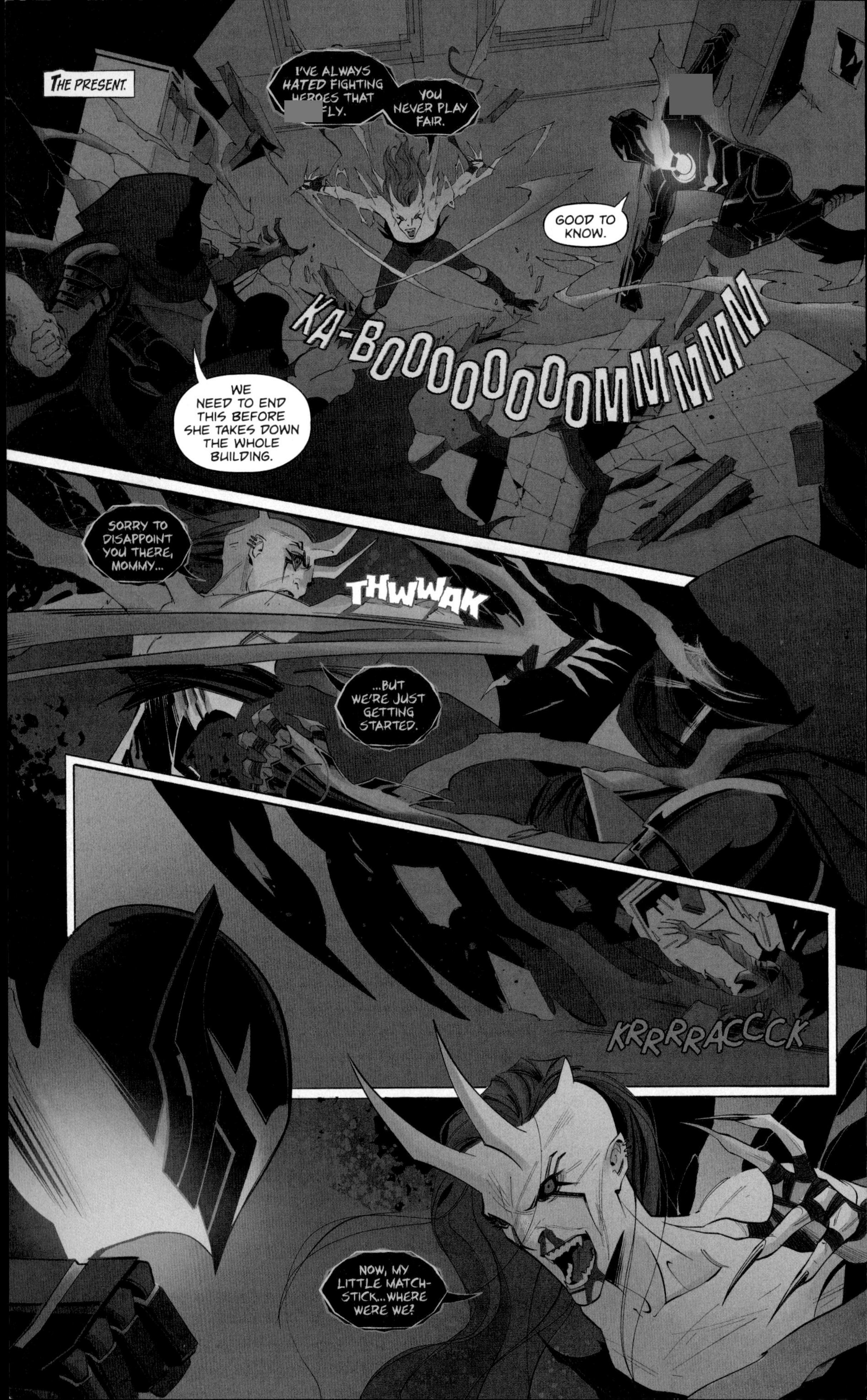
THE PRESENT.
I'VE ALWAYS HATED FIGHTING HEROES THAT [redacted] FLY.
YOU NEVER PLAY FAIR.
GOOD TO KNOW.
KA-BOOOOOOOOMMMMMM
WE NEED TO END THIS BEFORE SHE TAKES DOWN THE WHOLE BUILDING.
SORRY TO DISAPPOINT YOU THERE, MOMMY...
THWWAK
...BUT WE'RE JUST GETTING STARTED.
KRRRRACCCK
NOW, MY LITTLE MATCH-STICK...WHERE WERE WE?

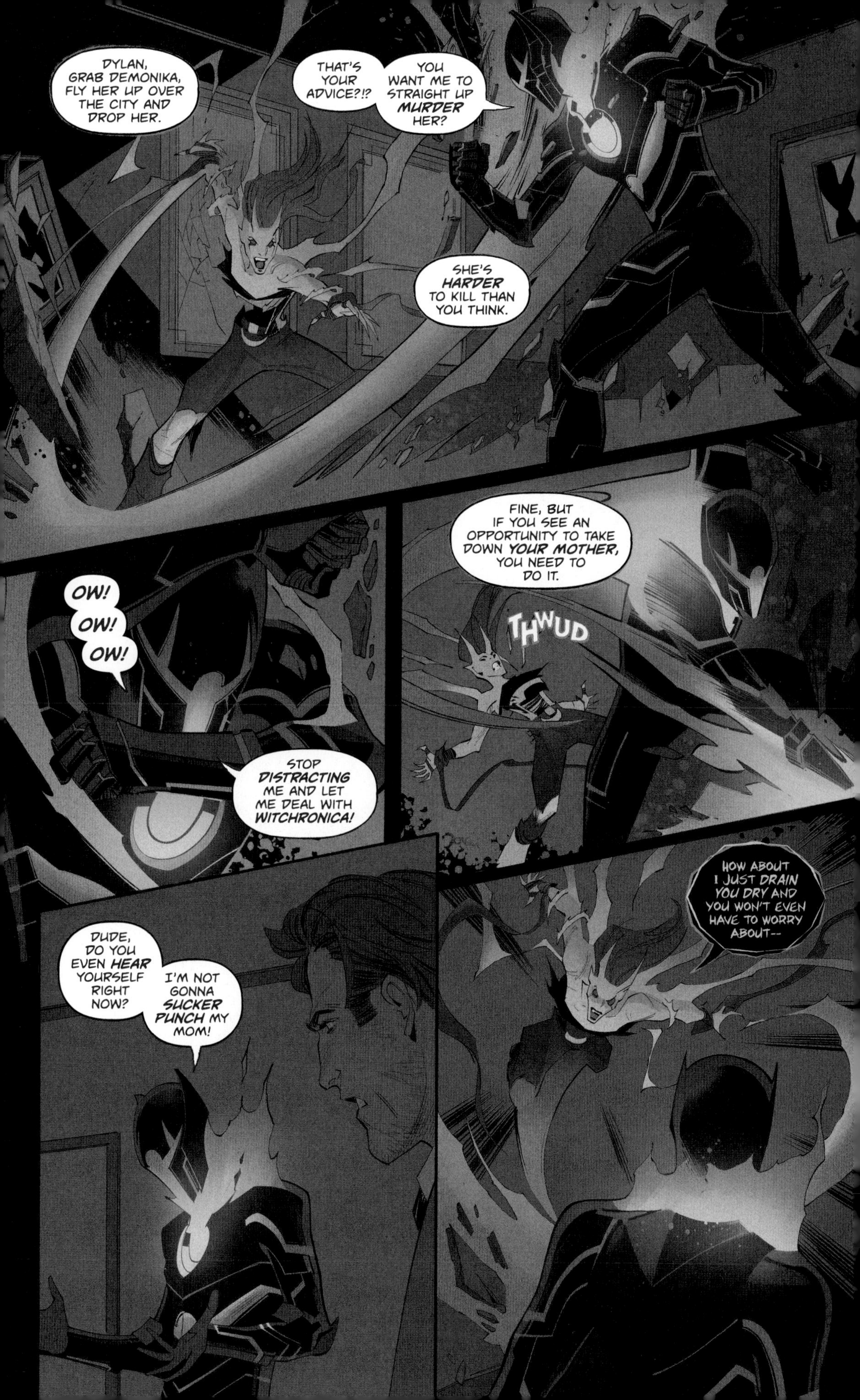
DYLAN, GRAB DEMONIKA, FLY HER UP OVER THE CITY AND DROP HER.
THAT'S YOUR ADVICE?!?
YOU WANT ME TO STRAIGHT UP MURDER HER?
SHE'S HARDER TO KILL THAN YOU THINK.
OW! OW! OW!
STOP DISTRACTING ME AND LET ME DEAL WITH WITCHRONICA!
FINE, BUT IF YOU SEE AN OPPORTUNITY TO TAKE DOWN YOUR MOTHER, YOU NEED TO DO IT.
THWUD
DUDE, DO YOU EVEN HEAR YOURSELF RIGHT NOW?
I'M NOT GONNA SUCKER PUNCH MY MOM!
HOW ABOUT I JUST DRAIN YOU DRY AND YOU WON'T EVEN HAVE TO WORRY ABOUT--

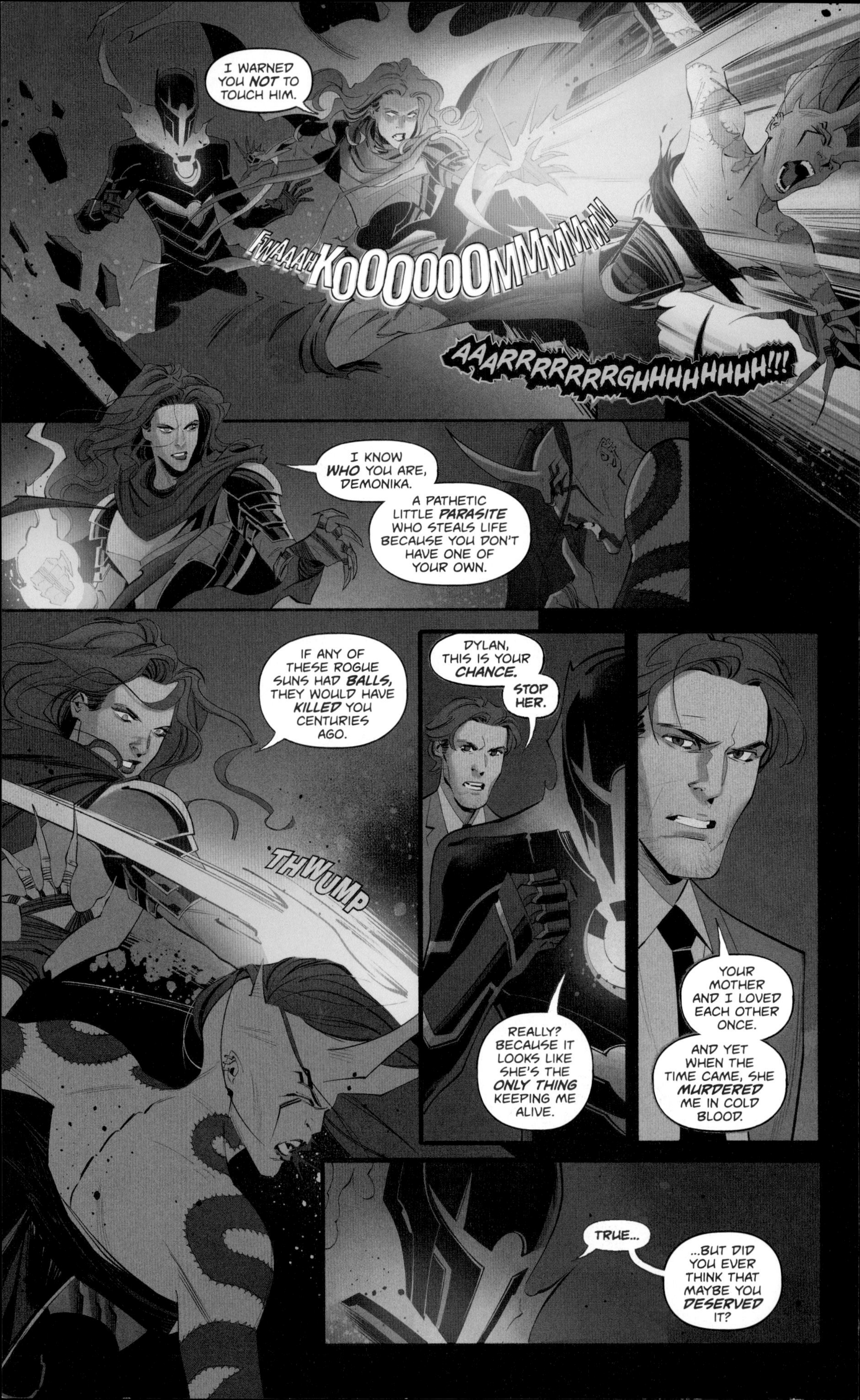
I WARNED YOU NOT TO TOUCH HIM.
FWAAAHKOOOOOOOMMMMMM
AAARRRRRRRGHHHHHHHH!!!
I KNOW WHO YOU ARE, DEMONIKA.
A PATHETIC LITTLE PARASITE WHO STEALS LIFE BECAUSE YOU DON'T HAVE ONE OF YOUR OWN.
IF ANY OF THESE ROGUE SUNS HAD BALLS, THEY WOULD HAVE KILLED YOU CENTURIES AGO.
THWUMP
DYLAN, THIS IS YOUR CHANCE.
STOP HER.
REALLY? BECAUSE IT LOOKS LIKE SHE'S THE ONLY THING KEEPING ME ALIVE.
YOUR MOTHER AND I LOVED EACH OTHER ONCE.
AND YET WHEN THE TIME CAME, SHE MURDERED ME IN COLD BLOOD.
TRUE...
...BUT DID YOU EVER THINK THAT MAYBE YOU DESERVED IT?

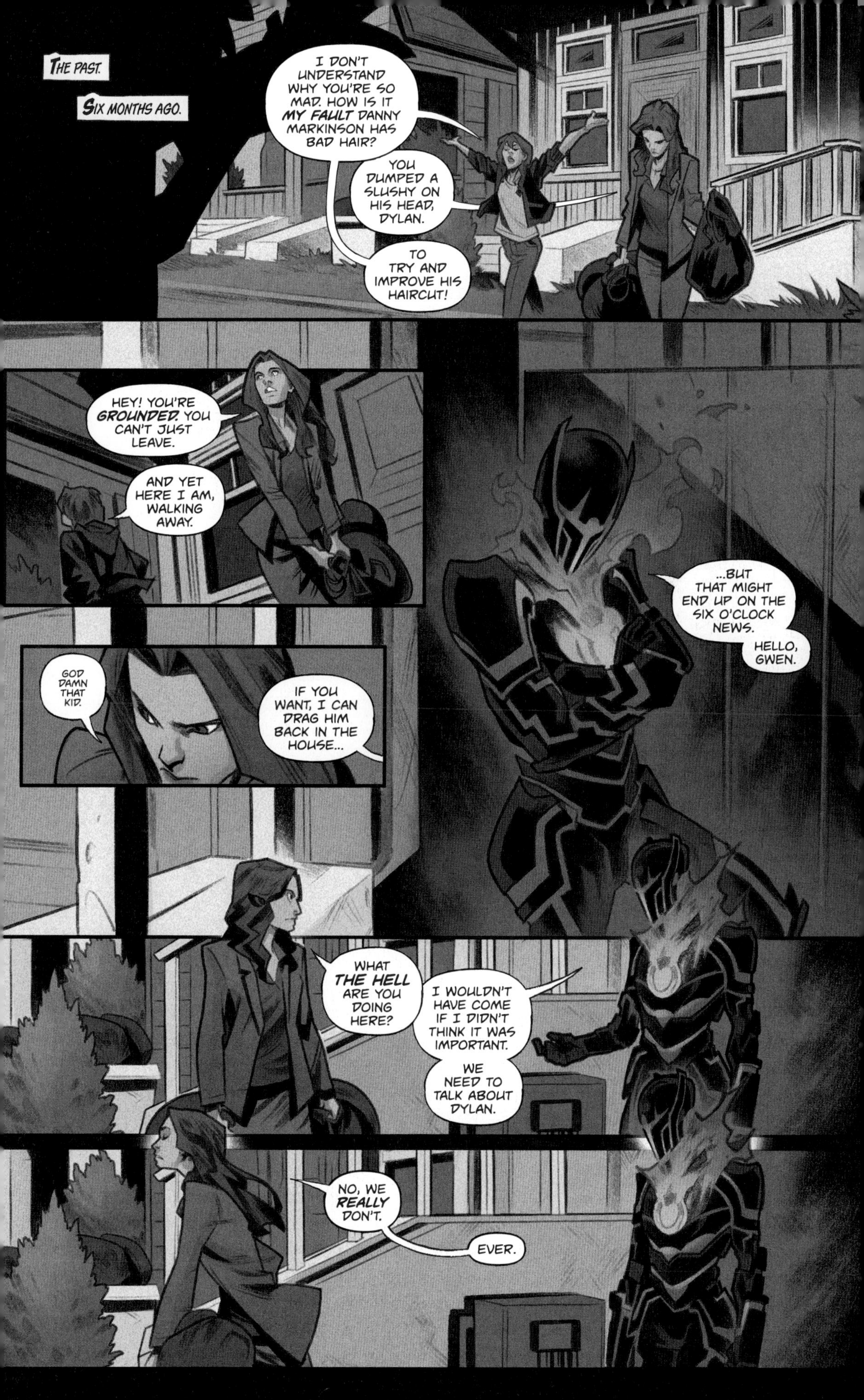
THE PAST.
SIX MONTHS AGO.
I DON'T UNDERSTAND WHY YOU'RE SO MAD. HOW IS IT MY FAULT DANNY MARKINSON HAS BAD HAIR?
YOU DUMPED A SLUSHY ON HIS HEAD, DYLAN.
TO TRY AND IMPROVE HIS HAIRCUT!
HEY! YOU'RE GROUNDED. YOU CAN'T JUST LEAVE.
AND YET HERE I AM, WALKING AWAY.
GOD DAMN THAT KID.
IF YOU WANT, I CAN DRAG HIM BACK IN THE HOUSE...
...BUT THAT MIGHT END UP ON THE SIX O'CLOCK NEWS.
HELLO, GWEN.
WHAT THE HELL ARE YOU DOING HERE?
I WOULDN'T HAVE COME IF I DIDN'T THINK IT WAS IMPORTANT.
WE NEED TO TALK ABOUT DYLAN.
NO, WE REALLY DON'T.
EVER.

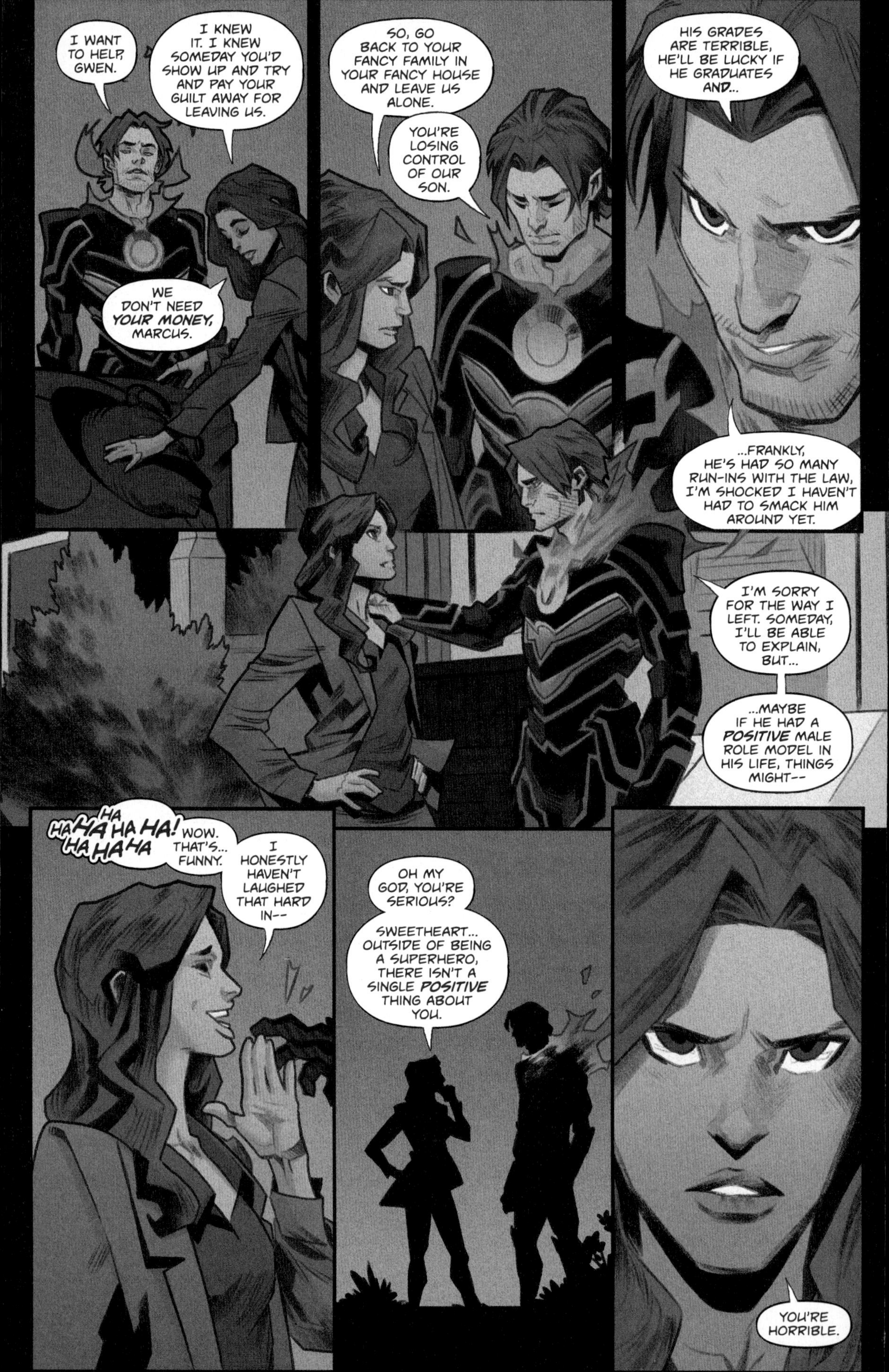
I WANT TO HELP, GWEN.
I KNEW IT. I KNEW SOMEDAY YOU'D SHOW UP AND TRY AND PAY YOUR GUILT AWAY FOR LEAVING US.
WE DON'T NEED YOUR MONEY, MARCUS.
SO, GO BACK TO YOUR FANCY FAMILY IN YOUR FANCY HOUSE AND LEAVE US ALONE.
YOU'RE LOSING CONTROL OF OUR SON.
HIS GRADES ARE TERRIBLE, HE'LL BE LUCKY IF HE GRADUATES AND...
...FRANKLY, HE'S HAD SO MANY RUN-INS WITH THE LAW, I'M SHOCKED I HAVEN'T HAD TO SMACK HIM AROUND YET.
I'M SORRY FOR THE WAY I LEFT. SOMEDAY, I'LL BE ABLE TO EXPLAIN, BUT...
...MAYBE IF HE HAD A POSITIVE MALE ROLE MODEL IN HIS LIFE, THINGS MIGHT--
HA HA HA HA HA! HA HA HA HA
WOW. THAT'S... FUNNY.
I HONESTLY HAVEN'T LAUGHED THAT HARD IN--
OH MY GOD, YOU'RE SERIOUS?
SWEETHEART... OUTSIDE OF BEING A SUPERHERO, THERE ISN'T A SINGLE POSITIVE THING ABOUT YOU.
YOU'RE HORRIBLE.

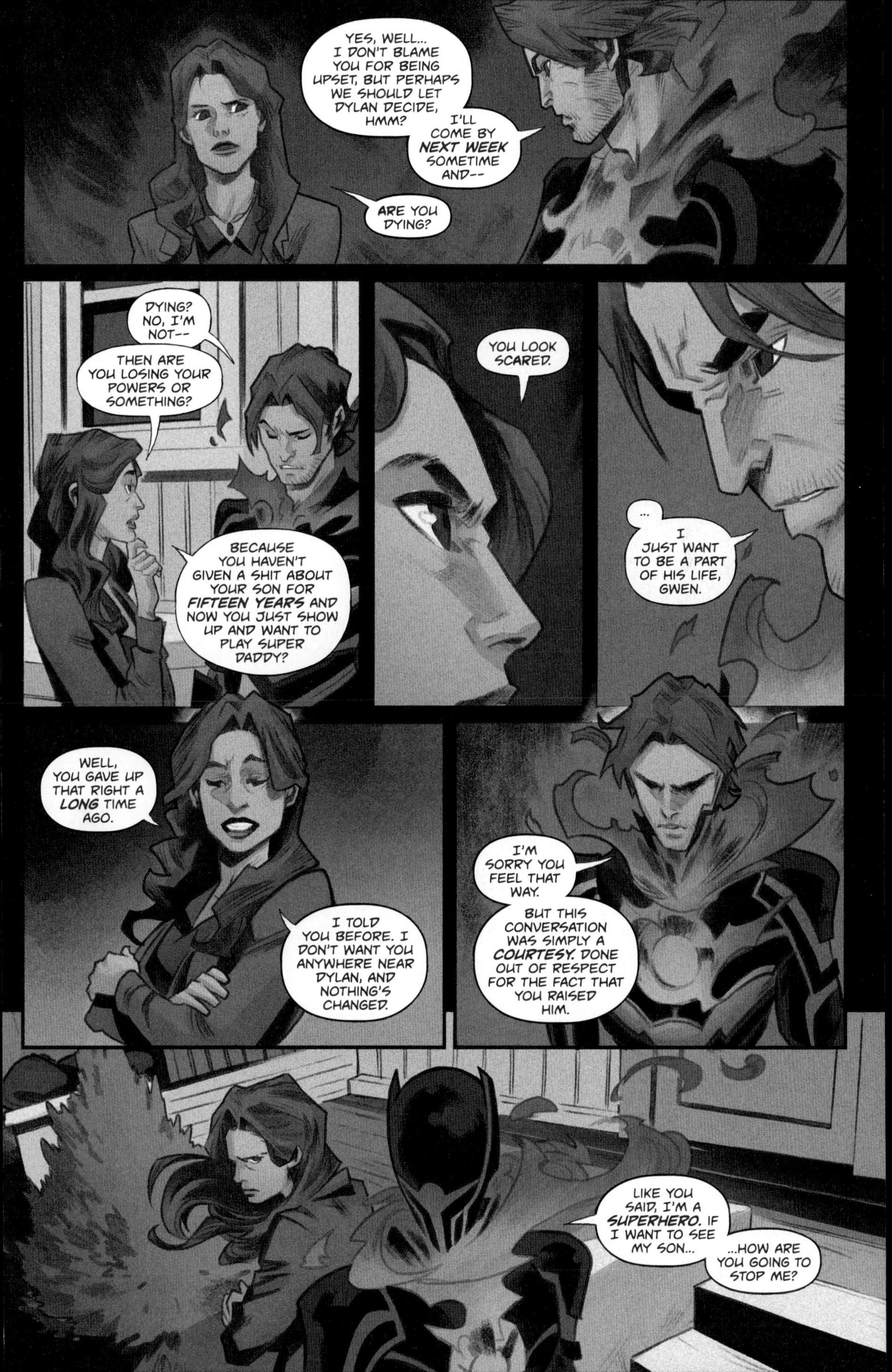
YES, WELL... I DON'T BLAME YOU FOR BEING UPSET, BUT PERHAPS WE SHOULD LET DYLAN DECIDE, HMM?
I'LL COME BY **NEXT WEEK** SOMETIME AND--
ARE YOU DYING?
DYING? NO, I'M NOT--
THEN ARE YOU LOSING YOUR POWERS OR SOMETHING?
BECAUSE YOU HAVEN'T GIVEN A SHIT ABOUT YOUR SON FOR **FIFTEEN YEARS** AND NOW YOU JUST SHOW UP AND WANT TO PLAY SUPER DADDY?
YOU LOOK **SCARED.**
...
I JUST WANT TO BE A PART OF HIS LIFE, GWEN.
WELL, YOU GAVE UP THAT RIGHT A **LONG** TIME AGO.
I TOLD YOU BEFORE. I DON'T WANT YOU ANYWHERE NEAR DYLAN, AND NOTHING'S CHANGED.
I'M SORRY YOU FEEL THAT WAY.
BUT THIS CONVERSATION WAS SIMPLY A **COURTESY.** DONE OUT OF RESPECT FOR THE FACT THAT YOU RAISED HIM.
LIKE YOU SAID, I'M A **SUPERHERO.** IF I WANT TO SEE MY SON...
...HOW ARE YOU GOING TO STOP ME?

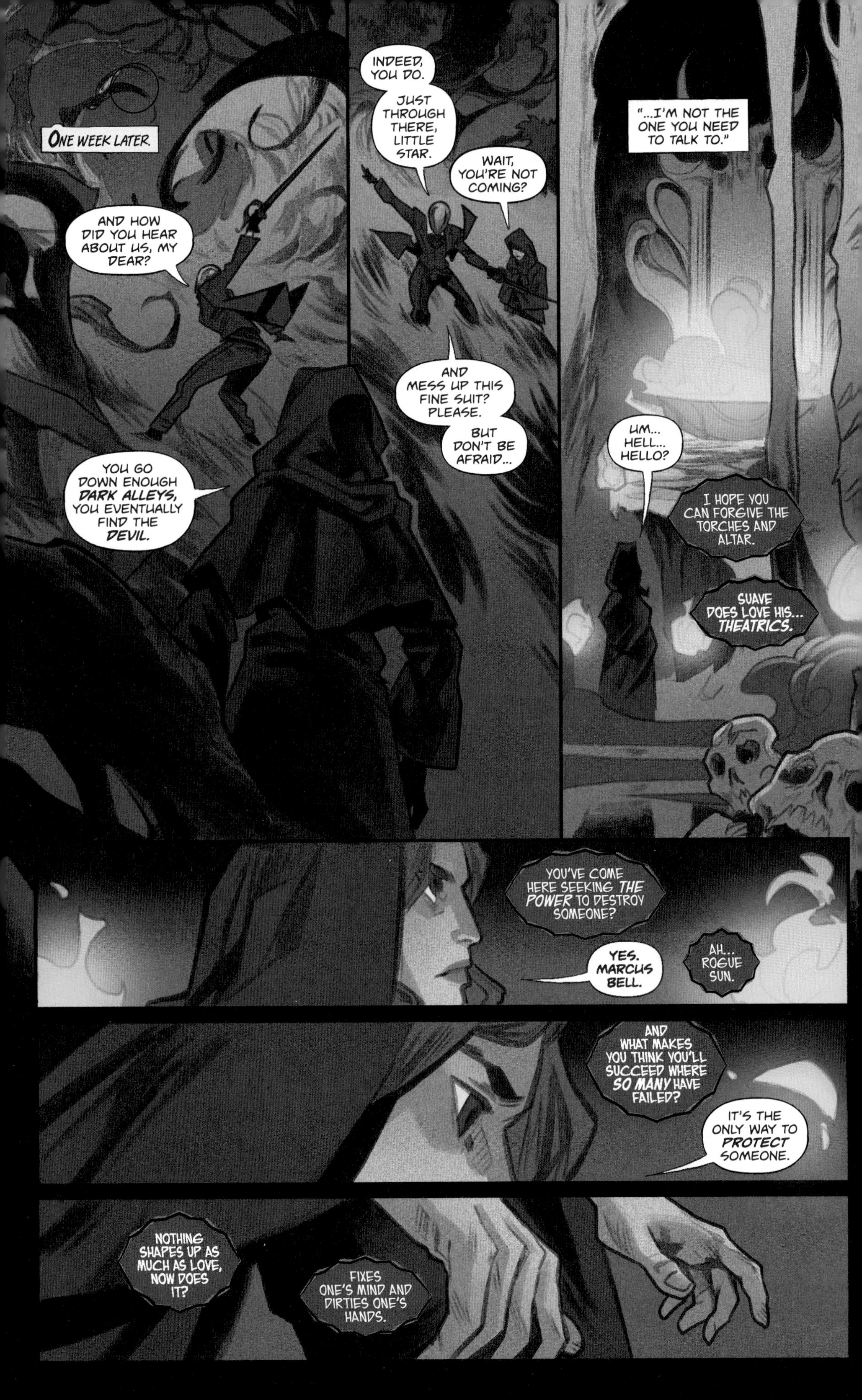
ONE WEEK LATER.
AND HOW DID YOU HEAR ABOUT US, MY DEAR?
YOU GO DOWN ENOUGH DARK ALLEYS, YOU EVENTUALLY FIND THE DEVIL.
INDEED, YOU DO.
JUST THROUGH THERE, LITTLE STAR.
WAIT, YOU'RE NOT COMING?
AND MESS UP THIS FINE SUIT? PLEASE.
BUT DON'T BE AFRAID...
"...I'M NOT THE ONE YOU NEED TO TALK TO."
UM... HELL... HELLO?
I HOPE YOU CAN FORGIVE THE TORCHES AND ALTAR.
SUAVE DOES LOVE HIS... THEATRICS.
YOU'VE COME HERE SEEKING THE POWER TO DESTROY SOMEONE?
YES. MARCUS BELL.
AH... ROGUE SUN.
AND WHAT MAKES YOU THINK YOU'LL SUCCEED WHERE SO MANY HAVE FAILED?
IT'S THE ONLY WAY TO PROTECT SOMEONE.
NOTHING SHAPES UP AS MUCH AS LOVE, NOW DOES IT?
FIXES ONE'S MIND AND DIRTIES ONE'S HANDS.

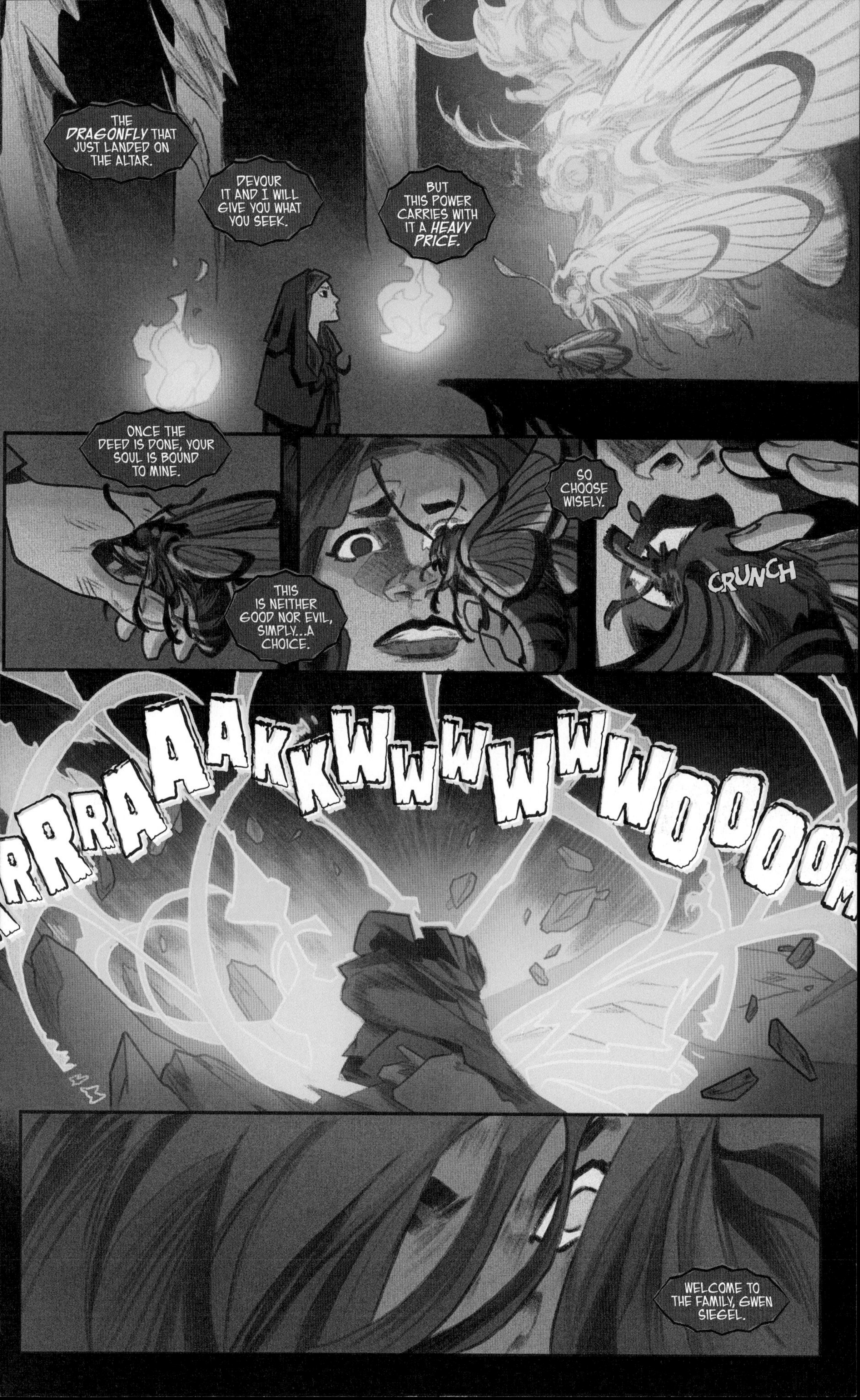
THE DRAGONFLY THAT JUST LANDED ON THE ALTAR.
DEVOUR IT AND I WILL GIVE YOU WHAT YOU SEEK.
BUT THIS POWER CARRIES WITH IT A HEAVY PRICE.
ONCE THE DEED IS DONE, YOUR SOUL IS BOUND TO MINE.
THIS IS NEITHER GOOD NOR EVIL, SIMPLY...A CHOICE.
SO CHOOSE WISELY.
CRUNCH
RRRRAAAKKWWWWWWOOOOM
WELCOME TO THE FAMILY, GWEN SIEGEL.

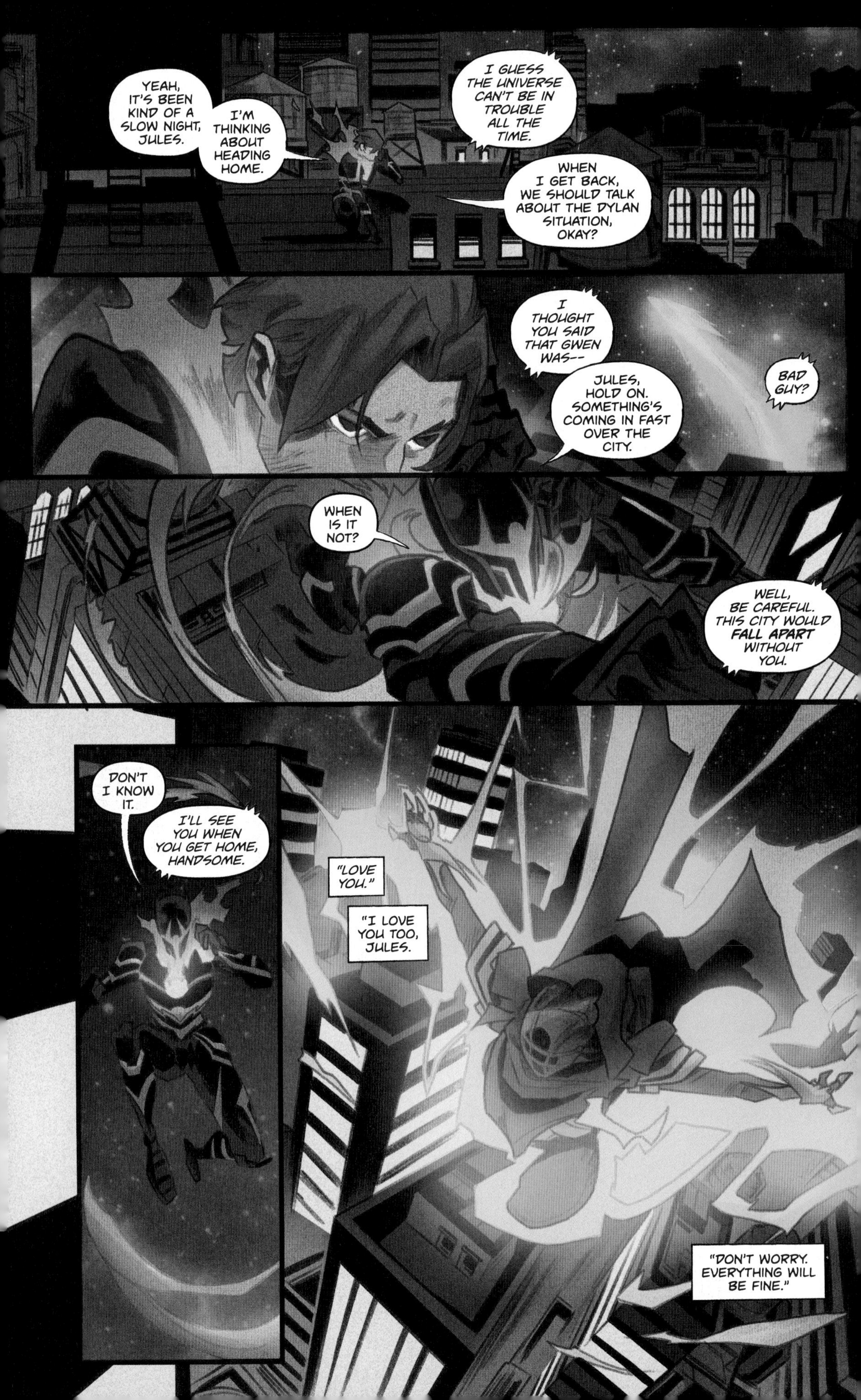
YEAH, IT'S BEEN KIND OF A SLOW NIGHT, JULES.
I'M THINKING ABOUT HEADING HOME.
I GUESS THE UNIVERSE CAN'T BE IN TROUBLE ALL THE TIME.
WHEN I GET BACK, WE SHOULD TALK ABOUT THE DYLAN SITUATION, OKAY?
I THOUGHT YOU SAID THAT GWEN WAS--
JULES, HOLD ON. SOMETHING'S COMING IN FAST OVER THE CITY.
BAD GUY?
WHEN IS IT NOT?
WELL, BE CAREFUL. THIS CITY WOULD FALL APART WITHOUT YOU.
DON'T I KNOW IT.
I'LL SEE YOU WHEN YOU GET HOME, HANDSOME.
"LOVE YOU."
"I LOVE YOU TOO, JULES.
"DON'T WORRY. EVERYTHING WILL BE FINE."

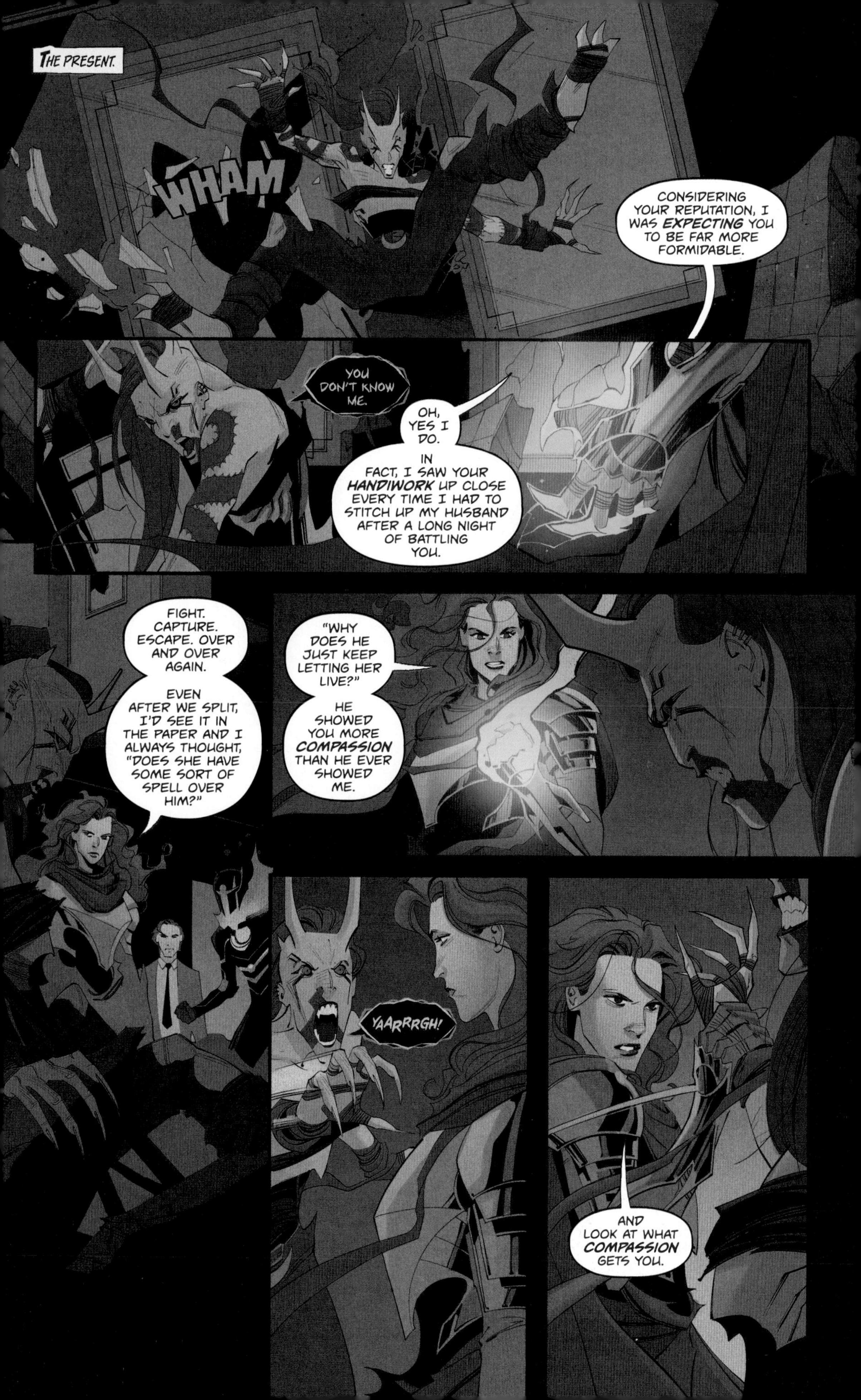
THE PRESENT.
WHAM
CONSIDERING YOUR REPUTATION, I WAS EXPECTING YOU TO BE FAR MORE FORMIDABLE.
YOU DON'T KNOW ME.
OH, YES I DO.
IN FACT, I SAW YOUR HANDIWORK UP CLOSE EVERY TIME I HAD TO STITCH UP MY HUSBAND AFTER A LONG NIGHT OF BATTLING YOU.
FIGHT. CAPTURE. ESCAPE. OVER AND OVER AGAIN.
EVEN AFTER WE SPLIT, I'D SEE IT IN THE PAPER AND I ALWAYS THOUGHT, "DOES SHE HAVE SOME SORT OF SPELL OVER HIM?"
"WHY DOES HE JUST KEEP LETTING HER LIVE?"
HE SHOWED YOU MORE COMPASSION THAN HE EVER SHOWED ME.
YAARRRGH!
AND LOOK AT WHAT COMPASSION GETS YOU.

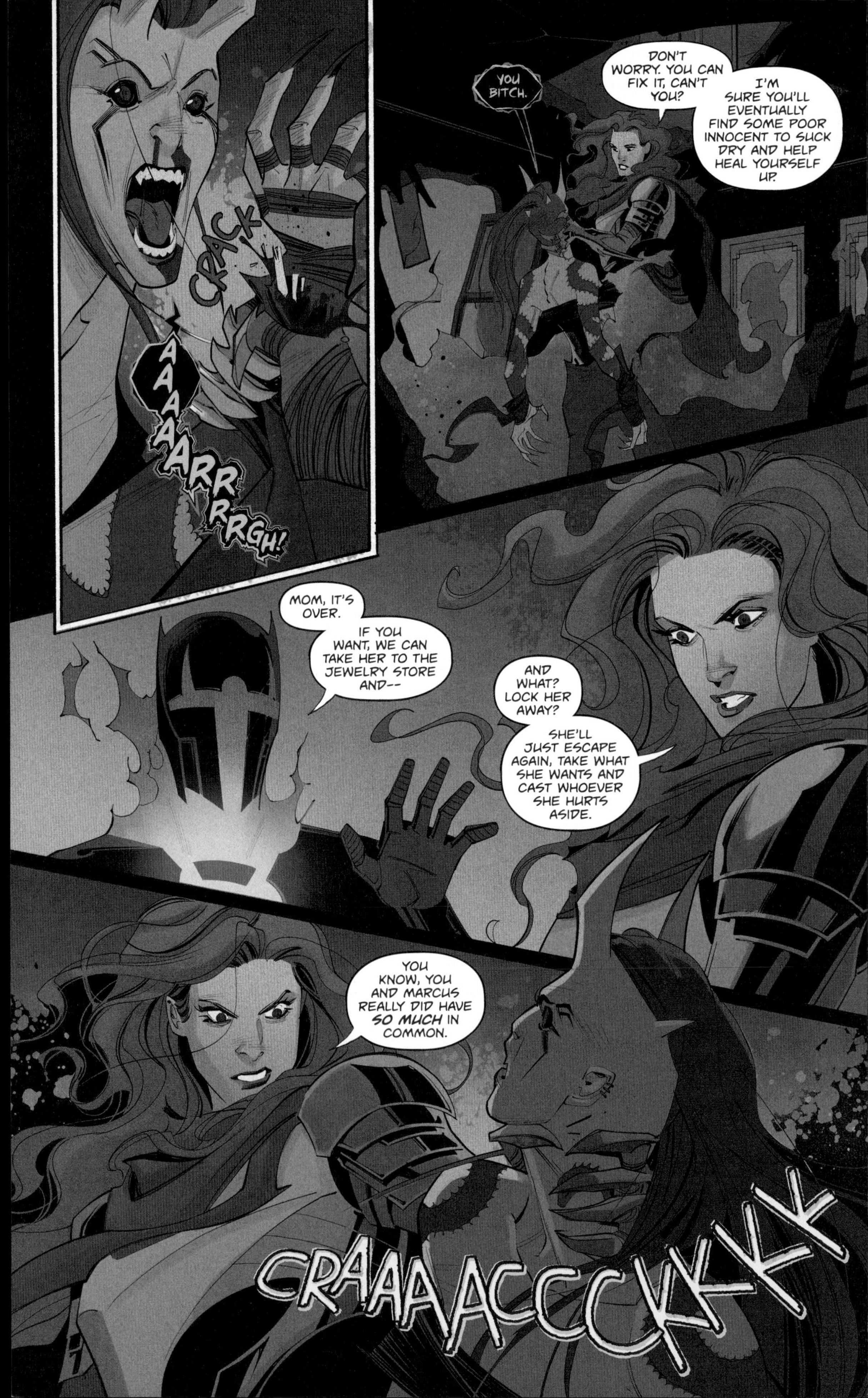
CRACK
AAAAAARRRRRGH!
YOU BITCH.
DON'T WORRY. YOU CAN FIX IT, CAN'T YOU?
I'M SURE YOU'LL EVENTUALLY FIND SOME POOR INNOCENT TO SUCK DRY AND HELP HEAL YOURSELF UP.
MOM, IT'S OVER.
IF YOU WANT, WE CAN TAKE HER TO THE JEWELRY STORE AND--
AND WHAT? LOCK HER AWAY?
SHE'LL JUST ESCAPE AGAIN, TAKE WHAT SHE WANTS AND CAST WHOEVER SHE HURTS ASIDE.
YOU KNOW, YOU AND MARCUS REALLY DID HAVE *SO MUCH* IN COMMON.
CRAAAACCCKKKK

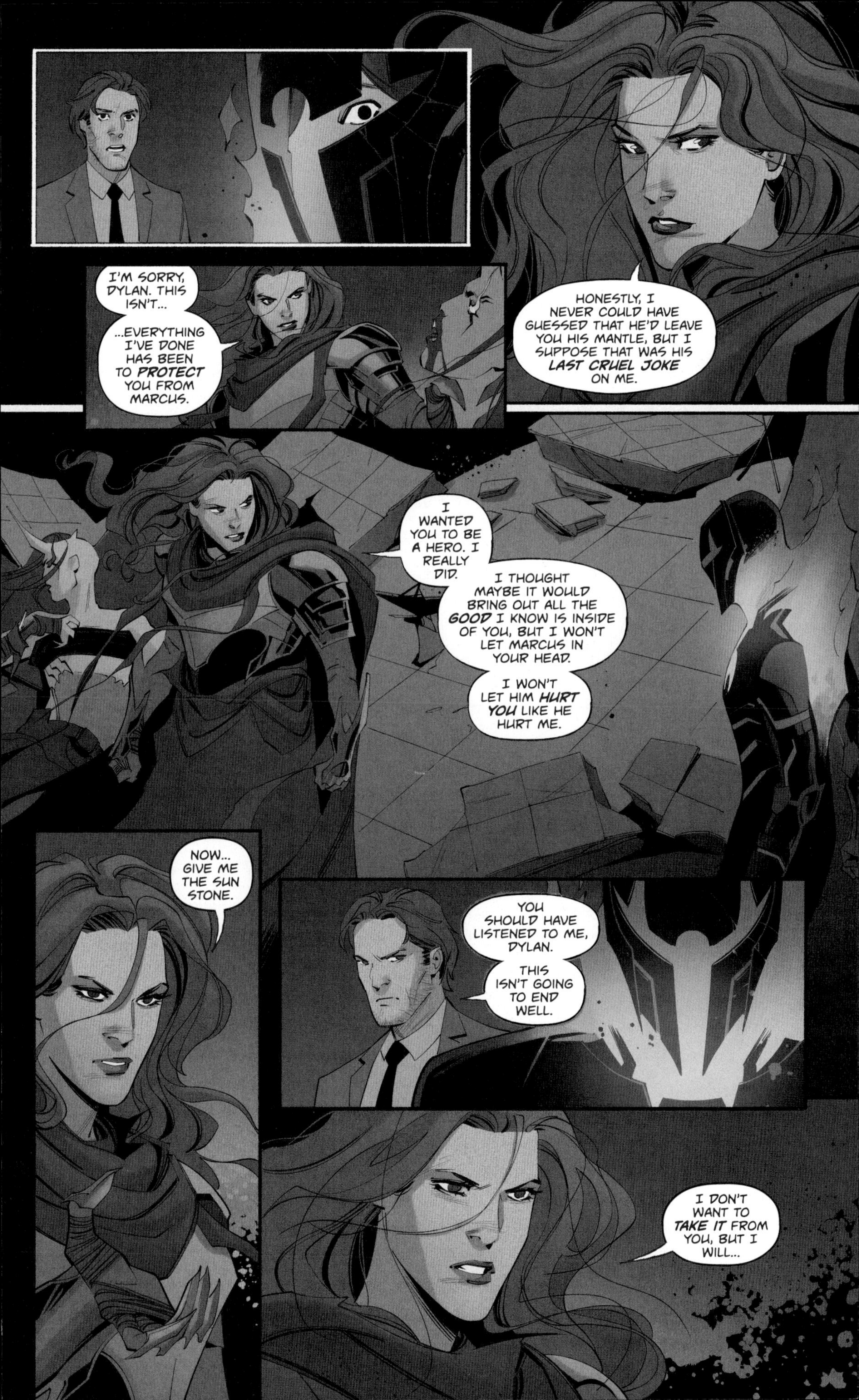
I'M SORRY, DYLAN. THIS ISN'T...
...EVERYTHING I'VE DONE HAS BEEN TO PROTECT YOU FROM MARCUS.
HONESTLY, I NEVER COULD HAVE GUESSED THAT HE'D LEAVE YOU HIS MANTLE, BUT I SUPPOSE THAT WAS HIS LAST CRUEL JOKE ON ME.
I WANTED YOU TO BE A HERO. I REALLY DID.
I THOUGHT MAYBE IT WOULD BRING OUT ALL THE GOOD I KNOW IS INSIDE OF YOU, BUT I WON'T LET MARCUS IN YOUR HEAD.
I WON'T LET HIM HURT YOU LIKE HE HURT ME.
NOW... GIVE ME THE SUN STONE.
YOU SHOULD HAVE LISTENED TO ME, DYLAN.
THIS ISN'T GOING TO END WELL.
I DON'T WANT TO TAKE IT FROM YOU, BUT I WILL...

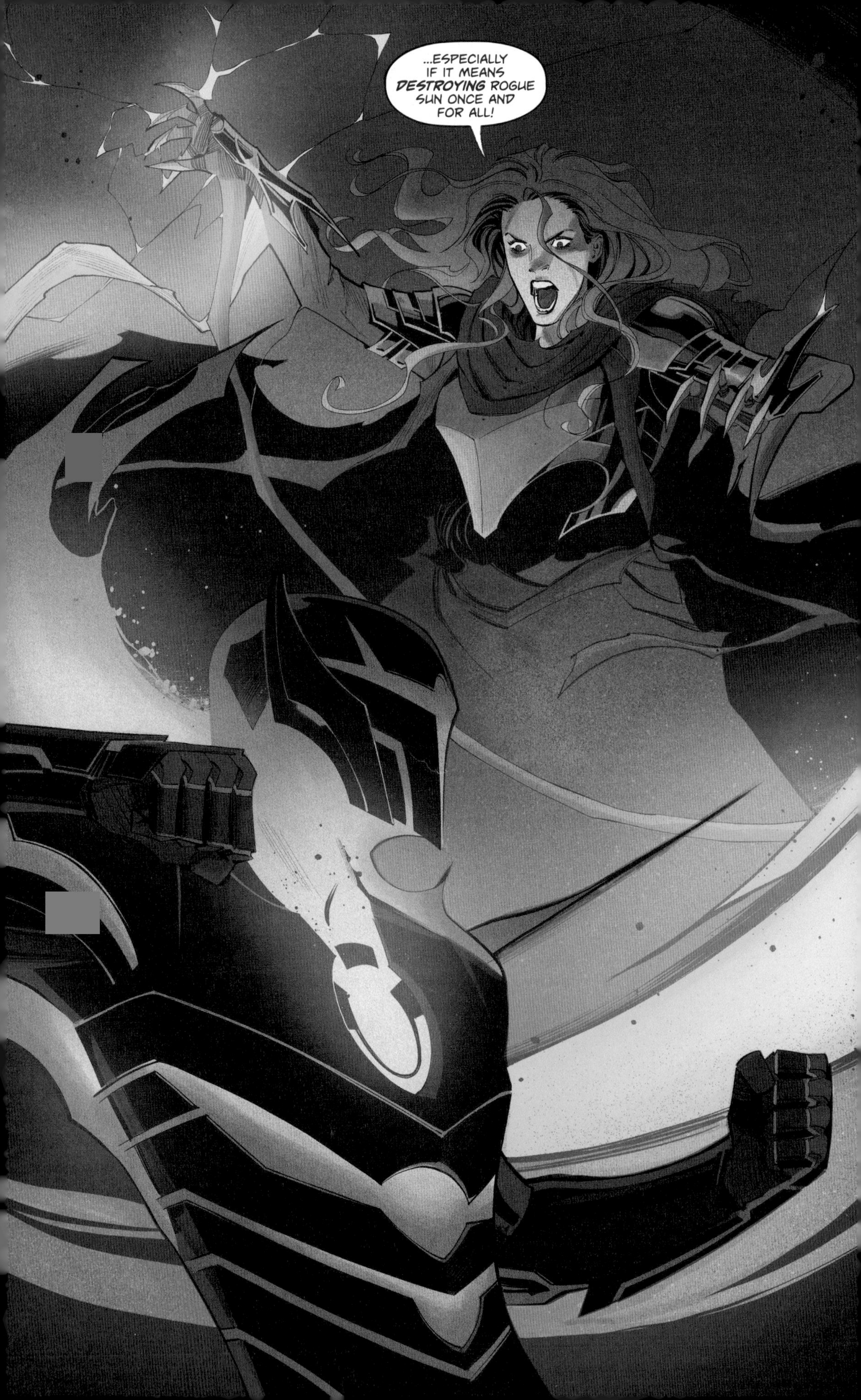
...ESPECIALLY IF IT MEANS DESTROYING ROGUE SUN ONCE AND FOR ALL!

Chapter Six
Family Matters

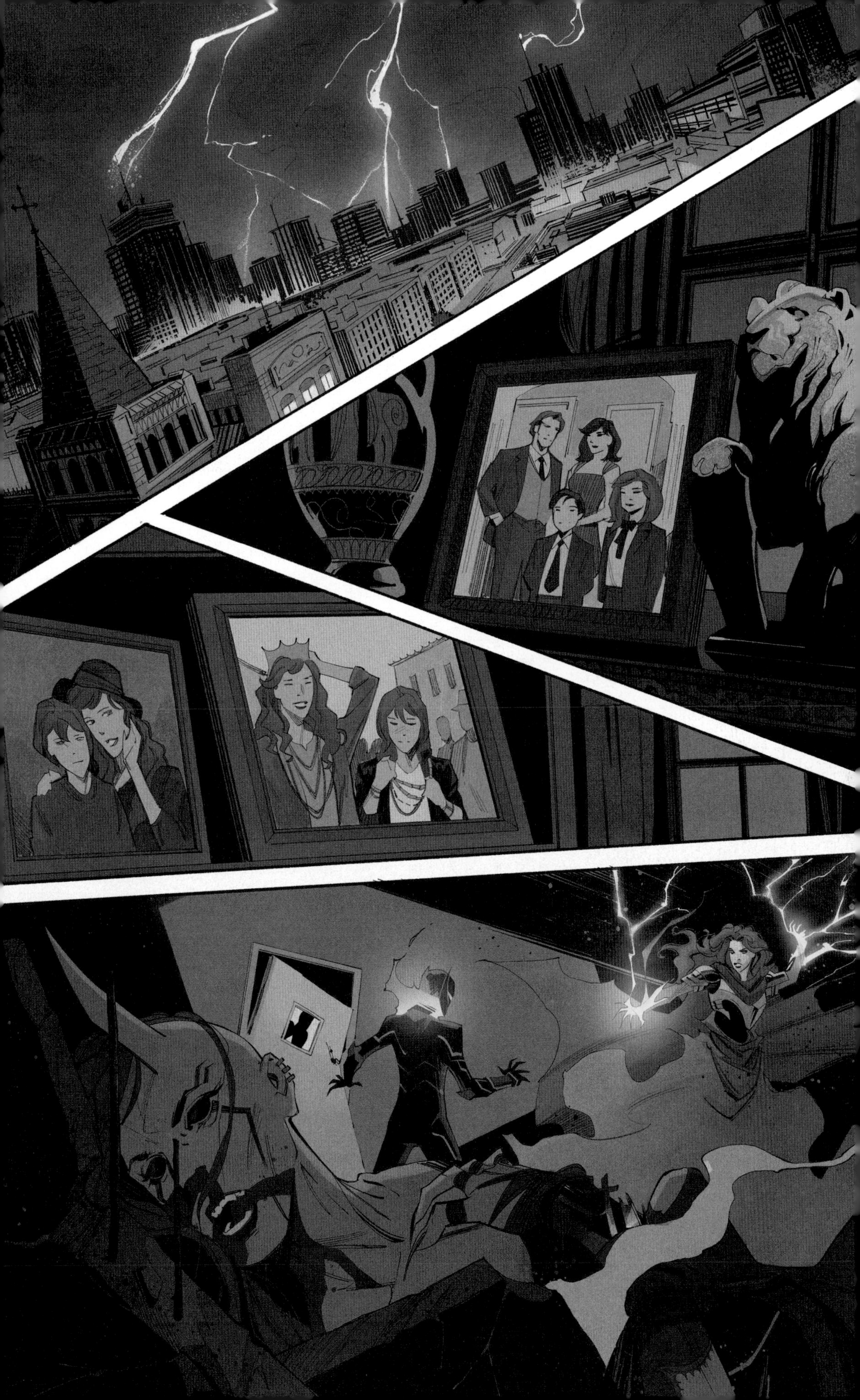

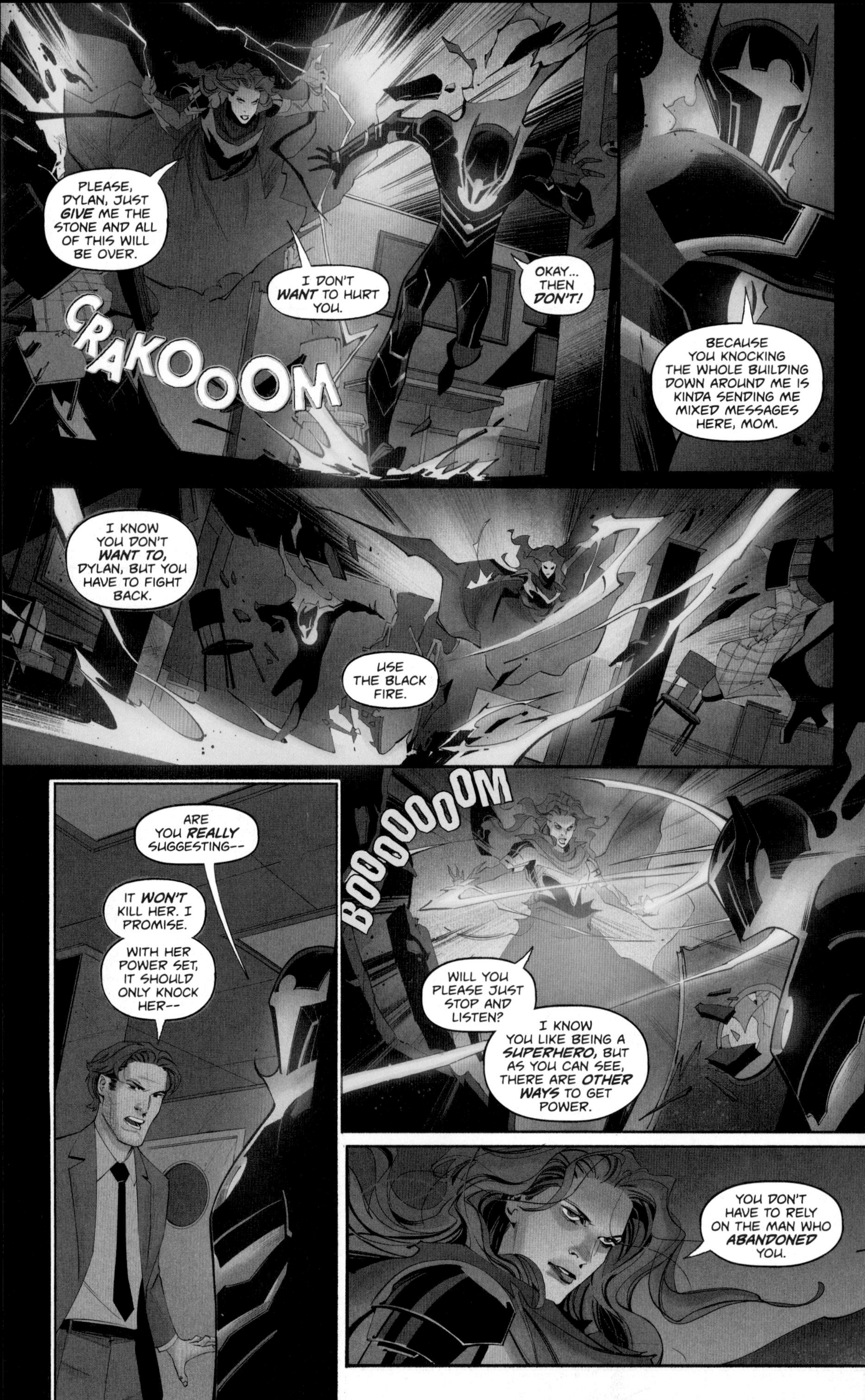
PLEASE, DYLAN, JUST GIVE ME THE STONE AND ALL OF THIS WILL BE OVER.
I DON'T WANT TO HURT YOU.
OKAY... THEN DON'T!
CRAKOOOM
BECAUSE YOU KNOCKING THE WHOLE BUILDING DOWN AROUND ME IS KINDA SENDING ME MIXED MESSAGES HERE, MOM.
I KNOW YOU DON'T WANT TO, DYLAN, BUT YOU HAVE TO FIGHT BACK.
USE THE BLACK FIRE.
ARE YOU REALLY SUGGESTING--
IT WON'T KILL HER. I PROMISE.
WITH HER POWER SET, IT SHOULD ONLY KNOCK HER--
BOOOOOOOOM
WILL YOU PLEASE JUST STOP AND LISTEN?
I KNOW YOU LIKE BEING A SUPERHERO, BUT AS YOU CAN SEE, THERE ARE OTHER WAYS TO GET POWER.
YOU DON'T HAVE TO RELY ON THE MAN WHO ABANDONED YOU.

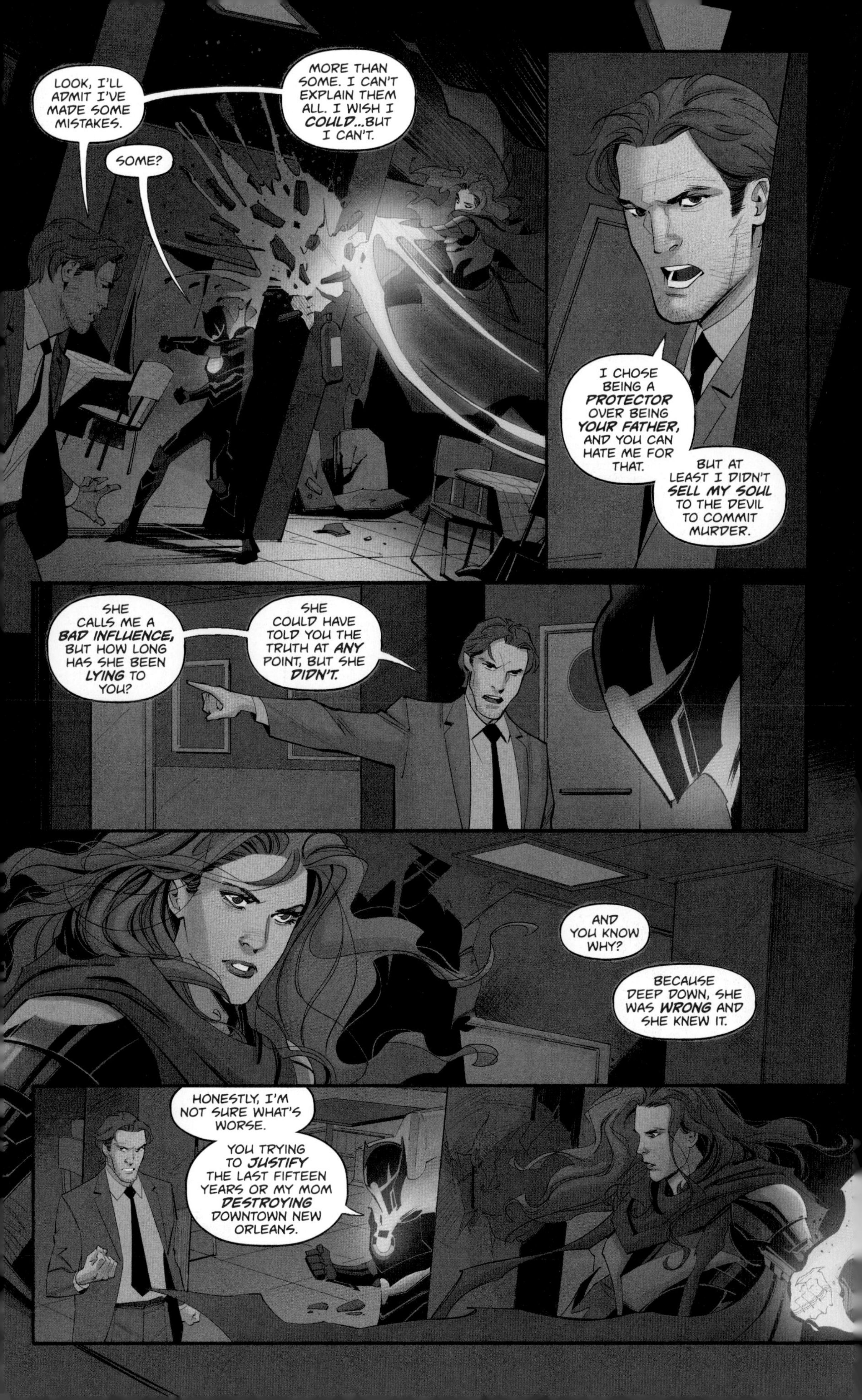
LOOK, I'LL ADMIT I'VE MADE SOME MISTAKES.
SOME?
MORE THAN SOME. I CAN'T EXPLAIN THEM ALL. I WISH I COULD...BUT I CAN'T.
I CHOSE BEING A PROTECTOR OVER BEING YOUR FATHER, AND YOU CAN HATE ME FOR THAT.
BUT AT LEAST I DIDN'T SELL MY SOUL TO THE DEVIL TO COMMIT MURDER.
SHE CALLS ME A BAD INFLUENCE, BUT HOW LONG HAS SHE BEEN LYING TO YOU?
SHE COULD HAVE TOLD YOU THE TRUTH AT ANY POINT, BUT SHE DIDN'T.
AND YOU KNOW WHY?
BECAUSE DEEP DOWN, SHE WAS WRONG AND SHE KNEW IT.
HONESTLY, I'M NOT SURE WHAT'S WORSE.
YOU TRYING TO JUSTIFY THE LAST FIFTEEN YEARS OR MY MOM DESTROYING DOWNTOWN NEW ORLEANS.

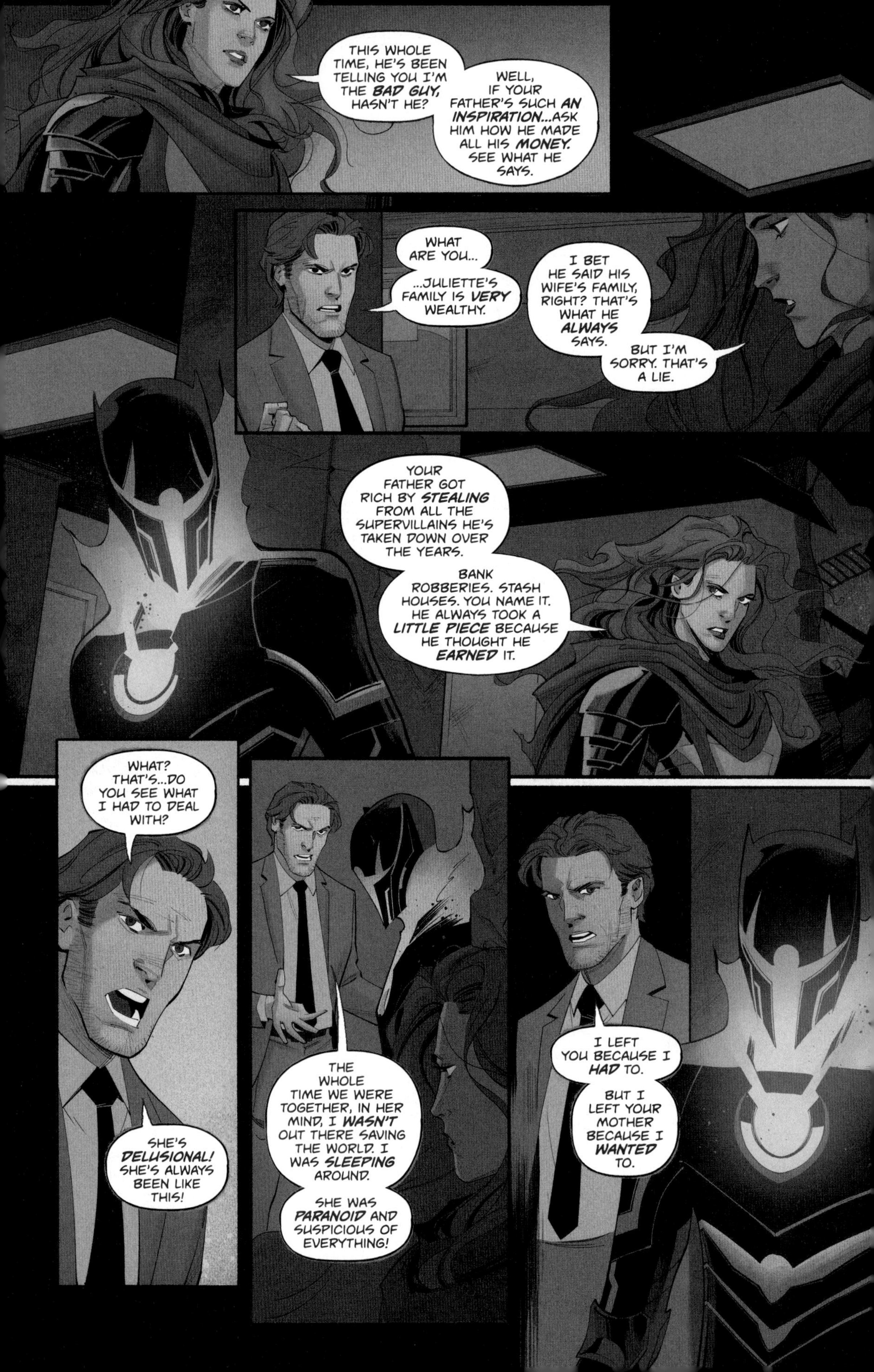
THIS WHOLE TIME, HE'S BEEN TELLING YOU I'M THE BAD GUY, HASN'T HE?
WELL, IF YOUR FATHER'S SUCH AN INSPIRATION...ASK HIM HOW HE MADE ALL HIS MONEY. SEE WHAT HE SAYS.
WHAT ARE YOU...
...JULIETTE'S FAMILY IS VERY WEALTHY.
I BET HE SAID HIS WIFE'S FAMILY, RIGHT? THAT'S WHAT HE ALWAYS SAYS.
BUT I'M SORRY. THAT'S A LIE.
YOUR FATHER GOT RICH BY STEALING FROM ALL THE SUPERVILLAINS HE'S TAKEN DOWN OVER THE YEARS.
BANK ROBBERIES. STASH HOUSES. YOU NAME IT. HE ALWAYS TOOK A LITTLE PIECE BECAUSE HE THOUGHT HE EARNED IT.
WHAT? THAT'S...DO YOU SEE WHAT I HAD TO DEAL WITH?
SHE'S DELUSIONAL! SHE'S ALWAYS BEEN LIKE THIS!
THE WHOLE TIME WE WERE TOGETHER, IN HER MIND, I WASN'T OUT THERE SAVING THE WORLD. I WAS SLEEPING AROUND.
SHE WAS PARANOID AND SUSPICIOUS OF EVERYTHING!
I LEFT YOU BECAUSE I HAD TO.
BUT I LEFT YOUR MOTHER BECAUSE I WANTED TO.

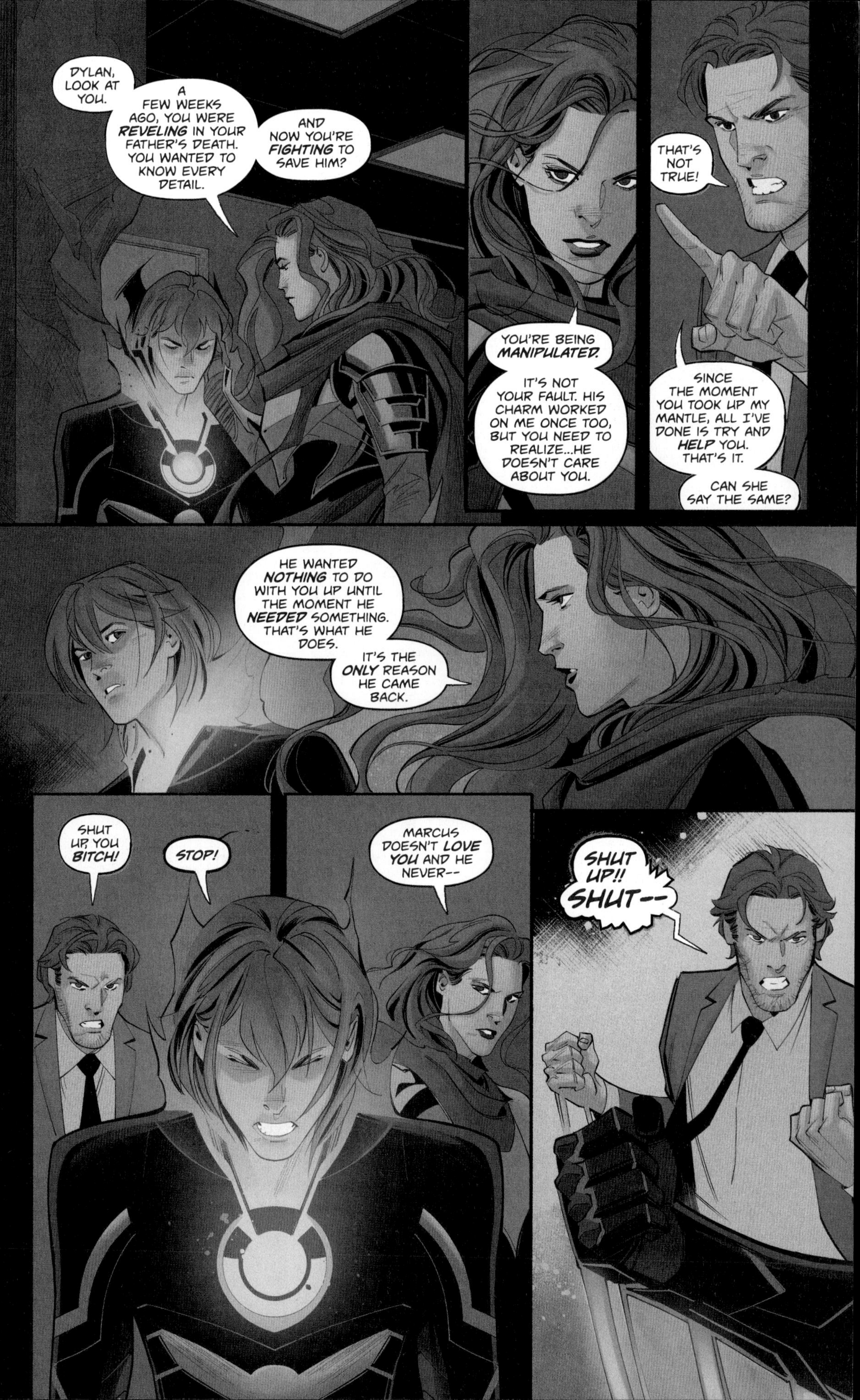
DYLAN, LOOK AT YOU.
A FEW WEEKS AGO, YOU WERE REVELING IN YOUR FATHER'S DEATH. YOU WANTED TO KNOW EVERY DETAIL.
AND NOW YOU'RE FIGHTING TO SAVE HIM?
YOU'RE BEING MANIPULATED.
IT'S NOT YOUR FAULT. HIS CHARM WORKED ON ME ONCE TOO, BUT YOU NEED TO REALIZE...HE DOESN'T CARE ABOUT YOU.
THAT'S NOT TRUE!
SINCE THE MOMENT YOU TOOK UP MY MANTLE, ALL I'VE DONE IS TRY AND HELP YOU. THAT'S IT.
CAN SHE SAY THE SAME?
HE WANTED NOTHING TO DO WITH YOU UP UNTIL THE MOMENT HE NEEDED SOMETHING. THAT'S WHAT HE DOES.
IT'S THE ONLY REASON HE CAME BACK.
SHUT UP, YOU BITCH!
STOP!
MARCUS DOESN'T LOVE YOU AND HE NEVER--
SHUT UP!! SHUT--

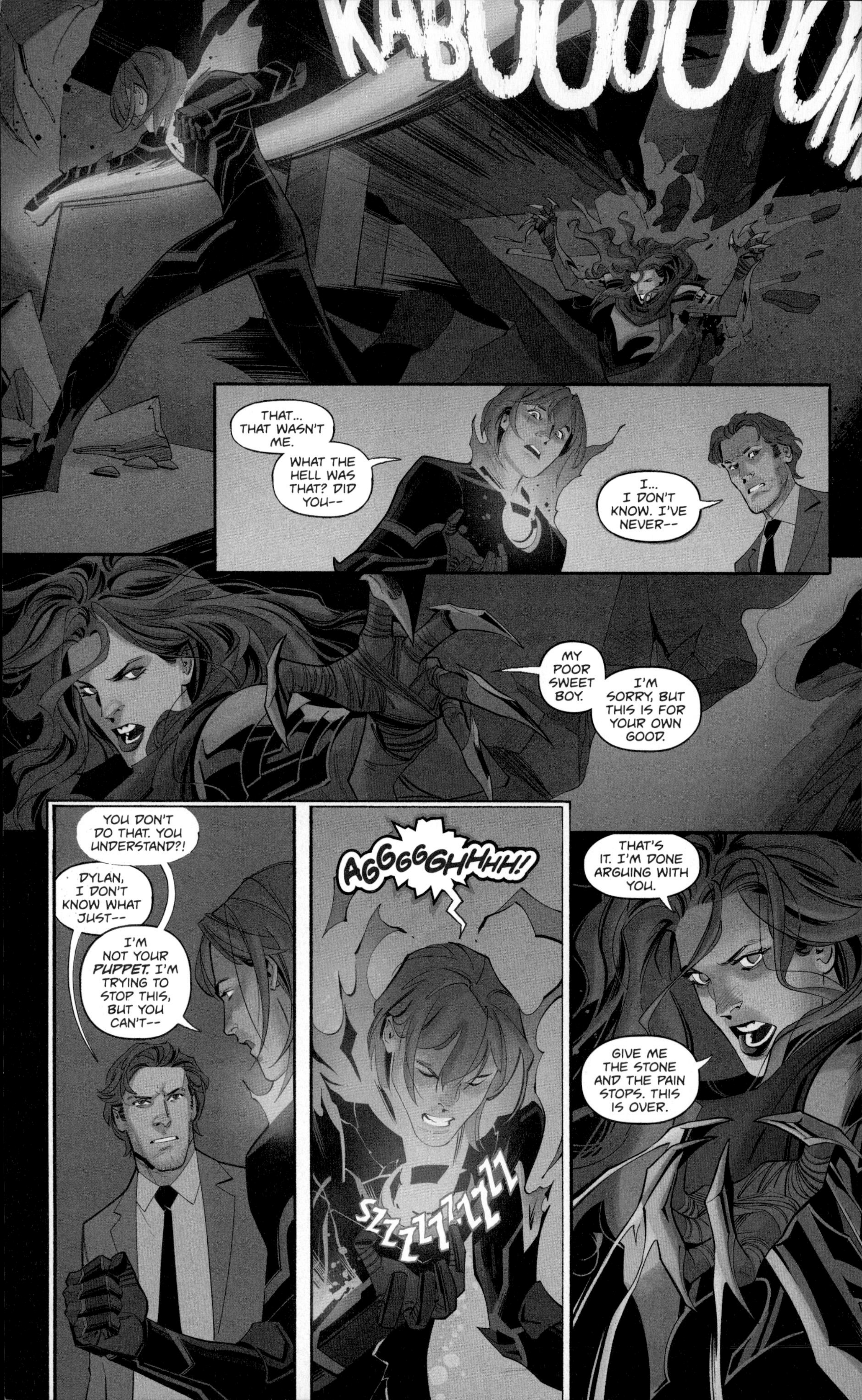
KABOOOOOOM
THAT... THAT WASN'T ME.
WHAT THE HELL WAS THAT? DID YOU--
I... I DON'T KNOW. I'VE NEVER--
MY POOR SWEET BOY.
I'M SORRY, BUT THIS IS FOR YOUR OWN GOOD.
YOU DON'T DO THAT. YOU UNDERSTAND?!
DYLAN, I DON'T KNOW WHAT JUST--
I'M NOT YOUR PUPPET. I'M TRYING TO STOP THIS, BUT YOU CAN'T--
AGGGGGHHHH!
SZZZZZZZZZ
THAT'S IT. I'M DONE ARGUING WITH YOU.
GIVE ME THE STONE AND THE PAIN STOPS. THIS IS OVER.

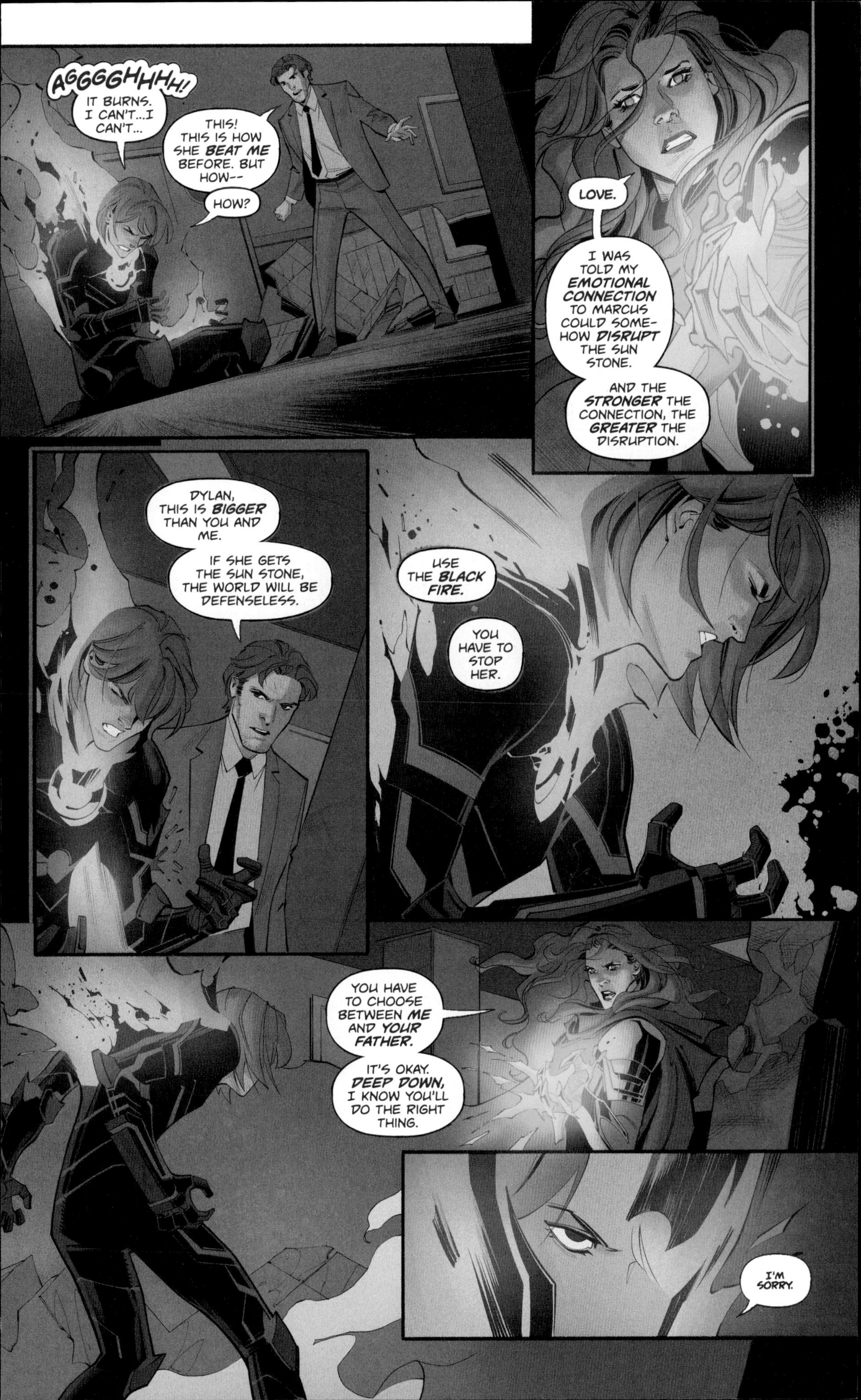
AGGGGHHHH!
IT BURNS. I CAN'T...I CAN'T...
THIS! THIS IS HOW SHE BEAT ME BEFORE. BUT HOW--
HOW?
LOVE.
I WAS TOLD MY EMOTIONAL CONNECTION TO MARCUS COULD SOME-HOW DISRUPT THE SUN STONE.
AND THE STRONGER THE CONNECTION, THE GREATER THE DISRUPTION.
DYLAN, THIS IS BIGGER THAN YOU AND ME.
IF SHE GETS THE SUN STONE, THE WORLD WILL BE DEFENSELESS.
USE THE BLACK FIRE.
YOU HAVE TO STOP HER.
YOU HAVE TO CHOOSE BETWEEN ME AND YOUR FATHER.
IT'S OKAY. DEEP DOWN, I KNOW YOU'LL DO THE RIGHT THING.
I'M SORRY.

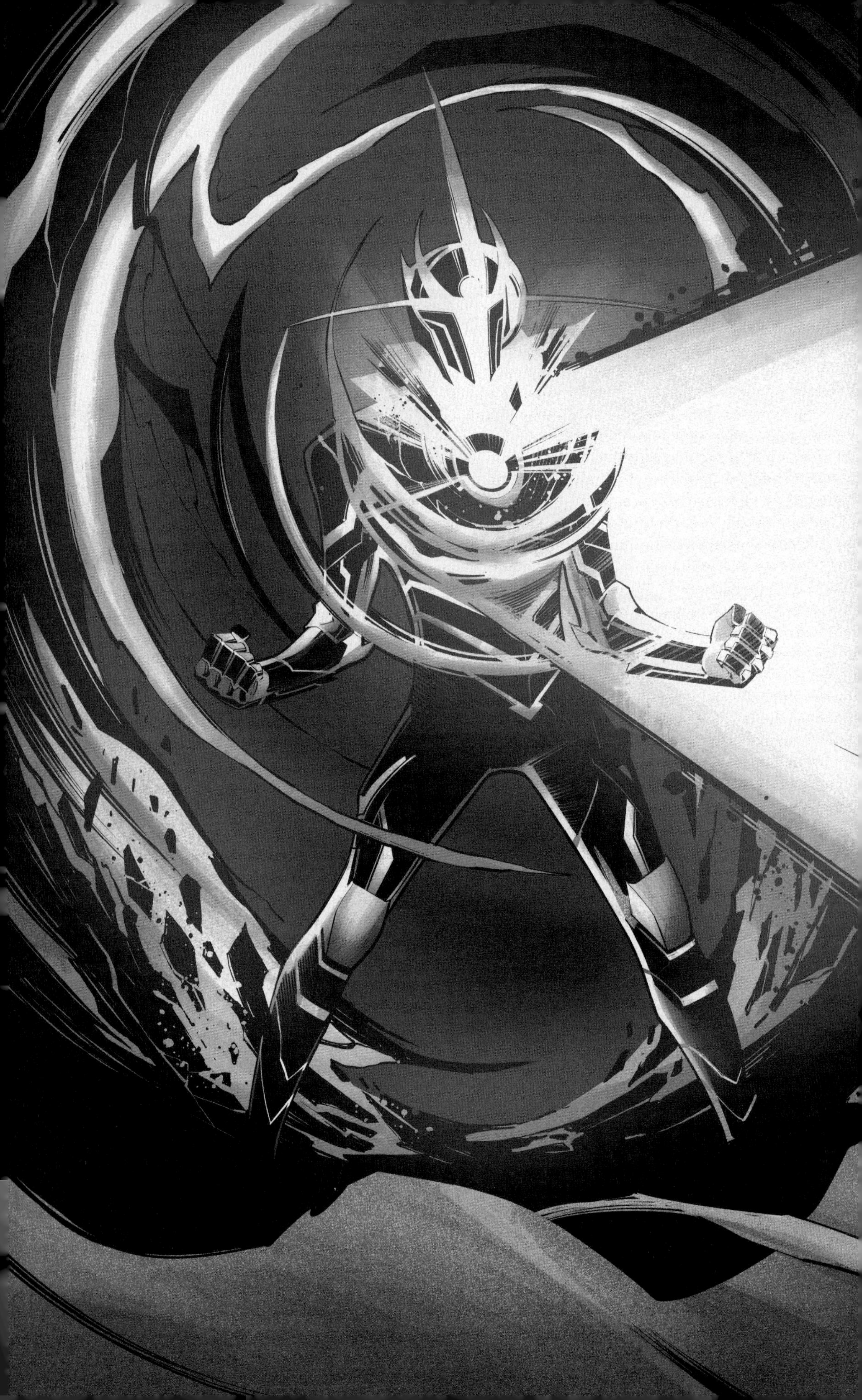

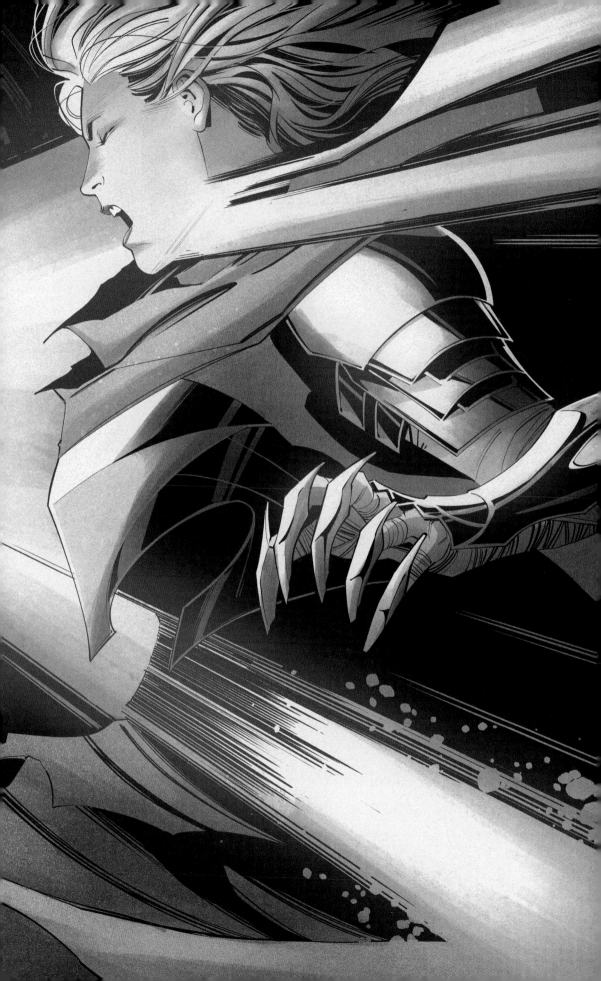

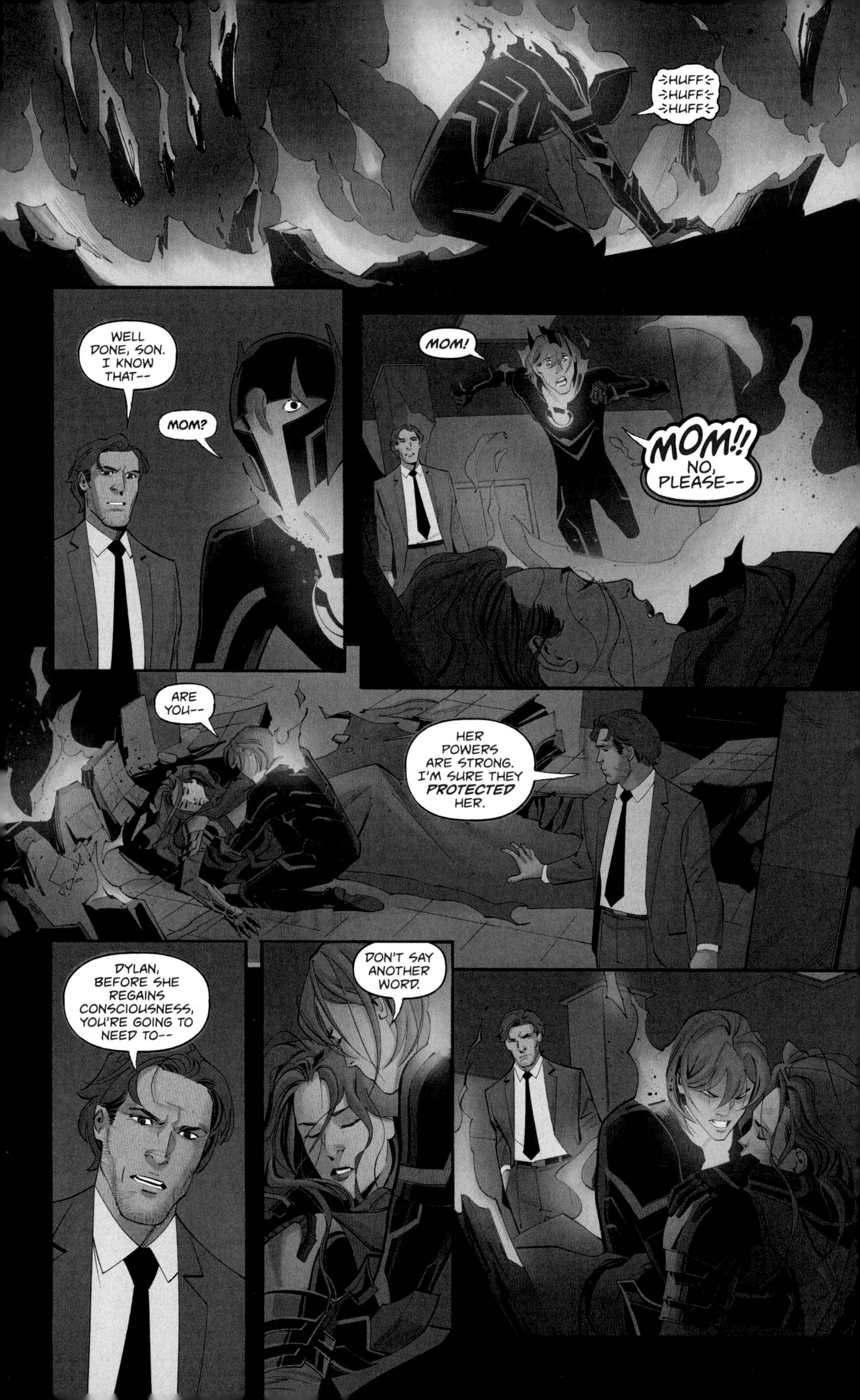
HUFF HUFF HUFF
WELL DONE, SON. I KNOW THAT--
MOM?
MOM!
MOM!! NO, PLEASE--
ARE YOU--
HER POWERS ARE STRONG. I'M SURE THEY PROTECTED HER.
DYLAN, BEFORE SHE REGAINS CONSCIOUSNESS, YOU'RE GOING TO NEED TO--
DON'T SAY ANOTHER WORD.

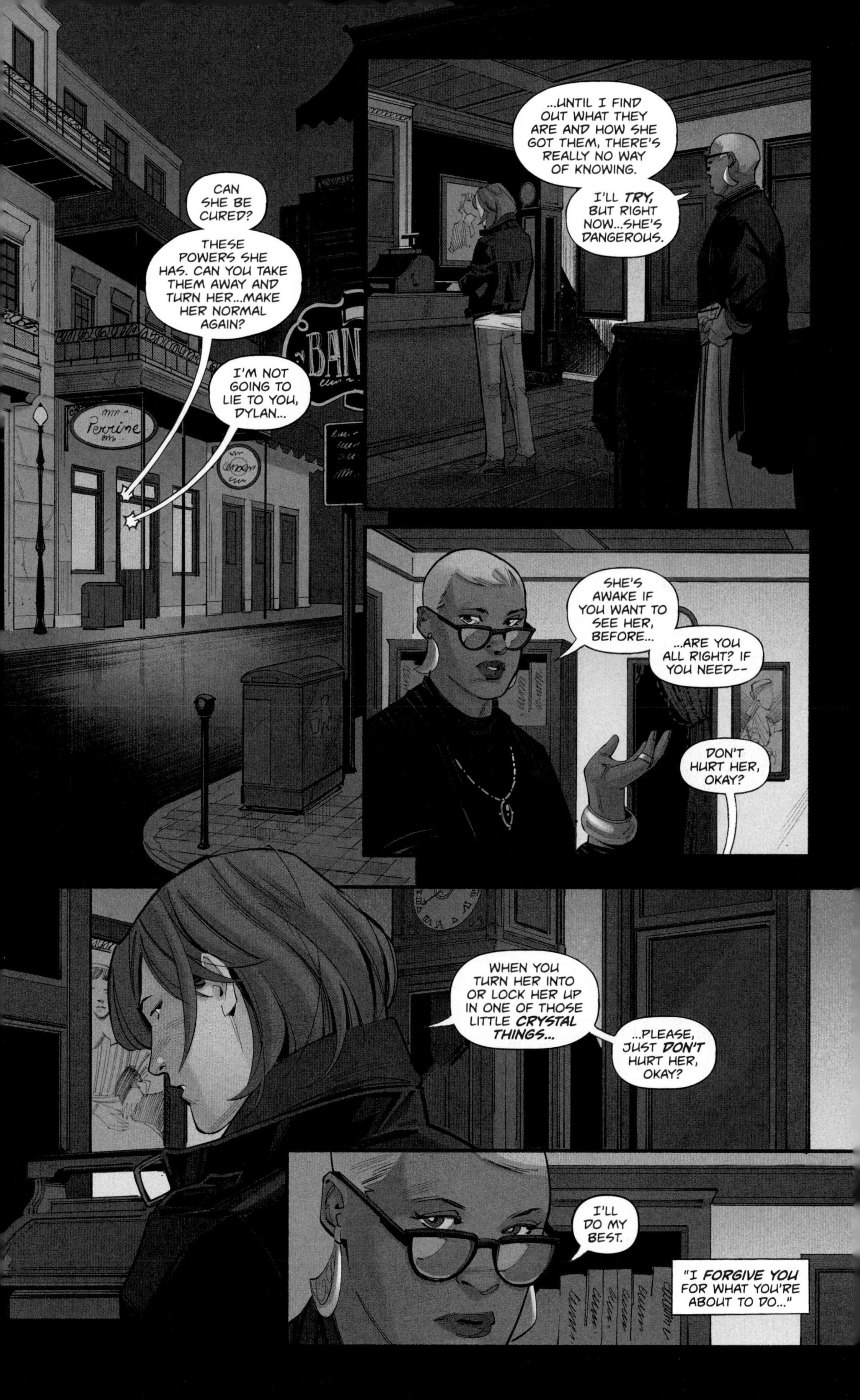
CAN SHE BE CURED?
THESE POWERS SHE HAS. CAN YOU TAKE THEM AWAY AND TURN HER...MAKE HER NORMAL AGAIN?
I'M NOT GOING TO LIE TO YOU, DYLAN...
...UNTIL I FIND OUT WHAT THEY ARE AND HOW SHE GOT THEM, THERE'S REALLY NO WAY OF KNOWING.
I'LL TRY, BUT RIGHT NOW...SHE'S DANGEROUS.
SHE'S AWAKE IF YOU WANT TO SEE HER, BEFORE...
...ARE YOU ALL RIGHT? IF YOU NEED--
DON'T HURT HER, OKAY?
WHEN YOU TURN HER INTO OR LOCK HER UP IN ONE OF THOSE LITTLE CRYSTAL THINGS...
...PLEASE, JUST DON'T HURT HER, OKAY?
I'LL DO MY BEST.
"I FORGIVE YOU FOR WHAT YOU'RE ABOUT TO DO..."

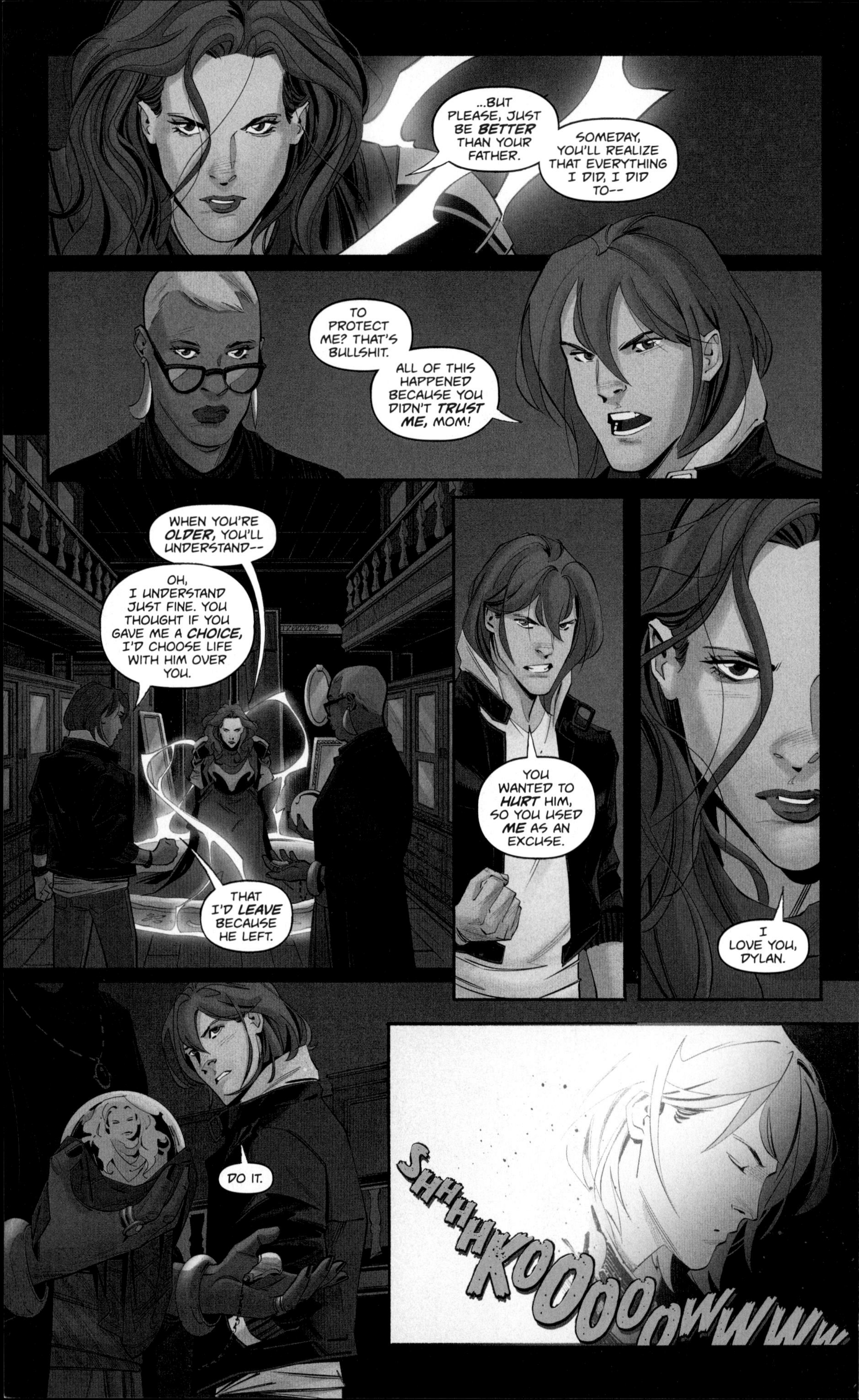
...BUT PLEASE, JUST BE BETTER THAN YOUR FATHER.
SOMEDAY, YOU'LL REALIZE THAT EVERYTHING I DID, I DID TO--
TO PROTECT ME? THAT'S BULLSHIT.
ALL OF THIS HAPPENED BECAUSE YOU DIDN'T TRUST ME, MOM!
WHEN YOU'RE OLDER, YOU'LL UNDERSTAND--
OH, I UNDERSTAND JUST FINE. YOU THOUGHT IF YOU GAVE ME A CHOICE, I'D CHOOSE LIFE WITH HIM OVER YOU.
THAT I'D LEAVE BECAUSE HE LEFT.
YOU WANTED TO HURT HIM, SO YOU USED ME AS AN EXCUSE.
I LOVE YOU, DYLAN.
DO IT.
SHHHHKOOOOOWWWW

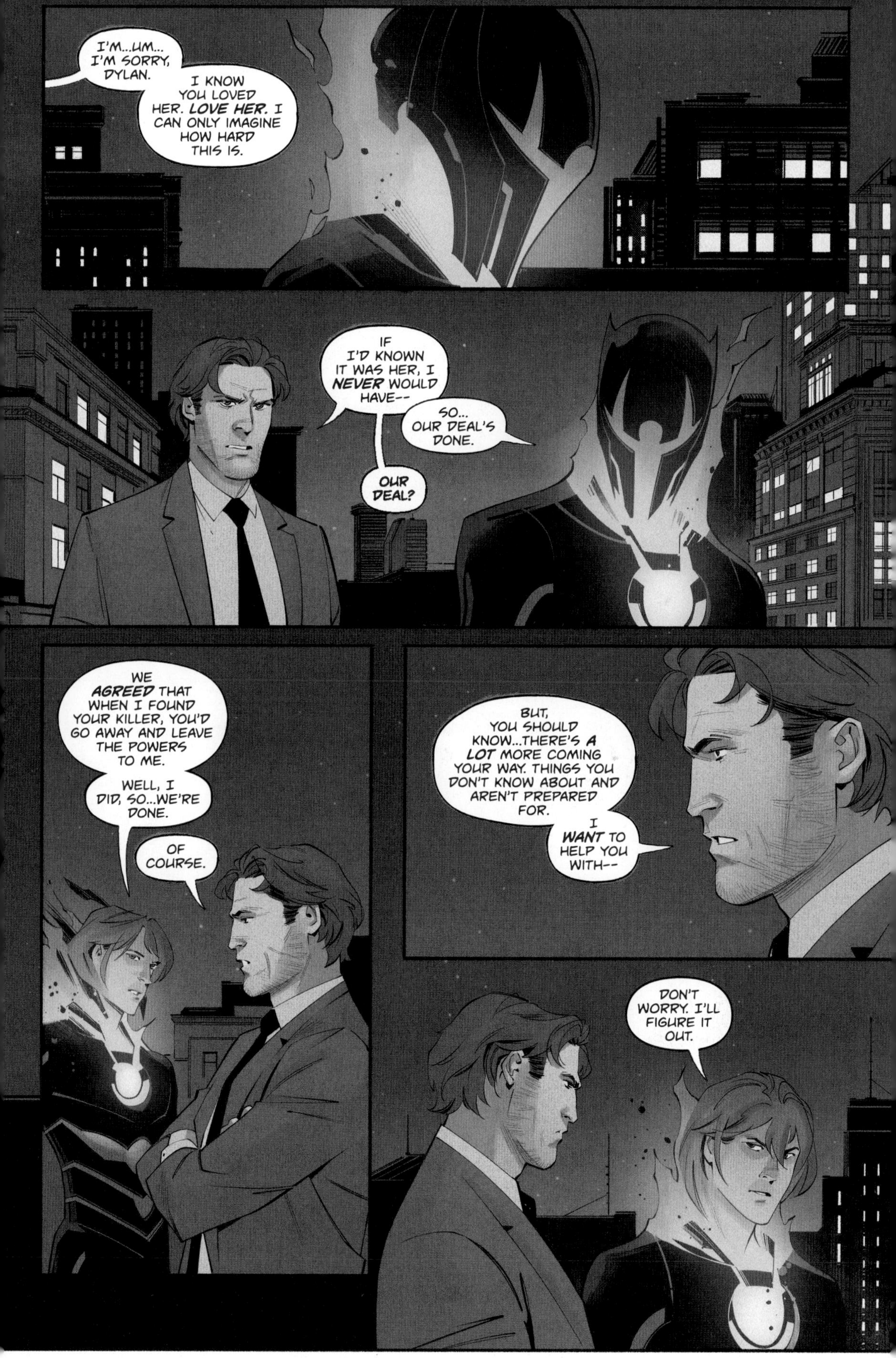

I'M...UM... I'M SORRY, DYLAN.
I KNOW YOU LOVED HER. LOVE HER. I CAN ONLY IMAGINE HOW HARD THIS IS.
IF I'D KNOWN IT WAS HER, I NEVER WOULD HAVE--
SO... OUR DEAL'S DONE.
OUR DEAL?
WE AGREED THAT WHEN I FOUND YOUR KILLER, YOU'D GO AWAY AND LEAVE THE POWERS TO ME.
WELL, I DID, SO...WE'RE DONE.
OF COURSE.
BUT, YOU SHOULD KNOW...THERE'S A LOT MORE COMING YOUR WAY. THINGS YOU DON'T KNOW ABOUT AND AREN'T PREPARED FOR.
I WANT TO HELP YOU WITH--
DON'T WORRY. I'LL FIGURE IT OUT.

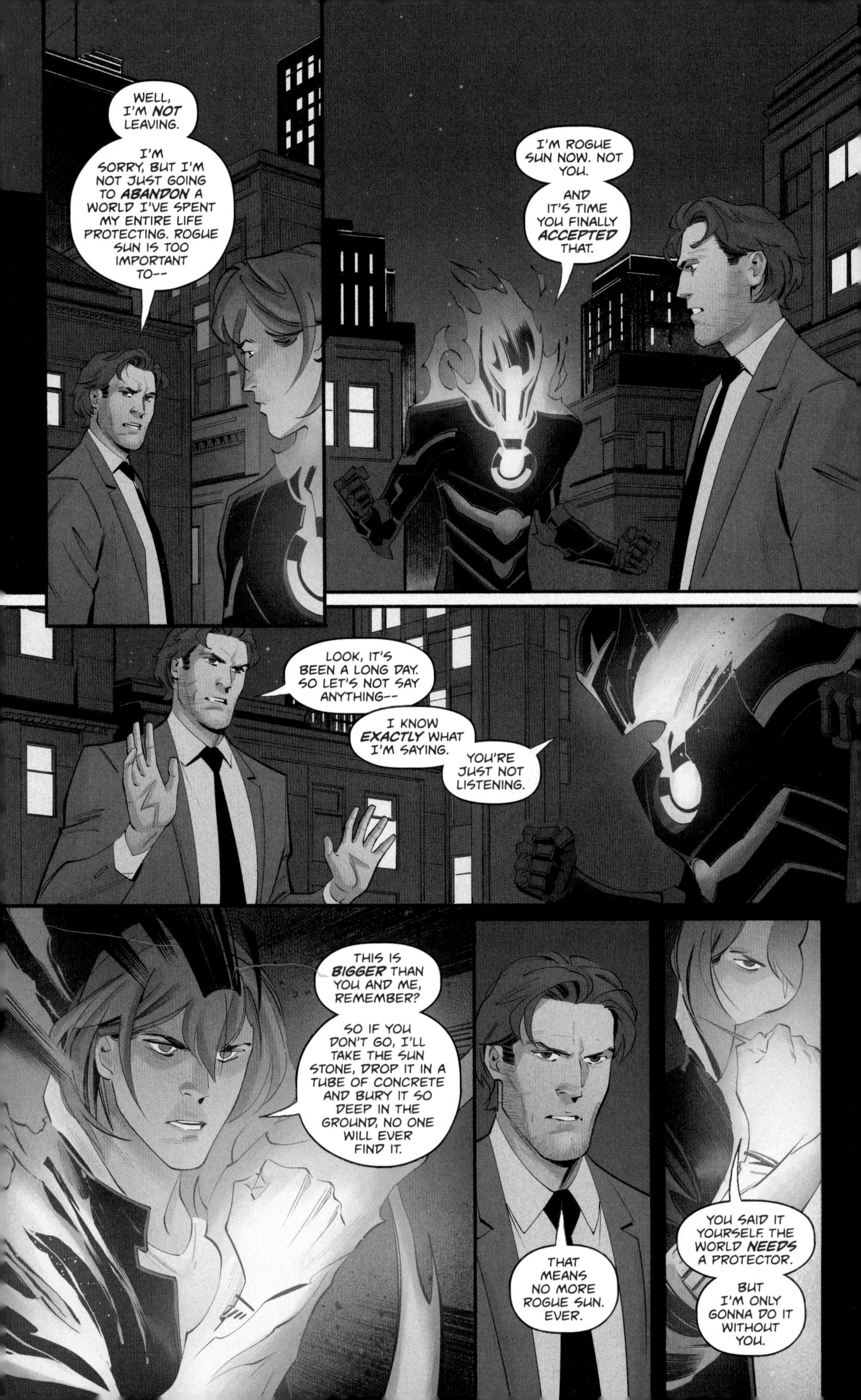
WELL, I'M NOT LEAVING.
I'M SORRY, BUT I'M NOT JUST GOING TO ABANDON A WORLD I'VE SPENT MY ENTIRE LIFE PROTECTING. ROGUE SUN IS TOO IMPORTANT TO--
I'M ROGUE SUN NOW. NOT YOU.
AND IT'S TIME YOU FINALLY ACCEPTED THAT.
LOOK, IT'S BEEN A LONG DAY. SO LET'S NOT SAY ANYTHING--
I KNOW EXACTLY WHAT I'M SAYING.
YOU'RE JUST NOT LISTENING.
THIS IS BIGGER THAN YOU AND ME, REMEMBER?
SO IF YOU DON'T GO, I'LL TAKE THE SUN STONE, DROP IT IN A TUBE OF CONCRETE AND BURY IT SO DEEP IN THE GROUND, NO ONE WILL EVER FIND IT.
THAT MEANS NO MORE ROGUE SUN. EVER.
YOU SAID IT YOURSELF. THE WORLD NEEDS A PROTECTOR.
BUT I'M ONLY GONNA DO IT WITHOUT YOU.

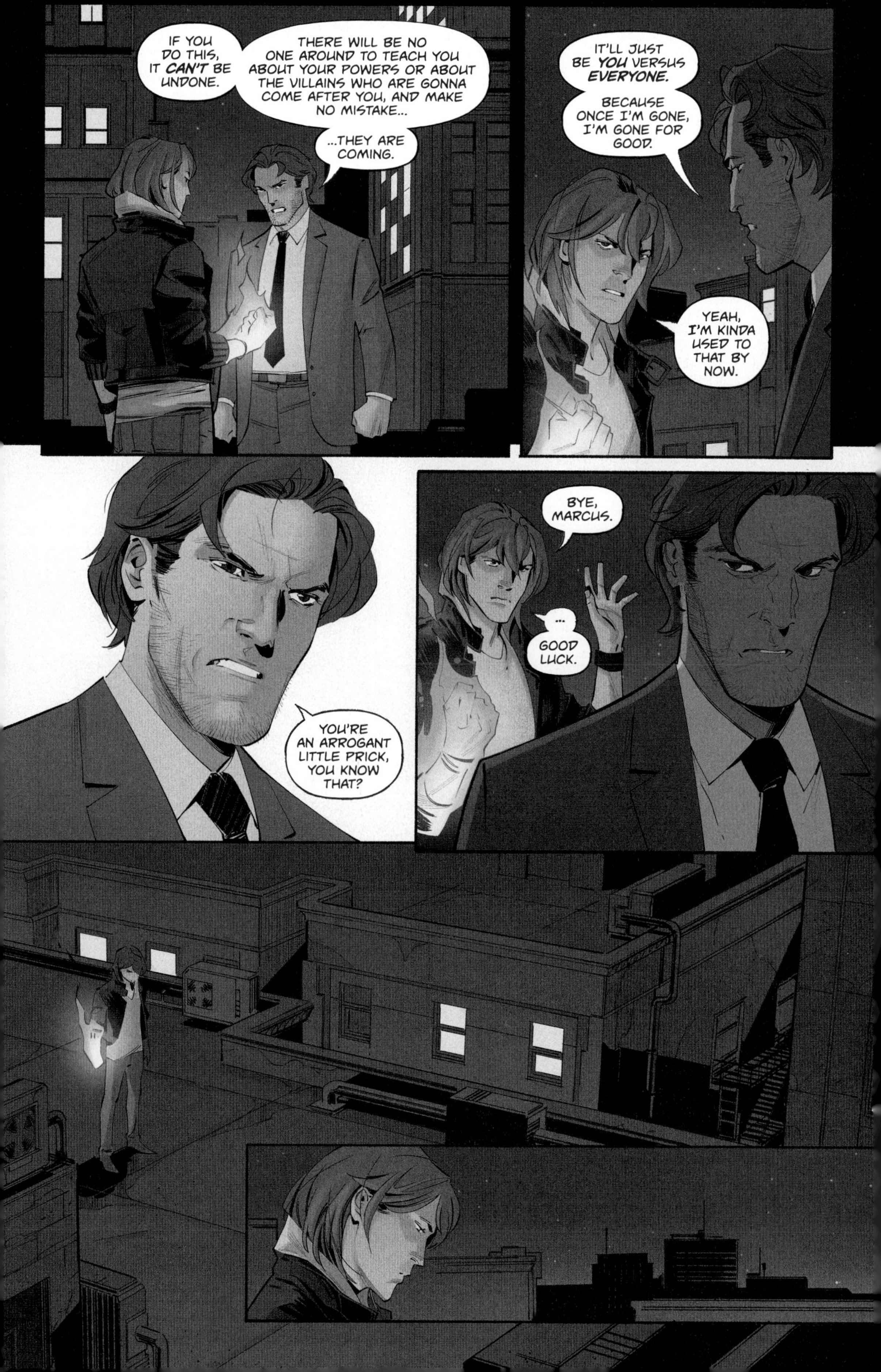
IF YOU DO THIS, IT **CAN'T** BE UNDONE.
THERE WILL BE NO ONE AROUND TO TEACH YOU ABOUT YOUR POWERS OR ABOUT THE VILLAINS WHO ARE GONNA COME AFTER YOU, AND MAKE NO MISTAKE...
...THEY ARE COMING.
IT'LL JUST BE ***YOU*** VERSUS ***EVERYONE.***
BECAUSE ONCE I'M GONE, I'M GONE FOR GOOD.
YEAH, **I'M** KINDA USED TO THAT BY NOW.
YOU'RE AN ARROGANT LITTLE PRICK, YOU KNOW THAT?
BYE, MARCUS.
... GOOD LUCK.

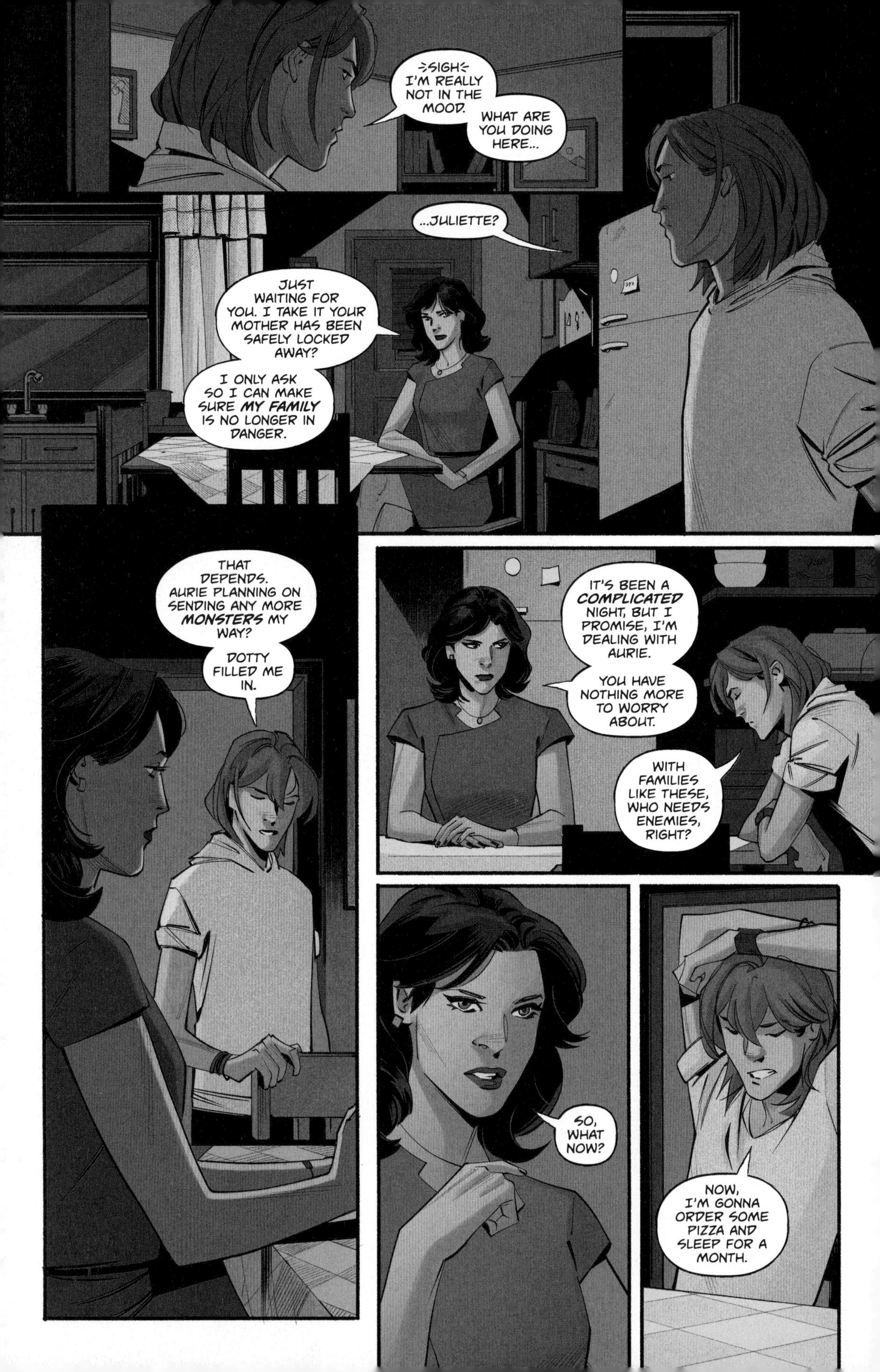

=SIGH= I'M REALLY NOT IN THE MOOD.
WHAT ARE YOU DOING HERE...
...JULIETTE?
JUST WAITING FOR YOU. I TAKE IT YOUR MOTHER HAS BEEN SAFELY LOCKED AWAY?
I ONLY ASK SO I CAN MAKE SURE MY FAMILY IS NO LONGER IN DANGER.
THAT DEPENDS. AURIE PLANNING ON SENDING ANY MORE MONSTERS MY WAY?
DOTTY FILLED ME IN.
IT'S BEEN A COMPLICATED NIGHT, BUT I PROMISE, I'M DEALING WITH AURIE.
YOU HAVE NOTHING MORE TO WORRY ABOUT.
WITH FAMILIES LIKE THESE, WHO NEEDS ENEMIES, RIGHT?
SO, WHAT NOW?
NOW, I'M GONNA ORDER SOME PIZZA AND SLEEP FOR A MONTH.

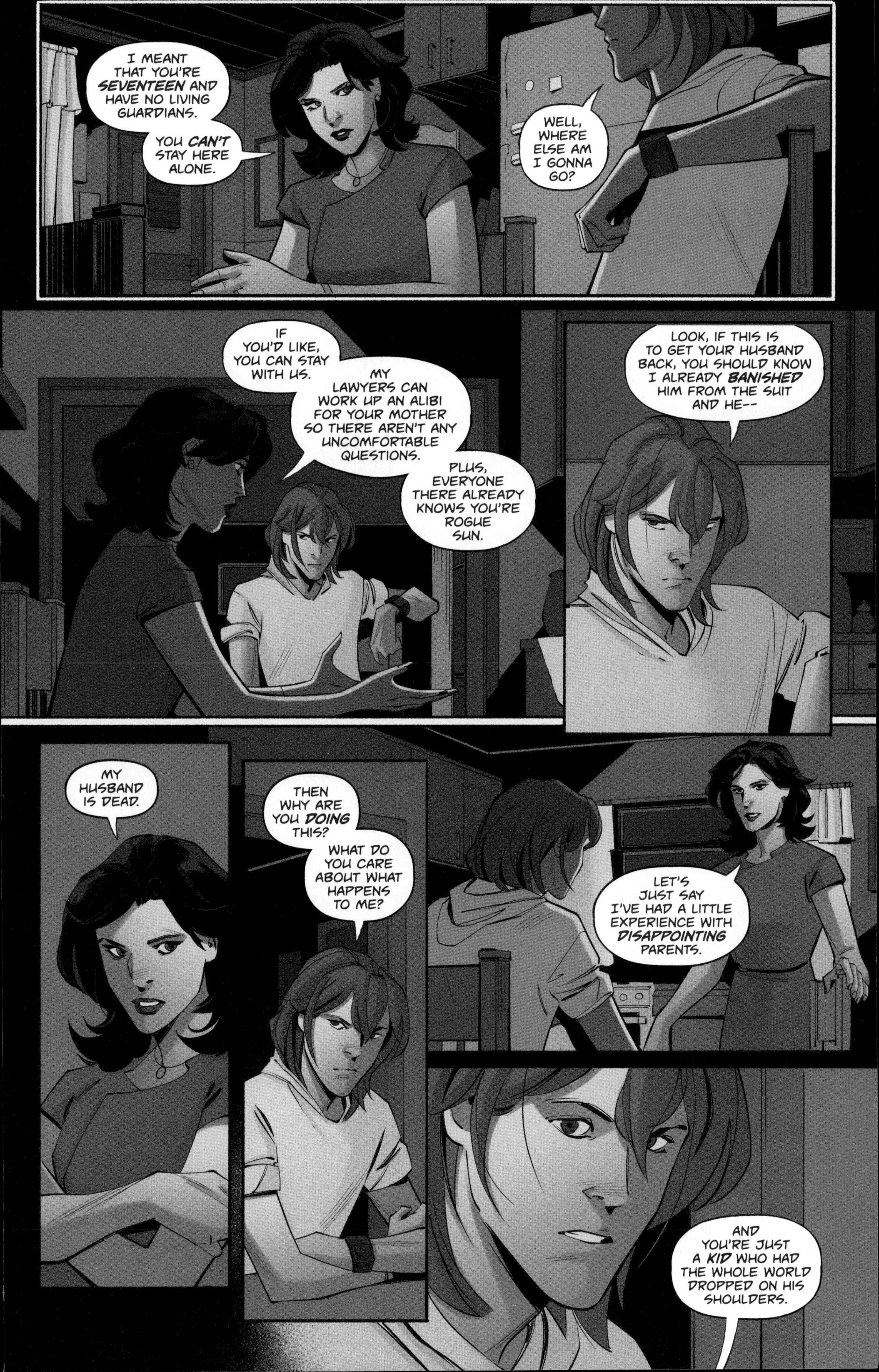

I MEANT THAT YOU'RE SEVENTEEN AND HAVE NO LIVING GUARDIANS.
YOU CAN'T STAY HERE ALONE.
WELL, WHERE ELSE AM I GONNA GO?
IF YOU'D LIKE, YOU CAN STAY WITH US.
MY LAWYERS CAN WORK UP AN ALIBI FOR YOUR MOTHER SO THERE AREN'T ANY UNCOMFORTABLE QUESTIONS.
PLUS, EVERYONE THERE ALREADY KNOWS YOU'RE ROGUE SUN.
LOOK, IF THIS IS TO GET YOUR HUSBAND BACK, YOU SHOULD KNOW I ALREADY BANISHED HIM FROM THE SUIT AND HE--
MY HUSBAND IS DEAD.
THEN WHY ARE YOU DOING THIS?
WHAT DO YOU CARE ABOUT WHAT HAPPENS TO ME?
LET'S JUST SAY I'VE HAD A LITTLE EXPERIENCE WITH DISAPPOINTING PARENTS.
AND YOU'RE JUST A KID WHO HAD THE WHOLE WORLD DROPPED ON HIS SHOULDERS.

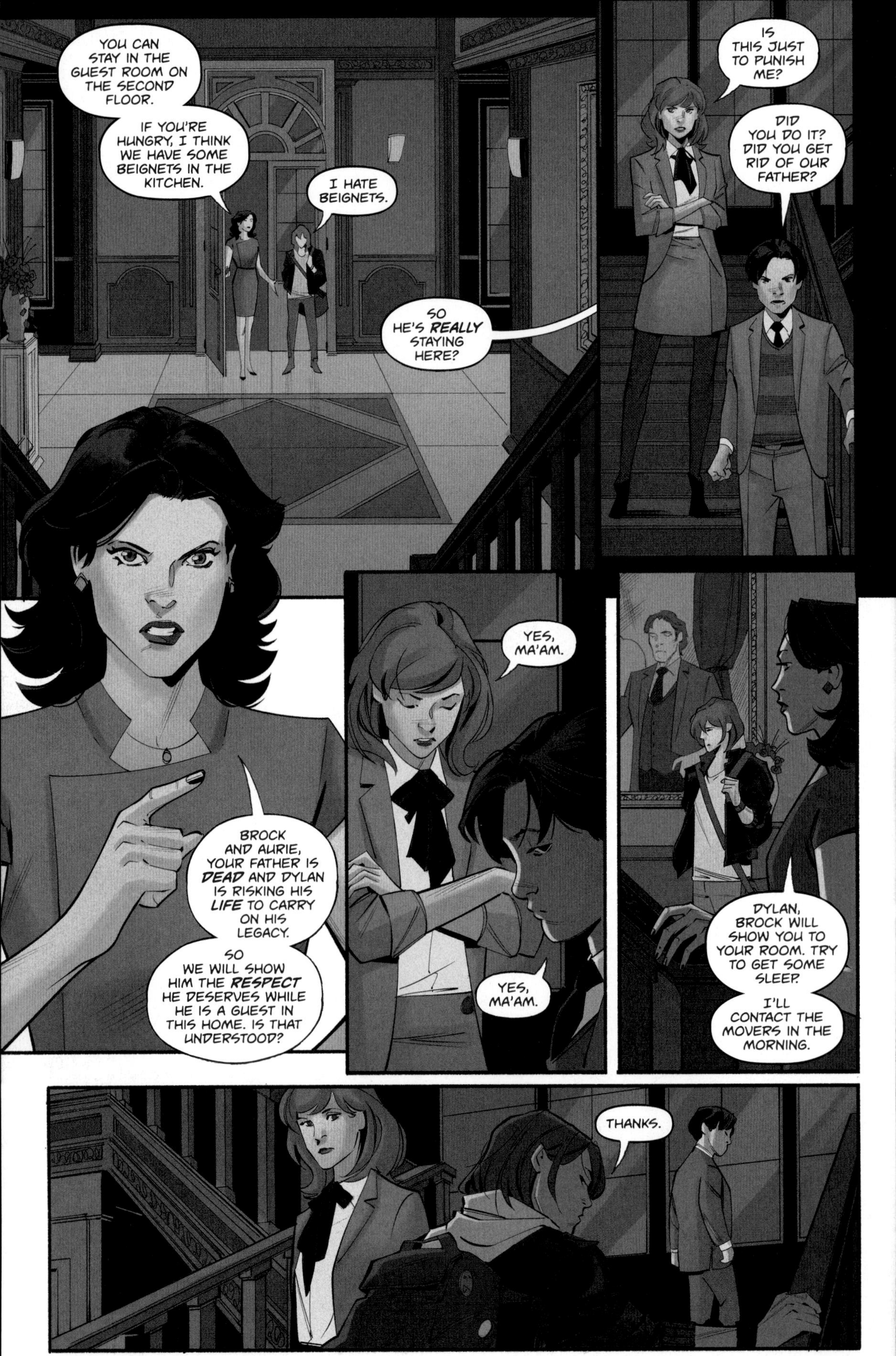

YOU CAN STAY IN THE GUEST ROOM ON THE SECOND FLOOR.
IF YOU'RE HUNGRY, I THINK WE HAVE SOME BEIGNETS IN THE KITCHEN.
I HATE BEIGNETS.
SO HE'S *REALLY* STAYING HERE?
IS THIS JUST TO PUNISH ME?
DID YOU DO IT? DID YOU GET RID OF OUR FATHER?
BROCK AND AURIE, YOUR FATHER IS *DEAD* AND DYLAN IS RISKING HIS *LIFE* TO CARRY ON HIS LEGACY.
SO WE WILL SHOW HIM THE *RESPECT* HE DESERVES WHILE HE IS A GUEST IN THIS HOME. IS THAT UNDERSTOOD?
YES, MA'AM.
YES, MA'AM.
DYLAN, BROCK WILL SHOW YOU TO YOUR ROOM. TRY TO GET SOME SLEEP.
I'LL CONTACT THE MOVERS IN THE MORNING.
THANKS.

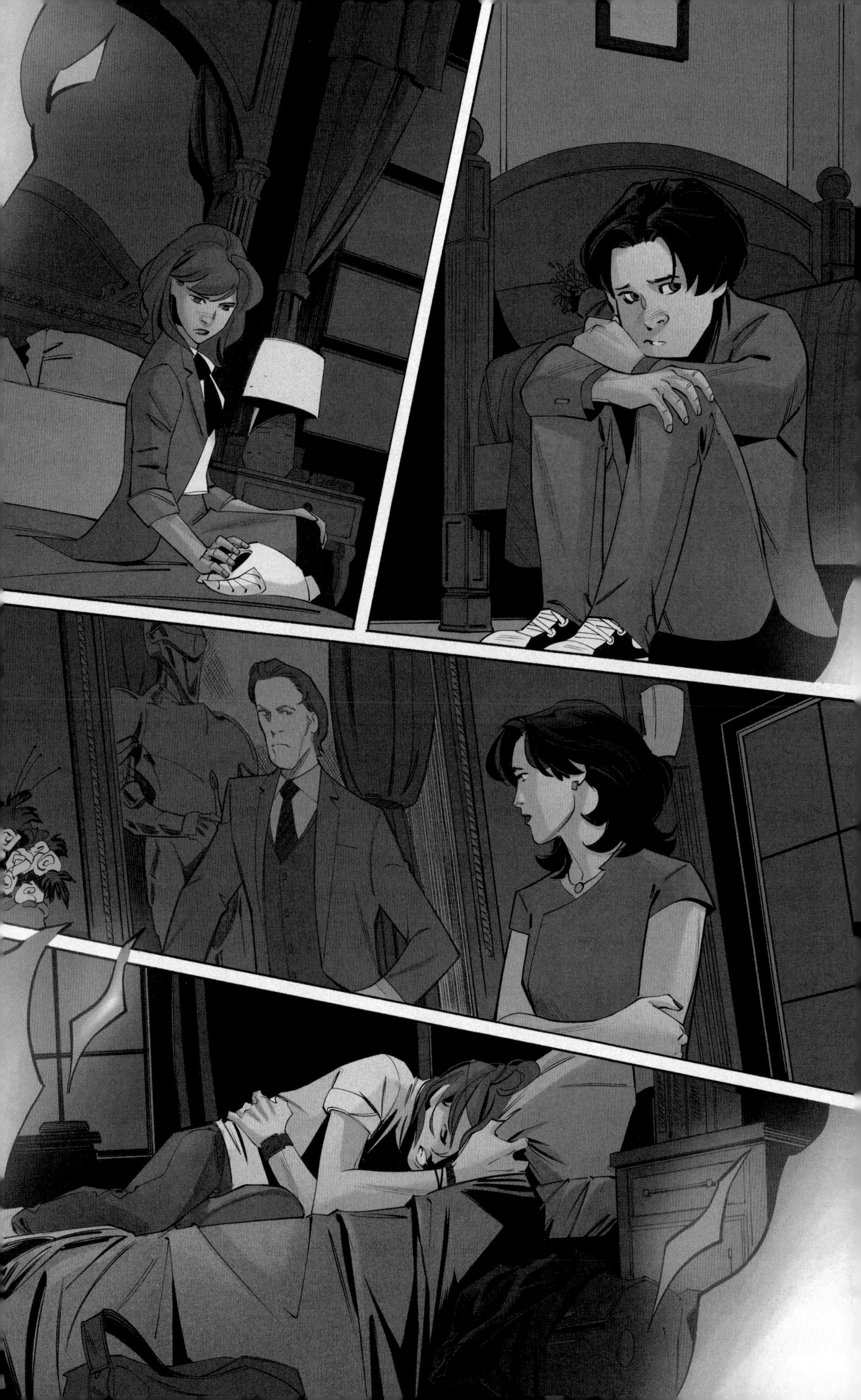

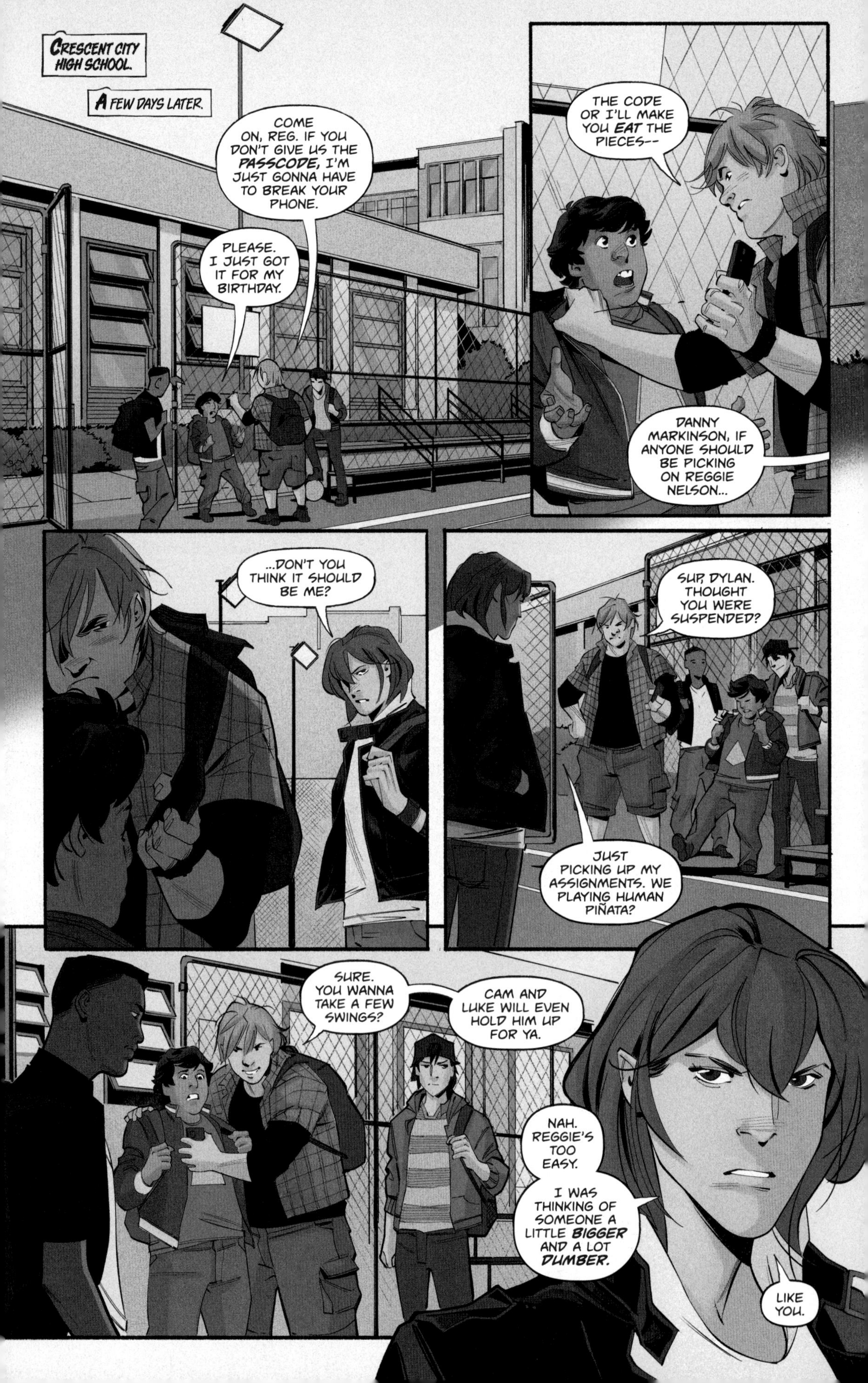
CRESCENT CITY HIGH SCHOOL.
A FEW DAYS LATER.
COME ON, REG. IF YOU DON'T GIVE US THE PASSCODE, I'M JUST GONNA HAVE TO BREAK YOUR PHONE.
PLEASE. I JUST GOT IT FOR MY BIRTHDAY.
THE CODE OR I'LL MAKE YOU EAT THE PIECES--
DANNY MARKINSON, IF ANYONE SHOULD BE PICKING ON REGGIE NELSON...
...DON'T YOU THINK IT SHOULD BE ME?
SUP, DYLAN. THOUGHT YOU WERE SUSPENDED?
JUST PICKING UP MY ASSIGNMENTS. WE PLAYING HUMAN PIÑATA?
SURE. YOU WANNA TAKE A FEW SWINGS?
CAM AND LUKE WILL EVEN HOLD HIM UP FOR YA.
NAH. REGGIE'S TOO EASY.
I WAS THINKING OF SOMEONE A LITTLE BIGGER AND A LOT DUMBER.
LIKE YOU.

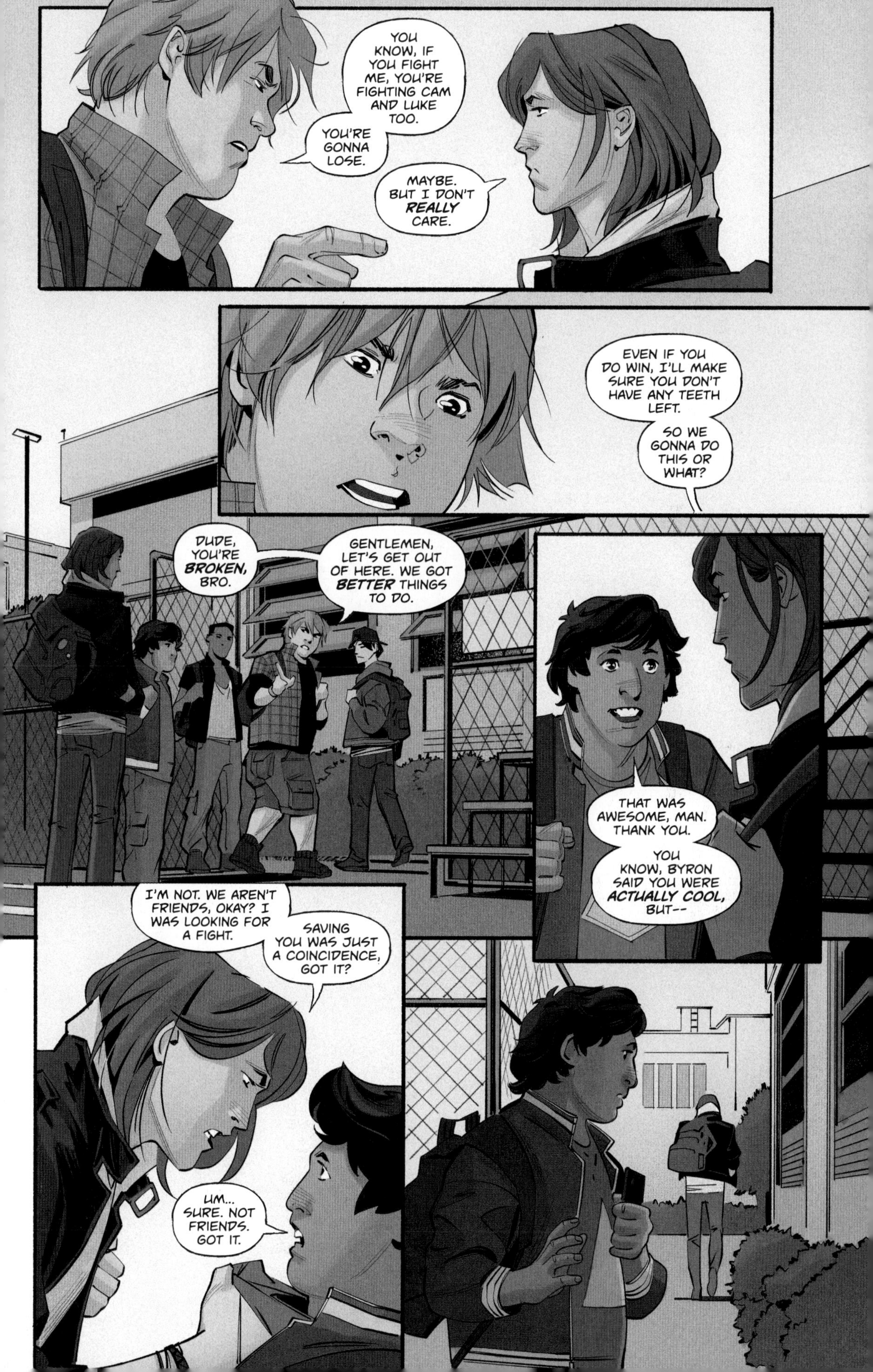
YOU KNOW, IF YOU FIGHT ME, YOU'RE FIGHTING CAM AND LUKE TOO.
YOU'RE GONNA LOSE.
MAYBE. BUT I DON'T *REALLY* CARE.
EVEN IF YOU DO WIN, I'LL MAKE SURE YOU DON'T HAVE ANY TEETH LEFT.
SO WE GONNA DO THIS OR WHAT?
DUDE, YOU'RE *BROKEN,* BRO.
GENTLEMEN, LET'S GET OUT OF HERE. WE GOT *BETTER* THINGS TO DO.
THAT WAS AWESOME, MAN. THANK YOU.
YOU KNOW, BYRON SAID YOU WERE *ACTUALLY COOL,* BUT--
I'M NOT. WE AREN'T FRIENDS, OKAY? I WAS LOOKING FOR A FIGHT.
SAVING YOU WAS JUST A COINCIDENCE, GOT IT?
UM... SURE. NOT FRIENDS. GOT IT.

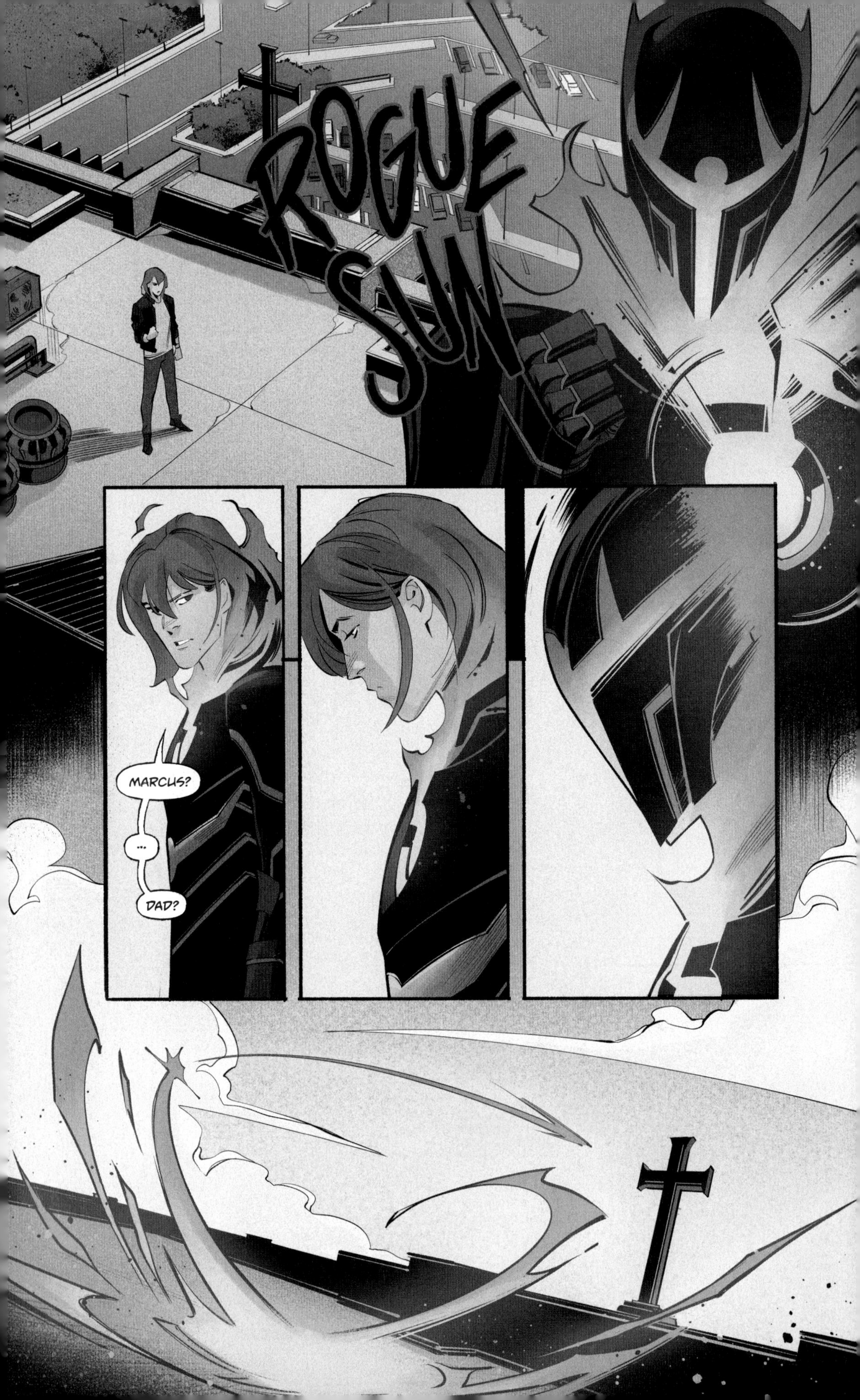
ROGUE SUN
MARCUS?
...
DAD?

Gallery
Covers

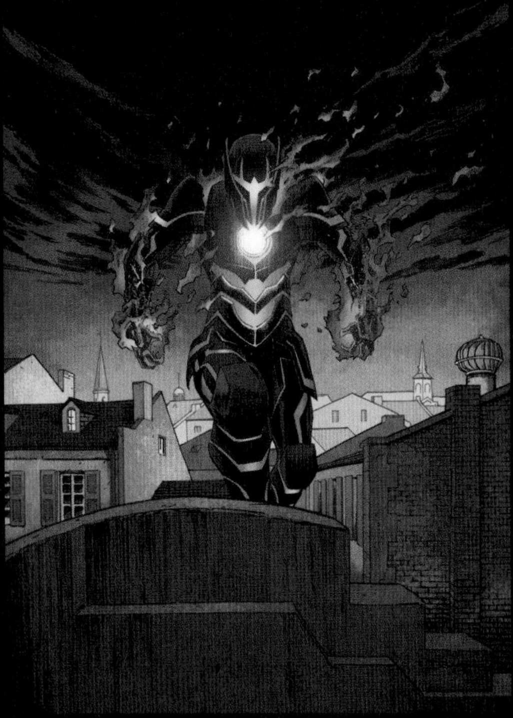

Issue One (A)
Declan Shalvey w/ Chris O'Halloran

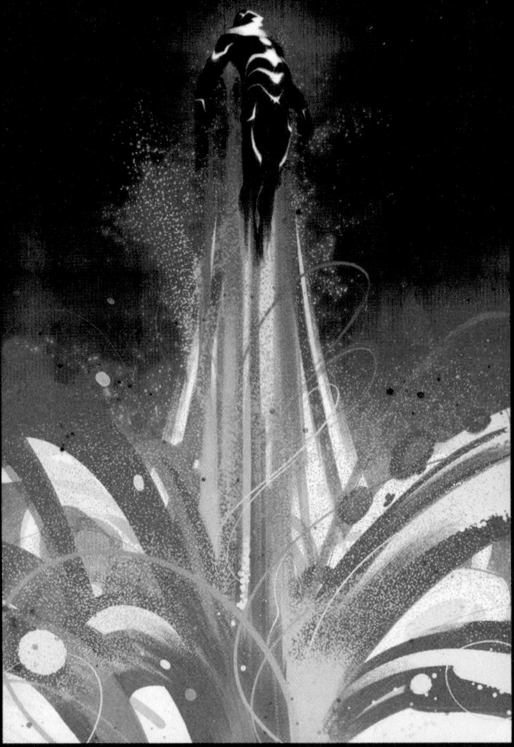

Issue 1 (b)
Goñi Montes

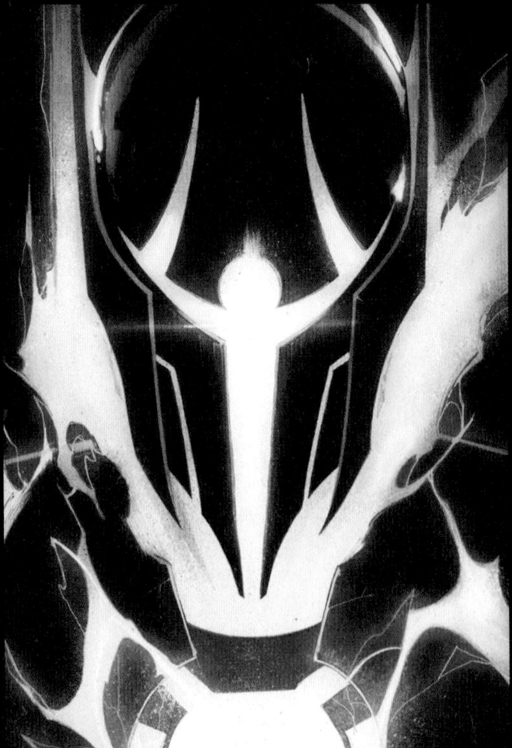

Issue One (C)
Abel

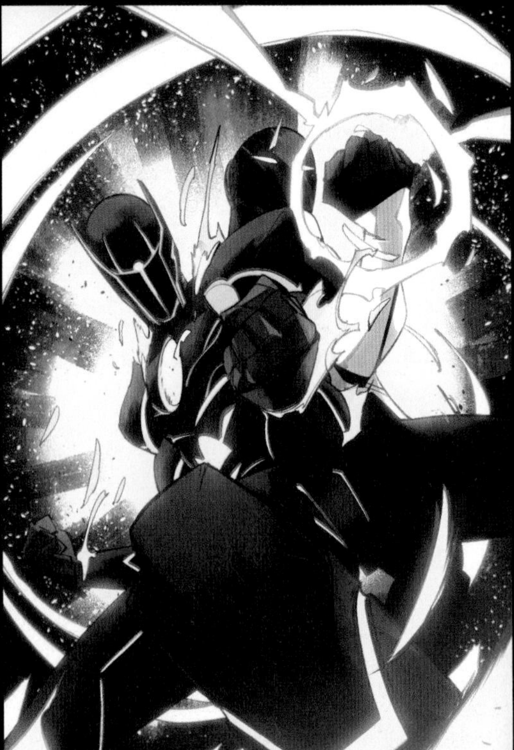

Issue One (D)
Daniele Di Nicuolo w/ Walter Baiamonte

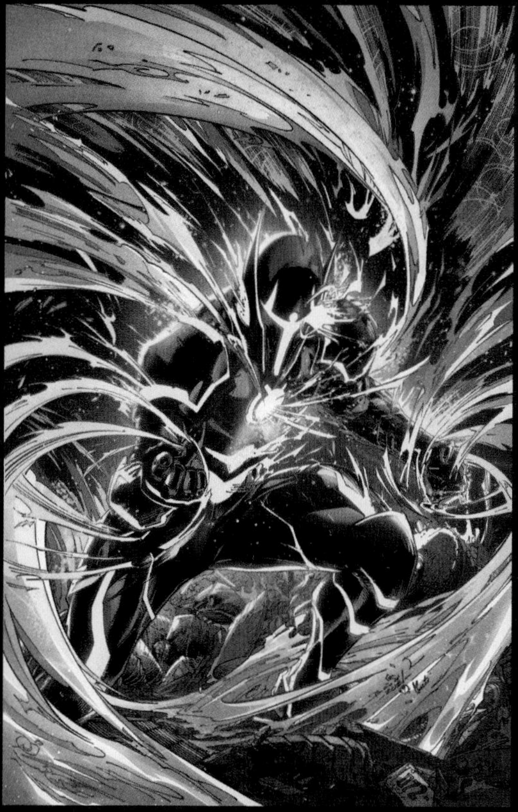

Issue One (E)
Brett Booth & Marc Deering w/ Igor Monti

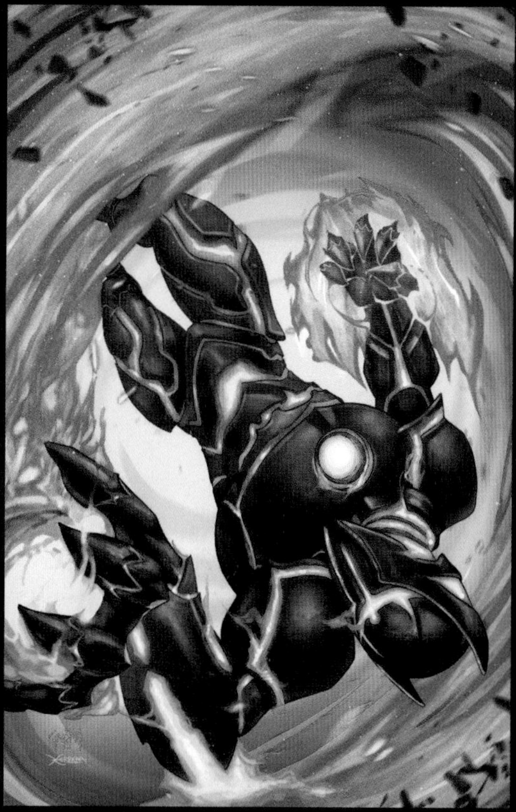

Issue One (Things From Another World)
Mauricio Herrera & DasGnomo

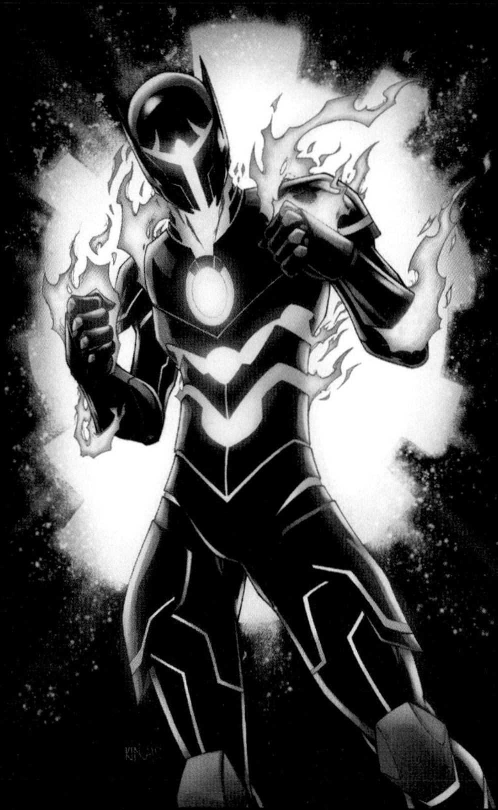

Issue One (Wally's World)
Ryan Kincaid

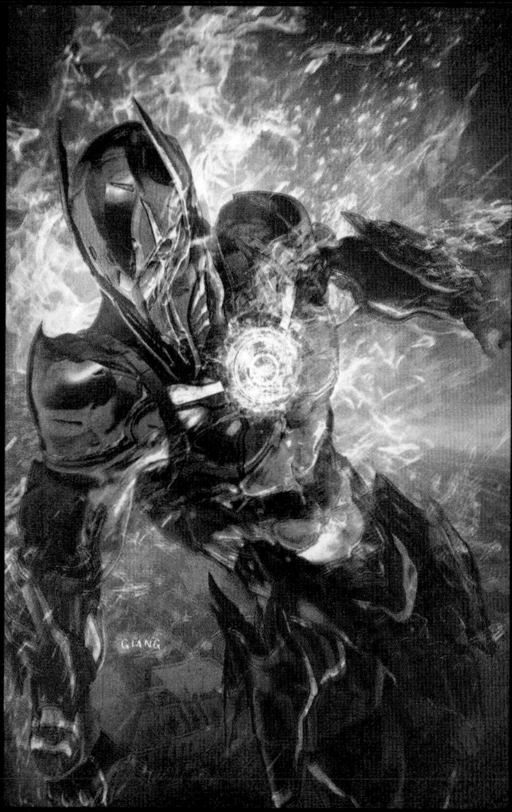
GIANG

Issue One (Comic Kingdom of Canada)
John Giang

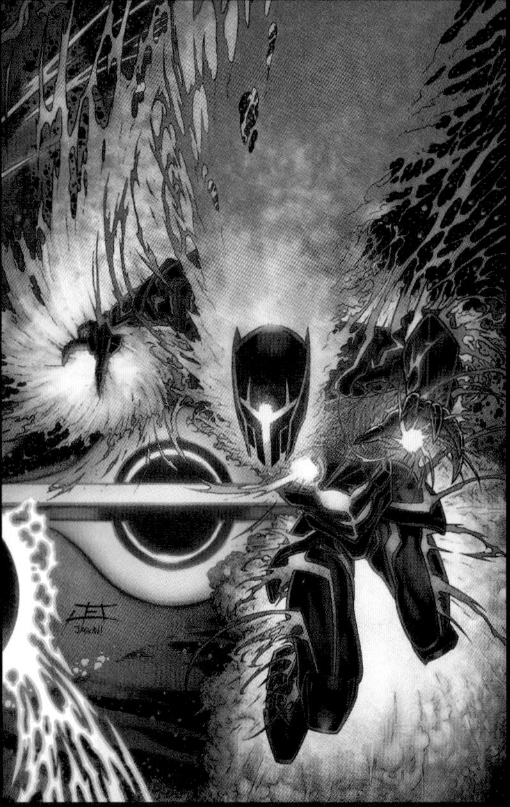

Issue One (One Stop Comic Shop)
Jeff Edwards

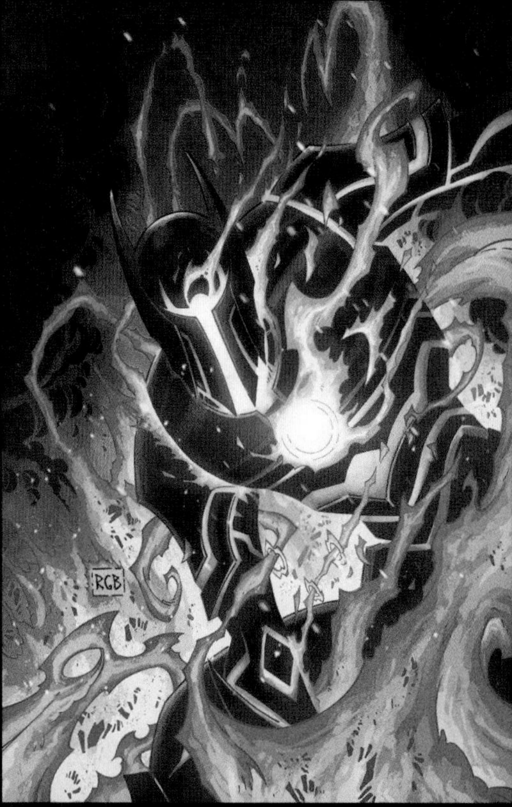

Issue One (Mutant Beaver Comics)
Ryan G Browne

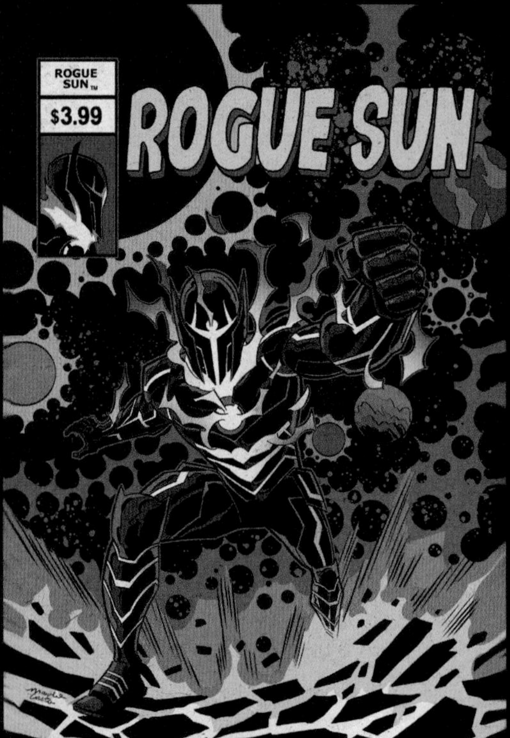
ROGUE SUN
$3.99
ROGUE SUN

Issue One (Stadium Comics)
Marcelo Costa

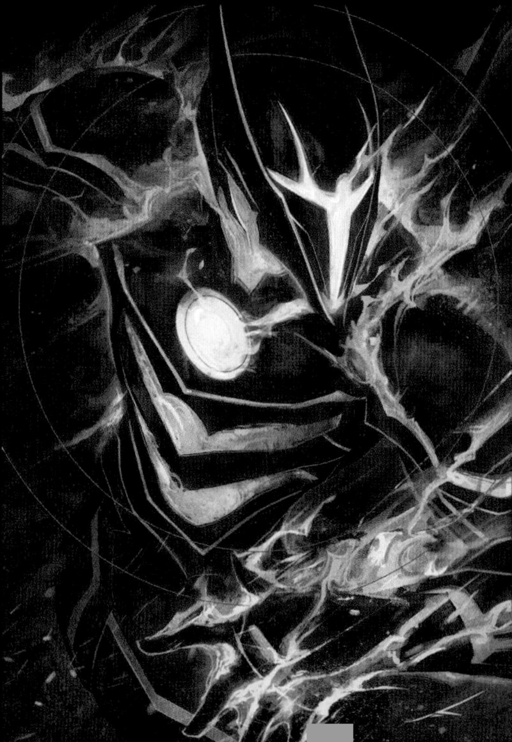

Issue One (Rabbit Comics & Wicked Gator)
Ivan Tao

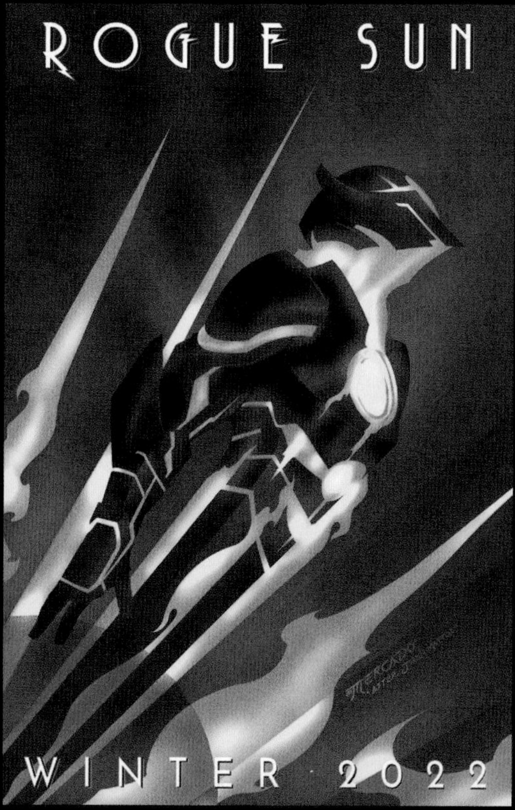
ROGUE SUN
WINTER 2022

Issue One (Spectral Comics)
Miguel Mercado

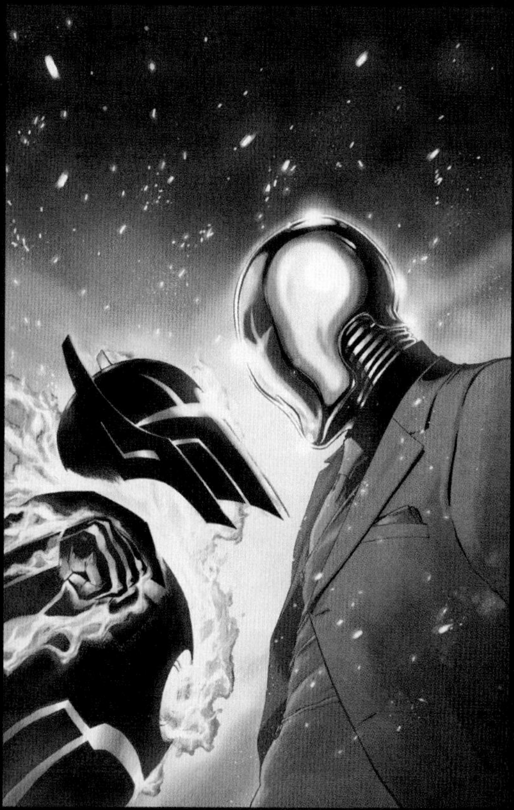

Issue One (Hive Comics & Whatnot)
Guillaume Martinez

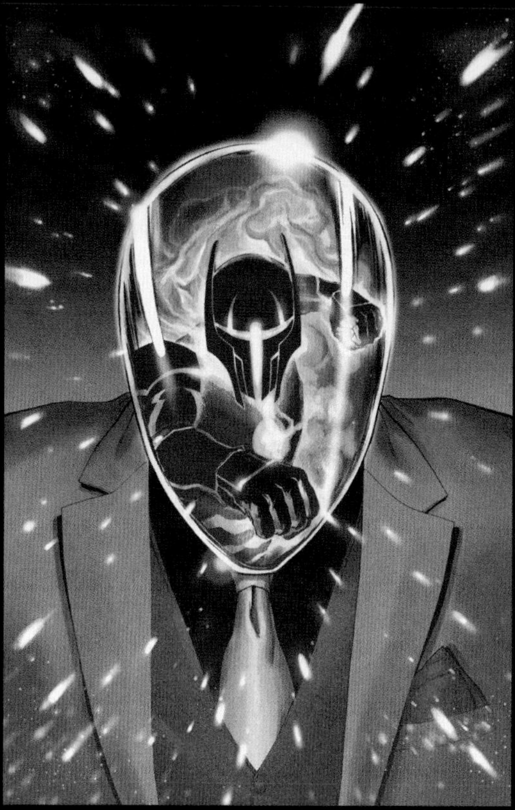

Issue One (Hive Comics & Whatnot)
Guillaume Martinez

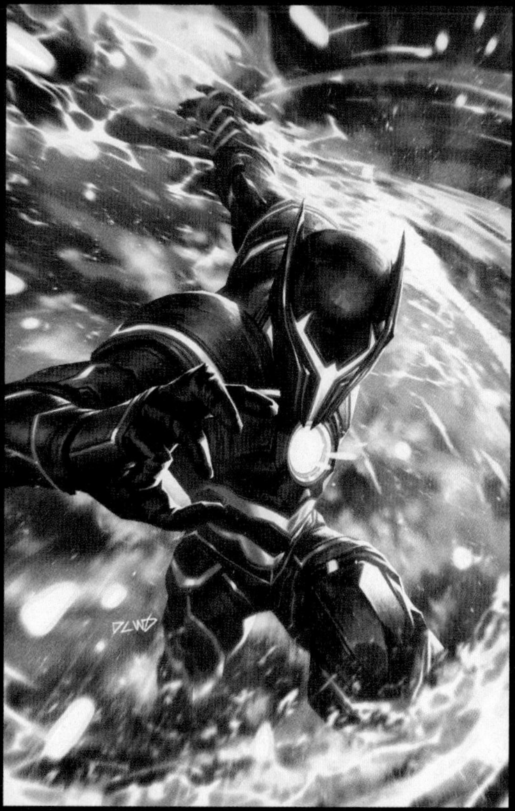

Issue One (Spectral Comics)
Derrick Chew

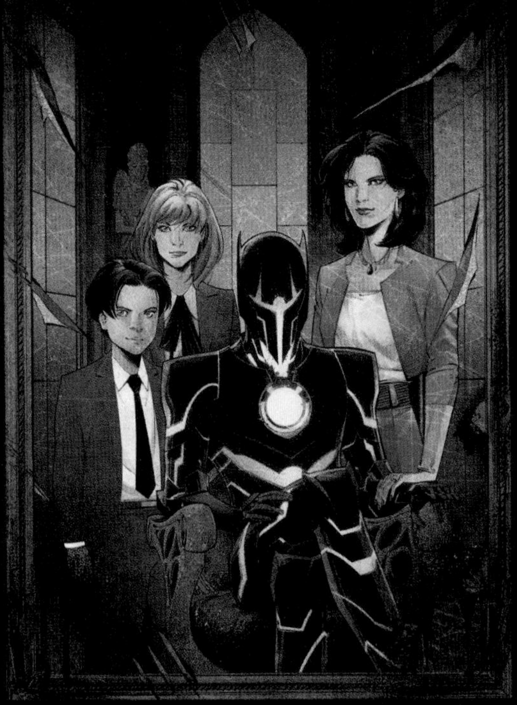

Issue Two (A)
Abel

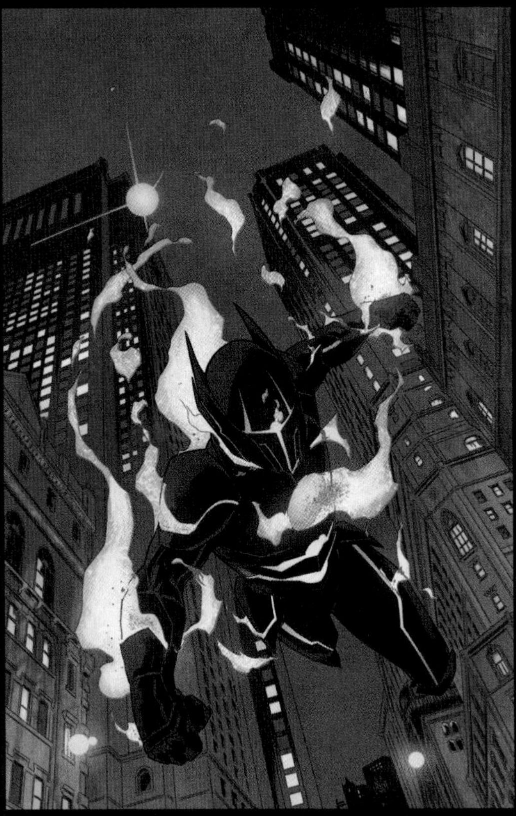

Issue Two (B)
Marco Renna w/ Chris Sotomayor

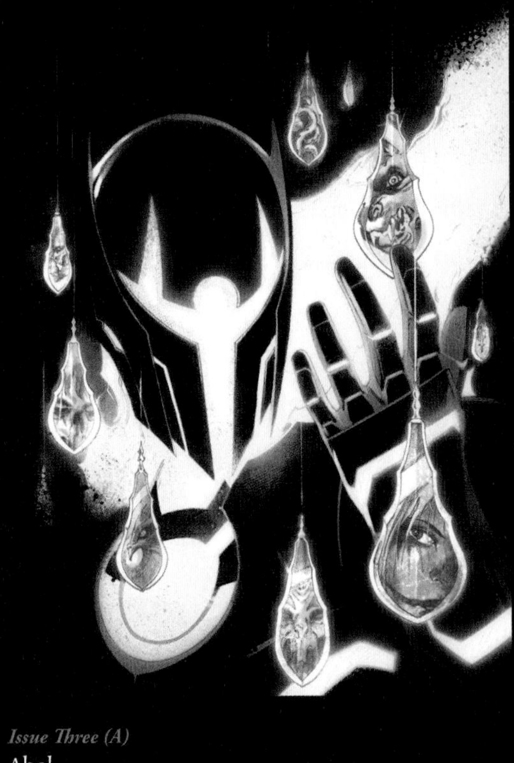

Issue Three (A)
Abel

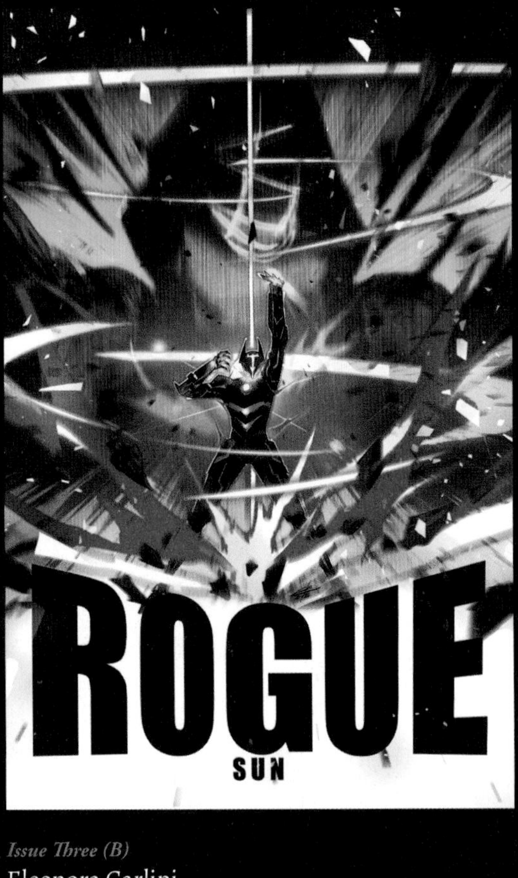
ROGUE
SUN

Issue Three (B)
Eleonora Carlini

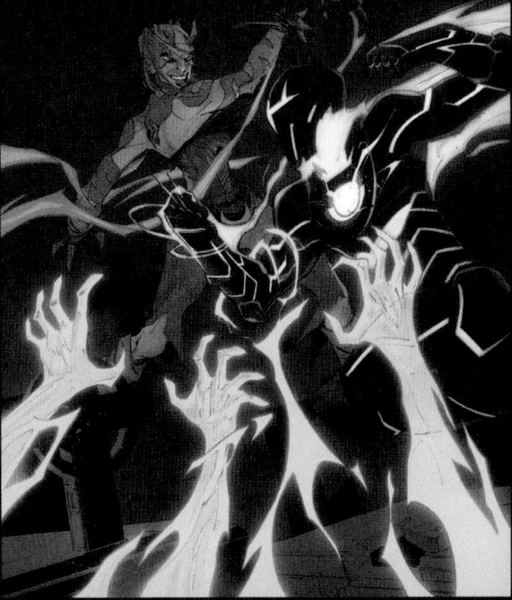

Issue Four (A)
Abel

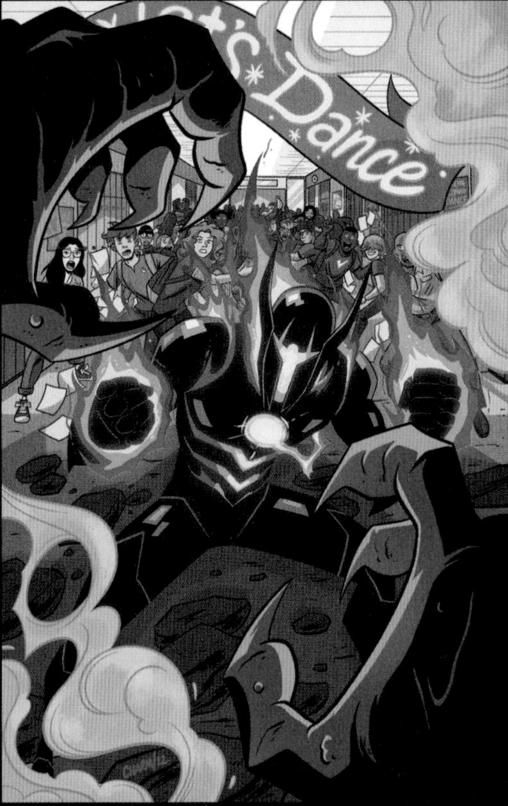
Dance

Issue Four (B)
Derek Charm

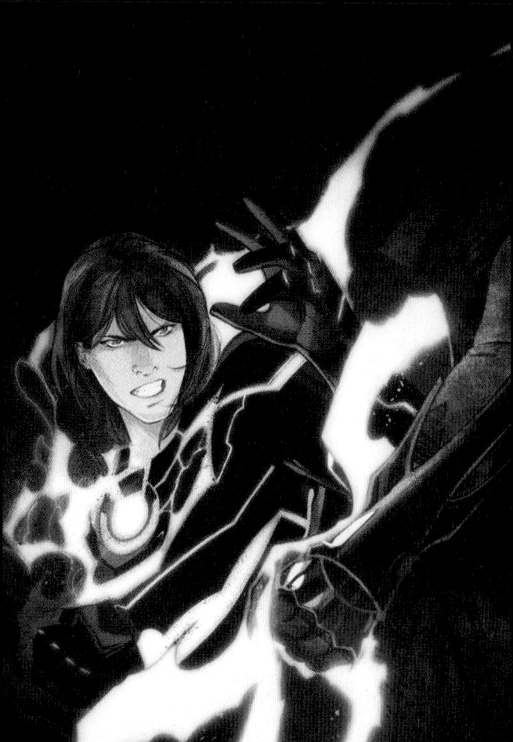

Issue Five (A)
Abel

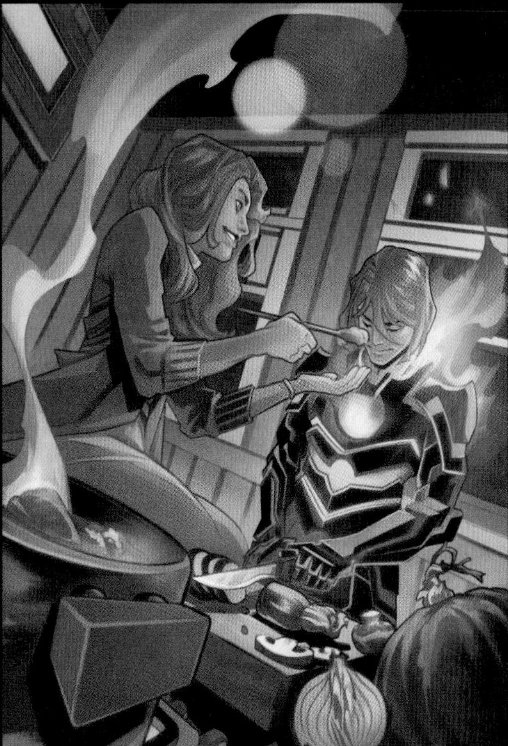

Issue Five (B)
Simone Ragazzoni

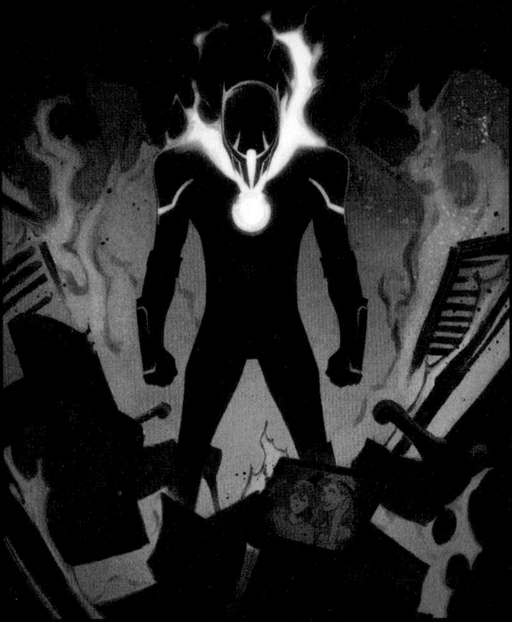

Issue Six (A)
Abel

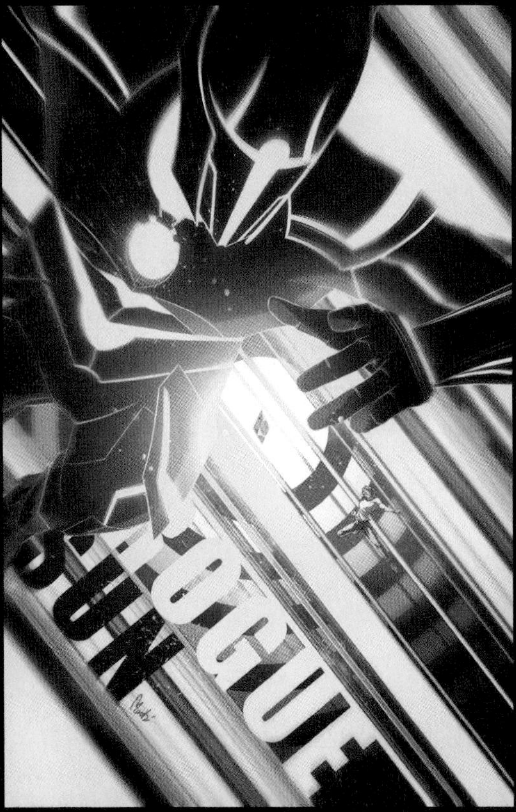
ROGUE SUN

Issue Six (B)
Igor Monti

Gallery
Character Designs

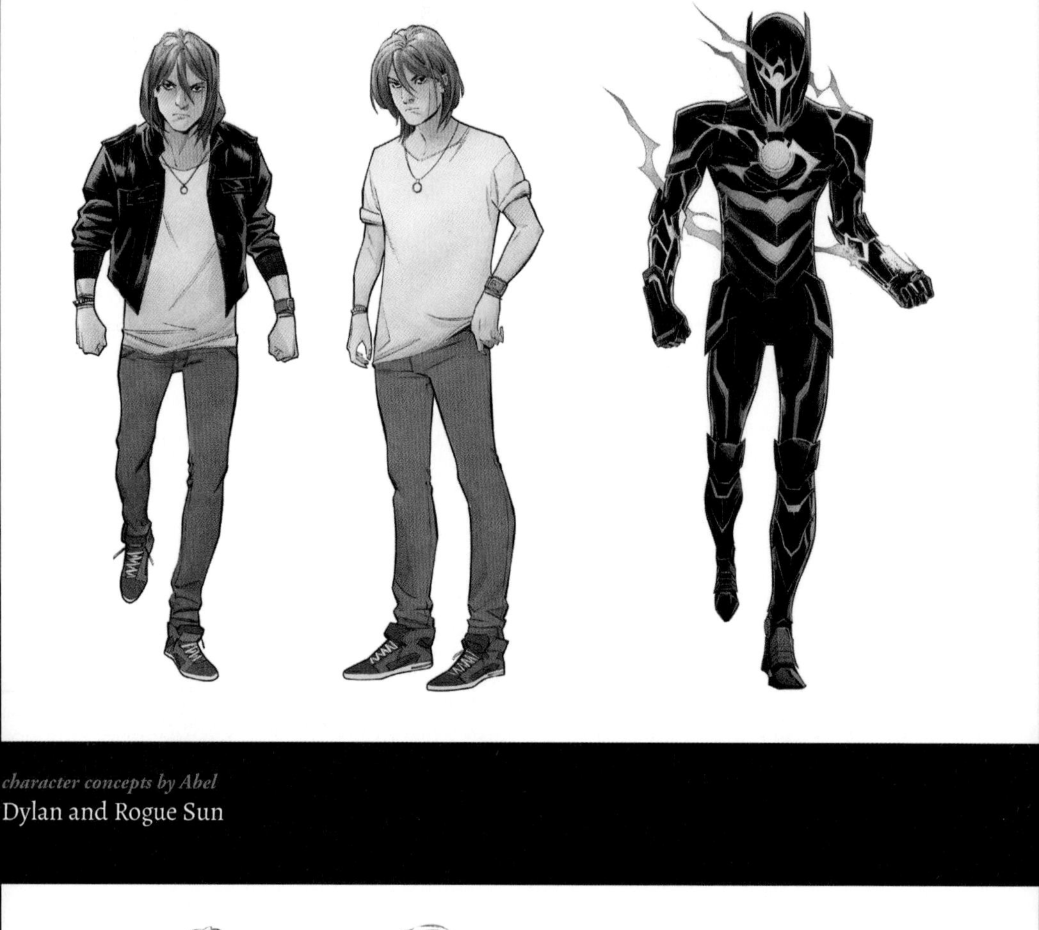

character concepts by Abel
Dylan and Rogue Sun

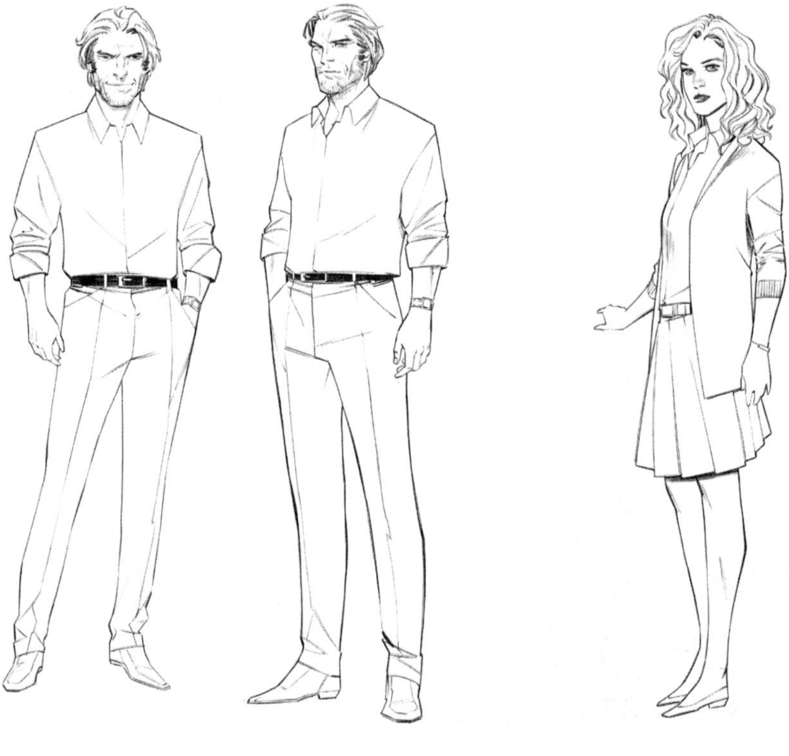

character concepts by Abel
Marcus and Gwen

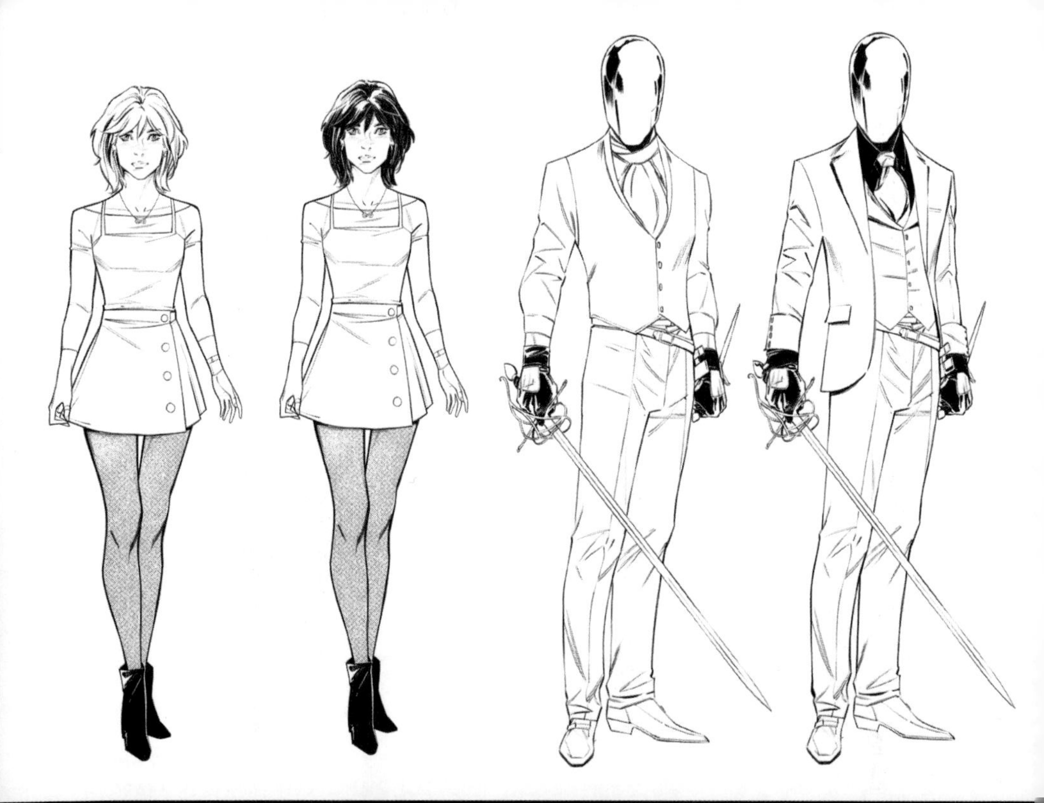

character concepts by Abel
Aurie and Suave

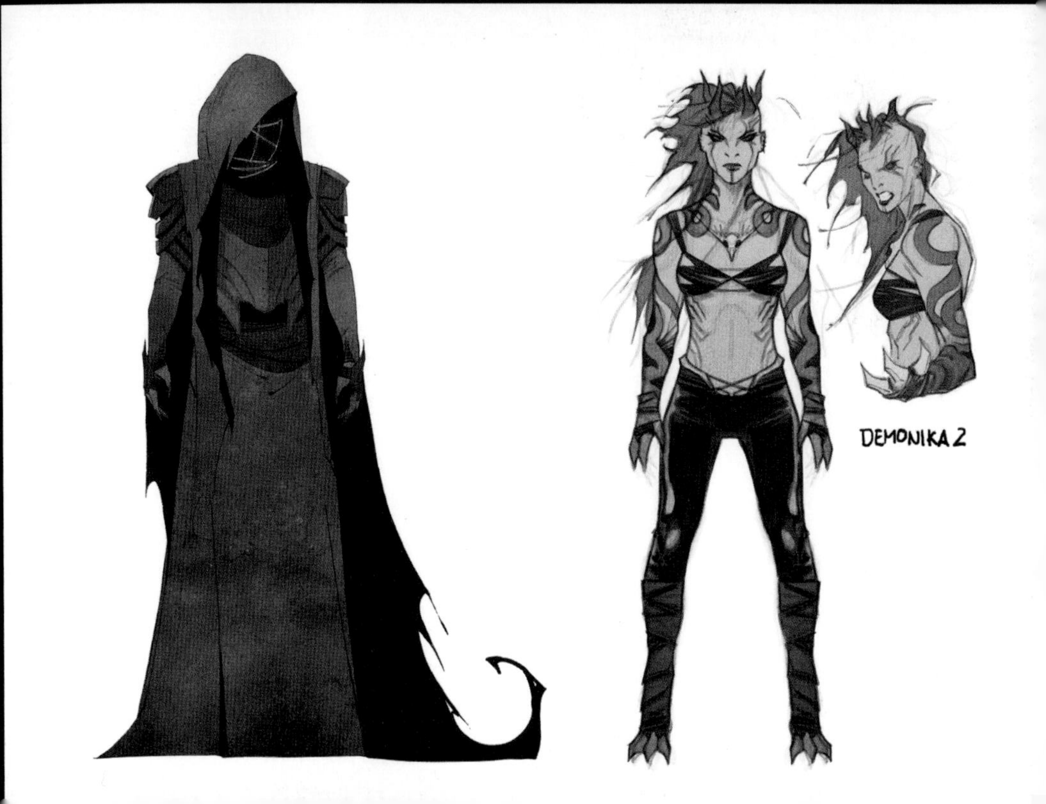
DEMONIKA 2

EXPLORE THE

MASSIVE-VERSE

RADIANT BLACK

VOLUME ONE: CATACLYSM
ROGUE SUN

RADIANT RED

THE DEAD LUCKY
FLORES
CARLOMAGNO
IACONO
CAREY
VOLUME 01

RADIANT BLACK
KYLE HIGGINS, MARCELO COSTA
VOLUME 1
ISBN: 978-1-53431-916-5
VOLUME 2
ISBN: 978-1-53432-109-0
VOLUME 3
ISBN: 978-1-53432-328-5

ROGUE SUN
RYAN PARROTT, ABEL
VOLUME 1
ISBN: 978-1-53432-237-0

RADIANT RED
CHERISH CHEN, DAVID LAFUENTE, MIQUEL MUERTO
VOLUME 1
ISBN: 978-1-53432-320-9

THE DEAD LUCKY
MELISSA FLORES, FRENCH CARLOMAGNO, MATTIA IACONO
VOLUME 1
ISBN: 978-1-53432-466-4

VISIT
MASSIVE-VERSE.COM

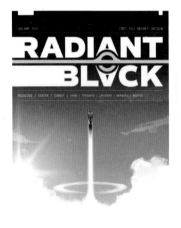

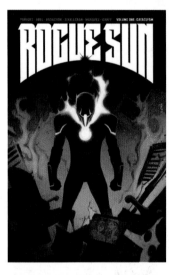

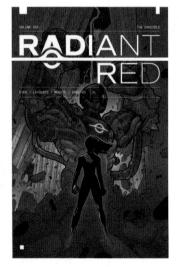

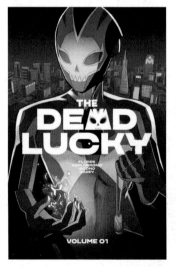